CONTENT ADVISORY

This book contains serious discussion of depression, suicidal ideation, homophobia, disownment, disability, and injury. A happy ending is absolutely guaranteed.

If you or someone you love is struggling with mental health, help is out there. Call, text, or chat 988 to be connected to trained counselors at the 988 Suicide & Crisis Lifeline or call 1-800-273-TALK (8255).

https://988lifeline.org
https://findahelpline.com/i/iasp

Copyright © 2022 by K. Evan Coles

All rights reserved.

No part of this book may be reproduced in any form or by any electronic or mechanical means, including information storage and retrieval systems, without written permission from the author, except for the use of brief quotations in a book review.

This book is a work of fiction. Names, characters, businesses, organizations, places, events and incidents either are the product of the author's imagination or are used fictitiously. Any resemblance to actual persons, living or dead, events, or locales is entirely coincidental.

This book contains erotic material and is intended for mature readers.

For information contact:

https://kevancoles.com

Book and Cover design by K. Evan Coles

Edited by Rebecca Fairfax

SUMMARY

Some hearts are made to be hopeful.

Ian Byrne is done with love. Or so he's been telling himself since his life crashed and burned. Ian got through his depression with help from friends and his career as an orthopedic nurse, as well as a big shaggy dog that's not really his. And if most days Ian feels just all right, he thinks that's fine.

He never expected to meet a guy on the train. Especially not a robot-building whiz kid like Tris Santos, fifteen years younger than Ian and in so many ways his opposite. But they agree that epic love is a myth and strike up an effortless friendship, the spark of attraction between them quickly igniting and burning hot over chat screens when Tris moves away.

Now, Ian can't imagine his life without Tris. Can't believe that what started as a fling became so much more and how deeply he feels for a man he doesn't even see in person. Ian thinks Tris might be the right guy; that he might be ready to risk his heart one more time. But ... is it too much to hope that Tris might feel the same?

Hopeful Hearts is an 85.1 K age gap sex-buddies-to-lovers novel. In it you'll meet a grumpy nurse practitioner recovering from heartbreak, a bright-eyed robotics genius who thinks epic romance is epically dumb, a huge wily dog in need of an owner, a 400-mile LDR, and a deliciously satisfying happily ever after.

HOPEFUL HEARTS

Stealing Hearts 4

K. EVAN COLES

For my son, who makes me laugh every day and answers my <u>many</u> questions about Gen Z language with surprisingly good humor.

My deepest gratitude to Randall Jussaume and Beth Greenberg who generously donated their time to help fix my words and provide feedback on covers, to Barb Payne Ingram and her eagle-eyed proofreading, and to Rebecca Fairfax, one of my favorite editors ever.

And for my newsletter subscribers who asked for a whole book and not a serialized story.

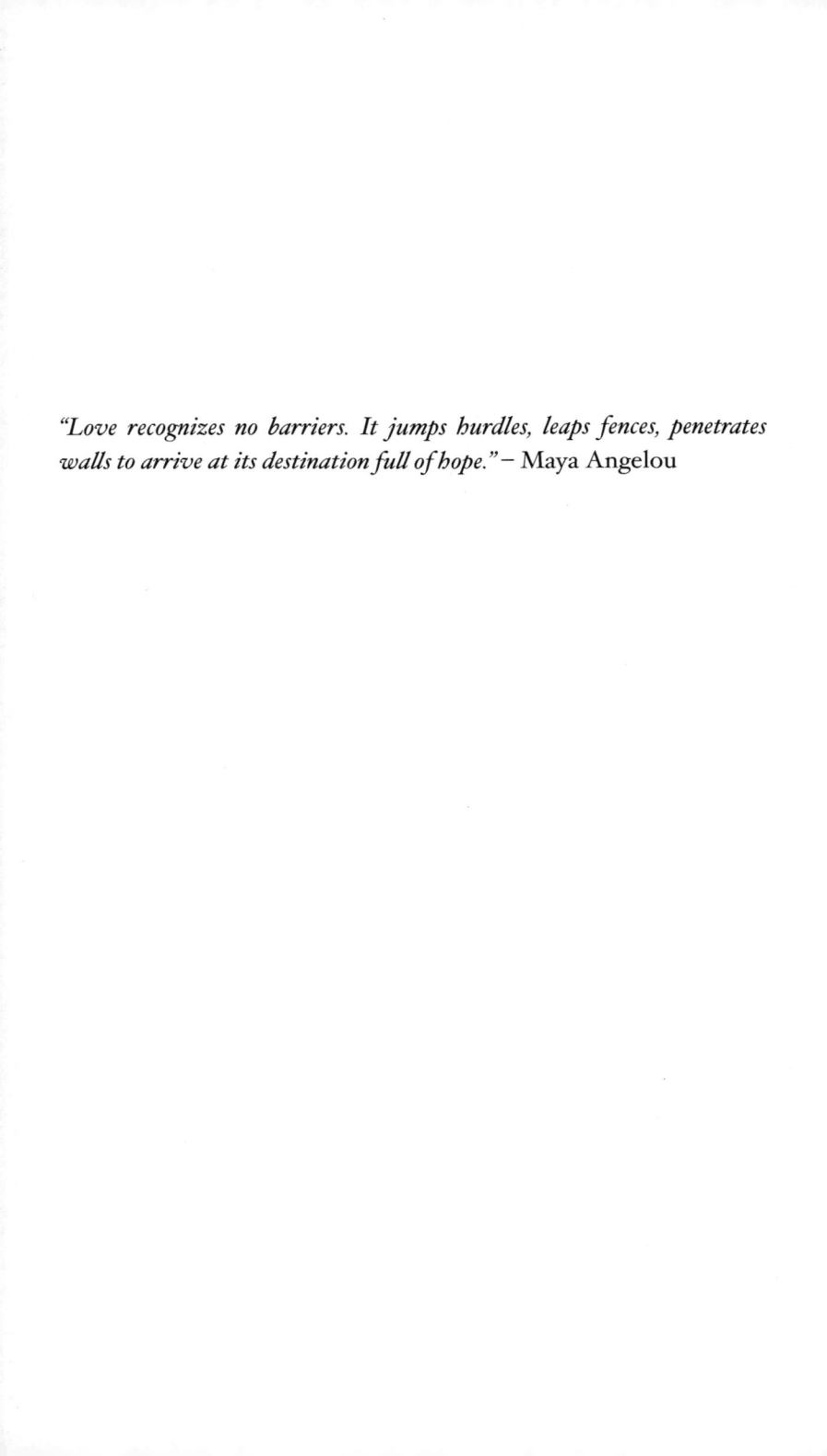

"Love recognizes no barriers. It jumps hurdles, leaps fences, penetrates walls to arrive at its destination full of hope." – Maya Angelou

1

February, 2022

"*Close your eyes and take this opportunity to connect with your breath. Inhale ... exhale.*"

Ian Byrne drew in a breath, mind attuned to the buttery voice floating through his earbuds.

"*Let us welcome this beautiful new day that has come upon us,*" the voice urged, and while Ian thought it was a bit early to be gauging what sort of day he'd have, he worked at keeping his mind open. "*Waking up to the feeling of being alive. Grateful to be here. To be able—*"

A distant noise snuck past the recorded track. Had that been a crash? Eyes still closed, Ian frowned slightly, attention wavering again when a shout reached his ears.

"Elliott! Give it back!"

"*—breathing in peace. Breathing out calm. Breathing in—*"

There was another thump, closer this time and accompanied by more yelling. Ian cracked open an eye.

"I swear to God, if that bag breaks, you're getting nothing but dry food from now on. Don't do it!"

"With your exhale, open your heart to gratitude. To this day full of—"

Ian opened the other eye. The commotion was closer now, a cacophony of clacking and stomping and laughter, first on the stairs and then nearing his door, and Ian didn't have time to scramble up before a big shaggy dog burst into the room carrying a plastic pouch in its teeth.

"Shit, I'm sorry!" Ian's housemate Marco skidded in next, still clad in his pajamas. He glared at the dog, but it was clear he was fighting laughter. "Fucker grabbed the food right out of my hand."

Ian didn't reply beyond an 'oof.' Couldn't actually, because the dog had just knocked him flat on his back, abandoning the bag of stolen dog food in favor of straddling Ian's body and huffing warm doggy breath into his face.

"I hate you both," Ian got out, then pulled his earbuds out. He didn't hesitate to bring his hands up to Elliot's scruff and scrub it with his fingers, though. The dog's coat spoke of uncertain heritage, light cream on the belly and legs but darker along his back and shoulders, gray and black mixing with sable, all gorgeously soft. Ian enjoyed running his hands over it. Even when doing so meant he'd miss his chance to meditate before work because dogs had zero respect for Monday morning rituals that didn't involve bounding around a yard or gobbling food.

Ian groaned as Elliott plopped down on top of him, chin coming to rest in the middle of Ian's chest. He'd meditate on the train ride into the city, he supposed. That'd be a better use of his time than staring out at however many feet of snow had fallen during the night.

"WEYMOUTH LANDING. DOORS OPEN ON THE RIGHT."

Ian slipped his earbuds in and called up the meditation track on his fitness app again. But he hesitated to hit Play when the train's conductor continued speaking, voice oddly friendly over the PA system.

"Passengers, due to the unusual weather conditions, this train will be taking on Red Line riders at some stations. We expect ridership to be unusually heavy during this time and the MBTA appreciates your cooperation in making room where you can."

In the seat opposite Ian, Marco heaved a sigh. "What fresh hell is this?" he muttered, turning to look out the window to the station platform that lay ahead.

Ian frowned, too. That announcement had sounded not awesome. Yes, back-to-back blizzards had buried the eastern half of the state, clogging highways and making streets impassible. And yes, the 'snowpocalypse' had heavily impacted 'the T'—as the transit authority was known—whole sections coming offline and stranding thousands without buses, ferries, and trains. That had happened with the Red Line, a subway route that serviced nearly a quarter of a million people daily and extended over twenty-two miles from end to end.

So ... if Ian's train was about to take on stranded subway riders, things were going to get—

"Ho, shit. There's, like, three hundred people out there."

—crowded.

Ian leaned over to get a look for himself and saw the platform was *packed* with hordes of passengers eyeing the train through the swirling snow.

"There are two stops after this," said their friend Dennis, who was leaning into Marco's shoulder and gawking, too. "Where the hell are they going to put everybody?"

"Wherever they'll fit, I guess." Ian gestured at the two empty seats beside him. "Sharing a few inches with strangers isn't going to kill us."

"It might," Marco countered mildly. "We're citizens of Massachusetts, Ian. We drive badly on purpose, drop consonants, and are selfish assholes about personal space."

"There's so much wrong there to unpack." Ian ignored his

friends' snickering as the doors at each end of the car thunked open.

People streamed in, coats encrusted with snow. Some found seats, like the tall guy in the dark ski jacket who sat on Ian's right, but most chose to stand, bodies rapidly filling the long car's narrow aisle. And the people kept coming, a clear indication the MBTA really was going to cram as many people on board as possible.

"Good morning and welcome aboard the Greenbush line," said the voice on the train's speakers. *"This train will make stops at Quincy Center and JFK/UMass, terminating at South Station."* The conductor paused, then sounded almost amused as he continued.

"Passengers, we understand conditions are more crowded than usual and appreciate your patience. Just, ah, squeeze a little closer. Maybe share the Sports section and make a new friend or two while we get you to your next stop."

Dennis's expression bordered on dazed. "Squeeze closer? Where?"

"On your lap?" Ian suggested, lips twitching when Dennis visibly recoiled. "What? You grouse all the time about not having time to meet men. This could be your chance."

That got a chuckle from the guy in the ski jacket beside Ian. "Not happening."

Ian and his friends raised their eyebrows at the guy.

"Oh?" Ian knew he sounded grumpy. But strangers in this town didn't talk to each other on public transit and this guy—this *kid*—had big pale eyes fringed with absurdly long lashes and was making all kinds of eye contact.

"People don't talk on trains," the kid said, echoing Ian's thoughts perfectly. "I've been here a year and all I get is 'scuse me' or 'your bag's on my feet,' or my personal favorite, 'move your fat ass.'"

Ian's lips almost twitched again. "Charming," he murmured. "Don't take it personally. Insults are kind of a side-hustle here."

His seatmate nodded. "Truth. Though you're talking to me and, so far, no insults."

"Give it time." Ian sat back in his seat, then surprised himself by asking, "Where're you from? You said you'd only been here a year," he added when the kid stared at him blankly.

"Oh! Well, I move around a lot so I'm not really from anywhere. Last place I lived before here was Chicago and that was for six months."

The kid pulled a messenger bag onto his lap and inched closer as a woman slid into the aisle seat beside him. Ian spied what looked like several Pride-themed pins attached to the bag's front flap, then heard a soft, "Ugh, sorry."

He frowned at his seatmate. "What for?"

"For possibly throwing up on you. I feel like crap." The kid appeared genuinely pained. "I'm not joking when I say I might barf."

The woman who'd just settled into the aisle seat side-eyed them balefully.

"Ah." Ian looked his seatmate over. Being blue-yellow color-blind, he didn't process some colors the way others did and while he knew the kid's eyes weren't dark, he couldn't guess their actual hue. The distress in them was real, however, as was the guy's pallor and the sweat dotting his full upper lip.

"Open your coat," Ian said, "and take off the hat if you can. You'll feel better if you're not overheated."

"Um. Okay." The kid pulled off the hat, revealing a shock of very light hair that was nearly white to Ian's eyes, a good deal of which flopped onto his forehead. "I'm Tristan," he said as he unzipped his jacket. "Figured I'd introduce myself since I just threatened to vomit on you."

"How ya doin'," Ian said, "My name's Ian." He turned to his backpack, which sported its own Pride patch, and withdrew a square red and white tin from one of its pockets. "Want one? Peppermint can help relieve nausea."

"Oh, man. Thank you." Tristan's smile completely changed his face, softening the elegant angles and making him look disarmingly sweet.

Not that Ian had noticed.

"Are you dizzy?" he asked.

"No." Tristan popped a mint in his mouth. "Just tired."

"Now arriving at Quincy Center," the conductor announced. *"Doors open on the left."*

Ian set his right arm on the table in front of them. "I know an acupressure trick you could try." He pulled his right sweater sleeve back. "The P6 point is about three fingers below the heel of your hand, in between the tendons." He indicated a spot on the inside of his forearm while the kid mimicked his actions. "You feel it?"

"Think so." Frowning slightly, Tristan glanced down at his wrist while the woman in the aisle seat watched them with interest. "Here?"

"Yup. Press that spot for a couple of minutes and you may feel a change. Not too hard but firm. I know it's sort of awkward but it works for me."

"Dude, I'll try anything that makes me feel less like death." Tristan dug his thumb into his forearm and sighed. "Are you a doctor?"

"Nurse practitioner," Ian replied. "Planes and boats make me motion sick, so I've learned a few tricks and keep supplies in my bag."

"Supplies?"

"Like the mints." Ian offered the tin to the woman in the aisle seat who smiled at him and took one. "Some ginger gummies. Probably have some sea bands in here somewhere and they're like acupressure cuffs. Oh, Dramamine for when I need the big guns. I'll sleep through anything after a couple of those suckers, including crying babies and alien abductions."

Ian furrowed his brow. Why the hell was he talking so much?

"I like how you make it sound almost fun." Tristan's eyelids fluttered closed. "Where're you from?"

"Virginia, originally. Why?"

"You're pretty friendly for a stranger on the train. Figured you might be from outta town."

Ian made a non-committal noise. Friendliness was the last thing on his mind at the moment; he just wanted a vomit-free ride. Oddly, he was okay with this kid thinking otherwise, and why that might be he couldn't guess.

"Doing okay?"

"Yeah," Tristan replied, though his sleepy tone made it clear he wasn't all there.

Slipping his earbuds back in, Ian cued up his meditation practice again, but kept his eyes open as the remaining miles passed. The train was nearing the terminus by the time he'd finished, and Ian cast a quick glance at his seatmate, noting that while Tristan still looked a bit pale, his face had relaxed as he dozed. Ian let his gaze linger on his sweep of long lashes and full lips before a flutter of nerves prickled his skin and he glanced away, unwilling to be the guy who perved on a much younger stranger who clearly felt like shit.

"He's cute."

Ian caught Chris's eye across the table. "Stop."

"What? You're the one flirting."

"Chatting. You could try it sometime."

"I don't chat with strangers."

"Not without an app," Ian replied, and Chris let out a snort.

"Hi, Pot. I'm the Kettle."

Ian ran his knuckles over his beard, lips pursed against a smile. He hadn't dated a ton since breaking up with his ex, but he used hookup apps and appreciated their uncomplicated convenience.

"Now approaching South Station," the conductor droned. *"Connections available for Red Line and Amtrak trains."*

"Jeez, that guy is loud." Tristan straightened, eyes open again and expression the slightest bit surly. "What's going on?"

"Ride's almost over." Ian watched him rake his hair back from his forehead. "You feeling any better?"

"Maybe a little."

"Nice." Ian slid the tin of mints over the table until they were in front of Tristan, and Tristan smiled down at it.

"These for me?"

"Figured you might want them for the ride back tonight."

"Ugh, can't wait for that. But thanks." Tristan shot him a smile. "I really appreciate it. Can't believe I fell asleep." His brow creased as the train slowly glided up to the platform. "I swear that's never happened to me before."

"Nausea makes some people drowsy," Ian replied, "and I'll take snoring over vomit any day."

"Bro." Tristan looked mortified, eyes flicking from Ian to Marco and Dennis and back. "I was *snoring*?"

"Some, yeah," Ian said.

"Oh, my God."

The woman in the aisle seat broke her silence, patting Tristan's shoulder as the train ground to a halt. "It wasn't too bad. At least you weren't drooling."

Tristan actually cringed.

"What's the big deal?" Ian asked. They got to their feet, watching the masses in the aisle slowly clear out. "You didn't plan to get sick, right?"

"Definitely not. But snoring!" Tristan slid the knit cap back onto his head. "I'll be less boring the next time I see you, I promise."

Ian could have scoffed. The ordinary madness of rush hour made it unlikely he'd ever see this floppy-haired kid again—a kid who'd nearly barfed on Ian and then fallen asleep. Add in the insanity that came with literal mountains of snow and dead train lines and the chances of their crossing paths vanished. Which was fine.

But Ian simply nodded. He hadn't minded the time he'd passed on this ride, despite the *extra* chaos brought on by the snowpocalypse. Tristan had been charming in spite of his nausea and talking to him had been sort of ... fun.

Something about that—something about Tristan himself, possibly—made Ian want to be kind with his goodbye.

"Okay," he said easily. "Maybe I'll see you around, Chi-Town."

A laugh came out of Tristan as they stepped out into the snow. "Not if I see you first, Ian!"

※

NINE HOURS LATER AND WITH HIS TRAIN HOPELESSLY DELAYED, Ian was feeling less kindly toward chaos. He worked his way through throngs of stranded passengers standing around South Station—most staring at the departures board that hung overhead as if the thing were an oracle—and headed for The Tavern, a minuscule, roofless pub located in the middle of the terminal's floor. If he was going to wait around for God knew how long, he wanted to do it with snacks.

Unsurprisingly, the place was packed to the gills, but he found a spot at the bar and hung his backpack from a hook beneath it. He'd no sooner pulled his phone from his pocket when an oddly familiar voice called his name.

"Ian! Hey!"

Ian's eyebrows traveled upward as a smiling face pushed through the crowd. It was Tristan, the kid from the train, looking much healthier, color back in his face and his eyes all bright as he sidled up to Ian's place at the bar.

"I'll be damned," Ian said. "What are you doing here, Chi-Town?"

Tristan wrinkled his nose. "You know nobody from Chicago calls it that, right?"

"Uh-huh. Nobody from Boston calls it Beantown either, but I'm not the one making the rules."

"That's fair." Smiling, Tristan pulled off his beanie and stuck it in his jacket pocket. "So, what's up? I was just trying to figure out how the hell to get home when I saw you."

"Can't believe you saw me at all through the crowd."

"Meh, it helps that you're tall like me. Plus, I was looking for you."

Tristan was indeed tall—he had a couple of inches on Ian's own six feet. But Ian had no idea what to make of the 'looking for you' comment, so he simply nodded in lieu of a reply.

"Can I buy you a beer?" Tristan asked. "It's the least I can do after this morning."

"Sure," Ian said, "but you really don't have to."

"I think I do." Tristan handed the bartender his driver's license—of course he'd get carded—and ordered up two pints of a local craft beer to go with a cheese platter. "Seriously, you saved me."

"More like saved myself and my clothing," Ian reminded him, and got a wry laugh in reply.

"I'm hoping it was a one-time thing." Tristan's mouth twisted. "I still need to get home and this shit with the Red Line—"

"Sucks," Ian finished for him. "I get it. My commute's all jacked up too, and that reminds me I need to make a call. Excuse me one sec."

Picking his phone up from the table, he thumbed past a message from his ex, Gus, then placed a quick call to Marco. The drinks and snacks had been delivered by the time he hung up, and Tristan was constructing a trio of neat little sandwiches from the crackers, sliced meats, and cheese.

"Everything okay at home?" Tristan asked, then bit into one of his snack stacks.

"Yup. There's a dog at the house and I wanted to be sure my housemate made it back and could feed him. You met Marco this morning," Ian added, "the Black guy with the short hair. Next to him was Dennis, who is redheaded and freckled."

"Ah. You all work together?"

Ian shook his head and started to build a snack stack of his own. "Dennis and I work at the Vanguard Clinic in Post Office Square, but Marco's over at Mass General. I'm in Orthopedics and Sports Medicine."

A playful grin lit Tristan's face. "Nurse Bones?"

Ian almost smiled. "Nurse Byrne, thank you very much. Although one of my younger patients calls me 'Bones' and I'm not sure how I feel about it."

"You should feel good. 'Bones' is great with the scowly, Grumble Bear eyebrows you've got going."

Ian narrowed his eyes. "What the hell is a Grumble Bear and what do they have to do with my eyebrows?"

They polished off the food while Tristan described the Grumble Bear, a boss from a PC game he'd been playing for years. Ian had made a note to check it out himself when the initial boarding call for their train was announced, and they and half the state's population scrambled to board.

Holy *fuck*, it was crowded. Ian and Tristan had found seats but just barely, and there were wall-to-wall bodies pressing in all around.

Ian exchanged a glance with the kid. "This is fun. You're not claustrophobic, are you?"

"Not that I know of," Tristan said with a laugh, "but I've never been motion sick before today and I ride the subway all the time." He tugged the zipper on his ski jacket open. "These big purple beasts suck."

Now Ian did smile. He'd known the commuter rail's color scheme used shades of purple, but to him the huge engines had always looked a bit gray or sometimes brown.

"Good evening passengers," boomed a voice through the overhead speaker, *"and welcome aboard what should have been the 6:20 train to Greenbush. Please be aware that we're almost at capacity and appreciate your cooperation in making room for your fellow passengers."*

Tristan pulled the tin of mints from his pocket and popped

one as the train glided out of the terminal. He started in with the acupressure on his wrist but quickly dozed off and missed the next press of passengers that stuffed the cars so full, people's bodies jammed the doors at either end of it wide open. Recorded warnings bleated pointlessly as the train traveled south, alerting the largely silent crowds of unsafe conditions while Ian read articles on his phone and Tristan slept on.

"Next stop, Weymouth Landing. Weymouth Landing is the next stop for this train."

Ian set a hand on Tristan's shoulder and squeezed lightly. "Hey."

"Whazzat?"

"Your stop is next, kid."

"Christ, this is embarrassing." Tristan made a face. "Sorry, baby," he said, eyes flying wide as he realized what he'd just said.

Ian barked out a laugh. "You'd better be. Are you okay to get home?"

"I'm okay, Bear. I mean Byrne! Oh, my God." Tristan's cackle was loud. "I swear, I can get myself home. My house is a short walk from the station, and I've done it in worse shape than this."

"Not reassuring."

"Totally true, though." Tristan held out a hand. "Gimme your phone."

Ian narrowed his eyes. "Why? I don't want a barf selfie."

"Yes, you do." Snickering, Tristan took the device Ian handed him and flicked open the chat. "I'll message myself, then hit you back when I get home so you know I didn't die." He smiled as he handed it back. "Do you guys sit in second car from the front every morning?"

"Generally, yup."

"Cool." Tristan got to his feet. "Guess I'll see you tomorrow."

"I guess you will."

Amused, Ian watched him walk off. It seemed he'd made a train buddy. Who was apparently immune to grouching and had

Ian's number, because Ian was an idiot who handed his phone off to strangers.

An idiot who full on grinned when his phone buzzed with a new message a little while later too, the declaration *Santos lives!* followed by a string of bear-faced emoji.

2

"Mornin', Chi-Town."

Tristan's nose and cheeks were flushed from the cold as he slid into the seat beside Ian. "Morning, Grumble Bear. Happy Tuesday."

Ian's stomach curled with dread at Dennis's slow grin.

"Grumble Bear?"

"We ran into each other at South Station last night," Ian said quickly. "Tristan bought me a beer."

"And remembered which car we sit in, obviously." Dennis turned his smile on Tristan. "So, is it Mr. Grumble Bear or Nurse Grumble Bear? Because I think the latter is wicked cute. Ooh." His eyes went wide. "We could just go with GB."

Ian shook his head. "No."

"Yes," Dennis said firmly. "I'm going to make you a special name tag when we get to work."

"Next stop, Quincy Center. Doors open on the left."

Ignoring his friends, Ian glanced at Tristan who'd pulled off his knit hat and was looking rather sheepish.

"Sorry, dude."

Ian waved him off. "Don't worry about it. Dennis was raised by wolves. We shared a flat once upon a time, this tiny two-bedroom out on Mission Hill. It went about as well as you might expect."

Tristan's eyes twinkled. "Hey, at least you're still friends. I have five housemates and—"

"Wait, did you say *five*? Why would you do that to yourself?"

Ian's head spun as Tristan described his many housemates—Gary, Haru, Ela, Sully, and Hannah—and the train sped toward Boston.

"There's a cat, too," Tristan said. He was working the acupressure point in his wrist and smiling. "But she doesn't take up much space."

Ian considered the spacious three-bedroom house and big yard he shared with just Marco and Elliott and had to shake his head. "There's really enough room in your place for so many people?"

"Yup. Three floors and the top one is like an in-law apartment with its own kitchen. Ela and Sully live up there. Plenty of rooms so we can get out of each other's hair when we need to. I like people and all, but I need a space just for me." Tristan covered a yawn with one hand. "Ugh, sorry."

Ian shook his head. "Even with three floors, I think I'd go nuts."

"I sort of like it. My dad died when I was eight and my mom was in the Navy, so there were long stretches when it was just me, my brother, and my grandma. It's nice coming home to a bunch of people."

"I'm sorry about your dad. Must have been hard."

"It was," Tristan agreed. "I'm not sure how my mom did it, but I know she was super glad to have Grandma around."

Ian didn't smile at Tristan's lightly joking tone. He'd been much older than eight when he'd 'lost' his own parents to their bigotry, and the experience—the pain at knowing they simply weren't going to be there for him anymore—had hurt Ian profoundly.

"I meant it must have been hard on you," he said gently,

unsurprised when Tristan's wry grin faded. "You were just a kid and a loss like that is never easy."

"You're right," Tristan said, quieter now. "It wasn't easy and my mom's deployments were the worst. She's a helicopter pilot and sometimes she'd be gone for months. You know she missed my whole fifth grade year?" He shook his head. "My brother and me, we got it. Knew she had a job to do that was bigger than just us. But it sucked knowing she had to choose between us and her job.

"Anyway, she met my stepdad around the time I turned eleven and it got easier. Well, maybe not for Rick." Tristan chuckled. "He's such a good guy. Put up with a ready-made family and seemed totally okay with all of it. He's the one who got Jim and me into STEM. Which Mom loved, even when Jim and I started building battlebots and staging fights in the backyard. One time, I reprogrammed the robot vacuum to scream when it bumped into the furniture." He smiled at Ian's laughter. "But the robots I build now don't scream."

Ian blinked. "You build robots?"

"Uh-huh. I work for a cyber-tech firm in Back Bay."

Tristan's raised eyebrow pricked Ian's conscience. He hadn't put much thought into what Tristan did for a living—he hardly knew the kid. He'd formed some assumptions, though. That Tristan was artsy or even still in school. Certainly not that he worked in robotics, a field that demanded serious brain power. And Ian's assumptions had been based on Tristan's good looks and very obvious youth, snap judgments he probably dealt with every day.

"Sorry," Ian said. "I've never met anyone who worked in robotics and, clearly, need to pull my head out of my ass."

Tristan huffed out a laugh. "No worries. I know I don't look the part, whatever the heck that means. My friend Gary thinks I should wear glasses because he says they make me look more serious." The air quotes he drew with his fingers around those final two words had Ian grinning.

"Do you actually need glasses?"

"No. But I like that he's trying to help. We've known each other a long time, had a thing for a while at school. But Gary moved here for a job while I moved around for mine. Silicon Valley for a year, then Austin and Denver and Chicago."

"Now arriving at JFK/UMass."

Ian scrunched up his nose. "Moving is the worst. I couldn't do it every year."

"It doesn't bother me much." Tristan shrugged. "Keeps me from getting bored and means I always get interesting work. Anyway, Gary and I kept in touch, and when I landed a job here last spring, he offered me a room at his house. He was with Haru by then and I hooked up with Hannah. Uh." His expression went sheepish. "I don't know why I told you that."

Ian flapped a hand at him. "People tell me stuff all the time—Marco calls me the guidance counselor because everyone's always spilling their guts. Doesn't bother me that you're ..."

"Bi," Tristan finished for him.

What the actual hell. Ian nearly winced. Why would he talk sexual identity with a near stranger? "I shouldn't have gone there."

"Nah, you're good." Tristan smiled. "I saw the Pride patch on your bag and figured you probably wouldn't care who I bang."

"Word."

"Like ... to your mother?"

Ian laughed out loud before he could stop himself. "Somebody's, sure. I don't know why anyone would ever care about how a person identifies."

"Same. People do though, and biphobia is totally a thing." Tristan shook his head. "A guy I was with in Austin suggested I date women so I can pass for straight, and Hannah the housemate thinks I go with guys because I'm kinky."

"That's not how kink works. Or has anything to do with being bi." Ian furrowed his brow. "She knows that, right?"

"I dunno. She says I'll meet the right woman someday and

turn straight." This time, Tristan scoffed outright. "Sexuality is fluid, but that's not even what she's talking about. Not to mention I'm twenty-five and know who I'm attracted to."

Twenty-five? Jeez.

Ian wanted to wince. He'd known Tristan was younger but confirming there were fifteen years between them made him feel positively ancient. Still, this conversation wasn't about him, so he seized the next easy topic and kept his tone light.

"No epic romance with Hannah, huh?"

"God, no. No epic romance with anyone. Hannah and I are just friends."

"Friends who happen to have sex," Ian suggested and smiled at Tristan's bark of laughter.

"Not for a while now." His eyes danced. "I'm not going to apologize for that either, no matter how judgy you get with those eyebrows."

"Totally not judging," Ian said. "I'm not going to tell you how to live your own life."

"I knew I liked you, GB," Tristan said. "This is why we're going to be friends."

Smiling, Ian just shook his head. He wouldn't see Tristan after the Red Line went back online. But saying the words felt negative and Ian wasn't feeling the downer vibe that morning.

Tristan, however, seemed to be feeling an abundance of negativity by the time they met up again at South Station for the evening commute, his forehead marred by a frown as they studied the departures board.

"Shit, that says our train's on time, right?" he asked, eyebrows shooting up when Ian immediately started backing toward the exits to the platform.

"That says our train is boarding, kid," Ian called out. "So get your ass in gear!"

They rushed through the falling snow with hordes of fellow passengers, making their way to the far end of the platform where the crowd became thinner. Ian felt more than saw Tristan lose his footing when he unknowingly crossed a patch of black ice and caught hold of his shoulder just in time to keep Tristan from falling ass over tea kettle.

"Son of a *monkey*," Tristan yelped, which just made Ian laugh.

"You okay?"

"I'm good. Thanks for that." Tristan clapped Ian on the back. "My ass'd be broken if it weren't for you."

Ian shrugged and waved Tristan aboard. They found seats in the center of the car, a minor miracle of timing given the number of people pouring in after them. But Tristan still seemed tense, mouth tight and usual sunny demeanor absent.

Ian watched him a minute, unsure if breaking the kid's mood would be wise, then almost laughed at himself. *He* was used to being the grouchy one; finding himself on the lighter side of a mood was a bit odd.

Carefully, he pulled his phone from his pocket and tapped out a quick message.

Wanna talk about it?

He added a robot emoji, hit *Send*, then heard a quiet buzz a moment later. Tristan shifted in his seat slightly so he could pull his own phone from his pocket and after checking the screen, slowly turned his head so he could meet Ian's gaze.

"Do I have to type my reply or can I just say it?" he asked.

Ian chuckled. "Whatever you want, kid. What's going on?"

"My day kind of sucked." Tristan sighed, dropped his phone to his lap. "Not so much this morning but from lunch on? Shitty. I wanted to chill with you at the pub for a while before having to ride a purple beast, and I feel like a giant dick for complaining about the train being on time." He grimaced. "Please punch me in the face."

"No." Snorting softly, Ian shook his head. "What happened? Did your robots misbehave?"

"Nah. The robots are never the problem—it's the humans you have to watch." Tristan pulled off his hat. "I spent an hour convincing a client not to make changes to a project that's eighty-five percent done. Problem is, I'm not sure I got through to them. Because I know they don't take me seriously." He frowned again. "I get that I look young. *Am* young. But I know robots and I'm fucking good at my job."

Ian didn't doubt it. Yes, Tristan's obvious youth and easygoing attitude probably made it easy to forget a big brain was hard at work behind his pretty face. There was no mistaking his intensity now, however, or that he took both his work and the client's slight seriously.

"The really frustrating part is that the changes the client wants are aesthetic and could affect the robot's performance. And that, my friend, is very much not okay because form *must* follow function. Shit, I'm sorry." Tristan seemed to pull himself up short. "I know robot talk is boring."

"Not to me." Ian shrugged. "I don't know a thing about what you do but it's still interesting to talk about. What sort of robot have you been working on?"

"A wearable exoskeleton. Its purpose is to help improve the mobility of people who've lost some of their motor function."

Ian's mouth opened and closed and he blinked. "Like a ReWalk?"

"Um, yeah." A wondering smile dawned on Tristan's face. "Exactly like a ReWalk, but thinner and lighter, and a little less noisy. Do you work with exo-suits in your job?"

"Sometimes, yes." Excitement sparked in Ian's chest. He'd had patients in therapy programs with bionic devices, seen people with spinal cord injuries able to move from wheelchairs and stand upright again, walk, and even climb and descend stairs. "You're *building* those kinds of robots?"

"Word," Tristan said, looking smug now. "What do you think of them?"

"I think they're mind-blowing. And, at sixty grand, not affordable for a lot of patients."

"Yup. I want to change that, GB." Tristan tapped the bag on his lap with his index finger like he was punctuating his own thoughts. "Build stuff that will change people's lives without killing their bank accounts. That's why my company also builds robots that behave like service animals."

Ian smiled, charmed and fascinated by the idea. "Do they walk on all fours?"

"Some do while others have wheels. Which is sort of the point. Assistive robots are more adaptable to their environments than animals and don't require rest or nourishment or even emotional stimulation. An AR can also perform tasks an animal just can't, like folding laundry or setting a table."

"Robots aren't cuddly at the end of a long day," Ian pointed out because he was a *giant* fucking sap who was way too fond of his four-legged housemate.

"The machines Off-World builds aren't supposed to be," Tristan replied. "They're meant to enhance the human experience while remaining in the background. Prosthetics and exo-suits that compensate for function or perform tasks too dangerous for humans. Like bomb disposal or reading radiation levels."

Ian hummed. This kid was so cool. "You really like your job, huh?"

"I do. The clients can drive me nuts, though." Tristan sighed. "If I shifted into pure research, I wouldn't have to deal with that as much. But unless I want to start my career over from scratch, I'd need to get an advanced degree and I don't know if now is the right time to do it. On paper, everything points to me going back to school."

Ian ran his teeth over his bottom lip. He didn't have a clue about Tristan's field of work; had never built anything mechanical that didn't come out of a box with a set of instructions. But he could talk about perfectly laid plans not always translating to real life and how sometimes less traveled paths worked out for the best.

You sound like a man who has read too many fortune cookies.

"Maybe what's on paper just isn't right for you." He kept his tone mild. "I thought I wanted to be a doctor. Had it all planned out and went into my undergrad studies believing I'd be in pre-med once I had that degree. Obviously, things turned out differently, but I have no regrets. I love my job, too."

"I can tell." Tristan smiled. "What changed your mind about being a doctor?"

"I realized the patients meant more to me than the science and medicine. I volunteered at a hospital during my undergrad," Ian said. "Did whatever was needed, mostly with the outpatient population—escorting them to the right departments, dropping off books or games when they got bored, that kind of thing. And I learned that doctors don't actually spend a lot of time with patients." He nodded at Tristan's questioning look.

"Ironic, right? Once a diagnosis is made and treatment begins, most of the patient care is left to the nurses and we're often the first and last people a patient will see. I like that. I can't do my job without the science and medicine, and I like that stuff too, a lot. But being there for my patients means more." He smiled. "You need to figure out what you want from your career —like, what makes you feel good doing it—and not just follow a plan someone else says is right."

Tristan shook his head slowly. "No one's ever put it like that before, Ian. Thanks."

"Sure. Can I call you Dr. Roboto if you do get more degrees?"

"Der, of course." Tristan laughed. "But I'll keep thinking about the school thing. I want to decide by the time the snow is finally gone."

"Meaning July," Ian teased, "when we'll maybe be able to put away our coats. Well, at least the trains should be back to normal by then."

"Yay." Tristan sat back in his seat. "Seriously, the current state of my commute is bullshit. Except for the part where I get to talk to you." His grin made warmth coil all through Ian. "You're fun under the grumpy. *Almost* enough to make me forget I might spew all over the place."

"Lovely." Ian rolled his eyes but he smiled too, liking the idea that he was a fun grump. "I think you're improving, y'know. You seem steadier now than you did yesterday and haven't fallen asleep. You didn't even do the acupressure thing tonight."

Tristan's mouth fell open slightly. "Huh. You think I'm cured? Because I'm taking the Acela to Philly in a couple of weeks for a friend's birthday."

"Now approaching JFK/UMass. Doors open on your left."

Ian winced. "You're going to ride a high-speed train?"

"Yup." Tristan's laugh sounded strained. "Just the thought of traveling over 60 miles an hour in a tin can like this kind of makes me want to die."

"You and me both. You should invest in the sea bands I told you about, just to be on the safe side."

"Or, I could pop a Dramamine."

"Might make you groggy."

"So? The ride to Philly is around five hours long," Tristan said. "The way things have been going with the stupid snow, it could take ten. I'd rather nap through it if possible."

Ian laughed out loud. "If you think your seatmate won't mind the snoring and drooling, I know you'll pull it off."

3

The next morning, Ian waited for Tristan to slide into the seat beside him before pulling a steel container from his backpack. "I brought you something."

"What, like a barf bag?"

"Please, God, no. It's ginger tea." Setting the thermos on the tabletop, Ian removed the cup and cap from its top. He paused a moment to enjoy the fragrant steam wafting from the bottle, then slid it over to Tristan. "Ginger can be soothing for the stomach, and I thought it might help with the nausea. Only if you want it, of course."

Tristan stared at the thermos with wide eyes before giving Ian the sweetest little smile. "Bro. This is so nice!"

Ian would have smiled, but a balled-up napkin bounced off the side of his face and he froze. Tristan pressed his lips tightly together, clearly fighting a laugh.

"It's rude not to bring treats for the whole class," Dennis said airily, and Ian had to count slowly backward from five before he shot a look over the table at his *ridiculous* friend.

"My apologies. I'll remember that in the future."

"Next stop, Quincy Center. Doors open on the left."

Ian turned back to Tristan who'd pulled the thermos closer and was breathing in the ginger-infused steam, eyes closed.

"Mmm. This smells so good."

"Please don't call me that." Ian looked away, very aware of Tristan pouring the pale amber tea into the cup. "Dennis really did make me a name tag at work because his one goal in life is to give me all of the shit."

Tristan tsk'd with his tongue. "Sorry, buddy. Do you want some of this?"

"I'm good. Had two cups of coffee before I even let the dog out this morning, but you drink up. You're looking a little tired if you don't mind my saying." On impulse, Ian reached over and pressed the back of his hand against Tristan's forehead to check for overheating. "You feeling okay?"

"Yup." Tristan smiled as Ian dropped his hand, but his face was indeed pale against his black shirt. "I can't blame the way I feel right now on motion sickness."

Ian cocked an eyebrow at him. "What did you do?"

"Had a tequila party at the house last night."

"I see. What was the occasion?"

"It was Tuesday," Tristan shrugged. "Hannah and Ela cooked enchiladas and Sully made killer margaritas. I consumed more than I should have of both and I swear, I can still taste tequila."

Ian had to laugh. He couldn't remember the last time he'd enjoyed a random midweek celebration involving too many cocktails.

"I'm a guacamole slut," Tristan declared. "There's a place in Weymouth Landing called El Jorongo that we hit up on the regular, but no one wanted to trek through the snow last night, so we threw a wee party at home instead." He frowned at the cup in his hand. "I miss going out. I don't even mean to party, either. Like, right now I'd be cool just being outside without having to stand in a snowbank."

"You've got cabin fever. We all do," Ian added. "I got way too excited to go grocery shopping last weekend and I think I'd actually sell my soul for a barbecue on the beach."

"God, a barbecue. And the beach," Marco said from across the table, his voice dreamy. "That sounds fantastic."

"Yo." Tristan's expression brightened. "You guys just gave me a great idea for this weekend."

"Yeah? You fixin' to set up a beach scene in the snow?" Ian asked.

Tristan's face scrunched up adorably. "Not sure I've ever been fixin' to do anything. But, no, not a beach—a barbecue pit. Shit, a *wintercue* pit."

Ian's mouth fell open a little. "You can't be serious. There's nine feet of snow on the ground." He snorted when Tristan nodded with so much enthusiasm, he looked like a bobble-head toy.

"There are also inventions called shovels, bro. And we have a gas grill in the garage and a full tank of propane left over from the summer—all we'd need to do is clear a space big enough to set it all up."

"Tristan."

"This is happening, Ian!"

Ian clapped a hand over his mouth to stifle his mirth, but knew he'd failed from the way Dennis and Marco were laughing too.

"You're ridiculous," he said to Tristan. "Please send me photos."

"Come see it for yourself!" Tristan urged.

"You want me to come to your house and watch you dig a hole in nine feet of snow?"

"Yes, you boob, because it's going to be hell of a lot more than a hole. Weymouth's not very far from Cohasset, and we can put you up if the trains get weird and you end up stranded."

"Bizarrely, this whole thing sounds pretty fun. I'm gonna have to say no, though."

Which was exactly what Ian knew he should say. Hanging

with a bunch of snow-bunny twenty-somethings would probably be all kinds of hilarious but he'd still feel—and certainly look—like a scout leader sent in to ensure the junior campers didn't burn down their cabins. His heart still did a funny little flip when Tristan's mouth turned down at the corners.

"Boo. You suck, GB."

"I'm working a double on Saturday," Ian countered. "Up at six, work till ten, then back on at seven the next morning."

"That sounds horrific."

"You get used to it. But with the trains being so shitty, I'm going to stay at the hospital which means I won't be anywhere near Weymouth or Cohasset."

"You're not going home at all? But where will you sleep?"

"In an on-call room." Ian chuckled at Tristan's wrinkled nose. "It's easier to stay sometimes than make the trip back and forth."

"Will you bring fuzzy bunny slippers to wear overnight? Because if you send me some sleepy-time selfies, Grumble Bear, I will forgive you for bailing on me." Tristan waggled his eyebrows and Ian's face went suddenly warm.

Wait. Was Tristan flirting with him?

Surely not.

Ian was a good-looking man—his mirror told him so when he could be bothered to examine himself closely. His eyes were expressive, and he'd heard often enough that their unusual shade of hazel was striking. An old rugby injury had left his nose a bit crooked, but he didn't think it detracted from his appearance, and his short beard complimented his grouchy bear vibe.

But Ian was also just days from turning forty and the floppy-haired kid sitting beside him was a full fifteen years younger. And *not* flirting, but simply being playful in the wonderfully open way Tristan had. Ian could work with that. Batting harmless remarks back and forth was a lot easier than wondering if a robot-building whiz kid could ever be interested in a well-preserved but still slightly broken-down guy like Ian.

"I don't own any animal slippers," he said to Tristan, "but I'll think of something. No pics for you unless you send some of the barbecue, though."

"Wintercue." Tristan knocked his shoulder gently into Ian's. "And of course, I'll send you pics. I want you to know what to expect during an actual barbecue at my place. Which won't happen until July." He dragged his hands down his face. "When the grass might start poking its way out of the snowbanks."

Ian laughed. They'd all lose their marbles if there was still snow to be seen during the dog days of summer. But he supposed hanging out with Tristan and doing anything might still be fun.

<hr />

"Hello, handsome."

Ian glanced up at his friend and fellow nurse, Mark Mannix, who took the seat across from him in the hospital cafeteria. Another friend, Jae-seong Bak, settled into the chair between them and smiled.

"Hey, guys," Ian said. "Thought you were standing me up."

"That's on him." Jae shot a droll look at Mark. "We walked out of the ED together ten minutes ago and it was like he disappeared in a puff of smoke."

"I had to pick up a curbside delivery." Eyes gleaming, Mark indicated a small duffel he'd placed on the chair beside him. "I'm here overnight and forgot to bring my go-bag so I had it dropped off. And the guy who brought it by? Mmm, hot as fuck. All tall and rangy with these amazing dark eyes and the best ass I've seen in a long—"

Jae held up a hand. "Okay, no. You could've just said 'I had to meet Owen outside.'"

"But that's very boring, Jae-seong," Mark said with a sigh.

Ian stifled a laugh. Mark was gone for his boyfriend. And while Ian typically found the idea of being gone for *anyone* annoying these days, he thought Mark's behavior was endearing.

Handsome and charismatic, Mark had once been the most enthusiastic hedonist Ian had ever met. He'd changed after meeting Owen though, and completely transformed into a loving, committed partner.

"Did you tell your man hello from us?" Jae asked him now.

"No, because I'm a terrible friend." Mark made duck lips with his mouth. "I'll message instead and send him your love. He was on his way to Haymarket to see Emmett actually, so he can pass some on to your man, too." Quickly, he withdrew his phone from his pocket and snapped a photo of Ian and Jae. "I'll just draw something lewd on that," he said, his delight obvious.

"If you must." Jae turned his attention to an insulated bag he'd set on the table. "Speaking of Emmett, I have a new recipe of his to share if you're in the mood to taste test."

"Like we'd ever say no," Ian said. Jae's partner Emmett was a chef at one of the hippest kitchens in the city, which meant Jae often came to work with enough fantastic food to feed a crowd.

"I can't wait for the new truck to launch," said a voice from behind them. Zac Alvarez's smile was wide under his trim beard as he pulled a chair up to the table, too. "Aiden's not sure if it'll be spring or summer before that happens but I guess we'll just have to see."

"They need to wait for the weather to stop trying to kill us," Jae replied with a laugh. "But for now, they're selling the Jeomsim food in Back Bay and Harvard Square a few days a week and the customers are loving it."

Ian had no doubt. Italian cuisine had put business partners Emmett and Aiden on the map, but they'd gone in a different direction with their latest venture selling foods inspired by Korean dishes Jae had been eating since childhood.

He served them small meat-stuffed buns that looked a bit like tacos and tasted unbelievably good. Notes of chili and ginger in the shredded meat made Ian's lips tingle, and the flatbread wrapped around it was beautifully soft and chewy. Serious heat lurked in a layer of crunchy kimchee, however, and he quickly found himself sweating.

"My face is on fire," he mumbled, "and I don't even care." On impulse, he picked up his phone and snapped a quick shot of his half-eaten plate for Tristan. "I know someone who would be all over this. What days do they sell Jeomsim in Back Bay? Am I saying that right?"

"It's more like 'juhm-sheem' with the way the Korean characters are placed," Jae replied at the same time Mark asked, "Someone who?"

Ian registered his friends' suddenly inquisitive looks. Oh, balls. "Uh. A guy I met on the train."

"I like this already." Mark grinned. "Tell us more."

Ian wiped his lips with a napkin. "There's nothing to tell. A guy sat next to me on the train, and we got to talking. He works in Back Bay."

"I'm glad *someone's* having fun on the T," Zac said, his arch expression making Ian snort.

"No one's having fun with so many lines out of service," he replied. "That's how I met Tristan. He and everyone else who'd usually take the Red Line out past JFK are riding *my* train until their service comes back."

"Gross. You should move back in here with us." Zac nodded. "That'd cut your commute down to almost nothing and you could skip the trains entirely. Besides, we miss you and Marco."

"We miss you guys, too. I don't miss the three-hundred percent rent hike, however, so thank you but no." Ian kept his voice mild, though his stomach still bottomed out. He and Marco *had* talked about moving back to the city, in fact, but they had no idea what to do with the beast dog and, oddly, that didn't sit well with either of them. "I'm fine with a longish commute."

"Because you met someone." Mark's face was smug. "When did this start?"

"I sat next to the guy on the train, Mark. And that was Monday." Ian rubbed the back of his neck with one hand. How could that be? "Honestly, my commute's been so screwed up, I feel like I've known him for longer."

His phone buzzed then, vibrating in quick bursts as message after message popped up on the screen, all from Tristan, whose interest had very obviously been piqued by Ian's food pic.

Omg.
What is this?
How?
Where do I get it?
Why are you eating without me??

"Jeez." Ian muttered scooped the phone up, cheeks heating as he tapped out a quick reply. "Guess he liked the look of your food, Jae."

Mark cocked his head. "How old is this guy?"

Ian stared at him for a beat, then the others. "Twenty-five. Why?"

"I figured as much from the buzz-buzz-buzz." Mark huffed a laugh. "Owen does that when he messages, like every thought has to go on a separate line."

Jae pointed at him. "Yes. The young people have their own ways." He shot a smile at Ian. "Do we get to meet him?"

"Yeah, no." The heat was creeping down Ian's neck now. "It's not like that. And Tristan's way too young for me."

"Says who?" Mark shrugged. "Owen was twenty-eight when we met. I'm not going to judge you for trolling a younger guy."

"Neither will we," Jae and Zac said together.

No surprise there. Their boyfriends were also barely past thirty and good friends of Owen's. Funny how that had worked out; this trio of friends finding happiness with younger men, all six growing so close they acted like family.

Because they are, Ian reminded himself. *Family isn't one-size-fits-all, and you know that better than anyone.*

Ian's chest ached a little. His friends had found lasting, real love in their May-December romances, but *he* hadn't been trolling a cute younger man. Much. He'd checked Tristan out after the imminent threat of being vomited on had passed, sure. And maybe the times they'd met at the pub. And in the mornings when he'd turned up at their table. Fuck. But only out of a desire to be sure the kid was healthy, Ian reminded himself, and now he could just stop doing that.

"Tristan's a commuting buddy," he assured his friends. "I doubt I'll see him again after the Red Line service goes back to normal."

4

"*This beautiful, peaceful energy is here with you always. You simply need to still the mind and reconnect whenever you need it. Always, by your side.*"

Ian opened his eyes as the track came to an end. The dog had been needy that morning, refusing to leave Ian alone, and he'd put off meditating until after he'd boarded the train with his friends. He felt mellow and pleasantly loose-limbed now as Tristan slid in beside him. "Hey, Chi-Town."

"Morning, GB." Tristan's eyes went round when Ian set not one but two steel canisters on the table. "Thank you. And what have we here?" He turned a bright look across the table onto Dennis and Marco. "Are these treats for the class?"

"They are indeed," Ian replied. "I didn't want to listen to Dennis whine for two days running so—" he slid the shorter of the thermoses across the table to his friend "—enjoy."

Dennis eyed the offering with a steely gaze. "I'm gonna be wicked pissed if this turns out to be poison."

"I think you mean you'll be wicked dead, but I swear it's just raspberry tea sweetened with honey." Ian handed a pair of silicone cups across the table too, while Tristan sat back in his seat and laughed. "There's enough for Marco if he'd like some. But no honey for you, I'm afraid," he said to Tristan. "You don't need the sugar what with the nausea."

Tristan waved him off. "You're right, I don't. This is perfect, GB."

Pleasure curled in Ian's belly, but he was distracted again by an impatient huff from Dennis.

"Just try it," he said, pushing a cup toward Marco. "Man can't live on coffee alone, you know."

"Man can try," came Marco's reply.

"If you don't like it, I'll buy you a goddamned coffee at South Station."

"A macchiato. *And* a chocolate croissant the size of my head," Marco bargained, making Dennis snort with laughter.

"Don't blame me if you lapse into a butter coma."

"Why would I blame anyone for feeding me butter?"

Ian exchanged an amused glance with Tristan. "What sort of mixed drinks were on the menu at your place last night?" he asked.

"None! Or none to *me* at least because I went to bed instead of playing Halo. Woo, I'm awesome." Tristan sipped his tea, but then his gaze zeroed in on Ian's shoulder and he furrowed his eyebrows over the rim of the cup. "Is that dog hair?"

"Probably." Ian glanced down at himself and sighed. "The beast dog was all over me before I left home. This is why I'm a wash-and-wear guy."

Tristan reached over and brushed at a patch on Ian's shirt where the hair was particularly thick, then gave his arm a quick squeeze. "I'm kind of jealous you have an extra layer that I don't."

Ian had to laugh. But then his phone buzzed in his pocket, and he frowned as he checked it, swapping a couple of texts back and forth with his ex about meeting up for lunch.

He'd just set his phone back on the table when the train's

motion changed and it quickly lost speed, eventually coming to a shuddering standstill in the middle of the tracks. Ian met Marco's eyes across the table, nodding as Marco mimed choking himself, and everyone froze when a voice came over the train's speakers.

"Passengers, we have traffic ahead. We expect to be moving shortly."

Ian crossed his arms over his chest. "'Expect to be moving shortly' means they don't have any idea what's in front of us. I'm starting to think I'm going to have to rent a hotel room in town and sleep over if I ever want to be on time for work."

"You could move closer to the city." Tristan looked past him to the window, face glum as he studied the frozen landscape. "You guys board at the far end of this line, right? So, your commute's what, an hour?"

"On the train, yes, if nothing goes wrong. We have to drive to and from Greenbush Station too, so there's that."

Tris pulled a face. "How do you stand it?"

"Outside of the current insanity, the commute's generally not a big deal. Driving into Boston can take a lot longer depending on traffic, and then you have to pay stupid amounts of money to park." Ian shrugged. "Besides, Cohasset is nice."

"I'm sure it's pretty and all, but it seems kind of remote for a friendly misanthrope like yourself." Tristan appeared almost scandalized. "What made you move out there anyway?"

Ian had seen the question coming a mile off; he'd practically invited Tristan to ask. But it still caught him off guard. Which was funny considering it was nobody's fault but his own that his personal life was still in the shithouse, long after he should have put it back together.

"I'm not a friendly anything." He knew he sounded gruff and, damn it, he could feel Marco and Dennis watching them. "But that's a story best told over beer and a basket of Buffalo wings. And only if you're buying."

"Deal." The grin that crossed Tristan's face was easy. An unfamiliar sharpness lingered in his gaze though, and Ian knew better than to think he'd stop wondering why Ian lived twenty miles outside of the city he worked in with a man who wasn't his partner.

Sure enough, Tristan asked about Ian's move to Cohasset later that day, when the two of them were polishing off a platter of spinach and artichoke dip at the pub. Ian was prepared for the question this time, but considered kicking himself in the ass nonetheless.

"I swear I mentioned needing hot wings for when I told you this story," he said, dragging a piece of celery through the bowl of dip. "I like to roll up my sleeves when I eat spicy pink sauce, by the way, so there should be a bulk of napkins and moist towelettes."

"You don't *have* to tell me any story you don't want to, GB. I'm not trying to make you uncomfortable."

Glancing up, Ian was struck by Tristan's serious face, no trace at all of his typical impish humor. He looked earnest and so fucking young as he watched Ian, despite the little line that had formed between his eyebrows.

"You're not making me uncomfortable." Ian paused, aware only as he said the words that they were absolutely true. "But if you really want to hear this, you should know I'm going to talk about a romance gone bad and we both know that's not your thing."

Tristan pushed a pita chip into the bowl. "Didn't think it was yours, either."

Ian licked his lips. "I wish it weren't. I got into the habit of saying I didn't believe in love after splitting up with Gus and guess I haven't had any good reason to stop."

"Gus is your ex?"

"Uh-huh. August James Dawson—Gus to his friends and family and Super Gus when he's feeling extra. He's an EMT." Ian sipped his beer. "We met when I moved up here to go to nursing school. He was a rookie with Boston Fire and rode with a rescue squad downtown until he had to find something new."

Tristan looked impressed. "Emergency medicine doesn't exactly sound like a step down from firefighting."

"Gus doesn't do anything by halves. He's intense. Passionate and one hundred percent committed. Unlike me, he doesn't have an Off button."

"My guy, you're a nurse. You're all of those things, too."

"I'm definitely passionate about my job and committed to my patients. But I like to unplug, too. My idea of vacation is to find a beach, plunk myself in a chair, and read between naps." Ian smiled down at his beer. "Gus, however, would be wanting to zipline and hike and eat foods that'd crawl away if you set them down."

"I can relate," Tristan said. "I like a mix of both, honestly. Play hard, then chill, preferably in the company of friends. Balance, y'know?"

The boarding call for their train sounded then, and they had to hustle out of the bar, hurrying into the snowy night with hundreds of others. Ian and Tristan were lucky to find seats on a bench on the upper level of the very last car, and Ian watched in amusement as Tristan sat on his messenger bag in a bid to free up precious inches.

"Please tell me there's nothing breakable in there," he said, "because you are gonna need more than a nurse if you take an iPhone up the ass."

Tristan's loud cackling made the guy on the bench beside him snort. "No worries," Tristan replied. "Nothing more dangerous in my bag tonight than some industry journals and what was once a bag of spicy cheese curls."

"Good evening, passengers, and welcome aboard the Greenbush train."

Tristan drew the tin of mints from his pocket. Opening it, he offered its contents to Ian, then the man seated by the aisle. When he spoke again, his voice was quieter, almost intimate, and something tight in Ian's gut relaxed just a touch. "So, you and Gus, huh?"

"Yup, me and Gus."

"You loved him," Tristan said, no question at all in his voice, and Ian absently stroked his beard with his knuckles.

"I did. We were doing the mate-for-life thing you spurn. Until we weren't." From the corner of his eye, Ian saw the guy in the aisle seat slip a set of earbuds into his ears and quietly thanked the universe. He didn't need an audience for this. "We started unraveling after Gus was injured. That's why he left firefighting and became an EMT. There was a structural collapse at a fire, see. He and some of the guys on his truck were pinned by debris. He lost his right leg below the knee. Another firefighter died."

Tristan sucked in a breath. "Fuck. I'm sorry, man."

"Me too," Ian said with a sigh. "It's been two years and it's still … a lot."

"I hear you."

Tristan's gentle tone told Ian he could keep talking or stop without being judged. And while Ian felt some surprise that he wanted to keep talking, he didn't question himself. He felt grateful instead. Tristan was really *listening*. Not just hearing Ian out. Or coming at him with opinions or attitude.

"Physically, Gus bounced back quicker than anyone thought he would—he's called Super Gus for a reason. But he had terrible phantom pain for a while. Struggled emotionally. He'd lost his career and his friend, and the grief and guilt ate him up."

"That must have been so hard."

"It was," Ian said quietly. "Gus didn't know how to handle his pain and I didn't know how to help him. We fought all the time. And I could feel him slipping away. One night I came home early from a shift and found him with someone."

He held up a hand at Tristan's stricken expression. "Now, hold on before you start with the sad eyes. It wasn't as terrible as it sounds. Gus and Ben weren't doing anything when I walked into the apartment—they were just eating dinner. And I knew Ben."

That weasel.

"He was a friend to us both and had been for years. But I could tell something was up. Saw it in their faces, felt it in the air between them." Ian licked his lips. "I was right. It wasn't physical then, but Gus was connecting with Ben in ways that went beyond attraction."

"That almost sounds worse." Tristan made a face. "Sex is just bodies, y'know? Emotions are way more complicated."

Privately, Ian agreed. He liked to think he could have dealt with a physical affair. Gotten through it somehow and been able to put it behind him. But he'd choked on the bitter pill of knowing Gus's *heart* had reached out to someone else.

The guy in the aisle seat stood as the train approached JFK station, giving Ian a moment to clear the tightness that had crept into his throat.

"After Ben left, I begged Gus to talk to me. And he did. Finally," Ian said when the train started moving again. "But everything just got more complicated. Because he started talking about wanting kids. Said that what we had together wasn't enough and he thought having a child was the answer. But neither of us had ever wanted kids, and all I could think was that Gus was looking to fill up the holes of his grief. Fuck, he was so pissed when I said that."

Ian scrubbed a hand over his hair. He and Gus had been on the same page about family and kids from day one. Until Gus had come out of the house collapse and ripped the page—shit, the entire book of life they'd been writing together—to pieces.

"It's still hard, you know? Wondering if I misjudged him. People come out of traumatic experiences all the time wanting to remake their lives," Ian said only for Tristan to shake his head.

"Yeah, they do. Doesn't mean the rest of the world is up for remaking itself along with them."

"Mmm." Ian looked down at his hands in his lap. "Gus and I

fought for weeks. And none of what he was saying sat right with me. He'd always been so adamant about not wanting children and now it was all 'life is too short and we need to make the most of ours.' I just couldn't go there with him." He sighed. "Call me a selfish ass if you want."

Tristan held up his hands in a gesture like surrender. "My stepdad never wanted kids, either. The only reason Rick *is* my stepdad is because he fell for my mom and got Jim and me as part of a package deal." He smiled. "He's super loving and a really good parent, and I can't imagine anyone being better at it. But if Mom hadn't already had kids when they met, Rick would've been happy it just being the two of them forever."

Ian's eyes stung. "Maybe that's me. I like children. And I know to never say never because life always throws curveballs when you least expect them. But I couldn't agree to what Gus wanted. Not then. Not with the way we were falling apart. And when Gus said he needed to be with someone who wanted the same things he did, I knew he didn't mean me."

"He meant Ben."

"Yup. That fuckface." Ian exhaled hard through his nose. "That was sort of the final blow. Gus was angry when he said it and just trying to hurt me, but I knew he meant it deep down. That he'd find someone else if I didn't bend. We tried for a while. Went to couples therapy and did the hard work. Said over and over that we wanted to stay together. But I don't think our hearts really believed we could do it. And in the end, I left."

"Next stop, Quincy Center. Quincy Center is the next stop for this train."

Ian leaned back against his seat, feeling every one of his almost forty years and the last ten hours he'd worked in particular. "I didn't want to lose Gus, but I didn't want to lose myself, either, and I knew that would happen if I tried to force myself into what he wanted. I mean ... a *kid*." He shook his head. "How the hell were we going to take care of a child when we could barely take care of each other? But it didn't matter what I thought or how much work we did, because in his head—in his heart—Gus was already gone."

A hand came to rest over Ian's, solid and warm. "I'm sorry."

"Thanks." Without really thinking, Ian flipped his palm up and wrapped his fingers around Tristan's. "For a while, I wished I'd had the balls to have at least tried. But I'm not wired right for kids."

"Ian. You're not wired *wrong*. People don't come with checklists. All that crap people feed us about needing to have kids and mate for life like freaking swans just to be happy is wrong. Sure, it works for lots of people, but not for everyone." Tristan's grip tightened around Ian's hand. "There's no such thing as a template for a happy life."

"You're right. We talk about that sometimes, Gus and me. What we wanted then, what we want now, and how everything's changed." Ian smiled. "Or how some things haven't changed. Like how he and Ben don't have any kids yet."

"You guys still talk?"

"Sure. Gus and I are friends. Took work to get to that point but ..." Ian shrugged.

"Huh." Tristan ran his bottom lip between his teeth. "I wouldn't have thought you'd want that."

"Well, Gus and I were friends before we ever got together." Ian cast a quick glance out the window before looking back to Tristan. "It's hard to imagine not having him in my life. And he feels the same. That hanging on to being friends is worthwhile."

"Now approaching Weymouth Landing. Weymouth Landing, next stop."

Tristan cocked his head. "Does he know you call his boyfriend a fuckface?"

The sheer absurdity of the question made Ian laugh. "I can't confirm. But that's what Ben is so, I don't care."

"I believe you." Tristan smiled. "Thanks for trusting me with this. I'm glad you did. And that you came out of that situation okay."

Truthfully, Ian hadn't. Leaving Gus had been one of the hardest things he'd ever done and left his heart in a million pieces. But these days, Ian felt like he was doing more than simply surviving the fallout. That made his heart feel good. Just like it did when Tristan looked at him the way he was now.

5

Friday dawned through another round of heavy snow that Elliott greeted with glee during his morning romp, bounding through the drifts like a big furry goofball while Ian tried not to straight up die from the cold.

He did his best to de-ice the dog once they'd gone back inside, but somehow lost hold of Elliott, who took off like a shot for the kitchen. When Ian tried to follow, he stepped wrong in a puddle of the ice Elliott had shed and went down like a ton of bricks, leaving him flat on his back and wondering where his life had gone wrong.

"What was that?" Marco's call was followed by a gasp. "Holy shit, dog. Did you try to build an igloo with your face?"

Elliott answered with a series of grumbly woo-woo noises and Ian quickly sat up.

"Watch it!" he yelled, but he was too late, and the unmistakable sound of a beast dog shaking itself dry was followed by a loud, shocked screech.

"Oh, my God! He shook all over me! There's snow everywhere!"

Snorting with laughter, Ian heaved himself up, kicking off his boots before he jogged into the kitchen where a snow-splattered

Marco was glowering at Elliott, who appeared both completely unbothered and still rather wet.

"It's like Dante's Ninth Circle out there," Ian said after they'd toweled Marco, Elliott, himself, and most of the kitchen dry. He leaned against the counter slurping coffee without shame while Marco scrambled eggs for them both. "I do not relish the idea of freezing to death at the station while the T decides if it's going to take its head out of its ass."

Marco made a face. "Balls."

"Indeed."

They kept an eye on the commuter rail app, tracking their train's repeated delays as they got ready to head out. But they still had a long-ass wait in Ian's ancient Jeep once they'd reached Greenbush Station and another on the platform when the train began its approach. It was almost eight o'clock when they finally stomped aboard a train and every body part Ian could name felt chilled.

"Holy hell." Dennis rubbed his mittened hands together as they sat down, face flushed. "Is my nose still attached to my face? I can't feel it at all."

"You're good." Ian pawed at the scarf covering the lower half of his face, then peeled off his mittens, flexing his icy fingers in an effort to get the blood circulating. "Fucking A."

"Yes," Marco muttered, arms still crossed over his chest.

"I brought tea," Ian told them. "Just give me a minute to defrost and we'll see if it's still hot."

"Good morning and welcome aboard the now very delayed 7:05 Greenbush train to South Station. We'll be departing shortly."

Ian unpacked the thermoses and cups, smiling as he slid them across the table. Dennis poured his tea with a heartfelt sigh but frowned before he'd even raised it to his lips.

"Think we'll see your boy Tristan today? This train'll be delayed over an hour by the time we get the fuck out of here."

"I think you mean *if* we get the fuck out of here. And I dunno about Tris—tan." Ian watched his friends eye him, knowing they'd caught his slight slip over Tristan's name, and silently cursed himself for being a dumbass of epic proportions.

Four days. He'd known Tristan Santos four days and eight train rides, around which they'd shared three thermoses of tea, several pints of beer and plates of snacks, way too many text messages, and a red and white tin of mints that had started the whole fucking thing. Ninety-six hours and *somehow*, Ian had grown almost fond of the kid, enough to start calling him by a nickname, at least in his head.

You are a putz.

Ian glanced out the window. Damn Tris—Tristan! —and his friendly, good-natured openness. The easy talk and laughter that came with his pretty eyes and mouth made it far too easy for Ian to ignore some things he shouldn't have.

Like how he hadn't quite recovered from the left turn his life had taken with Gus. Still needed to figure out who Ian Byrne was now that *he* was no longer part of a *we*. And, most importantly, had a messy, fucked-up life that not even a near stranger could fail to notice. That was what Tristan was to Ian. A lovely, personable guy whom Ian knew only slightly and would never see again once the subway resumed its regular service.

So, yeah; Ian was poised on the border of very dangerous territory. He could so easily become more than fond of Tris. Could really *like* him, and possibly already did, which explained why he'd word vomited so many details about his messy, fucked-up life during the train ride home last night.

And if Tristan ghosted him in response, Ian wouldn't blame him at all.

"He probably found a shuttle bus into Boston," he said as the train finally glided away from the station. "Better than dying of exposure."

Dennis grimaced. "I've heard people are calling out sick rather than riding those shuttles. Apparently, they're more terrible than these sardine cans we ride."

"Next stop, North Scituate. Doors open on the right."

Ian opened his tablet and immersed himself in nursing journals, but his attention wavered when his phone chimed with an incoming message. After reviewing it, he glanced up and caught Dennis's eye, and whatever Dennis saw in his face made him frown.

"What happened?"

"Doc Hennessey referred Jenna to oncology over at MGH."

"Aw, shit."

"Is this the kid you saw Monday?" Marco asked. "The one who comes in for PT and calls you Boner?"

Ian put a hand over his eyes. "Bones. She calls me Bones, you reprobate," he replied over Dennis's cackling. "Jenna just turned nineteen and is such a nice kid."

A guard for the women's basketball team at one of the local universities, Jenna Orloff had been referred to the clinic at Post Office Square following an off-season shoulder sprain. Like many of Ian's patients, she'd been scared and in pain at their first meeting and prone to surly moods. But he'd gotten to know her during her treatments, and she'd taken a shine to him too, seeking him out during every appointment if only to say hello.

"She came in Monday with a sore back," he said to Marco. "I noticed her lymph nodes were enlarged during the exam and that led everything in a whole different direction. She's on her own out here," he added. "Her dad lives in Michigan and can't just show up when she's got an appointment, even for something scary like this. I wish she had a friendly face in the crowd."

Dennis's smile was indulgent. "I think I can help. I've got a friend over in oncology at MGH—I could ask him to check in on Jenna."

"That'd be fantastic, thank you." Ian narrowed his eyes. "What do I have to do in return?"

"Mmm, nothing much. Maybe just listen to the *stellar* idea your friends have for celebrating your birthday."

Ian stifled a groan. This couldn't be good.

Dennis turned to Marco. "Zac and Mark want to throw a party at your place next weekend, starting Friday night."

Marco's eyebrows went up. "*Starting* Friday night? What the hell does that mean?"

Ian shot a look at his housemate. "Did you know about this?"

"Nope." Marco's headshake was firm. "I'd have told you if I had because I know how you feel about the b-word."

"Birthday." Dennis rolled his eyes. "It's a birthday, you bozos, not a b-word, and we all have one every year including you, my darling pain in the ass, grumpy-fuck friend. I swear, if I have to literally sit on you and make you blow out candles, I am going to make it happen."

He outlined the party plans through the next several stops, his chatter filling the miles, so Ian lost track of their travels, only to be startled back to the here and now when Tristan practically tumbled into the empty seat beside him.

"Jesus Hot Christmas Cake," Tristan muttered. "I can't remember the last time I was this cold. And I lived in *Chicago* for fuck's sake."

Ian quickly scooted over to give him some room. "Are you okay? You look half-frozen."

"I think I might be. I need help. Could you …?" Laughing, he angled himself toward Ian, who gave him a hand wrangling the strap of his messenger bag over his head as another person slid into the aisle seat. "Thank you."

Ian frowned at him. "Let's get you some tea. What are you even doing here?"

Tristan blinked a few times, clearly mystified by the question. "Commuting to work like I do every day of the week?"

"We figured you'd have found a shuttle to ride," Marco said with a smile. "No point in standing out in this cold if you don't have to."

"I didn't have much choice," Tristan replied. "The shuttles run out of the train stations, so I'd need to get to one of those first and then stand around hoping a shuttle showed up and that they'd have room for me. Either way, I'd still be playing a game of not freezing to death and I actually hate that game."

"Next stop for this train will be Quincy Center. Quincy Center, next stop."

Tristan's expression brightened as Ian handed him a cup of tea. "Thank you, GB." He took a greedy sip and groaned, cradling the cup to his chest with his hands. "Mmm. I think I love you in a very romantical way right now." He turned a grin on the group when they all cracked up laughing. "What?"

Dennis waved a finger at him. "Romantical is not a word."

"Is too. Of, relating to, imbued with, or characterized by romance. Also, given to thoughts and feelings of love, especially idealized or sentimental love." Tristan waggled his eyebrows at Ian. "Ooh, I almost forgot." Setting down his cup, he pawed at his bag and quickly withdrew out a thermal pouch. "I have treats to share with the class."

Ian raised his eyebrows. "Oh, do ya now?"

"Yup." He set the pouch on the table. "My housemate baked muffins and, if the universe is my friend, they won't be frozen solid."

Opening the bag, he showed off a half-dozen pinky-mauve muffins that smelled so mouthwateringly good Ian's stomach rumbled loudly.

"Jesus, Ian." Marco let out a laugh. "I can hear you from here!"

Tristan's obvious delight made it impossible for Ian to feel embarrassed. He picked a muffin out of the bag and bit into it carefully, mindful of how even a partially frozen baked good could fuck up his teeth. He made a happy noise as toffee and lemon notes burst onto his tongue followed by the more surprising flavor of ginger and it was all he could do not to groan.

"Not frozen. And *wow*, so good. I would marry your housemate right now if she asked me," he said around the mouthful. "If she didn't already have a boyfriend. And I wasn't irretrievably gay."

Tristan laughed. "I'll call that a win all around."

He handed muffins and napkins to Marco and Dennis, then shared a few extra with the woman in the aisle seat and some passengers standing nearby.

"What kind of muffins are these?" Ian asked, examining the last bite of the half he'd been eating. "The pink makes me think berry, but I can taste that I'm wrong."

"They're zucchini bread," Tristan said, brow furrowed. "But how are they pink in your world?"

"Shit, I'm sorry." Ian smiled as he realized his mistake. "I'm blue-yellow colorblind."

"Aha!" Tristan's whole face lit up. "The comment you made last night about spicy pink sauce now makes a lot more sense."

"Spicy sauce? Oh, right! The Buffalo wings you didn't buy. I forget their sauce is allegedly orange."

"Yeah, there's no allegedly about it, buddy."

"Says you," Ian replied. "Maybe you know this, but there are two types of light receptor nerves in our eyes, cones and rods. The cones allow us to process color and when you have tritanomaly like me, the perception of blue and green and yellow and red are different. Muddled, really, as opposed to a true color blindness. I see shades of green in places you don't, and a lot of pink."

"Huh." Tristan frowned. "The sky isn't blue for you?"

"It's not what you'd consider blue but to me it's just sky. Also, bananas are pink on Planet Ian."

"Well, I want pink bananas!" Tristan grinned. "The tritanomaly doesn't get in the way of nursing?"

Ian shook his head. "There are plenty of colorblind persons in healthcare. My eyes don't process color the same way yours do, but the spectrum I see makes sense in my head. I know what I'm looking at when I do an exam. Hey, what the latest on the wintercue?"

They talked details as the last miles spun out, Tris's obvious excitement spreading warmth all through Ian. Despite a firm belief that barbecuing in ass-deep snow was not a thing sane people should want to do, he'd started to see some appeal in the project.

Or perhaps the appeal was all Tristan, whose bright-eyed enthusiasm was so genuine it was honestly contagious.

"Thanks again for the treat," Ian said as they crept into the station. "It was really thoughtful of you."

"You're welcome." Tristan watched Ian wrap the remaining half of his muffin up in the napkin. "You liked it, right?"

"Very much." Ian smiled. "Processed sugars make me moody, so I try not to eat too much of them at once. This, however," he said of the little bundle, "will make my break a lot nicer."

They gathered their belongings and filed onto the platform, but Ian wanted to curse as a wind so bitter it stole his breath swirled around him. The foursome made a beeline for the terminal, scurrying in their race to find shelter. Once they were inside, Dennis's face grew so dejected Ian actually stopped walking and put a hand on his friend's arm.

"What's wrong?"

"This is going to sound stupid, but I don't know if I'm up for the walk over to Post Office Square." What could be seen of Dennis's cheeks over his scarf flushed with color. "Would you be mad if I just went back home?"

Marco held out his arm. "Buck up, buttercup. C'mon and I'll buy us some hot chocolate and Danish."

"Christ. Like we didn't just eat the best zucchini bread in the world," Dennis grumbled. But he took hold of Marco's arm anyway, expression growing a touch more sunny.

"Thanks again for the snack, Chi-Town," he said to Tristan. "Guess I'll see you next week."

"Later, nerds." Tristan watched Marco and Dennis head off before turning to look at Ian. "Think he's okay?"

"Yeah. He's just frustrated and cold and sick of being stuck indoors all the time. Exactly like the rest of us." Ian glanced toward the exits. "I'd call a Lyft to get us the rest of the way to

Post Office Square, but I doubt I'd be able to find one." He cocked a quizzical eyebrow at Tristan's smile. "What?"

"Mmm, nothing. Just that you're a nice guy under the surly Grumble Bear thing you've got going."

"Slander and lies, Tris. No one who knows me would ever believe it."

"I *know* that's a lie." Tristan gave Ian a doting look, then bumped their shoulders together. "I like it when you call me Tris, y'know. Only a few people in my life do and I've always liked it. I'm not gonna see you tonight, right?"

"Nope." Ian ignored his hot cheeks. "I'll be over at MGH after lunch and then on again tomorrow at ass o'clock in the morning."

"Then you should have the last of the muffins for breakfast."

"What? No."

"Yup." Smiling, Tristan handed the lunch pouch to Ian, then turned for the exits. "Don't work too hard this weekend, Ian. And don't forget to send me pics of your fuzzy bunny slippers!"

6

Tris—and he was definitely *Tris* now rather than *Tristan* in Ian's head—did not freeze to death while digging a hole in the snow.

Ian knew as much from the messages that began arriving only moments after he'd clocked in at MGH. They were simple observations at first, ranging from how much Tris enjoyed the test-break-fix part of working with robots to his current love-hate relationship with a series of novels he'd been reading. Some messages were composed of song lyrics and emoji while others held snaps of the world around Tris, including photos of a dark tabby cat in a variety of poses that started showing up around dinnertime. Ian sometimes didn't reply for long stretches, but Tris hadn't seemed bothered, and they kept the back and forth going until late into the graveyard hours.

Shots of the wintercue appeared at mid-morning on Saturday and continued for hours, though it was evening before Ian had time to look them over and truly understand what Tris and his friends had been up to. After excavating a pit for the gas grill, they'd built a near mountain with the snow they'd displaced, and there were photos of some housemates scaling it while others tended the grill, everyone bundled up in so many layers they were like shapeless blobs with eyes. Tris still caught Ian's attention in every shot, gaze bright and grin so captivating Ian had to smile back.

"What's got you all smiley?" Jae asked as they sat down to a very late lunch.

"Oh." Ian ignored the heat crawling up the back of his neck. "Remember the guy I told you about from the train?" He held up his phone. "He and his housemates went hog-wild in the snow. Dug out a huge pit and set up what they're calling a wintercue."

Mark's eyes gleamed. "That is *nuts* and I love it. Owen and Emmett would be all over a wintercue," he said to Jae. "Bet they come up with something just as bananas when we tell them about this."

Ian didn't doubt it. He could easily picture Owen and Emmett in among the wintercue crowd, Zac's boyfriend Aiden by their side as they scaled the giant snowbanks with Tris, towing the gas grill behind them.

He said as much as they went through the rest of the photos, and Jae swapped a smirk with Mark. But they kept their teasing gentle, suggesting that Ian being smitten was too cute for words. Ian shrugged them off easily and gave them each a muffin from Tris's stash, but the truth was he thought about Tris on and off for the rest of his shift, particularly during the quieter times between patients. And he felt positively distracted as he lay on a lumpy mattress in one of the on-call rooms that night, gritting his teeth against the arousal warming his belly and praying for sleep that only came in dribs and drabs before he had to get up and start a double shift.

All of which happened before he got home late Sunday night and found Elliott suffering from a stomach problem that made the rest of the evening endlessly gross.

By morning, Ian was so sleep deprived he thought he might die. He knew he looked it from the way Dennis was eyeing him as they boarded the train.

"No offense, Grumble Bear, but you look terrible."

"Please, stop calling me motherfucking Grumble Bear." Ian went to rub his eyes with his fingers but knocked his black-framed glasses askew in the process, smack into the bridge of his nose. "Ow."

Across the table, Marco huffed out a laugh. "Man, you are a wreck. You need to meditate."

"No, I do not." Ian groused. "If I start listening to the 'breathe in and breathe out' right now, I am never going to be awake for my shift. Oh, who am I kidding, I'm gonna pass out in a minute anyway." Sighing, he reached for his backpack. "Made some tea."

"Ian. Why?" Dennis accepted the thermos with a frown. "You could've slept another half hour."

"Sure." Ian made a face. "*If* the damned dog hadn't woken me up with his stomach drama. Funny how he never goes to Marco with any of that."

"It's because El wants his mama when he's not feeling good," Marco said, grinning wide when Ian flipped him off.

"I'm gonna check out for a bit." Wedging his bag against the car's wall, Ian crossed his arms over his chest, his body already melting into the seat. "Tris's thermos is there if he wants it and that's his lunch bag, too. Wake me before South Station if I don't wake up on my own, will ya?"

"Of course," Dennis replied, words soft and squishy to Ian's dozy brain.

It felt like only seconds before he surfaced again but, for a fleeting moment, he had no idea where he was. He opened his eyes, squinting against the light, and found Tris seated beside him, book in hand and a smile on his face.

"Good morning, sleepy."

"'Sup, Chi-Town," Ian murmured. "Were you watchin' me snooze?"

"Maybe a little."

"You're creepy."

"And you're cute. Especially with the glasses and the cozy

brown sweater. All rumpled and snuffly and curled up against the window like the grouchy bear you are."

"For the love of *God* stop talking." Groaning, Ian shifted and pulled himself straight. "What the heck time is it, anyway? And where the hell are we stopped?"

"Somewhere between JFK and South Station." Tris set the book down beside his cup of tea. "The driver said they're de-icing the tracks outside the terminal and we've been here a while. Also, it's 8:45."

Ian squinted at him. "Huh?"

"You asked for the time," Tris replied. "Thanks for the photos of your rainbow-striped socks, by the way. Fuzzy bunny slippers would have been cuter, but the socks are very you."

"Not sure that's a compliment. But shots of my socks seemed like fair payment for the wintercue pics you sent. Your party looked epic."

"It was. Pretty sure we're going to have to wait until the spring thaw before we'll be able to get the grill out of the pit, though." Smiling, Tris slid another insulated lunch bag over the table to Ian. "Want some breakfast? Ela made biscuits with almond flour and cheddar and they're really fucking good. Low carb too, which I think works with your no sugar rule."

Ian smiled, insides swooping goofily as he opened the bag. "I didn't say *no* sugar. I just try not to eat a ton of the processed stuff. Thank you for thinking of me."

"You're welcome. There's a cup of maple syrup if you want to drizzle or dip." Amusement stole across Tris's face as he watched Ian unwrap the package of biscuits. "Imagine my surprise when I got on the train and found you dead to the world. You're sneaky pulling the old role reversal there, GB."

"Holy hell, this is delicious," Ian mumbled around a mouthful before looking askance at him. "And what do you mean, role reversal? I didn't plan to pass out."

"I figured you were biased against biscuits and didn't want to hurt my feelings."

"You're not making sense. I didn't know you were bringing biscuits and I'm literally making out with one now."

"This is a disturbingly erotic image, Ian." Tris leered. "Especially from the guy who was snoring a minute ago."

"I was *asleep*. I didn't get back to Greenbush until almost nine last night and we had to dig the Jeep out for the nine-hundredth time because Marco was with me at the hospital." Ian wiped his mouth with a napkin. "Then, the freaking dog was up all night with a stomach problem I'd really prefer to wipe from my memory banks, *and* I spent the whole goddamned weekend sleeping on a piece of shit mattress composed of petrified sawdust and ping-pong balls."

The corners of Tris's lips tilted up in a full-on grin. "Jeez, you kiss your mother with that mouth?"

"Don't bring my mother into this, Santos."

"That's a yes, then?"

"*Guys*."

Ian froze as Dennis's voice cut through the back-and-forth and Tris's eyes got big. Their voices sounded *loud* against the heavy silence in the train car, and together they looked across the table to their friends. But not before Ian noticed the passengers standing in the aisle who were totally staring at Tris and him, every one of them smiling.

"Oops," was all Ian said before he sent a sidelong look back to Tris who cracked up laughing.

The PA system let out a strangled-sounding chime.

"Passengers, apologies for the delay. We've been informed that the ice has been cleared from the tracks ahead and we should be moving in about ten minutes. Or fifteen. So ... sometime today, South Station will be the last stop for this train."

"Yay," Ian muttered, then tucked into a second biscuit.

"I WISH WE HAD TIME FOR A BEER," TRIS SAID AS THEY boarded a train that evening, and while his tone was easy, something got Ian's hackles up.

"Tough day with the robots?" he asked.

"Nah. It was okay. Some interesting projects came into our pipeline, including a few for work out of state."

"Ah." Well, now Ian knew what was probably coming. "Anything you'd want to take on?"

"Possibly. We'll see." Tris gave him a crooked smile as he slid onto a bench.

Ian nodded. "Don't let me fall asleep, okay? I caught a second wind after lunch today but with my luck the balloon will pop, and you'll have to scrape me off the floor."

"Are you okay to drive tonight?"

"No, but Marco's got the Jeep anyway and he's picking me up." Ian smiled at Tris's uncharacteristically stern demeanor. "I'm beginning to think you're right about the role reversal thing. It's starting to weird me out."

Tris raked his floppy hair back from his forehead. "All I need is a backpack and a pair of scowly eyebrows and it'd be an alternate universe where I boss people around and you pass out whenever you're seated."

"I fell asleep *one time*," Ian protested. "You'd be a zombie too if you had to sleep on the rock slabs that pass for beds in the on-call rooms." He groaned as what felt like a full-body yawn seized him. "Crap."

Tris put a hand over his mouth, trying to hide his own sympathetic yawn and failing. "Ugh, sorry."

"Not your fault. Just keep talking so I don't melt into a puddle of goo. You got any mints left?"

"Yup." Tris produced the tin in an instant, then reached over and tugged Ian's coat zipper open. "You feeling okay?"

"Meh. Thought a mint might perk me up."

"Eat as many as you want. I have an extra tin in my bag. I had some ginger gummies too, but they were so good I ate the whole bag. You should have warned me about their deliciousness." The tips of Tris's ears colored. "Anyway, the birthday party in Philly is this weekend and I figured I'd start gathering my supplies."

"Wicked smaaht."

"I love it when you do the accent. Oh hey, I just remembered you never answered my question last week."

"You asked me a thousand and ten questions last week, Tris, I'm going to need you to narrow it down for me."

"That's fair." Tris laughed. "I meant the one about living in Cohasset. I know *why* you moved but not what made you pick Cohasset. You could have moved to Cambridge, Brighton, Quincy ... a bunch of places closer to where you work."

Ian ran his knuckles over his beard. "I rented a studio in Beacon Hill at first, actually. But after a while, paying a ton of money for a four-hundred- square-foot box got to me, and I decided to move someplace cheaper."

There was more to Ian's story, of course. Issues more serious than high rents had pushed him into the house he shared with Marco and a shaggy dog. But Ian wasn't ready to spill those gory details, not after he'd already laid so much bare to a guy he'd only known a week. The urge to keep the conversation going was still there though, so strong Ian had to wonder what it was about *this* guy that made him want to open up.

Oblivious, Tris was nodding. "Rent in this area is bananas. I know you think I'm nuts for sharing a space with five other people but, for real, I'm not paying a bajillion dollars every month to some jackass I'll never meet.

"Tell me about this dog of yours," he said then. "You complain about him a lot, but I know it's all for show. Just like the rest of your grumping."

"Elliott's not my dog—he came with the house."

Tris's expression turned dubious. "I hate to break it to you GB, but from everything you and Marco have said, Elliott thinks he's yours and by 'yours' I mean you specifically."

"No."

"Yes. Stop deflecting and tell me about him."

Ian rolled his eyes and tried to ignore the way Tris's shoulder was pressed against his. "The vet thinks Elliott's around three. He's probably a Malamute-Husky mix based on his coat and behaviors. He doesn't bark but sort of yodels with these woo-woo kind of noises, and he'll howl when he's really feeling it. He fucking *loves* snow. He's big and strong as hell but generally easygoing, and smart, too, like worryingly so." He laughed. "I mean it when I say he came with the house. He was there when we moved in and clearly at home."

Tris brought his eyebrows together, looking like he didn't know whether to be angry or saddened. "Someone left him there?"

"Yes and no. According to the neighbors, the people who leased the house previously found El in their backyard. They took him in and did a search for his owners but came up empty. Pretty sure they'd have kept him, but they moved overseas and couldn't bring him along. So, the neighbors took care of El until Marco and I showed up and boom, there he was, the beast dog welcome wagon."

"You could have taken him to a shelter or put him up for adoption." Tris was smirking now. "But you let him stay. Which tells me you knew you and Elliott were made for each together from the start. How'd he get a name like Elliott?"

"It's Elliott Stabler, actually, a.k.a., Wonder Dog, sock liberator and stealer of dog food."

Tris stared at Ian blankly for a beat before his face lit up. "Elliott Stabler, like the detective on *Law & Order: SVU*?"

"Uh-huh. Marco likes to hum the theme song while the dog eats," Ian said. "It's like he's conducting the dumbest Pavlovian experiment in the galaxy because now when the show comes on TV, Elliott grabs his bowl from the kitchen and brings it to us."

Tris lapsed into a fit of giggles. "You guys are dorks."

Ian had to smile. "We started throwing out names at random

to see how they fit and one day he yodeled when one of us called out 'Elliott' and we figured it was a good a sign as any."

"There is something so wrong with you."

"You love it."

"You know I do!" Tris gave him a sweet smile. "You wanna grab dinner the next weekend we're both free? Like a real dinner, not just snacks and beer in between train rides. We can meet up somewhere in between Cohasset and Weymouth and not talk about snow. I could meet Elliott!"

Ian ignored his stupid heart as it tried to beat its way out of his chest. "Yeah, sure. I'd like that," he said, and leaned a tiny bit closer into Tris's shoulder. "I'm sure the dog *who is not mine* would enjoy it too." A jaw-creaking yawn seized him, so huge it made his eyes tear. "Ugh, fuck all the things."

Tris shushed him gently. "Think standing would do you some good? We can hang by the doors and get some fresh air." He stood and held his hands out, hauling Ian up when he grabbed hold. "Maybe it's wrong, but I kind of like you this way. All loopy and open and a big fucking wreck."

"It's sort of humiliating."

"Nah. You put the hot in hot mess, GB. And you were always nice when I was the one staggering around half awake—now I can do the same for you."

Ian grunted as Tris fussed over him, straightening Ian's coat and backpack in a way that might have been annoying had he been less tired and Tris not so cute. Together, they pushed past the passengers standing in the aisle toward the nearest door, which already stood half-open thanks to the overflow of people. Unsurprisingly, the air in the vestibule was *many* degrees cooler and rendered Ian instantly more awake.

They chatted for the next several minutes until the approach to Weymouth Landing station was announced, and Tris pulled his hat on.

"I'll call you from the street," he said, frowning when Ian waved him off.

"You don't need to do that. I'm fine, really."

Tris didn't reply, but his expression remained doubtful, and he held Ian's gaze without wavering. Ian fell into those pale eyes. He was aware of the passengers around them preparing to debark, of the train's gradual slowing, of another announcement over the PA. But he couldn't look away from the man standing in front of him.

Tris leaned in closer, bringing a hand up and brushing his knuckles over Ian's bearded cheek, imitating the gesture Ian used so often to self-soothe. The moment stretched out, sweet energy buzzing between them, Tris's fingers warm against Ian's skin. Tris waited until the train had slid to a stop before dropping his hand, and the softest of smiles touched his full lips.

"I'll see you tomorrow, Ian," he said over the train doors thunking open, and then he was gone the next instant, out into the frigid night.

Ears filled with the thunder of his own heart, Ian stepped back to allow the passengers who were streaming toward him to pass. But they were just a blur, and he really was so very fucked. Of all the people on the planet to crush on—Lord, that he was crushing at all was humiliating—he'd picked a guy way too young and even more unavailable, the perfect recipe to leave Ian hating himself when Tris rode off into the sunset for a new job or a program that would bring the advanced degree he wasn't yet sure needed. Surely one or both of those things would come to pass soon, and Tris would be gone; that was just how Ian's world worked and he knew better than to get attached.

He really did.

He didn't fight his smile at all when his phone buzzed with an incoming call though, insides swooping with a foolish, giddy rush when he heard Tris's breathless laugh.

"So, I'm up to my ass in snow and, of course, I thought of you."

"That sounds like the start of a bad joke. And you should be thinking of yourself," Ian chided him. "Using that big brain of yours to get home in one piece."

"Oh, I'm doing that," Tris replied. "But since I've got a ten-minute walk through the aforementioned ass-deep snow, how 'bout you quit complaining and keep me company while I do it?"

Ian's body felt toasty, like laundry fresh from the dryer. "Okay," he said, and did.

7

Eyes closed, Ian coasted on surf sounds gently pierced by the mellow tones of meditation bells. He felt the train's stop-and-go motions beneath him, doors clunking open and closed as passengers boarded and debarked. But time was immaterial, and he stayed focused on the ocean noises and soft-spoken voice of his guide.

"Know that you are a blessing to this earth. Believe in yourself and your power and radiate that surety out into the world. Inhale a few, deep breaths."

Ian did so, holding each inhalation for a count of four as he savored the sense of being still while also in motion. He became aware of someone on the bench at his side, close enough to touch.

"Breathe. Think. Enjoy. And when you are ready to resume your day, open your eyes."

Tris was there when Ian did, and the sight made him smile. "Morning."

"Good morning." Tris's eyes crinkled at the corners with his grin. "I have lemon poppyseed bread flavored with the finest agave syrup money can buy. Except that's a lie because it was just the bottle of syrup we already had in the house for margaritas. The bread still tastes amazing."

Ian nodded. "I can't imagine otherwise."

Leaning back slightly in his seat, Tris gave Ian a once-over, his glance approving—appreciative, even—and set the insulated lunch pouch on the table. "Tuesday looks good on you, Grumble Bear."

"Thanks," Ian said and quickly turned to his backpack for the thermos of tea. He was blushing for Christ's sake, like he'd never been paid a compliment in his life. "I was asleep by nine. Didn't move for eight hours."

"He was so out of it, he didn't notice the dog." Marco smirked at the scowl Ian sent across the table. "Elliott usually sleeps out on the landing in between the bedrooms," he said to Tris.

"On a *giant* dog bed that's probably softer than mine," Ian added.

"But last night he parked himself in front of Ian's door, crying and pawing until I let him in."

"After which he apparently climbed on to the bed and did his best impression of a fur rug." Ian scowled at him again. "I still can't believe you let him stay there."

"What was I supposed to do?"

"I don't know, Marco, make him get down?"

"Pretty sure he was checking you weren't dead," Marco said over Tris's and Dennis's laughter.

Ian pursed his lips. "He almost scared me dead this morning. I woke up and couldn't move my legs and it took me a minute to understand I'd been pinned by the heaviest canine on the planet."

He and everyone else fell silent as the train's motion changed without warning, decelerating at a rate that wasn't typical. A mad scramble began, all of them trying to secure the items sitting atop the table while Ian's insides flopped around and the passengers standing in the aisle grabbed hold of the seatbacks nearest them. They came to a sudden stop, the change in momentum enough to jerk Ian and Tris hard into the table while gasps rose from the passengers. In the ringing silence that followed, Ian met Marco's eyes over the table.

"Jeez," they said, almost in unison.

"Blargh," Tris said weakly.

Frowning, Ian looked him over, noting the color had drained from his cheeks. "Okay?" he asked in a low voice.

"I guess?" Tris's smile was more like a grimace. "That sucked."

"Yup." Reaching up, Ian gave Tris's shoulder a quick squeeze, then turned to the table at large. "This happened yesterday, didn't it? While I was sleeping?"

"Uh-huh. There was no slamming of brakes, however," Marco said, "or people hanging on for dear life."

"The tracks could be iced over again," Tris murmured. He was staring out the window now, watching the snow swirl lazily over the frozen landscape. "I was reading some stuff online about how the T has to send crews to chip out the crossings by hand."

Ian snorted out a laugh. "This is *nuts*." He looked round the table at his friends who'd started smiling, too. "I'm not the only one who thinks so, right?"

"Not the only one." Tris mussed up Ian's hair, laughing when Ian immediately went on the defensive and swatted at Tris's hands with his own.

"Why are you like this?"

"Because you love it. And, while my guts feel like they've been to a barn dance—" Tris swallowed "—this isn't bad compared to the bus shuttles running in place of the Red Line. That shit is a nightmare."

Ian cocked his head. "When did you take the shuttle?"

"Last Friday night. I got cocky without you, GB, and thought I'd try to find a different way to get home." He sighed and turned back to the insulated bag, a light, lemony smell filling the air as he unpacked the bread. "I paid for my hubris for almost five hours."

"Oh, Lord." Propping his elbow on the table, Ian set his chin in his hand and smiled at him. "What the hell did you do?"

"WHAT DO YOU THINK ABOUT INVITING YOUR TRAIN BUDDY to your dinner party this weekend?" Zac asked as they stood in line with Marco in Riquísimo, a taco joint halfway between Post Office Square and Mass General Hospital.

Ian looked at him askance. "I think you mean *your* dinner party. You and Mark picked the date, invited everyone, and planned the menu."

"Yes, but you and Marco are hosting so, technically, it's your party. Not to mention your birthday."

"Hey now, we agreed—nobody says the b-word out loud."

"You are ridiculous." Zac laughed. "And sadly mistaken if you think Dennis is going to wish you a *Happy B-Word* instead of saying the word all the way out."

"You can all send whatever wishes you want from your phones and all will be well."

"Not promising anything." Zac's little grin was wicked. "Can we invite your guy anyway?"

"Tris is not my guy."

At all. It wasn't hard for Ian to picture the kid at the Cohasset house, patting the goofy beast dog and chatting with his friends. But that didn't matter, given Tris would be out of town during the b-word weekend Ian's friends seemed so intent upon having. And while Ian should have felt good about that because it meant he'd be able to put Zac and Marco off without even trying, he didn't. Because Ian sort of wished he *could* invite Tris to the party and, boy, that was a huge red flag. He needed to do more work keeping Tris in the friend zone and away from flirtation.

Especially after the way Ian's whole freaking body had responded to Tris simply touching his face last night.

"Tris's in Philly this weekend for somebody else's birthday." Ian made his tone casual. "I know for a fact he's been looking forward to it."

"Damn." Zac frowned at Marco. "I wanted to get a look at the hot as fuck kid myself."

Ian blinked at his friend. "How do—?"

"Jae and Mark told me about the wintercue photos," Zac replied.

"Well, of course they did."

"And how handsome this Tris is, something you conveniently neglected to mention."

"Sounds like Mark."

Zac tutted. "Jae had observations of his own, my friend."

Ian glowered back but then Marco's expression turned thoughtful, and a familiar sense of dread crept over him. Marco liked to play at being super chill, but he was both perceptive and candid. If he had an opinion about anything at all, Ian was going to hear it whether he wanted to or not.

"What?" he huffed out, then scowled at Marco's knowing gaze.

"Are you going to keep hanging out with Tris after the trains go back to normal? Assuming they go back to normal ever."

"I don't know. I can't see why not." Ian brought his eyebrows together at Marco's quick nod. "Why?"

"No reason. I hope you do."

"Yeah?"

"Uh-huh. The guys are right—Tris is gorgeous, with the blue eyes and the smile, and don't get me started on that supernaturally blond hair." Marco chuckled. "Don't tell me you haven't noticed either, because I've seen the way you look at him."

Ian picked up a taco. "I didn't know his eyes were blue but, yes, I've noticed he's attractive. I just hope *he* hasn't noticed me noticing."

Marco and Zac exchanged 'what-the-fuck' looks. "Why not?" Marco asked. "He's talked to us about his ex-boyfriend, so you know he's into guys."

"Doesn't mean he's into *me*." He took a bite of food and chewed as Marco pursed his lips.

"You're either lying to yourself or dumb as a box of rocks."

"Hey!"

"Seriously." Marco shook his head while Zac smothered a laugh behind one hand. "You're not the only one making cow eyes on the train every day. Tris goes out of his way to find us when we both know he doesn't have to and it's *not* to see Dennis or me. He's into you, dude. And he makes you laugh, which I like hearing more than you know."

Ian took all that in. When he'd been at his lowest after the breakup with Gus, he'd worked hard to seem 'normal.' Most of the world had bought the act and few people even now knew how hard he'd been struggling. His friends had known, though. They'd seen past his mask. Reached past it really, and grabbed on to Ian, made sure he stayed afloat.

He tried to smile. "Is this your passive-aggressive way of telling me I need to chill?"

"Nothing passive-aggressive about it." Marco forked up some refried beans. "But I think 'lighten up' might be more accurate, and you are a lot lighter these days."

"I see it, too," Zac said. "The fun guy peeking out from behind the grumpy eyebrows."

Ian touched a hand to his forehead. "My eyebrows do not have moods."

Zac smiled. "Yes, they do. Our point though, is that you've been different recently and it could be that this guy, Tris, has something to do with it."

Balls.

Ian knew denials wouldn't get him anywhere; his friends wouldn't buy one word. But he didn't want to lie to them, either, because he tried never to lie to the people he loved.

"You could have a point," he said carefully. "Tris is easy to be around, and I have fun when we hang out. For the record, I think he's just being friendly. Save it," he warned when Marco opened his mouth. "I love that you want there to be more between him and me, but I don't think it's there. I'm okay with that, by the way. But you're right. I like being around him. And a lot of it is because Tris never knew the guy I became after my life went south. The moody, bitter asshole who wanted everyone to just keep away."

Ian ran his fingers over his mouth a moment before he continued. "Hopefully, I never end up back in that hole. But the weight of the memories I carry around from that time isn't there when I'm with him. Honestly, it feels good letting go of the burden, just for a while."

Distress flashed over Marco's face. "Do you think we see you that way? As someone who doesn't deserve to have friends who care about him? Who doesn't deserve joy? Because we don't, Ian. We love you." He glanced at Zac who was nodding vigorously.

"You went through some really serious shit," Zac said. "None of us held it against you then or ever would now, not when we're just glad you're ..." He smiled crookedly. "You, again."

Ian's heart gave a squeeze. He drew a breath in through his nose, then held it for a beat before exhaling. "You're right. I'm not that guy anymore. Down and ... fuck, so hopeless. I guess it's just easy to forget I ever was around Tris." The admission stirred a lightness in his chest.

Marco nudged his foot under the table. "Even more reason not to lose touch with the guy."

"You're right. Could be easier said than done, though ..." Ian tried not to grimace. "He's so young, guys. I know you think it's not a big deal because Zac has Aiden, and Mark and Jae have Owen and Emmett and you all make it work. But this is about more than just Tris's age. It's like he's poised for flight. He doesn't have roots tying him to Boston or anyplace he'd ever call

69

home, and I can tell he's still trying to figure out where he belongs."

"He can do that and still be here," Marco pointed out, which, while true, Ian thought unlikely.

"Why would he?" he asked. "Especially for me. Tris is young and gorgeous and out to conquer the world while I'm none of those things."

Zac waved him off. "Girl, please. So, you're older than Tris—"

"By fifteen years."

"Which is how much older I am than Aiden. I'm cavalier when I say it now, but I wasn't in the beginning, at all. Let it get into my head so much I screwed everything up and almost lost him."

Ian frowned. "I didn't know that."

"It happened." Zac nodded sagely. "I was lucky he gave me a second chance, and luck is something you have to grab when you can. Why not give Tris a first chance?" he pressed. "Marco says he's into you, and why wouldn't he be? You know you're even more attractive today than you were ten years ago. Which is annoying actually, and if I didn't adore you so much, I'd hate you."

"My ego aside, I've only known Tris a week," Ian said through a laugh. "And, from what he's told me, he's already looking to move on to another city."

"So, use the tech God gave you." Marco threw his hands up to express his frustration. "Two people don't need to be in the same city to stay friends or go for more, and you know he's good for you, Ian. I'm not asking for miracles, but promise me you'll try, no matter where Tris ends up."

Ian could do that. Despite feeling like he was dabbling with a dangerous recipe for a whole bunch of dented feelings. He recognized the restless energy in Tris that meant he already had one foot out the door. And if Tris wasn't going to stick around, Ian couldn't go getting attached.

Too late, he reminded himself and oh, yeah, it was.

8

Ian looked up from his tablet as Tris slid in beside him, red-cheeked and smelling oddly delicious. "Did you dip yourself in cinnamon and butter before leaving the house?"

"Possibly." Tris smiled at him cheerily. "No Marco today?"

"He's on call. Stayed overnight at the hospital."

"Too bad for Marco then, because he's about to miss out on some cinnamon roll goodness." Plunking the pouch onto the table, Tris waggled his eyebrows up and down. "Ela got up early to bake and made me help her."

"Poor you." His eyes went wide as Tris opened the pouch though, revealing four beautiful pastries drizzled with icing. "Or maybe I'm wrong. Because wow."

"Yup." Laughing, Tris slid some napkins over the table to Dennis who was already making grabby-hand motions. "She used maple syrup and coconut sugar and I do have an extra for Marco if you think you can get it to him."

"I'll do my best." Lifting a roll from the tub, Ian tore it in half and set one portion down, then bit deep into the other. He fought not to groan. "Shut the front door."

Tris nodded. "Sounds about right."

"Happy Wednesday to me," Dennis murmured around a mouthful of pastry. "I swear I taste orange?"

Ian muttered his agreement, but then he eyed Tris, noting the ever-so-slight downturn of his mouth. "You're going to miss Ela's baking when you move, huh?"

"Definitely. I asked her if she'd send me boxes of cookies every now and then." The tips of Tris's ears flushed dark, but his grin didn't quite reach its usual megawatt brightness. "Not sure she took me seriously, but I need her baking in my life."

Ian took another bite of his roll. He suspected there was more to Tris's turn of mood than the prospect of missing homemade sweet treats, but he wouldn't call his friend out. If Tris wanted to talk about whatever was bothering him, he would when the time was right.

"You don't need to convince me," Ian said. "Based on the things you've been bringing to share, I understand perfectly."

Tris smiled again, softer this time. "I figured you would. You've got a little icing on your face, right here."

Reaching up, he thumbed the corner of Ian's mouth, touch gentle, and came away with a rogue smear. Ian's cheeks warmed at the intimate gesture, the heat going all through him as Tris held his gaze. He did his best to school his expression, hoping he looked less dazed than he felt and so, *so* glad Dennis stayed mercifully quiet in his seat across the table.

Ian didn't need a reminder of how very screwed he was, not even from a friend.

⁂

W*hat's up for the b-word?*

Ian managed a half-smile at the message on his screen. Gus didn't understand his disdain for his birthday any better than the rest of Ian's friends, but he'd always respected the ban on the word 'birthday.'

Dinner with the nurses, he wrote back, downplaying his weekend plans to do ... he had no idea what. *Lunch next week?*

Glancing up, he got a look at the departures board and quickly flipped to the thread he shared with Tris.

Where are you?

The reply came only seconds later. *Chinatown. Why?*

6:20 on time, Ian wrote back, and was unsurprised by the string of wide-eyed emoji he got in return.

Sweet baby cheeses, Tris replied. *There in 10.*

Ian cast a wary glance at the people around him before firing off a final message. *Less talky, more walky, Chi-Town. Place is packed.*

The crowd had thickened further by the time Tris pushed his way through it, looking harried and oddly rumpled.

Ian eyed a large stain across the front of Tris's jacket. "What the hell happened to you?"

Tris grimaced. "Bumped into a guy at Downtown Crossing when I got off the subway. He had a Big Gulp filled with Mountain Dew."

Ian barked out a laugh. "Ho, shit. Was he pissed?"

"Yup. He called me a hipster douchebag. Blew it off when he realized I got the worst of it."

"I was going to suggest we stand outside but that's probably a bad idea."

"Why?"

"Because it's eight degrees and you're wearing a bucket of soda?"

"Meh." Tris looked down at himself. "The wet spot's on the outside of the jacket but my sweater's dry underneath. Let's go."

Hustling outside, they gathered with a different crowd of travelers clustered near the platforms that typically serviced the southbound trains. The brutal cold ate its way through Ian's thick boots and parka, and his eyes watered as they watched a smaller departures board. He frowned when he remembered Tris's jacket was wet.

Before he could suggest they head back inside, the 6:20 train's status flipped to *Boarding* and Tris's hand was on Ian's elbow, tugging him toward the right track. The train was packed, of course, but still somehow cold, even with the two of them squeezed onto a bench alongside a tiny woman swathed in an enormous puffy parka.

"Good evening, passengers, and welcome aboard the 6:20 train to Greenbush. We are aware of heating problems in some of the cars and apologize for any discomfort or inconvenience."

"Surprised they let us board at all," Ian muttered, then frowned when he realized the quiet clicking noise he'd been hearing of the past several seconds was Tris's teeth chattering. "You okay?"

"Yup. Definitely applying to master's programs anywhere desert."

Resisting an urge to wrap an arm around him, Ian had to laugh at the obvious disgust rolling off his friend. "Ready to start the journey to become Dr. Roboto?"

"No. But if I start applying anyway, I don't have to make any decisions until the fall and there'll be plenty of time to figure out which place will keep me warmest." Tris spent a minute reeling off a list of schools on the West Coast, his demeanor growing almost defiant. "Well?" he asked at last, tone so challenging, Ian understood it was expected he would disagree.

"Er." Ian noted the woman seated beside Tris eyeing them both. "Don't look at me," he said. "Far as I'm concerned, you should apply anywhere and everywhere you want."

"Yeah, well. You're a good friend." Tris's expression turned glum in a heartbeat. "Everyone else thinks West Coast would be a mistake. Well, except for Haru. And my boss at Off-World."

Ian swallowed a sigh. Again with the 'everyone else.' "What's your boss say about it?"

"That I shouldn't make decisions based on climate and instead figure out what I really want. Like I didn't know this already." Tris's eyeroll was epic. "I do respect the guy, though. Consider him my mentor. He's always looking out for his staff, finding us interesting projects and opportunities." He bit his lip. "He got me on an exo-suit project at the giant Navy hospital down in Bethesda. As in co-leading a team to help the c-spine injury unit evaluate how to make the suit available to patients."

Ian could feel his eyebrows going up. "You're leading a project team at Walter Reed? Tris. This is *big*."

"Right?" Tris made an 'eep' kind of face. "I'm sort of freaking out. Like I don't even know what to do with myself."

"Next stop Weymouth Landing."

A complicated mix of emotions bubbled up into Ian's chest. This news had surely been at the root of Tris's earlier odd mood; he'd simply been waiting to get Ian alone to tell him that his path away from Boston was about to begin. With an opportunity that could—would—be a game changer for him and shape Tris's career in ways he truly wanted. *That* was where Ian had to place his focus and not on the certainty that he wasn't ready to say goodbye.

"Well, I'm happy for you," he said, and meant every word. "You've been itching to work on a project like this, and you know this could open up all kinds of doors. How long do you think you'll be in Maryland?"

"The Off-World offices are actually in D.C., which means I'll be commuting back and forth a fair bit. So yay, more trains," Tris joked. "I'll be there nine to ten weeks we think, longer if stuff goes sideways. Which, since I'm involved, will probably be the case."

"Shut it—you're going to kill it." The knot in Ian's chest twisted slightly at Tris's wry laugh. "When do you go?"

"Next week. We were supposed to start in mid-March, but the timetable's been moved up. Basically, I'll get back from Philly on Monday, pack up my stuff, then turn around and leave again." The cheer on Tris's face faded. "I hate to do it, Ian, but I'm going to have to give you a raincheck on dinner and meeting the beast dog."

Ian gave him a nod. "We'll do it when you get back," he said, heart dipping a little at the way Tris was looking at him, eyes shadowed. "What's wrong?"

"Nothing? It's just the whole thing took me by surprise. Last week I was stuck on figuring out how I feel about grad school, and today I'm researching apartments in a new city. Parts of my brain are still catching up, you know? And ... well, I'm junior for this team."

That tiny pause spoke volumes to Ian. Told him Tris was nervous. And no wonder. The exo-suit could improve people's lives, a thing Tris clearly felt driven to do. But perhaps understanding that there were actual *people* on the other end of the project was more sobering than Tris had ever imagined.

That made Ian more sure than ever that this opportunity was going to change Tris's life, too.

Pride surged through him. "I know you are. But I also *know* you're going to kill it, Tris. I meant that."

"I know you did." Tris blew out a breath. "I love how you say it with zero hesitation. That you believe in me. Usually, I'm all about believing in me too, but I don't want to fuck up and let people down. Including myself."

"You won't. On this project or grad school or anything else you want to do." Ian swallowed at the gratitude he read in Tris's face. The guy just needed someone to listen and be there for him, without getting down in the weeds about careers and best-laid plans. Which Ian could one-thousand percent do, even if the idea of Tris being gone made him feel hollow. "I haven't known you long, but I am dead certain you can do anything you set your mind to."

"Thanks." Tris's lips quirked up in a shy smile. He seemed on the verge of speaking again when a heavy metallic clank rang out and the train's momentum changed, jerking Ian and Tris forward as it decelerated at an alarming rate.

"Balls," Ian breathed. He pressed his palms into the seatback in front of him bracing himself for impact, aware of Tris and the woman beside him doing the same. Passengers in the aisle scrambled for purchase, many crouching down close to the floor.

The train jerked hard, brakes groaning loudly, walls shaking as it ground to a tortuous halt. Head bowed, Ian listened to the passengers' gasps and curses, then clenched his teeth at Tris's sharp hiss. And then they were really stopped, the silence that followed deafening.

Swallowing hard, Ian straightened up and set a hand over Tris's. "Fucking A," he muttered and glanced sideways at Tris's shaky breath.

"Yup." Tris's voice was a croak. "You good?"

"Peachy." Ian glanced past Tris to their seatmate. "How about you, ma'am? Are you all right?"

She nodded, face weary as she leaned back in her seat. "What the ever-living fuck?" she asked no one in particular and Ian barked out a laugh.

Around them, passengers were righting themselves, expressions ranging from wary to confused to angry, but no one appeared injured or ready to fall apart, at least for the time being. But as this was a snowpocalypse evening in mid-January, the moments stretched on and on and an hour later, the train still hadn't moved. Ian and Tris huddled up close, murmuring back and forth about Tris's upcoming move and project for Off-World, and though Ian tried to stay upbeat, his energy continued to wane. By the time another train finally arrived to tow them into Weymouth Landing Station, he was too weary to comment beyond a muted 'yay.'

Frowning, Tris slipped an arm around his shoulders. "Is Marco at home for Elliott?"

"Yeah."

"Call and tell him you're staying with me."

"Huh?" Ian blinked at him, sure he'd misunderstood. "Why?"

"Because I'm not letting you wait outside in the cold for a goddamned train or bus coming who knows when. My house isn't far from the station and we both know there's plenty of room. If we're lucky, Ela will be cooking and Sully pouring drinks when we get there. Plus, it's Wednesday," he added, which only increased Ian's confusion.

"Okay. And what do we do on Wednesdays?"

"Wear pink and drink Cosmos, der."

The woman in the aisle seat snorted a laugh and Ian did the same.

"I guess I could go for a cocktail." He smiled at the way Tris's eyes glowed. "But I draw the line at Cosmos because this brain does not like the clear liquors."

Tris gave a quick nod. "Your wish is my command."

If only, Ian thought. It took some effort not to feel a little melancholy at that. Tris was leaving in just a few days. But then the train gave a jerk and started coasting, and Tris and the passengers around them burst into applause.

Thick flakes fell—because of course they did—as Ian and Tris walked the paths carved into the snowbanks lining the sidewalks outside Weymouth Landing station. But at last, they were standing inside a solid, unmoving structure that was both cozy and unexpectedly quiet.

"Showers," Tris said, tone decisive as he hung his coat on a hook by the door. "We need to get warmed up."

Stooping to untie his boots, Ian thought this a most righteous idea. "Yes, please."

Having expected a literal crowd, the silence of the big house around them came as a surprise, but Ian found it almost comforting as he followed Tris up a staircase set on the left side of the foyer.

"I'll put our stuff in the wash afterward," Tris said. He guided Ian into a room off the long hallway, going immediately to a large dresser and pulling open drawers. "I have my own bathroom— you use the shower in there and I'll grab one down the hall. We both need hot water, strong drinks, cheeses, and meats."

Ian cocked an eyebrow. "In that order?"

"Yup. And hey, I didn't have to give you a raincheck on

dinner after all!" Bundles of clothing in his arms, Tris crossed the room and handed a stack of items to Ian, then nodded to a door on Ian's right. "Shower, get comfy, and I'll meet you back here in a few minutes."

It was a sign of just how wrung out Ian felt that he didn't even notice his surroundings after Tris left the room. But fifteen glorious, steam-filled minutes later, he was clothed in a set of soft dark sweats and pair of thick socks, and he'd started to get a handle on his bearings. He was looking around at the bedroom's tastefully understated decor when a knock sounded at the door.

"You decent, GB?"

Ian glanced down at himself. "I dunno about decent, but I'm dressed."

"Boo, you whore." Tris pushed the door open and grinned at him. "C'mon. Let's forage."

After sticking their discarded clothes in the wash, Tris got Ian seated at an island in a large airy kitchen, a glass of red wine in his hand. Ian still felt slightly off-balance, however, and it quickly manifested in his mouth getting away from him.

"I figured you'd be drinking a Cosmo. Or something exotic from a coconut cup."

"There *would* be coconut cups if Sully were here to mix up the tropical."

"Well, the wine is delicious." Ian sipped from his glass again, savoring the rich notes of dark cherry and raspberry. "Are we really alone? How is that possible with so many people living here?"

"Most of the house is at a bar near the station. They sent messages while we were walking up here, but all I wanted was a shower and sweatpants." Tris held up a package wrapped in white butcher paper. "Smoked turkey with bacon okay?"

"Absolutely okay."

A plaintive meow echoed through the kitchen and Tris's smile lit his face. "This is Miss Ginger," he said as a gorgeous tabby cat made its way toward them. "Like magic, she always appears when a package of bacon is opened."

"I recognize her from the wintercue pics." Setting his glass on the island, Ian bent and ran a hand over the animal's head. "Is she yours?"

"Technically, she belongs to Sully and Ela, but I am totally her favorite." Tris sounded smug. "Ela's here actually, upstairs finishing paperwork. I ran into her when I was loading our stuff in the washer." He reached for a wheel of brie.

A peaceful feeling fell over Ian as they talked, and he couldn't help reveling in it. He found charm in the quiet house and Tris's lilting laughter, as well as in the deep red wine and even the goddamned snow still falling outside.

I could get used to this.

And boy, did Marco's and Zac's words from the previous day ring true. Ian felt relaxed and open around Tris, heart and spirit light in ways he'd almost forgotten they could be. None of which was remotely okay given Tris would soon be living over four hundred miles away.

Casting his gaze down, Ian stared at the sandwich Tris placed in front of him like it might give him the answers he needed. He didn't look up again until Tris was seated, too.

"This looks fantastic, Tris. Thank you."

"You're welcome." Tris picked up the bottle of wine and topped off Ian's glass. "You okay? You kind of went away there for a minute."

"I'm a little tired, I guess. And maybe tossing around some ideas in my head."

"I get it. You think a lot about your patients when you're not at work?"

Ian didn't bother correcting Tris's assumption; answering questions about nursing was a hundred times simpler than talking about his jumbled-up feelings. "Yes and no. You learn to compartmentalize because you have to. It's impossible to do the job unless you can pull back enough to look at the patients with your whole brain and not let your feelings take over."

Funny how Ian kept forgetting not to lead with his heart when it came to Tris.

He ran his fingers over his lips. "Sometimes I need the reminder to not get too close. Sort of an occupational hazard," he added with what felt like a crooked smile, because he wasn't talking about patient care anymore. Which Tris didn't know, so Ian seized upon the first thing he could think of to change the subject.

"Where do you want to live while you're working at Walter Reed?"

That was enough to have Tris off and running and soon they were exchanging stories about cities he'd lived in and still wanted to visit, lingering on their stools as they shared a plate of sliced fruit and cheeses and Tris finished his glass of wine. It was with real reluctance that Ian finally pushed back from the island.

Tris's face went pouty. "You calling it a night?"

"I'm afraid so." Ian gave him a smile. "I'm over at MGH tomorrow, assuming I can get into Boston at all. But *your* night doesn't have to be over. I'll just crash on the couch in your room."

"Mmm, no." Standing, Tris picked up the glasses, then carried them around the island to the sink. "You're bunking with me."

9

Ian's brain stuttered and stopped and, for a second, it felt like his heart had too. "I ... er," he got out. "You sure you don't mind?"

"Why would I?" Tris set the glasses in the sink. "My bed is a queen, and I just changed my sheets. There should be room for us both unless you're prone to night terrors." He raised a brow. "You're not, are you?"

"No. I have been known to be a bit of a blanket hog, however." Ian smiled at him. "I don't mind staying the night on the couch. Definitely don't want to put you out any more than I have."

A frown marred Tris's features. "You're not putting me out. I'm happy I can give you a place to stay tonight," he said, and the sincerity in his voice warmed Ian all over.

"All right. As long as it's no trouble."

Tris came back around the island to stand at Ian's side. Slipping his hand into Ian's, he held his gaze, and the world seemed to slow around them. Tris's eyes were wide and unguarded, lingering on Ian's before dropping to stare at Ian's mouth.

"You're no trouble at all," he murmured.

And just like that, the temperature in the kitchen seemed to increase by several degrees.

Awareness raced along Ian's spine. He twined his fingers around Tris's, his pulse speeding up. When he wet his lips with his tongue, Tris gave a very quiet hum.

"Would it be all right if I kissed you?"

"Yes." Ian smiled, heart turning a giddy flip as Tris leaned in and brushed his mouth against Ian's.

Heat raced all through him. Raising his free hand to Tris's cheek, Ian kissed him deeper, and was rewarded with another soft, pleased-sounding noise. Tris let go of Ian's hand, only to wrap Ian up in his arms and oh, Ian liked that. He dropped his hands to Tris's waist, aware how much he'd missed this kind of simple contact in the months since his last hookup. Ian loved being held, especially by a man who was taller than him, and having to tilt his head slightly back to be kissed. Then Tris's groin pressed against Ian's through their sweatpants, and the teasing press made Ian's already half-hard cock twitch. He groaned softly into Tris's mouth, delight raising the hair on his arms.

Tris sounded positively dazed when they finally came up for air. "Fuck. I've been wanting to kiss you for ages." Without opening his eyes, he set their foreheads together, a tiny smile on his lips. "Wanna do it some more?"

Ian couldn't help his soft laugh. God yes, he did. Kiss Tris some more and sink down with him onto the nearest flat surface and follow up those kisses with a whole host of deliciously dirty things.

Except this was a bad idea. Terrible, in fact, and one Ian knew he needed to put a stop to right now. He knew better than to risk being hurt just to feel good. He couldn't get wrapped up in a guy literally on his way out of town and he already liked Tris far more than he should. The fact Tris seemed to like Ian too, at least a little ... well. Maybe Ian's feelings weren't the only ones in danger of being dented.

But Ian shut off his brain and kissed Tris again anyway. Because now that he knew how Tris tasted, he couldn't imagine doing anything else.

He ran his hands over Tris's back and arms, greedy for the contact and loving the strength he sensed there. Tris was lean and broad shouldered, built like a swimmer, and his muscles lay in hard, flat planes beneath his clothes. He drew Ian closer, movements unhesitating, and brought an arm up to cradle Ian's shoulders, hand coming to rest over the back of Ian's neck. Ian groaned at that firm grip, heat gathering in his belly.

How long they stood there, kissing and touching beside the kitchen island with a tabby cat as their witness, Ian didn't know or care. God knew, it felt like they had lost time to make up for. But Tris drew back slightly at last, eyes blazing as he and Ian stared at each other, both breathing faster. Without speaking, they linked hands again, then walked to a second staircase at the back of the kitchen, padding in their thick socks over the hardwood floor.

Once the door to Tris's room had closed with a firm click behind them, though, Ian's nerves kicked up with a vengeance that made it hard to meet Tris's eye. He licked his lips, ready to offer once again to sleep on the couch, but said nothing when Tris turned and faced him, hands reaching again for Ian's waist. He kissed Ian, softer now, but the urgency in them was incendiary. Those kisses silenced the sensible thoughts in Ian's head clamoring to be heard, and he stepped in closer, insides going all gooey as Tris slid his tongue over his.

Somehow, they crossed the room to the bed, still kissing as they stripped each other down to their boxers, movements hurried as if they were desperate for touch. That was how Ian felt—desperate for skin and sensation with this man who seemed just as eager for more of the same with Ian. He gasped when Tris palmed him through the cotton of the underwear and Tris let out a groan.

"Jesus, GB," Tris muttered. "I really like touching you."

Ducking his head, Ian kissed along the line of Tris's jaw, in awe of how fucking good he felt, like he couldn't stop smiling. He aimed a mock glare at Tris anyway and turned on his not-so-inner grouch.

"You call me Grumble Bear again while we're kissing and see what I do," he warned, grinning as another groan mixed with Tris's laugh.

"Not sure I can help it," Tris said, "but I'll try."

At his urging, Ian got himself settled in the center of the mattress before Tris climbed on too, kneeling beside Ian's hip. Unsurprisingly, his body was beautiful, long-limbed and lean but broad enough through the chest that he didn't appear delicate. Gold touched Tris's creamy skin and the fine hair smattering his chest muscles, so different from Ian's more bulky, much fuzzier body. He traced a path with his gaze over Tris's abdomen to the trail beginning just below his navel that led to parts farther south, his mouth going dry.

"Mmm." Tris was smiling when Ian looked up. "You're gorgeous."

Ian huffed a laugh. "Was just thinking the same about you."

Lifting a knee, Tris straddled Ian's thighs, eyes aglow as he settled into Ian's lap. Ian let his head fall back a bit, whole body already buzzing. He set his hands on Tris's waist as Tris ran his palms over Ian's torso, trailing fire with his touch. Ian's eyes slipped almost closed, and he was awed by the electricity arcing between them, so intense he already felt seconds away from losing it.

Tris stroked Ian's shoulders and chest with his palms, the movements crushing Ian's control just a bit more. His breath hitched when Tris slid a hand around the back of Ian's neck and pulled him up for a kiss, delving deep with his tongue. Ian groaned into it, twining his arms around Tris tighter so their chests met, and Tris rocked against him, the pressure sweet torture against Ian's ready cock.

"God," Ian gritted out. "Can't believe Marco was right."

Pausing, Tris leaned backward, brow furrowed as he stared down at Ian. "Why are we talking about Marco right now?"

"We're not." Reaching down, Ian grabbed Tris's ass with both hands, then smiled at the hiss he got in return. "Just acknowledging he was right when he said you might want me like this. I didn't believe him," he explained to which Tris responded with a scoff.

"Well, that's just stupid. Why wouldn't I want you? You're hot as fuck, and I saw it the second I sat down next to you on the train."

Ian didn't know how to answer. He watched Tris instead, admiring the way his muscles flexed as he sat back on his haunches.

"It took work to get you to smile," Tris said, still stroking Ian's skin lightly. "But then you did and the way it changed your whole face ... well. I wanted to do it again."

Smiling faintly, Tris rose up on his knees, then slipped his fingers under the waistband of Ian's shorts. Shifting his weight, he climbed off Ian and drew the shorts down over Ian's groin and thighs, making a pleased sound when Ian lifted his hips to make the task easier. Tris took his bottom lip between his teeth as Ian's cock was revealed, lying rigid and thick against his abdomen, and Ian hissed when the air met his overheated skin.

"Fuck," he muttered, heart pounding so hard he felt dizzy.

"Fuck, yeah," Tris countered.

Ian reached for him, smoothing his hands over those long muscled thighs and delighting in the contrast of crinkly hairs over warm skin. A smile teased the corners of Tris's mouth as he laid Ian's boxers over the foot of the bed, then reached for the waistband of his own shorts. In seconds, he was nude too, cock jutting out from the thatch of brown curls at its base, long without being scary, a pearl of liquid glistening at the head. Ian's mouth watered for a taste.

"I'm clear, just so you know," Tris said as he turned to the nightstand, "but I've got everything we need to be safe." A drawer scraped open and closed before he turned back, holding up a small bottle of lube and some condoms so Ian could see them.

Ian's body thrummed as he watched Tris set down the condoms and pop open the bottle. "I'll keep that in mind." The laughter and teasing felt wonderful, filling him with happy feelings, the way he so often felt around Tris. And somehow, being naked together underscored even more how comfortable Ian felt with this man, like he could talk about absolutely anything and know he'd be heard. Lust overcame Ian's amusement when Tris took him in hand, however, palm slick and hot and so, so good.

"I'm clear too," Ian managed, breath jumping as Tris closed his fist a bit tighter, and he gave up the fight to keep his eyes open. "Tris," he murmured before Tris was kissing him again, and Ian lost himself in it.

They explored for a long while, learning what made each other gasp and writhe and groan. Ian hummed when he discovered Tris's nipples were sensitive, then kissed and licked them until Tris was squirming, teeth clenched against a torrent of curses. Tris battled back, playfully wrestling Ian until he lay flat, then teasing him, dragging his tongue along the length of Ian's sternum and belly before dipping into his navel, just to hear Ian gasp.

Ian hovered on a knife's edge, close to coming though all they'd done was kiss and pet. And he loved it. Couldn't remember the last time he'd felt this good and so connected to a person, and like he could go on kissing and holding Tris forever and never get enough.

"*Fuck*, Ian."

Breaths coming fast, Tris covered Ian's body with his. And yeah, Ian wanted more of that. The delicious weight felt amazing on top of him, his pleasure zooming into overdrive when Tris dropped a hand and cupped Ian's balls. Groaning, Ian arched up into him, trembling when Tris reached farther back and rubbed slow, maddening circles into the soft skin of Ian's taint.

Ian should have been embarrassed at his throaty whine, but he was too fucking out of his head to care.

"You like this?" Tris asked, voice a growl Ian had never heard before.

"Yeah." Turning his head, Ian peeled his eyes open, sucking in a breath at the lust he glimpsed in Tris's gaze. "Love being fucked."

Tris groaned in response. "Christ. I'd like that too. But I want to taste you first," he said, and the words had Ian reaching deep for control, the mere idea of Tris's mouth stretched around him almost enough to undo him utterly.

"Want it," he whispered, his own voice stretched tight. "Want your mouth."

Releasing Ian's wrists, Tris rose back up onto his knees. He reached for the lube, then shot Ian a mischief-filled grin. "You want me to use a condom? I have cherry and bubble-gum flavored," he said, before Ian lost it laughing.

"Holy shit, you *are* a frat boy."

"Don't knock 'em till you've tried 'em," Tris scolded, laughter in his voice. "But was that a no? Because I feel like maybe—"

"It was a no," Ian grunted. He licked his suddenly dry lips as he watched Tris wet his fingers again. "Don't want a condom, just you," he said, voice wavering when Tris bent and pressed his lips into the tender spot where Ian's hip met his groin. "Oh, fuck."

"Uh-huh. Open for me," Tris murmured. He tapped Ian's knee gently, humming as Ian spread his thighs, and when he sat up, his smile was so goddamned fond it made Ian's chest ache. "That's it."

Ian's throat went too tight for speech. Not that he could voice the words racing around in his head. Words like *mine* and *yours* and *stay*. Because he wanted more than pleasure from this young man who was all wrong for him. Ian wanted to make Tris his. Keep him here among places Ian had called home for more than half his life and couldn't imagine leaving.

Tris wasn't going to stay put. And Ian would never ask him to. They didn't have a future together. But they did have tonight.

Tris shifted so he could settle between Ian's thighs. Eyes locked with Ian's, he teased Ian's rim with his fingertips, waiting until Ian had dropped his hands to grab fistfuls of sheets before he pushed a finger inside. Ian welcomed the burn and the stretch with soft moans, and when Tris bent and took Ian into his mouth, the overwhelming combination of being filled and sucked at the same time took most of his brain offline. He uttered a low cry when the tip of Tris's finger brushed against his gland.

Eyes squished closed, he brought his hands to Tris's head. Instantly, he felt a change in Tris's body and heard a plaintive groan. The noise vibrated around Ian's cock, amping his arousal up even higher, and he gasped, his eyes flying open. He slid his fingers through Tris's silky hair, breath catching as he took in the sight of Tris's lips stretched over his shaft, eyes shining with moisture as he looked up at Ian, his gorgeous ass held high. He was debauched and so fucking beautiful, and without meaning to, Ian thrust up. Tris groaned again, an eager, needy noise that said he liked having his face fucked. Ian gasped, pumping into Tris's mouth again and again, his ragged breaths mixing with Tris's hungry sounds.

A tenderness too large to ignore cracked Ian wide open. Dropping a shaking hand, he cupped Tris's cheek, eyes locked on his. Tris's pupils were blown wide, only a thin ring of iris remaining, and he leaned into Ian's touch, eyelids fluttering closed. After a few moments, he snaked his free hand out of sight, and the lazy, rolling motion of his hips told Ian he was fucking his own hand.

Ian's pleasure swept through him suddenly, taking him off guard. He jolted, muscles strung tight and chest arching up as he unraveled, coming harder than he had in a long, long time. Sensation washed over him in bright, devastating waves, and he heard himself gasp through the white noise in his head.

Tris was there beside him when he floated back down, a panting, boneless wreck, unable at first to return the kisses Tris dropped on his lips. Ian hadn't noticed him moving, his brain too scrambled by orgasm, but he welcomed Tris's solid weight, loving the way Tris lay half on top of him, his dick like hot steel against Ian's hip.

"You feel so good," Tris murmured, sounding just as dazed as Ian felt.

Turning his head, Ian kissed him deep, tasting himself on Tris's tongue. New heat licked through him, and he pushed at Tris's shoulder, urging him onto his back. Tris's hold on Ian stayed tight as Ian rolled them, as if he thought Ian might pull away, and Ian smiled into the kiss, awash again with tenderness.

Not going anywhere.

Ian knew those words sounded way too fucking serious, so he pushed them aside and skimmed a hand over Tris's body, admiring the flush that was spreading from Tris's neck down to his chest. He kissed him again, slower and more languid now, until Tris's hold on him gentled.

"I've got you," Ian said against Tris's lips, and Tris murmured his agreement.

Ian raised a hand to his mouth, slicking his palm with his tongue, then reached between them to take Tris in his fist. He sighed at Tris's full body-shiver. "This okay?"

"It's fucking awesome." Tris's voice was thready. "Almost lost it blowing you and—" He groaned again, eyes rolling slightly in his head.

Ian's dick made a valiant attempt to get back in the game. Knowing Tris had gotten so turned on simply sucking dick? Feeling a little flattered wasn't out of line. Ian still tried to school his expression, wanting badly to make this good for the kid. Something must have shown on his face though, because Tris let out a laugh.

"You smug motherfucker, GB," he said. "I'd say you were

adorable if I wasn't about to fucking shoot so hard I could scream."

"I'd rather hear your scream than that ridiculous nickname," Ian teased, getting another, decidedly breathless, laugh out of Tris.

"You think I'm joking but ... Oh, fuck." Tris's voice wavered as Ian sat up, then shifted on the mattress so his face was over Tris's groin. Bending low, he blew a stream of air over Tris's cockhead and Tris gasped, his grip on Ian's waist bruising. "*Ian. Please. Need to come.*"

"I know," Ian crooned. Fisting Tris tighter, he darted his tongue out to tease his slit and fuck, the bitter-salt taste sent the inferno in him soaring higher. "That's it," he said before wrapping his lips around Tris just as he'd been dying to since their clothes had come off.

Tris didn't last more than a few minutes. He'd been close to orgasm for too long, and soon he was thrashing and moaning Ian's name, the warning in his tone clear. Ian pulled off just before Tris's cock pulsed, and he did indeed shoot so hard the first spurt streaked his chest. Ian leaned in again quickly, licking Tris through his orgasm and reveling in the cum streaking his lips and chin. Tris's hands shook as they came to rest on Ian's head, and when Ian finally sat back up, there was awe in Tris's gaze.

"Think you broke my brain," he said, lips curving up as Ian swiped at the mess on his chin and lips with a corner of the sheet. "How are you so fucking hot?"

"Practice," Ian shot back, then laughed at Tris's eyeroll.

"Get up here, please."

Tris pulled him into a hug and they lay together, sticky with sweat and lube and cum, chatting about meaningless things until Ian smothered a yawn behind one hand. Tris made a grumpy noise when Ian tried to sit up.

Chuckling, Ian relaxed back into him. "Wouldn't have pegged you for a cuddler."

"I think you mean yourself, Huggy McSnuggles." He pressed a kiss against Ian's head as Ian broke up laughing. "And you're harshing my afterglow, so I'm gonna kiss you to shut you up."

Eventually, they did rouse so the washing up could commence and Ian stowed his contacts in a travel case he kept in his bag. Still nude, Tris climbed back into bed, watching Ian draw the boxers back on.

"Do you not like sleeping naked? I can put mine back on too if you want."

"You don't have to." Ian switched off the bedside lamp and got in beside him. "I got into the habit of wearing something to bed because of the beast dog."

"What, Elliott's modest?"

"No, Elliott is an asshole," Ian retorted. "He likes to lick bare skin, especially legs, and he's uncannily good at being stealthy about it. He sneaks into the bedrooms sometimes and noses around under the covers, and I honestly couldn't tell you why." He felt Tris shrug.

"Sounds like he wants to sleep with you."

"Dogs on the bed are against the rules, the other night notwithstanding. The licking doesn't just happen when we're sleeping, by the way," Ian added. "He made Marco scream so loud the other day while we were making breakfast, I almost dropped my coffee." He grinned at Tris's helpless laughter.

"I *have* to meet this animal," Tris declared once he'd finally calmed down. "We could get the pets together when I get back into town. Unless you think Elliott would eat Ginger?"

"He wouldn't hurt a fly," Ian replied. "But getting him together with Miss Ginger sounds fun."

It was an easy promise to make. Far easier than ignoring the way his chest twisted as Tris nuzzled sleepily against Ian's neck. They didn't know when Tris would be back in Boston or if he'd even return at all. And there wasn't a thing Ian could do about it but close his eyes and breathe in the scent of Tris's skin.

10

"Grumble Bear."

For a few seconds, Ian couldn't place where he was. The room around him was dark, but its smell wasn't familiar, just as the bed beneath him didn't feel quite like his. There was a snug weight curled along Ian's back though, and the unmistakable shape of a hard cock resting against his ass cheeks. Soft lips nuzzled the nape of his neck and fingers slid along his belly, trailing soft fire over his skin as the pieces fell into place.

Tris.

This was Tris's room and bed, and the kiss that landed against Ian's ear signaled a continuation of the very bad idea Ian didn't want to end, an impulse he quickly shut down. Even thinking about permanence was dangerous around this man.

"Tris," he muttered, voice a low rumble. "You can't call me that in bed."

"Get naked and I'll stop."

Heat curled through Ian at the husky demand. Getting naked was a far better idea than talking. Being sleep-muzzy made Ian want to say things he knew he shouldn't, so he turned his head on the pillow and let Tris kiss him, groaning deep in his chest when Tris's hold on him tightened.

With some fumbling, Tris found the lube on the nightstand and the quiet click of the cap set off a bloom of desire in Ian's groin. They threw off the bedding, and Tris slid Ian's shorts off him again, so they lay on their sides facing each other, their breaths mixing in the dark. Ian inhaled sharply as Tris took their cocks into one slick hand and immediately reached down too, sliding his own fingers among Tris's.

Their kisses were lingering, each one bruising in its intensity, and Ian lost track of time as they moved in the dark together. He swallowed hard when Tris whispered how much he loved doing this with Ian, because those words felt dangerous too, way too close to something big that was simply out of reach for them both. He silenced Tris with small kisses along his cheek and the corner of his mouth, each one holding a sweetness Ian craved as much as he did Tris's hands and tongue on him, and the throaty murmurs he uttered as Ian writhed against him.

"Love the sounds you make, Ian. So fucking hot and hungry and God, you're gonna get me off."

He brought a hand to the back of Ian's neck and held on, movements growing more urgent when Ian gasped, his body coming alight with shattering pleasure. He panted against Tris's lips as he tipped over the edge, dick pulsing over their joined fingers. It was enough to send Tris flying too, face buried tight against Ian's neck while his body trembled and Ian held him close, uncaring of the mess between them.

"We're so disgusting right now," he murmured at last, and smiled at Tris's chuckle.

"You wanna do something about it?"

"Not really."

"Thought so."

Propping himself up on one elbow, Tris reached over Ian into the dark, and a second later, the blue-white light of a phone screen bathed them. Ian grinned as Tris's spectacular bedhead was revealed yet, somehow, the kid still looked good.

"And now your phone is disgusting," he observed, watching amusedly as Tris shifted his focus to groping around under the sheets. "What are you doing?"

"Looking for something to clean up with," Tris replied, "I'm too tired to change sheets again and besides I'm out of clean sets. Aha!" he exclaimed, dragging Ian's boxers out with one hand.

They'd started a half-hearted attempt to clean up when Ian heard laughter from somewhere downstairs.

"Sounds like your housemates are back," he murmured. "What time is it?"

"After two. They're probably raiding the kitchen." Tris tossed the boxers in the direction of the bathroom, then dragged the bedding back up over their bodies. "Don't worry. The door's locked so anyone who's feeling extra friendly tonight will just need to fuck off."

Ian rolled onto his side so he was facing Tris, unsure he wanted an answer when he made himself ask, "Your girl Hannah's not going to get bent out of shape about me being here, right?"

"You know she's not my girl." Tris sounded sour. "She's been known to knock now and again but, like I told you, it's been a while since I let her in. We were always casual, even before she told me I needed to grow up and get a real job and I told her to fuck off and die."

Ian raised his brows. "How is the job you already have not real?"

"I dunno." Tris rubbed a hand over his hair, mouth pulling down at the corners. "God knows why, but she's got a bug up her butt about me working in STEM. I build robots to make people's lives better, but she acts like I spend my day playing with toys."

"That sucks. But do you really care if she approves of your job?"

"No. I'm not changing my career just to please someone, but it wouldn't kill her to show some respect. I do *not* play with toys for a living."

"Tris."

"I know, I'm salty." Tris sighed. "I suppose it's dumb of me to expect loyalty from someone I've only known a year. But Gus never crapped on your job, right?"

"Never." Ian set a hand on Tris's hip. "He told me often he didn't know how I did it every day, but I felt the same way about his firefighting and then the EMS work. We don't disrespect each other—just the opposite, really. I admire the hell out of Gus for doing what he does on the job, and I know he feels the same about nursing."

"Well, Hannah told me once that if she had to do my job, it'd be like having her soul sucked from her body every day." Tris made a face. "And I get it, okay? She's a photographer and doesn't want to work in tech—cool. She doesn't have to say that shit out loud and make it sound like I'm wasting my life. As if she could even *do* my job," he scoffed. "Pretty sure the fucking robots would turn around and kill her if she tried."

Ian pressed his lips together hard to keep his laughter at bay, but it was too late, and he made a snuffling sound. "Dude. Remind me never to piss you off."

"Not sure you could," Tris murmured, the surliness in his face going gentle again. "We should sleep," he said. "It's only a few hours till sunrise and we'll need to be up first if we want a shot at a hot shower and coffee." He smiled, then reached over Ian to the nightstand, tapping his phone back into darkness.

Ian closed his eyes. "Any chance Ela might do some baking?"

"Dunno. But I know where she keeps her stash. I'll cut you in if I'm feeling properly motivated."

"You asking me to slut around for baked goods, Santos?"

"Never. *Spontaneous* sexual acts are encouraged, however."

Ian blinked at the gray light filtering past the shades on the windows then quickly closed his eyes again. Sometime during slumber, they'd turned on their sides with Tris spooned up behind Ian in a way he liked too goddamned much.

"You awake, GB?"

"No." A cozy feeling lapped through him at Tris's low chuckle.

"It's quarter past five. Time to get in the shower before the hot water runs out."

Ian opened his eyes wide. "That's really a thing?"

"Yup." Tris sat up, pushing the bedding away from their bodies. "But don't panic yet. No one else should be up for another hour and I can tell they're all still asleep from the way the house sounds." He was smiling when Ian rolled onto his back. "Are you pro or con when it comes to blowjobs in the shower?"

Just the idea of six-foot-three of wet, soapy Tris made Ian's dick perk up well past the point of morning wood. "Pro," he said evenly. "Not sure my knees will be happy about reciprocating, but I'll make you feel good."

Forty-five minutes later, Ian's knees did indeed ache and so did his jaw. He didn't have trouble ignoring the minor discomforts, however, because his body was still buzzing as he brewed a cup of coffee in the kitchen downstairs. It was going to be a long time before he'd shake the image of Tris watching Ian suck him under the spray. Water had shone on his long eyelashes and skin, and his plush mouth had fallen open when Ian had reached around and teased his fingers along the crease of Tris's ass. Tris's groan had been throaty and loud, and his touch exactly what Ian had craved, strong and still tender as he'd gripped Ian's head, shuddering hard when he came.

"Morning."

"*Gah.*" Ian's hand jerked at the unfamiliar voice, nearly upending the cup he'd just filled.

"Shit, I am so sorry! I thought you heard me come in."

Glancing up, Ian met the gaze of a dark-haired young woman clad all in black. Her skin was a lovely tawny brown and her smile irresistible, and Ian easily recognized her from the wintercue photos Tris had sent him the previous weekend.

"Not your fault," he assured her. "I'm not really awake until I've had caffeine."

"Same." She crossed the room toward him. "Are you Ian?"

He gave her a smile. "Yes, ma'am. Ian Byrne."

"Ela Naqvi." Ela held out a hand, her grin getting wider. "And listen to you with the ma'am. It's good to meet the guy who's been keeping Tris sane on those rides into town."

"Trust me, the feeling is mutual," Ian replied, cheeks going warm as he shook hands. "I'd have lost my marbles by now if I didn't have Tris to commiserate with."

Ela nodded at his cup. "Would you like milk or creamer?"

"Milk if you have it, please."

"Of course." She moved to the refrigerator and popped open the door. "Where's Tris gotten himself off to?"

"He was packing for his trip to Philly when I came down. And still doing his hair." Ian smirked at Ela's knowing laugh. "Not sure why he bothers since it just needs to go under a hat, but I wasn't gonna give him a hard time."

"He'll look annoyingly good regardless," Ela replied, jug of milk in one hand and creamer in the other. She let the refrigerator door close under its own weight. "It's a goal of mine to get him to stop going platinum, just so I can see what his real hair color looks like."

"Okay, now you've got me curious, too." Ian slid the freshly brewed cup of coffee toward her.

"Ah, thank you," she murmured, "you're sweet. Tris said your train broke down when I ran into him last night—was it as awful as it sounds?"

"Yup. We were half frozen by the time we got to Weymouth Landing and Tris—"

"—told you to come drink Cosmos with us," Ela said, no question at all in her voice, and Ian had to smile.

"More or less. We actually went with wine."

"And it was glorious," Tris threw in, striding toward them with an armful of cable-knit sweaters. "One of these is for you," he said as he laid the bundle on a stool at the island. "It's minus five out there and I think we need extra layers."

They had a meal of Ela-baked sourdough bread studded with golden raisins and cranberries that they layered with thick slices of cheddar, while around them the house buzzed with the sounds of many people starting the day. Ian startled slightly when a door at the other end of the kitchen popped open without warning, and a figure emerged wrapped in a plaid flannel bathrobe.

"Morning," said a bleary-eyed young man, rubbing a hand over a headful of light-colored curls as the others echoed his greeting. "Missed ya at the pub last night, Tris. Y'mind if I use yer shower?"

"Do it," Tris said with a wave. "I'd hurry if you want it hot."

Amused, Ian watched the young man bustle off, keenly aware he'd forgotten what it was like sharing food and space and utilities with a crowd. He and Marco did fine and had more space than they knew what to do with, but it'd been almost twenty years since Ian'd had multiple roommates. Another sign the shelf life on this thing he had going with Tris was bound to be short, one Ian didn't need.

"Rory, a new housemate," Tris said with a nod at the door.

Ian sipped his coffee and swallowed. "Number six, huh? Is his bedroom the only one on this floor?"

"Yup. It was actually an office," Ela said. "But we stuck an air mattress in there and he says it's more than comfortable until Tris's room is free."

"He's subletting my space while I'm out of town," Tris added. "Saves me paying rent on a room I can't use."

He stood and began stacking the empty plates and cups, talking about how they needed to leave for the station. Ian nodded without replying. He tried not to mind the repeated reminders that Tris wouldn't be around for much longer, but it was fucking hard now that he'd gotten too close and had no way of walking it back.

He'd watched Tris thrash under him, begging to get off, and watched Tris sleep, head pillowed atop Ian's shoulder. Held Tris while he'd dreamed. Woken in Tris's arms. Laughed with him and told stupid jokes and talked about everything and nothing at all. Ian had told Tris things he didn't usually reveal to others. He knew how Tris sounded when he was happy or upset, and the desperate timbre that colored his groans when he was ready to come.

And fuck, but the melancholy threatening at the thought of losing it all felt very, very real.

The inbound train schedule was already hopelessly wrong when they walked onto the platform at Weymouth Landing, but they lucked out when a train showed up randomly. The thing was crowded of course, and they didn't bother trying to find seats, instead standing together with their backs against the car's wall while more passengers packed in around them with each stop. Which left Ian trapped when a woman wearing a knitted hat with a giant fluffy pom-pom at its crown stood in front of him, the pom-pom knocking into the tip of Ian's nose every time she moved just so.

Ian grimaced, unsure if he could ask a person who had nowhere to go to please back the fuck off or if he should just slide down the wall and sit on the floor. And then he noticed that Tris was red-faced with suppressed laughter, his eyes practically dancing as he watched the scene unfolding before him.

"Not funny," Ian muttered out of the side of his mouth, a

second before the hat lady took a half step back and closer to Ian.

"Boop," Tris whispered when the pom-pom connected again, and then Ian was laughing too, his chest twisting painfully.

He was going to miss this far more than he'd ever admit. He really *liked* Tris, even outside of the unexpected attraction that had blossomed between them. Enough that he was starting to put serious thought into how they could keep their friendship alive, just as Marco and Zac had suggested.

You know it'd never work.

Ian drew a deep breath in through his nose. Yeah, he supposed he did. The deck was stacked against them, starting with the fifteen years sitting between his and Tris's birthdays. Fifteen years that were now official since Ian had crossed into forty during the night he'd slept beside Tris.

"You okay?" Tris's low voice was just for Ian. "You've been quiet since breakfast."

Ian made himself smile. "Sure. I don't know if I thanked you for letting me stay last night though," he said, pretending his cheeks weren't blazing. "So, thanks. It was nice."

Tris's expression softened. "It was. And you're welcome." Without looking down, he found Ian's hand and held it, his grip firm through their mittens. "I'm glad you said yes. Wanna do it again tonight?"

Ian bit his lip. He'd love to spend more time with Tris. Push off the melancholy a while longer and not think about what was going to be missing from his life in a matter of hours. Tris's grin. The cheerful chaos he brought with him wherever he went. These effortless conversations. The knowing looks that warmed Ian, even when no one spoke a word. Knowing what he wanted didn't guarantee Ian would get it, however, and in the meantime his life needed tending.

"I'm sorry, but I can't. Marco's working a double starting this afternoon and I have to be home for Elliott."

"Dang, of course." Tris wrinkled his nose. "How about this,

then? I should be back in Boston for at least a month after the Walter Reed project wraps, maybe longer. You can feed me then. Because you'll be glad to see me again, of course."

"Der." Ian made his voice teasing. "Yes, I'll be glad. We can do dinner then, Chi-Town, unless you want to come out to my place tonight?"

He had time to wonder where the hell that'd come from —*What the fuck are you doing?* —as well as answer himself—*Being an idiot, obviously*—before Tris's face lit up with a smile so big, Ian felt it down to his toes.

"I'd love it. Especially since I'll get to meet El."

Still reeling inwardly at what he'd done, Ian licked his lips. "Cool. Um. Fair warning you'll have to help me dig the Jeep out tonight before we can actually go anywhere."

Tris snorted a laugh. "I dug a wintercue pit out of nine feet of snow, bro. I can handle a Jeep."

"Okay then," Ian replied, just before that goddamned pom-pom hit his nose again.

11

"Holy balls." Tris said from the sunroom off the kitchen that evening. "There are freaking deer in your yard!"

Ian chuckled down at the vegetables he'd been slicing. Tris had nodded and hummed in all the right places as Ian had shown him around the Cohasset house but eventually he'd drifted back to the sunroom that looked out onto the expansive back yard. There wasn't much to see of said yard currently, given it was buried in massive snowdrifts, but the local wildlife was undeterred, much to Tris's delight.

"They'll wander off in a bit," Ian called back, "after they poop in the driveway. Just to make digging out in the morning extra fun."

Tris cackled loudly. "That sucks. Shoveling is bad enough without shitty surprises, pun totally intended. I can't believe you have to do it twice a day, what with driving back and forth to the station."

"That's why Marco and I started sharing the Jeep. Digging two vehicles out every day felt like an exercise in stupidity when it's simple enough to share the work on just one plus save money on gas. It could have been worse tonight, y'know. Marco drove out to catch the train at midday, so we only had to dig out a few hours of snowfall."

"I think you meant to say four inches."

"I don't even see it anymore. Stuff falls from the sky and I move it, end of story." Ian grunted. "It's just like taking the dog o-u-t, a thing that needs doing so you do it."

Tris laughed. "Did you just spell to throw Elliott off?"

"Uh-huh. But I think he's got me figured out because I hear him coming."

And yes, there were dog nails clicking over the floor, followed by Tris's measured steps. Dog and human entered the kitchen together, Tris immediately joining Ian at the counter.

"You haven't even started cooking and it already smells fantastic." He sniffed the air appreciatively, then set a hand on the small of Ian's back. "Sure you don't want any help?"

Ian set down the knife. "I'm sure. Almost ready to cook actually, and I need to start the rice."

Something warm nudged his hip then, and a solid shape insinuated itself into the narrow space between him and Tris. A telltale snort followed, and Tris set down his glass of beer so he could squat and fawn over Elliott, who instantly plunked his butt on the floor *right* against Ian's socked heels.

Ian rolled his eyes. There'd been a clear case of insta-love the moment Tris and Elliott had laid eyes on each other and they were pretty cute, Tris scrubbing his fingers through Elliott's thick fur while the animal let loose a litany of happy, rumbling groans. Ian could have done without being pinned against the counter, however, or with Elliott tipping his head back and literally bracing himself against the backs of Ian's thighs.

"Uh, guys?" Ian watched the dog and human look up at him from their positions on the floor, eyes wide as if only just remembering his presence. "Could you move the lovefest somewhere else? Can't get anything done with you up my ass."

Tris's laugh was wry. "Sorry, GB. We'll give you some space. What were you saying about rice?"

"That I wanted to make some," Ian replied. He made a dopey face at the dog, who was still staring up at him, mouth open now and long tongue hanging out of one side. "Yes, doofus, I'm gonna feed you, too."

Tris stroked Elliott's head. "You want me to do it so you can keep cooking?"

"Deal." Ian held up a fat chunk of carrot that got the dog to his feet, tail wagging hard. Elliott accepted the snack, crunching and smacking loudly as Ian gave Tris a hand up next. "His f-o-o-d is on the bottom shelf of the fridge," Ian said, "and he's incredibly unpicky so just grab any bag."

He walked to the pantry, aware of Tris popping open the refrigerator door.

"The stuff that looks sort of like chunky baby f-o-o-d, right?"

Ian laughed. "Yup." A box of rice in hand, he glanced over in time to see Elliott step up beside Tris and stick his snout into the still open refrigerator. "Watch yourself, Tris," Ian warned, but it was too late.

"Hey!" Tris squawked. "He grabbed a bag with his teeth!"

Elliott took off running and Tris tore after him, leaving the refrigerator door still standing open behind him while Ian laughed his head off. After tossing the rice box onto the counter, he jogged out too, knowing there'd be a dog food explosion and a zillion itty-bitty pieces of ground meat and veg to clean up if he didn't intervene.

"I should have warned you," Ian said a few minutes later, once they'd rescued the food pouch and all trooped back to the kitchen. They were at the sink now, Ian filling Elliott's bowl while a harassed-looking Tris watched and Elliott leaned against Ian's leg. "El's easygoing like I said, but faster than he looks and wily as hell."

"Apparently." Tris fixed the animal with a mock-glare. "I think your dad lied about you being dumb," he murmured, scritching Elliott's ear.

Ian leaned over and gathered more carrots from the cutting

board. "I said he was *goofy*, not dumb," he said, tossing them into the bowl. "He does stuff all the time that surprises us."

Once Elliott had his face in his dinner, the humans turned back to the task of preparing their own meal, Ian sautéing ground beef and vegetables with garam masala and spices while Tris made a cucumber salad dressed with a peppery vinaigrette. As usual, they talked a wide range of topics, touching on work and housemates and the party in Philly Tris would attend over the weekend. They interrupted each other and teased, sometimes going off on wild tangents just to make each other laugh, and it all felt so wonderfully familiar, Ian's heart buzzed with a pleasure he tried to resist but just couldn't.

He liked this so much. The ease with which he and Tris fit, puzzle pieces coming together with an almost audible click. He'd felt this way at Tris's the night before too, a sense of rightness that was as natural as breathing and possibly just as vital.

Man, he was sappy. And very much in trouble, too. Because sappy or not, this was going to be the last time he hung out with Tris until the exo-suit project at Walter Reed was finished and the kid came back to Boston. If he came back at all.

"Marco's going to give me so much crap for making curry without him," Ian said as they tucked into the meal. "Keema is his favorite."

"It might be a new favorite of mine, too. Damn." Tris took another bite. "This is fucking delicious."

"Glad you like it. I had beef jerky and an apple for lunch, and I'm going to eat the heck out of this."

"I could tell from your face when we met up at South Station that you had a crappy day. What happened?"

"Nothing outlandish, really. We were short-staffed at the clinic and had a ton of patients, and Dennis was annoyed with the planet at large. Gus called about his mom—she hasn't been feeling well and I can tell he's concerned—and Marco messaged about El being an even bigger weirdo than usual."

Not to mention you'll be gone in a couple of days and I really hate thinking about it.

Tris's eyebrows went up. "That's a lot. What happened with the dog?"

"Madness." Ian smiled. "I guess he pulled everything off my bed last night and got stuck in the fitted sheet, then scared the absolute crap out of Marco by crashing into the hall looking like a four-legged ghost."

Tris belted out a loud laugh. "Holy shit. Sounds like he missed you enough he found a bunch of stuff that smelled like you and went to town."

"Possibly. Ugh." Ian picked up his glass. "I think he needs to be out in the yard more."

"The yard is stellar, even under the ice. I get why you like it here now, what with all this space and being able to share expenses with Marco. I'm sort of the same about the Weymouth house if I'm honest. I like the cheap rent and how it's easy to get around, plus I get to hang with my friends every day."

Ian didn't taste his next bite of food. He'd heard similar comments from his friends and co-workers who assumed he'd moved out here with Marco to save money. Some thought it was about Gus too, and that Ian had exiled himself from the city to put distance between them. Ian never bothered to correct either assumption, because it was hard to talk frankly about how he'd ended up living in Cohasset and not be candid about the state of his mental health at the time.

But Ian wanted Tris to know the truth. Wanted him to understand the good, bad, and worse parts of a story Ian didn't often share. And while he didn't know *why* the urge to talk had come over him yet again, he went with it anyway.

"I didn't move out here to save money." He set down his fork. "I needed a soft place to land after ending it with Gus."

Immediately, the air around them felt charged, Tris's easy expression shifting to wary. "What do you mean?"

Ian wet his lips with his tongue. He could still change course.

Steer the conversation in a different direction and away from a dark time in his life. No need to lay a ton of personal baggage on a freaking kid—

—*who is a grown man*, Ian reminded himself, *and may know himself better at twenty-five than you do most days.*

Might know Ian, better too. Perhaps that was why Tris had circled around to the question of where Ian lived more than once. Because he'd sensed Ian was holding something back and his problem-solving, linear brain wanted to poke at it.

"I was depressed after Gus and I split," he said. "It's typical to feel loss after a breakup, to grieve and be sad. And I did feel all that. But there was something else happening, too. I felt flat. Like I'd been emptied out. And heavy. I don't know how to explain it, but even moving through space was so *hard* I was wiped out all the time.

"There's a TED talk by this author, Andrew Solomon, where he says 'the opposite of depression isn't happiness. It's vitality.' I think that's really true." Ian picked up his fork again, more to keep his hands busy than any desire to eat. "It'd take me a half-hour to convince myself to get out of bed so I could go to work. I kept going in because I didn't want to let my patients down, but also because being around them helped me get out of my own head for a while. I could breathe without all this weight pressing me down." He set a hand on his chest absently.

"I'm sure you've figured out by now I'm an extrovert, even when I'm complaining about humanity." He met Tris's eyes. "I mean, I'm sarcastic and grouchy but I enjoy being around people, even when I'm ignoring them."

Tris's mouth moved like he wanted to smile. "I know. There's a nice guy lurking beneath the eyebrows, just like I said."

"Yeah, well. That nice guy wasn't around much then. I was a miserable ass to anyone who wasn't my patient and my friends fucking exhausted me. Dennis would give me these terrible pep talks, telling me to snap out of it and quit sulking." Ian frowned. "We shouldn't say things like 'This too shall pass' to someone who's having a hard time. Trouble passes, sure. But it's fucking hard to embrace that philosophy when there doesn't seem much point in even opening your eyes every day."

"Jesus, Ian."

Shit. Tris looked spooked. And Ian got why. For a while, his depression had swallowed him. He'd woken up every day, wondering why he couldn't just sleep. Felt suffocated by an awful gray weight of sadness. And thought all the time about how it might be easier to drown in it than fight to keep his head above water.

Ian hadn't planned to harm himself. But he'd thought about *making* a plan fairly often. Worse, he hadn't been enough himself to understand why those thoughts were a problem.

He ran his knuckles over his beard. Thinking back on that time always felt surreal. As if his struggles had happened to someone else rather than himself. And while Ian knew it was his brain's way of coping, it left him unsettled every time.

"Dennis thought I was just bitching. But I was *down*. And it was different from anything I'd ever felt before. I was living on my own at the time," he said, "which meant no one was around to see how bad it was getting. That if I had a day off from work, I might not get out of bed until after four, and then I'd just park myself on the couch and stare at whatever was on the TV without really seeing it for a couple of hours before going back to bed. There were days I didn't get up at all."

Ian breathed in and out. "I don't know for sure what made me spiral. The breakup with Gus was probably a tipping point, but I think I was already depressed and not aware of it. I mean ... Gus almost died. And we were under a lot of stress around finances and the future while he recovered." He shrugged. "I really don't know."

Tris took hold of Ian's hand and folded his own around it, face more solemn than Ian had ever seen it.

"I'm sorry," Tris said. "Sorry you went through that and how much you hurt. But you know you sound like you're apologizing, right? And you shouldn't be. Don't feel bad about hurting, Ian, or needing time to get through it."

The conviction rolling off him surrounded Ian like an embrace, warm and protective. Tris got it, somehow. Listened and didn't judge, which was what Ian needed.

"My friend Zac says the same." Ian looked down at their joined hands. "He was the one who noticed I wasn't myself. Talked to Marco and some others and worked out a schedule so I was never alone. Man, that pissed me off. Could hardly turn around without literally bumping into one of my friends."

Ian laughed softly. "But having them there helped. They made sure I got up every day and ate, made me go outside for fresh air. Zac talked to me a lot about being depressed and I listened."

Holding Ian's hand tighter now, Tris leaned in so their temples met. "I'm glad."

"Me too." Ian rubbed his thumb over Tris's. "I found a therapist. Got on some meds. And when Marco invited me to move out here with him, I said yes because I already knew isolating myself didn't work for me."

"And you got a third roommate in Elliott," Tris teased, though his voice still sounded strained. "That was lucky."

"It was. El's been a big part of me getting back to being myself again," Ian admitted. "My therapist helped me with an action plan to find ways to feel good, and spending time with the beast dog is high on the list."

"So, it's better, huh? The depression?" Tris drew back and met Ian's eyes, worry evident in his pinched expression. "Maybe that's not okay to ask."

"You can ask," Ian assured him. "My depression is better, yes, and I'm recovering. I don't feel the way I did back then, hollowed out and just done with everything. I use exercise and diet to manage my moods and meditate to recharge. I've been thinking about living alone again, too. Marco and I rent month-to-month out here and we talk sometimes about change and when that might happen. Not sure what we'll do with the dog but—"

"Um, yes, you do." Tris frowned at him. "You can talk out your ass all goddamned day about how El belongs to the house, Ian, but nobody's buying it."

"You suck at the sweet talk."

"Maybe so, but that dog is yours."

"I guess." Ian squeezed Tris's hand. "Listen, I'm sorry I laid all this shit on you tonight. But it didn't feel right letting you think stuff about me that just wasn't true."

"Don't apologize. I'm just glad you're doing better."

"I am doing better. And that's enough."

Tris nodded slowly. "Yeah, it is."

They resumed eating, the conversation lighter as they discussed the latest film in an action series and whether the aging but still very hot actor playing the titular role would remain or hand off the torch. Tris seemed subdued though, like he'd been drained slightly of his typical cheery spirits and Ian couldn't help feeling guilty. He'd wanted tonight to be enjoyable, regardless of whether everyone's clothes stayed on or not. And then he'd started in with the way heavy talk and probably spoiled everything.

"There's ice cream in the freezer if you want something sweet," he said on his way to the sink with plates in both hands. "Or, if you're itching to get back to Weymouth, I'm happy to run you home in the Jeep."

He set the plates on the counter and turned, fully expecting to glimpse relief on Tris's face at having an out. But Tris surprised him again, stepping forward to wrap his arms around Ian, and the relief that swept through Ian at knowing he was still wanted was almost as sweet as the kiss that came next.

"Yes to ice cream," Tris said when they came back up for air. "But only if you can eat it, too."

"I can. It's a low sugar brand." Ian hummed into another kiss, several moments passing before he forced himself to draw back. "Totally okay doing this, too."

"Good." Tris laughed. "I'd like more. With ice cream. And a movie and making out until we're both too tired to move."

"Mmm, okay. But what about your trip to Philly? You don't need to pack before tomorrow?"

"I packed this morning, remember? I'll message Gary and ask him to bring my bag with him tomorrow so we can do a hand-off."

"So smaaht."

"You know that missing 'r' makes me hot." Tris's leer made Ian laugh. "I'm where I want to be, Ian, and I'm not changing my mind."

They kissed some more, cycling between sweet and scorching, until Ian's dick was like an iron rod in his jeans. Tris took over loading the dishwasher while Ian got the dog out for one last pee, and by the time he and Elliott had trooped back inside and de-iced, Tris was camped out on the couch with a movie going, the tub of ice cream, two spoons, and a smile Ian didn't hesitate to return.

I really could get used to this.

12

Ian basked in having Tris near. Hunkered down beside him and shared mango vanilla swirl ice cream while the movie unfolded and good feelings ran through him. They made out a long time, but instead of feeling tired, Ian got drunk on sensation, head swirling like he'd had too many cocktails. Tris sounded equally wrecked if his low pleasured noises were anything to go by and oh, how Ian loved those little gasps and groans. Craved them the way he did the touches Tris gave so freely as he stroked Ian's face and kneaded his muscles.

"Shit." Ian grunted. "You are going to kill me."

"Not before we get naked again." Propping himself up on an elbow, Tris stared down at him through the TV's flickering light. He spread a hand over Ian's belly, fingertips teasing under his waistband. "*If* you want."

"Oh, I want. Can't promise the dog won't follow though, so I'll apologize in advance for weirdness that occurs."

"I can handle doggy weirdness. I just want you in bed."

"Aw, fuck. My bed still needs to be made."

Tris laughed. "C'mon, then. I'll help you do that and then we can mess the sheets up all over again."

Arms full of bedding, they climbed the stairs, sharing one of those comfortable silences Ian loved. They got the sheets and pillowcases on, and Ian was drawing the comforter up when Tris stepped up beside him and pulled it from his hands. He gave Ian a beautiful smile, and Ian sank into his kiss the way he would a warm bath.

They didn't speak while Tris undressed him, touches as reverent as they were hungry. Ian fought to keep his eyes open, intent on not missing anything as Tris swept his eyes over Ian, expression rapt.

Like he's memorizing you.

In that moment, he knew neither of them would walk away from this night completely unaffected. Not with the way Tris was looking at him while Ian's heart beat so hard, he wouldn't have been surprised if Tris could hear it.

"Ian," Tris whispered, so hushed it was a mere breath.

Ian gathered him close and poured everything he was feeling into his kiss. Tris groaned, then guided Ian onto the mattress. After hurriedly stripping off, he climbed onto the bed and settled over Ian, kissing him slow and deep.

Jesus.

Ian practically melted under the onslaught of fevered flesh. He rolled them onto their sides, then worked a hand between them so he could wrap his fingers around Tris's shaft. Tris mimicked him, stroking Ian lazily, the motions exactly the right combination of pressure and pace to drive Ian wild. In no time he was panting, body a tangled mess of need.

"Want you so much," Tris murmured. "To feel you around me."

Ian bit back a gasp. Thinking about Tris inside him was almost too much. "Want that. Need you in me, Tris, I ..." He quivered as Tris tongued his collarbone, raising goosebumps over Ian's skin. "Oh, fuck."

"Okay." Smiling, Tris pulled back to meet Ian's gaze, eyes crinkling at the corners. "You want that, baby?"

Ian nodded and brought his free hand to Tris's lips, tracing them with his fingers. Tris's eyes flared bright. He kissed the tips of Ian's fingers, then took the first two into his mouth. Transfixed, Ian groaned. It had been a long time since sex with anyone had consumed Ian like this, made his dick leak just by having his fingers sucked. It hit him square in the chest when Tris pulled away, the loss of the closeness and heat so jarring it felt like a blow.

Who am I right now?

Rolling onto his stomach, Ian closed his eyes tight, bundling the pillow close as he fought for control. "Stuff's in the nightstand," he said, relieved his voice didn't betray the way his insides were wobbling.

He heard the nightstand drawer open and close, and then Tris was beside him again, pinning Ian down with his body. The strength left Ian's limbs in a rush, and he lay still, goosebumps rising over his skin as Tris skimmed a hand over Ian's ass, fingers already slick. Ian closed his eyes and slowly spread his legs, shivering as Tris's fingertips met his rim, desire pooling deep in his groin.

"God," he whispered, burying his face in the pillow when Tris shifted, sliding his free arm under Ian's chest.

His touches leveled Ian, melting his bones like ice under fire as he worked Ian open. Ian couldn't stop his soft moans.

"You're so sexy, Ian."

Tris slid a finger slowly into Ian, and the singular sensation of being filled rippled all through him. He panted and swore as a second finger breached him, and he arched into it, groan throaty, reveling in the pressure that made his balls throb. It was several seconds before Ian noticed Tris had gone very quiet.

"Tris?" Opening his eyes, Ian stole a quick glance over his shoulder, insides going tight at the picture Tris painted, face slack as he stared at his own hand fucking in and out of Ian's ass. "Tris?"

"Huh? Sorry." Tris's gaze flicked to Ian's, and then he was laughing, breaths gusting over Ian's shoulder. "*Damn.*" He slid his fingers deeper and they groaned as one. "You are a fucking sight, GB."

"No." Ian huffed out a shaky laugh of his own, panting as he struggled to string words together. "Do not ... call me Grumble Bear ... while we are in bed."

Tris kissed the meat of Ian's shoulder. "Fine. But I wish you could see yourself. You're so fucking beautiful."

"Sweet talker," Ian got out, though Tris shook his head.

"I'm not. This is totally going in the spank bank and there's nothing you can do about it."

That got them both cackling and God, Ian loved that. The enjoyment looping between them, so pure and heady, heightening each caress and making them both infinitely sweeter and bone-meltingly hot. Then Tris crooked his fingers, searching out Ian's gland and a jolt of pure pleasure rocked through Ian.

"Nuh-h-h." Eyes squished shut, he rolled his hips into the sheets, mindlessly seeking out friction as words tripped out of his mouth. "*Tris*. Need you inside. Gotta ... fuck. I—need it."

"Me too," Tris soothed. "I'm gonna get us there."

Sliding the arm out from under Ian, he pulled his fingers free too, then coaxed Ian up onto his hands and knees. Eyes still mostly closed, Ian swayed slightly under the force of his want, and he sensed more than saw Tris turn back to the nightstand for the condom.

His skin prickled as Tris settled behind him, thighs pressing against the backs of Ian's as he lined their bodies up. The head of his cock met Ian's rim before Tris pushed forward slowly, a steadying hand on the small of Ian's back. The stretch split Ian open and he bore down, aware the strength in his limbs was fading. He swore, voice tight, and lowered himself to the mattress on shaking arms. Tris rubbed circles into Ian's back.

"Okay?"

"Yeah," Ian gasped out. He needed this. Needed more. Needed Tris to fill him up and make them both fly. Resting his forehead atop his pillowed hands, he rocked back, urging Tris on. "Need you to move."

Hand moving to grasp Ian's waist, Tris pushed forward, bottoming out in a single deep thrust. The burn in Ian's ass changed immediately, becoming a deep, delicious ache. Another lusty moan tore out of him as pleasure rippled outward in waves from his ass to his balls, and he gave himself over, surrendering utterly.

It was perfect. *They* were perfect. And Ian was going to remember this night for a long time.

"More," he pleaded, the word a mere puff of air. Tris still heard him, letting out an honest-to-God growl as he fucked into Ian, his rhythm so deep and hard Ian's toes curled.

Tris dropped kisses along Ian's shoulders and back as they moved together, sometimes cursing softly against his skin. The ache in Ian's body expanded, lighting him up stem to stern. He grunted when Tris reached down and took him in hand, the simple act enough to have Ian's balls drawing up tight.

"Yeah," he said, voice stronger now. "Fuck me harder."

Tris pushed Ian down onto the mattress, pinning him there with his full weight. The motion fucked Ian's cock into the fist still wrapped around him, and he soared, body skirting the edge of oblivion but not quite able to make that final leap.

"Love this," Tris ground out, his breath hot against Ian's ear. "Fuck. Gonna get me off. Make me come so fucking hard."

The words scraped Ian raw. "*Please*. Want it," he babbled. "Want to feel you in me."

A bone-deep shudder shook Tris's frame. "God, Ian."

Ian made a broken sound and craned his head back, gasping as Tris took his mouth in a bruising kiss, his grip on Ian ferocious. His thrusting rhythm faltered, whole body arching into Ian's with near crushing intensity. He tore his mouth from Ian's, voice shaking around a curse.

Ian forced his eyes open, intent on watching Tris's pleasure consume him. Face twisting, Tris closed his fist reflexively around Ian's dick with just the right pressure and damn, Ian was *there*, right up to the edge and hurtling over it.

"*Fuck!*"

He jolted, pleasure coiling so tight in his groin he hurt before it exploded outward with staggering force. A cry rose in Ian's throat, choking him as he shot hard over Tris's fist, body jolting with each spurt. Tris held him through it, nuzzling Ian's cheek and neck as he shook, until Ian lay boneless against the sheets.

He was aware of Tris pulling out. Of him rolling Ian away from the wet spot and wiping him down with a discarded t-shirt. But Ian was too goddamned wrecked to even open his eyes.

Maybe he was hiding a little, too. Avoiding his own treacherous thoughts. Distancing himself from the persistent beat of 'I want this every night' drumming in his head. Ian did want more with Tris. And had no idea how the fuck he was going to let him go.

"You should come visit me in Bethesda."

Ian blinked at the casual offer. He'd drifted for a while, Tris spooned up behind him like the world's most perfect man-blanket. But Ian felt wide awake now, pulse picking up at the knowledge there was only one way he could answer.

"That's not a good idea."

"Why not?" Tris tugged Ian's ear. "You're not thinking I'd ghost you, right? Or not come back from D.C. at all?"

"I don't believe you'd purposely hurt anyone," Ian murmured. "But you've said yourself that you don't know when you'll be back here, and I can't ignore that."

"Why not? I like spending time with you. Hanging out and sharing laughs. Making each other feel good."

"I like spending time with you, too."

So much, Ian thought. Doing just about anything with Tris Santos was fun, but that didn't change a thing.

"I'm all for hanging out and sharing laughs," Ian said. "But I want to be realistic about what we've been doing. This fling. Between friends," he added quickly, his insides shrinking on themselves. Reducing the connection he shared with Tris to mere physicality felt shitty. And the humor in Tris's voice when he spoke landed with a bittersweet sting.

"So, we're friends who happen to have sex?"

"I suppose." Ian didn't like having those words tossed back at him, even gently, but what else could he say with Tris smiling at him?

"I'm on board if you want that, Ian."

And that was exactly the problem Ian was grappling with as he rolled over in Tris's embrace and looked at him.

"I'm not sure I do." Ian sighed. "I thought I was done with the mate-for-life stuff after Gus, but it turns out …"

"You still want it," Tris finished for him, brow puckering as he understood where Ian was going. "Jeez, GB. You really are a hopeless romantic. What am I going to do with you?"

"I have no idea." Ian smiled. "But I can't help wanting to find the right guy, even now."

Can't help wanting forever.

And damn, there it was. Ian Byrne putting his heart before his head because that was just how he rolled. Not that he'd say it out loud, of course—Tris was already staring at Ian like he doubted his sanity. But rather than rolling his eyes at Ian's obvious folly, Tris grimaced like he'd tasted something bitter.

"So, I guess I'm not the right guy, huh?"

"Um, no?" Ian jerked away from a finger poking his ribs. "Ow."

"That's what you get."

"For agreeing with you? Tris. You're not into the whole mate-for-life plan and you know I'm okay with that."

Tris frowned. "Pretty sure you just insulted me twice."

"I don't mean to insult you at all." Ian pushed a lock of hair back from Tris's forehead. "Doesn't mean I'm wrong about you not wanting a serious relationship."

"True. But we could have a blast together anyway."

Ian almost sighed. "Not sure I'm in the right headspace for just having a blast."

Not with you.

"Is it because of what happened with Gus?" Tris gave him a narrow look. "I can understand being cautious. But I'm not Gus and I wouldn't fuck you over the way he did. I wouldn't hurt you."

"I appreciate that," Ian said softly. "Truthfully, I'm more afraid of hurting *myself*. We want and need very different things, Tris. If you were more settled—"

"That's not code for older, right? Because I really don't give a crap that you're, what, forty? My stepdad's eighteen years older than my mom and they make shit work."

Ian made a face. "I'm not talking about your folks while I'm naked. And how do you know how old I am?"

"I looked you up on LinkedIn. Wasn't hard to do the math using your undergrad dates. Your profile is really robust, by the way, so good job."

"Do you have *any* shame?" Ian said through a laugh, insides flipping madly when Tris's gaze grew unbearably tender.

"No, I don't." He laughed. "But what else was I going to do? I meet this guy on the train who's all grouchy and hot as fuck, and he's smart and funny and makes me freaking ginger tea in a thermos. How could I not be interested?" Tris shook his head. "I really don't give a shit that you're older than me. It's been a long time since I met someone who I can talk to the way I do you and who *gets* me. I like having that in my life."

Ian liked it, too. Liked the laughs they shared and the lightness that filled him just hanging out with Tris. But those feelings —lovely, bubbly, and so very new—weren't enough. Because Ian *did* get Tris and knew that for in all the ways they connected, they were not on the same page about some very critical concepts.

"I feel the same way. But God. We're at such different places in our lives. And looking for different things from the people we get close to. You know I'm right," he said, despite the disappointment creeping over Tris's expression. "You don't want a serious relationship or to stay in one place and put down roots. That's what I meant when I said you weren't settled. You like chaos and thrive on change."

"I'll own that, yeah. I don't understand what it has to do with us, though."

"A lot, I think." Rolling onto his back, Ian studied the ceiling. "Chaos is *not* my thing. I manage with the levels that come from just living life, but that's what I'm doing—managing change so it doesn't throw me. I both like and need familiarity. Like feeling settled. I see myself here into the future. Not in this house," he added quickly, "and not living with Marco either, bless his patient ass. But I have a place here in Boston with my career and my life I don't see giving that up. Which is *so* not who you are."

He turned his head so he could see Tris's eyes. "I like that about you, you know. The way you go after what you want. That you're true to yourself. A rulebreaker." Ian smiled. "That you don't settle because you don't want to. Just knowing you has got me thinking about what I want, too."

"Shit, I hope that's a good thing." Tris flashed a quick grin, but Ian saw the little line between his eyebrows and carefully reached over to smooth it away with the pad of his thumb.

"It is. I put a lot of my life on hold when I went off the rails. Dropped hobbies and chunks of social life because I couldn't handle them and myself at the same time. Managing *me* was the hardest thing I did every day for a long time, and I needed buffers to help me get through it. Living out here with Marco made it easy to focus on myself, but I don't think I need to do that anymore. I'm ready to handle myself and the rest of the world at the same time."

Propping himself up on one elbow, Tris stared down at him. "I love that you're saying this."

Something unfurled in Ian's chest, a tightness he'd been carrying so long he'd almost lost track of it.

"Me, too. I told you that Marco and I are thinking of moving back into the city and I'm excited about that. The thing is, giving up this place will mean uprooting my life again and it's going to be a lot for me. Not a fan of chaos, remember?" Ian kept his voice light but meant every word. "I could promise to visit you in Bethesda or Pasadena, or wherever you lay your hat next but I'm going to have a lot on my plate making rent *without* inter-state booty calls complicating everything."

Tris's mouth thinned. "Bro. Not what I was asking."

Ian wasn't so sure. But he hated the way Tris's shoulders had gone stiff and rubbed Tris's chest with his knuckles in silent apology.

"I shouldn't have said that," he murmured. "But this just brings me back to where we started, Tris. I don't even know where you'll be after the project at Walter Reed is done."

"I could be *here*, at least part of the time. Off-World wants to keep me, and they'll do a lot to make it happen." Tris covered the center of Ian's chest with one hand, face softer now. "They'll let me travel for project work as much as I want while making Boston my home base. Honestly, it sounds like a dream job for someone like me. The work will change and I'll be able to hop in and out of different cities, but still get to see my favorite people back here. And if you can't come out to the project sites where I'll be working, we could connect when I'm in town."

If he has time to spare.

Ian tried to push the unbidden words out of his head. "What about the graduate program? Or your plan to relocate back to the west coast?" he asked. "I'd never tell you not to go for the things you want, but I also don't know if I like the idea of having to schedule time to meet up."

"Would you have done it for Gus?"

The question raised the hairs on Ian's arms. "What?"

Tris had the grace to look abashed, but that didn't stop him from replying. "If Gus had gotten a different job that required him to travel, would you have stuck it out or told him to fuck off because it was too hard?"

"That's not fair." Ian swallowed hard and would have turned away if Tris's hand on his sternum hadn't stopped him. "Gus and I were together for years. We built a life together."

"Epic love and all that."

"I know you think it's dumb, but—"

"It doesn't matter what I think. I get it, Ian. Gus was more than your fuck buddy."

Guilt slid through Ian. Tris really had no idea how Ian felt about him at all; how could he when Ian could hardly acknowledge the sweet, scary feelings bouncing around in his heart?

"Don't freak out, but I'd say you're more than a fuck buddy to me, too." He smiled softly. "You're my friend and I care about you, sex notwithstanding."

"I care about you too." Tris smiled too, an easy and surprisingly not-freaked-out-at-all smile. "I'm not sure what that means, but I'm down to find out."

Ian rolled his eyes. "You're down for anything."

"And you are made of lies." Tris leaned down and pressed a quick kiss against Ian's lips. "Look, I'm not saying I'm exactly the right person for a romantical guy like yourself, but I don't want to say goodbye."

"I don't want that either. I just don't know how this would work with you gone most of the time and me here. And what if you meet a person you want to get serious with?"

"I'd still want to be friends with you. Besides, it's more likely *you'd* be the one to meet somebody," Tris said. "And while I guess the sex part of our being friends would change at that point, we'd figure it out."

"You really think so?"

"Uh-huh. I think we could try this, Ian. *If* you want to, I mean."

"I ... don't know how to answer." Ian frowned. "I've never done a long-distance thing with anyone."

"Then we make it up as we go. It doesn't have to be complicated if we keep talking and are up front with each other." Tris smiled down at him. "Besides, what do we have to lose?"

My sanity for one. And as for my heart ...

Ian stayed quiet as Tris settled back down beside him. Being friends who had sex would take getting used to. Especially since they were going to have to figure out how to keep it going over long-distance. Still, Ian thought Tris could be right and they might pull it off. Ian wanted to if he was honest. He liked Tris that much.

That knowledge kept Ian awake long after Tris had dozed off, thinking about how they might make this thing work and how they could keep the connection—wonderful, addictive, mind-blowing—between them alive.

13

Dennis strolled up to the nurses station and parked himself beside Ian. "Can we talk about Tris?"

Looking up from his chart, he blinked at his friend slowly. "What's there to talk about?"

"Well, how about that you turned up at Greenbush Station with him this morning, both of you smiling and looking incredibly well fu—"

"Hey." Glowering, Ian glanced around to make sure no one was within earshot. "Keep your voice down."

"Sorry." Dennis's cheeks took on a dusky shade, but that fucker was smiling. "I shouldn't have said that here."

"Or at all."

"But why? It's obvious you're perfect for each other. Like, I want to push your faces together so you kiss and I don't ship real life people."

"Yes, you do." Ian set down his chart. "Look, it's both nice and weird that you'd say all that, but Tris is leaving town on Monday and has no solid plans to come back. We're not 'together' and don't have plans to be."

Except that was a lie. Tris had said he'd come back, last night and again that morning, after he'd woken Ian with kisses. Ian had liked hearing it. A lot. They'd talked about how a long-distance thing would work until Elliott jumped up and joined them on the bed, snuffling and making increasingly louder woo-woo noises until the humans had gotten up, Tris laughing so hard he'd nearly cried. They'd taken the beast dog out for his morning run through the snow, then made breakfast together, still chatting and plotting over their eggs. Then Tris had led Ian to the shower where they'd brought each other off, Tris's gaze so intense Ian couldn't look away, not even when his knees had wobbled under the force of his orgasm.

Ian didn't want to give any of that up. But he also didn't want to talk about a back-and-forth thing where Tris traveled and Ian stayed in Boston. Not with Dennis or anyone else. Not right now, when Ian was still trying to figure out how it was all going to work.

Oblivious, Dennis frowned at him. "So, what—it's going to be like you and Tris never met?"

As if that could ever be possible.

Ian's chest fluttered as he glanced up at his friend. "I didn't say that. We're going to keep in touch. God knows it's easy enough with apps and phones."

"Maryland's not very far, you know." Dennis's expression turned sly. "You can be there in half a day by train or by car, and way less if you can stomach a flight."

"Stop." Ian bit back a chuckle. "I get what you're saying and love you for it. But Tris needs to focus on the exo-suit project, and I have stuff of my own to get through. And you know he talks about moving out to the West Coast all the time. He might be there by fall. The last thing either of us needs is to make life complicated and mess up our friendship."

Dennis sighed. "We should have invited him to the party at your place this weekend. He would have said yes."

"I told you, he already has plans to be out of town."

The receptionist poked her head around the corner then and

gave him a small smile. "Hey, Ian? Jenna Orloff is here asking for you. She's not on the schedule today."

Ian exchanged a look with Dennis. "Will you cover for me? Not sure what this is about, but I think we can both guess."

A half-dozen patients were in the waiting area when Ian walked out, but he spotted Jenna immediately, standing by the front desk with her coat folded over one arm. Ian could tell with one glance she was tense even as she gave him a small wave.

"Hey, Bones."

Ian smiled at the nickname. "Morning, Jenna. I didn't see your name on the schedule."

"Oh, I'm not here for Doc Hannity. I, um, have to see someone else." Jenna glanced away, expression turning inward. "Over at Mass General."

"I see." Ian kept playing dumb. "You here by yourself?"

"Yeah. My dad can't fly in until next week and Coach and the rest of the team are away at a game. I was going to ask my roommate to come but ..." Jenna blinked rapidly, her dark eyes gone suspiciously bright. "I don't know if I can do this, Ian," she murmured, voice wobbling dangerously over his name.

"You can," he said quietly. Shit, his heart went out to the kid, and he tilted his head toward the door. "Want me to keep you company? I was about to start my break and I don't mind walking over there with you."

Jenna's face crumpled, and for a second Ian thought she might bolt. But he knew from experience she was much stronger than people might guess, so he silently offered his hand and let Jenna squeeze it. He waited as she hauled in one deep breath after another, and though Jenna was still pale when she looked up at last, she was back in control.

"You sure you want to do that?" she asked, a trace of her sassy grin crossing her face. "It's gonna take longer than your break for us to walk over there."

Ian gave her a smile of his own. "I'm sure. But Dennis owes me, like, five hundred favors and I'm going to cash a bunch in."

He wished he had more favors to cash in by the time he entered the pub in South Station that evening. Ian wasn't much in the mood for company, even with friends he loved, and he really wanted to tell them that he didn't need a b-day dinner or weekend or anything but to chill with a dog that wasn't his but made for excellent company. That was impossible given Marco and Dennis were already out at the house with one group of friends and another contingent was on their way to meet Ian right now. And Ian knew he shouldn't be alone just then anyway. Not when he was feeling broody about work and life and a pale-eyed guy who'd gotten under Ian's skin enough he was ready to use chat apps to keep in touch.

"Ian! Hey!"

It took a second before Ian registered the hand on his elbow.

"There you are." Tris's smile warmed him a bit. "Really glad I caught you! I messaged earlier, but you didn't answer."

"Shit, I'm sorry." Ian had stopped checking his phone at around midday, what with being busy with Jenna and his group chats blowing up with hundreds of messages about how the weekend would play out. "Everything okay?"

"Yeah." Tris cocked his head, brow furrowing. "Are *you* okay?"

Ian gave him a fast nod. "Long day. Really glad it's over. But what are you doing here? Shouldn't you be headed for Philly?"

"Just waiting on the Acela with my partners in crime." Tris inclined his head toward some tables on Ian's left, where several people sat among platters of food and pitchers of beer.

"Ah. Didn't realize it was a group trip." Ian nodded to Ela, who'd caught his eye and was waving.

"Gary and Haru mentioned tagging along," Tris replied, "then Sully started in and so did Ela and Hannah. You know how it is."

"Not really. But you know me. No fun and all that." Ian

smiled to show he was teasing, but the concern in Tris's face didn't lessen.

"You sure you're all right? Because you look kind of wrecked."

"Thanks." Ian sighed. "That's just what I needed to hear." He made to move past Tris but paused again when the hand on his elbow squeezed lightly.

"Whoa, wait. I didn't mean that the way it sounded." Tris's earnest expression zapped Ian's annoyance utterly. "I meant you look upset and I want to know you're okay."

"I am." Ian made his tone gentle. "I had a shitty day and I'm taking it out on you. That's not fair."

"What happened?"

"A patient—the kid who calls me Bones—she had an appointment with oncology today and it didn't go well."

"Oh, damn." Tris's brow furrowed further. "You want to talk about it?"

Ian shook his head. He loved that Tris cared enough to ask, but no one needed to hear about how he'd held Jenna's hand while she'd been diagnosed with a form of anaplastic large-cell lymphoma; talking about a nineteen-year-old needing to start chemo was a shit story to start off a party weekend. Predictably, Tris waved Ian off when he tried to say as much.

"The weekend is happening GB, stories or not. But I'm more concerned about how you look like you hate life in general." Tris gestured toward the table with his hand. "Wanna sit down for a minute?"

"Nah. I'm meeting some friends and I don't want to butt in with yours."

"You won't be. Besides, I saw from the board that the 6:20 train is delayed, so you and those friends will have time before you start battling for seats."

Biting back a sigh, Ian allowed Tris to steer him to the table and seat him beside a dark-haired young man with laughing eyes who immediately poured Ian a glass of beer. Tris made introductions as he settled into the chair on Ian's other side, and Ian tried his best to summon a tiny bit of charm.

Thanks to the wintercue photos, the faces around him were vaguely familiar, and each was achingly young. The guy with the beer pitcher was Gary and beside him sat Haru, both terribly handsome and very into each other. Ela and her boyfriend sat across the table from Ian, each dressed in black and a study in contrasts, Sully pale and angular where Ela was curvy and brown, but the friendliness Sully showed Ian was a perfect mirror of his girlfriend's.

And then there was Hannah, fair and quite pretty, her pale, knowing eyes a great deal like Tris's, though lacking his ever-present warmth. She regarded Ian with a friendly expression as she wound a long, blonde curl around one finger, but she didn't quite smile and something in her cool appraisal made his skin prickle. Left Ian feeling scruffy and worn and really fucking *old*.

Which he was of course, at least compared to this crowd of very attractive, very young people, and it didn't help at all that his afternoon had been a suckfest and now he looked like he'd been ridden hard and put away wet. Ian had never been particularly vain; he liked looking good but didn't think much about it beyond making sure he was well groomed and his clothes didn't clash. He felt out of place among Tris's fashionable friends, however, and telling himself it was all in his head wasn't doing a damn thing to change that.

His chest tightened as he looked Tris's way. They'd spent enough time together in the last two weeks it'd gotten easy to forget just how young Tris really was. But watching him here with his friends brought that awareness back in glaring detail Ian couldn't ignore, and it was like Ian was seeing him for the first time all over again. Floppy, stylish hair. Long lashes around those big, pretty eyes. The easy grin that changed his face, lighting up his elegant features with an unguarded cuteness Ian liked way too much.

"You want some wings?" Tris nudged a platter of food in Ian's direction. "I promise there are plenty of moist towelettes to mop up the spicy pink sauce."

That made Ian smile. "No, thanks. The friends I'm meeting are cooking out at the house tonight."

"Oh, right—the guys who work at a restaurant?" Tris plucked a piece of chicken up for himself. "Dennis mentioned you and Marco were hosting a dinner."

"Did he now?" Ian pursed his lips. That figured. Dennis had probably blabbed during the Monday morning commute while Ian had been out cold. Tris hadn't mentioned anything birthday-related in the days between, however, which meant not all of the gory details had been spilled. "Some friends of my housemate's and mine did all the planning," he said to the table at large. "We're just giving them space to party. For the weekend, actually."

"Sounds fun." Ela smiled at him. "Like a slumber party?"

Ian chuckled. "Basically. A bit like your trip to Philly."

"I don't think we'll be in the house much, other than to sleep," Hannah said, then leveled a look at Tris. "I *need* a Halo-free weekend."

"You know Gia has Xbox, right?" Gary asked, eyes gleaming with mischief when Hannah rolled hers.

"I'm sure we'll be gaming at my place too," Ian said, "and there'll be an army of snowmen in the backyard by Sunday. I still draw the line at an ice luge."

"Smart." Ela grimaced. "The one Haru carved for the wintercue got pretty gross. Are you also planning to roast meats out in the snow?"

Laughing now, Ian held up a hand. "I don't but who knows what the others have planned. The food'll be good regardless and I'm not going to complain about the company either."

"See, I knew you'd come around," said a familiar voice and Ian glanced up to find a snowy Mark smiling at him, Zac and Jae at his sides, all of them rosy-cheeked and loaded down with bags.

Ian couldn't help grinning back. "Hey, y'all. About time you got here."

"That's my bad." Jae made a face. "My last surgery went longer than it should have and put us behind." His dark eyes twinkled when his gaze landed on Tris. "You're Tris, right? I was on shift with Ian during your wintercue and made him show us the photos."

"He's not kidding—totally grabbed the phone out of my hand and started flipping through them himself." Ian thought Tris looked very pleased with himself. "These are the party planner friends," he said with a wave at the trio, "or half of them, anyway. Where are your men?"

"On their way," Zac replied. "Emmett went to the Test Kitchen for a couple of things and Aiden and Owen kept him company." He glanced over his shoulder and smiled. "Here they are now."

Ela's eyebrows went up as three more snow-spattered figures walked into the tiny bar carrying yet more bags. "Your friends who work at the restaurant," she said slowly to Ian, "are the guys who own Endless Pastabilities?"

"Uh-huh," Ian said, a second before the penny dropped. "Oh heck, you're a food person—you totally care about that kind of thing." He grinned as several in the party broke up laughing. "Ela's a fabulous baker," he said to his friends, "and she knows way more about what Aiden and Emmett do than I ever will."

At hearing their names, Aiden smiled and Emmett rose up on his toes behind Aiden, offering a cheerful wave over his shoulder. But Emmett's demeanor changed when he spotted Haru, whose face lit up in a similar fashion.

"Yo!" Emmett called. "I know you from the boxing gym downtown, right?"

He walked around Aiden and the others to Haru while Jae watched him with an indulgent smile. "I swear, he knows everyone," he said. "Anytime we go out, he runs into people he's met through the food scene or random connections like fitness."

"Mark is the same." Owen exchanged a loving look with his partner. "Your connections are always people you know through the bar scene, though—"

"All of whom I met in the ancient days before you, my love," Mark declared with a wink.

If Ian hadn't turned his head at just the right moment, he would have missed the disdain that crossed Hannah's face. Still, he heard her voice without trying, and didn't have trouble imagining she'd wanted him to.

"Why are the hot ones always gay?" she asked Ela, who furrowed her brow. "It seems like such a waste for the rest of us."

"Emmett is pan, actually." Ian met Hannah's startled eyes over the table. "That means he doesn't let gender influence his choice of partner. Some people are wired that way." He glanced at Tris who was equally wide-eyed, before looking back to Hannah. "The rest of us are totally wicked gay though, and not a waste of anything."

Hannah's cheeks flushed a deep red. "Of course," she said hastily. "I didn't mean—"

Ian's shrug cut her off dead. She clearly hadn't expected anyone to call her out, particularly a stranger she'd only just met. But Ian had met too many passive homophobes over the years to dismiss the half-hearted excuse and he wasn't about to hesitate speaking up for himself and his friends. If Hannah despised him for it, Ian would consider it a win. He just hoped he hadn't pissed off Tris in the process.

"The 6:20 train to Greenbush is now boarding on track 11, with station stops at—"

Ian cut a small smile at Tris and picked up his backpack. "That's my cue." He looked at Mark and the others. "You need me to carry anything? It's like you packed for a world tour."

"Honey, we have to make merry for days." Mark passed him a bulging cloth sack. "That's all mochi from Sweet Garrett's," he said, "and the bulk of their cookies."

Ela let out an audible 'ooh.' "I'm officially jealous," she said. "The strawberry mochi at Sweet Garrett's are luscious."

Mark favored her with a mega-watt grin. "*Yes*. But the birthday boy prefers the purple sweet potato, so we loaded up on those, too." He waggled his eyebrows at Ian. "I'm hoping he lets me stick candles on some of them before he starts eating."

Ian narrowed his eyes. Fucker. "Why are you like this?"

"Wait," Tris said over Mark's laughter. "Is today your birthday, GB?"

"No. It was earlier in the week. And we agreed there would be no candles or cake or sappy b-day greetings," Ian said with an accusing look at his friends.

"That was just you, big guy." Jae's voice was mild. "We didn't agree to anything."

"I suppose you didn't." Ian glanced around at Tris's friends. "Nice meeting you all." *Or most of you,* he thought as he stood, surprised when Tris also got to his feet.

"I'll walk you out," Tris said. "I need to use the restroom and I want a goodbye hug."

Nerves fluttered in Ian's chest as he and his friends headed out, a chorus of goodbyes ringing out behind them. They'd made it to the terminal doors when Zac stopped walking without warning.

"I'll take this—" he plucked the cloth bag from Ian's hand "—and you say goodbye to your friend." He turned a smile on Tris that made his brown eyes dance. "Great to finally meet you, Tris. If Ian hasn't already mentioned it, he'd love to keep in touch."

Ian raised a brow. "Zacarías, would you mind your own business, please?"

"Awesome meeting you all, too," a grinning Tris said to Zac, exactly as if Ian hadn't spoken. "Will you make sure this guy blows out lots of candles?"

"We'll try!" Zac replied with a jaunty little wave, then headed off to join the others who were waiting by the doors.

Tris's smile softened as he watched the group walk off and Ian thought he looked almost wistful. "Your friends seem cool."

"They are," Ian said. *I'd love for you to get to know them.* "They keep me sane, even when I make it hard on them. Maybe especially then."

"I think I see that." Tris frowned. "Thanks for what you said back there to Hannah. I never know how to react when she says stuff like that. No one does. But we shouldn't let her talk about people that way."

Ian wet his lips with his tongue. "She was talking about *you* that way, Tris. Not just people." He watched, heart wincing, as emotions streaked across Tris's face—sadness, chagrin, real anger —and reached out, grasping his arm gently. "It sucks calling people out for shitty behavior, particularly people you know and even like. I hope I didn't make your life harder."

"You didn't." Tris huffed a humorless laugh. "I don't care if she's mad. I do care that you had a birthday this week and didn't tell me." He bit his lip, hurt filtering over his face. "Why is that?"

"I knew you already had plans for the weekend. And I don't make a fuss about the day anyway, haven't for years. This whole thing is literally Mark and Zac's doing with Jae and Dennis on the side."

"You still should have told me. I'd have done something understated and totally not embarrassing to help you celebrate."

"Uh-huh. Because understated is your default."

"Okay, now you're just being mean." Tris gave him a mock glare, but the hurt was mostly gone from his eyes. "I can do subtle, GB."

"I'm sure you can. And you're right, I could have mentioned the birthday. We did celebrate, though." Ian held Tris's gaze. "We ate curry and rice and a cucumber salad and shared a tub of my favorite ice cream."

Understanding dawned on Tris's face like the sun peeking out from a rain cloud. "Your birthday was yesterday?"

"Yup. Best birthday I've had in a really long time." He smiled, whole body thrumming when Tris pulled him into a hug.

"Good."

The terminal around them receded and Ian closed his eyes. Winding his arms around Tris, he pressed his nose against Tris's neck and breathed him in, wrapped in a complicated mix of good feelings and melancholy. His throat was as thick as his favorite wooly sweater when he finally pulled back.

Tris's eyes shone. "Ian, I—" He seemed to shake himself. "This is going to sound dumb, but I can't believe I'm not going to see you on Monday morning."

Ian rubbed his arm. "I know. Message me. Call, anytime. Just to talk if you want or whatever."

"We'll start there and see what happens, okay? Figure it out, just like we said."

"Yeah. We can do that."

Tris smiled wryly. "But I want you to remember you're the one who said, 'call anytime.' Because when I have my first freak out at ass o' clock in the morning—"

"I'll listen." Ian raised a hand to Tris's cheek. "You're entitled to freak out. But you are going to kick ass on this project and I can't wait to hear all about it." He sighed. "I'd better go."

"Okay."

It took everything Ian had in him to step away. "There are going to be at least twelve people in the house tonight," he said, walking slowly backward. "Elliott's gonna go nuts."

"Yup. He's going to love it too, same as you." Tris gave him a lopsided smile. "I'll see you later, Ian."

"Not if I see you first, Chi-Town."

The old joke got a laugh out of Tris that Ian carried with him out into the snowy night.

14

March, 2022

"Come on, GB."

"No."

"Yes. Get up off your ass and show me your apartment."

Ian glared at Tris, who grinned at him through the chat app on Ian's tablet. "I was on call this weekend," he grumbled. "I'm *tired*. I need food and many hours of sleep and to sit like a lump on this couch until further notice."

"You will have all of those things after you show me your place."

"There are boxes everywhere and the place is a mess."

Tris rolled his eyes. "That is bullshit and you know it. Jae told me the guys helped you unpack Thursday night, and Owen claims the place was as neat as a pin when he left."

"Not hard when all you own is a bed, a desk, a five-year-old futon, and a TV that is, apparently, too fucking small," Ian muttered. "Do you really have *all* of their numbers? Because I swear I only gave you Zac's."

"He added me to a group chat along with Gary and Haru."

"So, there's ten of us in there now? Jesus fucking Christ."

"Pretty sure Marco's in there too, so it could be more. Aiden said something about ten players making up a lacrosse team and this morning Mark renamed the chat LAX Dat Ass."

Ian belted out a laugh. "I noticed my phone said I had four hundred fucking new messages and thought I got hacked."

"I like how the idea of being hacked doesn't faze you at all." Tris shook his head. "But somewhere in those four hundred fucking new messages are a few that make it clear you are lying to me about the place being a mess."

"F-i-i-i-ne." Ian hauled himself upright. Striding into the tiny kitchen, he held the tablet up and faced it away from himself so Tris could see. "Here you go."

"Your appliances are shiny!"

Tris kept up the oohs and aahs as Ian moved from the kitchen to the main living space, his enthusiasm contagious enough that Ian, tired as he was, caught a spark of energy.

"The whole wall is windows, huh? And damn, the balcony is baller."

"That's a good thing, yes?"

Tris chuckled. "Yeah, it is. I still can't believe you found a studio with a freaking outdoor space in that neighborhood, GB."

Ian had trouble believing it himself. When he and Marco had agreed they'd leave Cohasset, they'd nearly despaired of finding places near Mass General that were nice yet still affordable. But Mark and Emmett had gotten involved, mining their extensive social networks for every available apartment in the city. Which was how Marco had found a one bedroom in Beacon Hill and Ian a studio located in a renovated brick building smack on the edge of the West End.

"Are you gonna buy more stuff?"

"I'm going to have to," Ian said. "I didn't take much with me when Gus and I split, and the place in Cohasset was already furnished. I need a better couch. And dishes. Actual pots and pans so I can cook in my own kitchen and stop using Mark and Owen's."

"They're your friends, dude. You know they don't care."

"Yeah, I do."

Ian smiled to himself. A pleasant little thrill ran through him as he looked around the space, trying to see it as Tris might. Other than the television and futon and Elliott snoozing in a patch of afternoon sun, there wasn't much in the room. Ian was still acclimating to how much his life had changed in just a few weeks. He missed seeing Marco outside of work every day and not having a yard for the dog. But he already felt at home. Loved the energy the city fed him and being able to commute to work in under ten minutes. And especially having his friends close, Mark and Owen just a few buildings to the west and the others in nearby neighborhoods.

If only Tris was equally close.

"Do you want me to go upstairs?" He turned the tablet around so he could see Tris's face. "There's not a ton there either, but it still looks nice."

Tris beamed at him. "You know I do."

Ian climbed the narrow staircase that ran along the right side of the studio, then faced the tablet away from him, turning slowly in a circle to give Tris a look at the loft.

"I love it up here."

"Shit, I do too." Tris's whistle sounded tinny through the tablet's speaker. "Hey, what was the fence thing at the foot of the stairs?"

"A dog gate," Ian replied. "The couple who lived here last had two Jack Russell terriers and the gate was the only reliable method of keeping the dogs out of the loft. There's also a sliding glass door to close off the room but they clearly had rules about pets on the bed."

"Unlike you, of course."

"Oh, I have rules. They just go unfollowed."

"You're a mess, man. But your place totally isn't. This is *nice*, GB. Almost like another balcony but inside."

Ian thought Tris had described the loft perfectly. The space wasn't huge, but it felt airy, the glass wall and door providing privacy without blocking out the light. "I'd take you out on the actual balcony if it wasn't still covered in snow."

"I'm sure. I miss a lot about Boston but not the snowpocalypse."

"Word." Moving to the bed, Ian sat down, settling with his back against the headboard and the tablet in his lap. A wholly different kind of thrill made his skin prickle when Tris's smile morphed into a leer.

"I like this view even better, Ian."

Ian ignored his hot cheeks. "Uh-huh. Jae wants to hit up some home decor stores tomorrow," he said in the blithest tone he could muster. "Hopefully, I'll find a bistro table and chairs and other things to help make the place seem less empty. Oop. Hang on. I hear doggy feet approaching."

Tris's frown was instant. "Is he okay on the stairs?"

"Yup." Ian laughed and Elliott appeared as if summoned, hopping up onto the bed with a confidence that said he knew he wouldn't be ordered off. Tris didn't hide his delight at seeing him, crooning when Elliott nosed at the screen, mouth stretched wide in a silly dog grin.

"I'm so glad you brought him with you," Tris said as the mutt settled onto the mattress beside Ian's knee, tail whapping his thigh.

"Me too. I feel guilty sometimes because I know Marco misses him and we always said El belonged to the house. But I couldn't leave him behind."

"Of course not. You need El more than Marco does, and you know he would have been miserable without you."

Ian slid his fingers into Elliott's scruff. "You were right when you said he claimed me. And Marco comes over all the time to visit and take him o-u-t."

Elliott's low woof made the humans laugh.

"Your dog can totally spell, GB," Tris said, smile so brilliant it almost hurt to look at him

"Yup. But he can wait a while longer to climb assloads of snow if you've got time to talk."

"I always have time to talk to you."

They'd messaged for the first few days following Tris's move, and Ian had done his best to enjoy the little speech bubbles and emails and not think about how much he missed just being close to Tris. Missed his bright eyes and his clear, contagious laugh, and the easy, friendly touches he'd been so free with both in and out of bed. But Tris was working flat out getting organized with his project work and his new apartment and Ian hadn't wanted to be a distraction.

He'd been mid-commute on the fifth day after Tris's move when his phone had buzzed with a different sort of insistency, the chat app they used bouncing with an incoming call, and then Tris grinning at Ian through the wee screen.

They chatted several times a week now, cooking dinner together in their respective kitchens or taking turns picking out films and TV shows to watch. They talked about work and friends and caught up on the mundane little moments that somehow made life richer. And despite the initial oddness of relying on tech, the conversations were easy, sometimes enough Ian could ignore the fact Tris wasn't in the room with him.

"Well, I have time to talk until my ladies get here," Tris clarified.

"Your ladies, huh?" Ian cocked his head. He'd noticed Tris was rather dressed up, wearing a dark jersey and jeans instead of the usual t-shirt and joggers he wore after work. "What have you got going on, Santos?"

"Dinner with Hannah and Ela," Tris replied. "They have tomorrow off and flew into town, commanded we go out to eat and then dancing."

"I take it you do not have tomorrow off?"

"Sadly for me, no. But whatever, I'll make it work. Ela's heading back to Boston tomorrow night and I'm not sure when we'll get a chance to hang in person again until I get back myself."

Awareness prickled across the nape of Ian's neck. "What about Hannah?"

"She's looking for an apartment in D.C., actually. I guess she figured why not with everyone else at the Weymouth house talking about moving."

Ian blinked a time or two, then climbed off the bed, Elliott close behind him. "I hadn't heard that. Did something happen?"

"Nah. I guess it's just one of those times." Tris shrugged, the movement careless, but his normally open expression was stiff. "Gary's firm transferred both him and Haru to the offices downtown, so they're already scouting out places, and Sully and Ela are looking in Cambridge."

"Huh. I didn't see that coming."

"Same. One day things were status quo at the house and the next, everyone had a plan to get out."

"Could be they had enough of the never-ending housemate situation," Ian teased on his way down the stairs. "But what about Rory? And Hannah's really looking to move down there?"

"Rory's moving in with the guys next door and Hannah just wants away from Massachusetts. Her career didn't go anywhere up there, and she thinks a move would be good to get it back online. It'll be nice for me having an old friend around the new town I guess."

A friend who treats you like crap.

"Cool." Ian thought he'd kept his voice light, but something about that one word—or possibly his stupid eyebrows—caught Tris's attention and he cocked his head.

"What?"

"Nothing."

Damnit. Walking into the kitchen, Ian went to the cabinet where he kept a few mugs, hoping Tris would just let it go.

Which didn't happen of course because Tris was not only perceptive but persistent.

"Ian? You know your poker face is for shit, right? So how about you tell me what's got you scowly."

Ian set down the tablet before grabbing a mug. "You don't always sound happy after you spend time with Hannah," he said. "With her and, more importantly, with yourself. I guess I wonder why that is."

"I don't think that's true." Tris's reply was quick, but he was frowning lightly now, the little line back between his eyebrows. "I mean, Hannah and I argue sometimes, but so do lots of friends."

"Sure. Look at Dennis and me." Ian filled the mug with water, then stuck it in the microwave. "Bickering has always been our primary mode of communication. But I still have fun with him. Even when he's under-caffeinated and snarky or all up in my grill about ... anything."

"You hate when he's like that, GB."

Ian laughed. "It's more a love-hate sort of thing. The guy can be the biggest pain in the ass on the planet, but I've never doubted he cares about me. And he for sure never gives me shit about who, as you'd say, I want to bang."

A laugh came out of Tris and made his eyes dance. "Point. Hannah and I don't agree on a lot of stuff including my choice of partners."

"Or your job, Mr. Guy Who Plays With Toys."

"Ugh, yeah. But whatever, she's entitled to her opinion."

"Sure. Doesn't mean she's entitled to share it."

"Agreed. Hannah's not the same kind of friend to me that Dennis is to you." Tris shrugged. "Doesn't mean we're *not* friends. It's not deep and profound or whatever, but we can still hang and have fun."

Point. Tris was right. Ian didn't know Hannah or much about the complicated history she shared with Tris. A history that might be about to pick up again by the sounds of it and if Ian didn't much like the idea, that was too bad. Jealousy was not a good look on him and there was fuck all he could do about who Tris wanted to have in his life.

Or his bed, not that Ian was asking. Even though he sort of wanted to.

"What's for dinner?" Tris asked as Ian went to the refrigerator.

"A sleep smoothie."

"A what? And why?"

"Because I don't have anything but breakfast cereal in the house and don't want to order takeout. It's kiwi, banana, and almond milk, and some other yummy shit. Like peanut butter. And chamomile tea which I will brew now." Ian picked up a box of teabags from the counter and held it up for the camera. "Jae gave me the recipe and says it'll put me out like a light. Not that I generally need help falling asleep, but whatever. He also loaned me his blender, so that's another thing I need to put on the shopping list. What about you? Where are you going for dinner? You've been there long enough to find some good Tex-Mex—you going to slut around for guacamole tonight?"

"My guy, I'm slutty for guac every night even if I don't actually eat it. I'm still looking for a fave Tex-Mex spot in this city, though—need to do some more research before I can claim I've found the best." Tris's smile became sly. "You should come and help me."

Ian hummed in lieu of a real reply. But before he had to shut down the idea once again, a chime sounded from behind Tris, saving them both from Ian's awkward bumbling. He gave Tris a quick wave.

"That must be the ladies," he said. "Tell them I said hi and have fun tonight, kid."

Tris's grin lit up the screen. "Talk to you soon, GB. And quit calling me kid!"

Ian went back to his meal prep after Tris's image on the screen had faded, keenly aware how quiet the apartment became after these calls. As if on cue, Elliott trotted in and settled himself by Ian's knee, offering up a grumbly whine.

"You hungry, buddy?" Ian grinned as the dog thumped his tail against the wood floor. "Should I get you dinner?"

Elliott's next much louder woo made Ian laugh and get busy with the dog bowl. He finished up the rest of the smoothie ingredients while the dog smacked away, peeling and slicing kiwi and bananas, then blending them with the almond milk, vanilla, and peanut butter. Knowing the tea needed time to cool before it could be added to the mix, Ian set everything in the fridge and said the magic o-u-t word to Elliott, who took off for the door in a flurry of clicking nails.

A shock of bracing air greeted them as they made their way outside, but the month of March had been milder and less snowy thus far, a combination that made long walks with Elliott easier, first around Cohasset and now through Boston, where finding paths among the towering snow piles clogging the city's sidewalks and streets became its own adventure.

Ian's brain wandered all over during those walks, turning over thoughts about work or his new apartment and certainly of friends, both longtime and newer. And always of Tris, longing and affection mixing with a peculiar lonesomeness Ian couldn't always shake.

They were figuring it out. The LDR, as Tris liked to say, throwing yet another acronym into Ian's life because saying the words 'long-distance relationship' took up unnecessary time. Ian had a hunch using an acronym lessened the impact of a world like *relationship* for Tris too, and that made sense with Tris hundreds of miles away, another topic they discussed on the regular.

Though 'discussed' wasn't the right word when really it was Tris encouraging Ian to visit while Ian made excuses not to. The excuses came easily with so much of their lives outside of work being disrupted now that both of them had moved. Ian was working more hours too, since 'affordable rent' didn't mean 'cheap,' and he still needed to buy more furniture and take care of the dog on his own.

But Ian was doing okay with all of it, even missing Tris. Which he did far more than he'd expected to.

Missed the way Tris smelled after a morning baking session with Ela and his habit of drawing pictures in the air with his hands as he spoke. The way he practically bounced when an idea took hold of him. The flirty shoulder bumps he gave Ian, for no other reason than because he could. Kissing Tris. Stretching out beside him on a bed or a couch or who the fuck cared as long as it was flat. The weight of Tris's body on his, pressing Ian down.

Christ.

The memories swamping Ian heated his blood and made his stupid heart thump.

His heart didn't care that the LDR thing between Tris and him was still very fragile. Mostly likely temporary. Because Ian had been gone for Tris Santos before the kid had even left town.

15

Ian dropped spaghetti into a pot of water he'd brought to a boil, aware of Tris's eyes on him through the tablet's screen. Tris was at a bar in D.C., waiting for people he worked with, and this was the third time that week their plans to hang out had been squashed.

"So, what are you doing tonight instead of hanging with me?" Ian was trying hard not to be grouchy. Tris couldn't help having to work when there was so much going on with the exo-suit project, and he looked pouty enough for them both.

"Working dinner with some subcontractors," Tris said. "Who are clearly running late." He made a show of checking his watch. "Which just makes me even more pissed that I didn't catch you last night because you never came online. What did *you* do instead of hanging out with *me?*"

"Shitty movie night at Mark's with his family and some of the guys." Ian grinned at the way Tris's eyebrows went up. "They do a big dinner and screen a terrible film once a month and it's actually fun if you embrace the idea you're going to watch something so bad it's good."

"I am in love with this idea."

"I knew you would be. Gary and Haru say hi, by the way."

"Because of course they were there." Tris scrunched his nose. "Did they decide on a new place? Last time I talked to Gary, he said they were down to two apartments, one in Chinatown and another in Bay Village."

"They're going with Bay Village, and they'll be two blocks from Jae and Emmett." Ian stirred the spaghetti. "Someone put my name on a list to help paint, which I don't appreciate at all."

Tris smiled. "They'll make it fun. Stuff you full of pizza as a thank you and probably turn it into a game night. I'm almost sorry I'll miss it." The little crease appeared between his eyebrows again, nagging at Ian.

It had to be strange for Tris, knowing the place he'd expected to return to was about to disappear whether he liked it or not. Ian had been in a similar place after Gus, thrown completely off kilter when he'd moved out of the apartment they'd shared. His circumstances at the time couldn't have been more different from Tris's now, but Ian remembered well how much that sense of uncertainty—the feeling that he had no control, even over the place that he'd live—had bothered him.

"Do you want me to get your stuff from the Weymouth house?" he asked. "Zac and Aiden offered me a corner of the storage locker they rent out in the Seaport and I'm happy to share it with you."

The unease in Tris's face vanished under a flash of genuine surprise. "Um. That'd be awesome. What made you think of it?"

"Nothing specific," Ian fibbed. "I just didn't want you to have to worry about it while you were out of town. I'll make Gary and Haru help me to get back at them for signing me up to paint, too."

"So smaaht. This is just another reason I don't miss anyone else's face half as much."

Ian felt the same. He adored spending time with his friends, but there wasn't any one person he looked forward to seeing more than he did *this* particular friend. Who was now miming petting him through the tablet's screen and making him laugh.

"Don't be weird."

"This is nothing," Tris said with a smirk. "If you're ever up for cyber, you know I can show you weird."

Ian's laugh sounded strangled. He didn't think he was ready for that. He'd adjusted well to chats over dinner and streaming but the idea of trying to be seductive on screen—of trying to be anything other than his grumbly, awkward self while actually engaging in cybersex—made fire lick up the back of his neck.

Still ... he was done pretending he wasn't curious. Or that he wanted to be with Tris again quite badly. Even if it had to happen through screens. And the sudden thought of watching Tris come apart without being able to touch him sent a bolt of lust to Ian's groin that took him off guard.

Okay, maybe he was more ready for cyber than he'd originally thought. Too bad he didn't know the first thing about it.

He cleared his throat. "I'm up for TV tonight if you're not too tired after your dinner. Something with lots of pretty people that isn't set in a hospital."

"I like the sound of that." Tris gave him an easy smile. "Not sure when I'll be done tonight though, so how about tomorrow?"

"Sure," Ian said. "I'll pick a show out."

"M'kay. Oop, my people are here. G'night, GB, give the Wonder Dog kisses from me."

After dinner and Elliott's walk, Ian stretched out on his bed and immersed himself in a police drama, becoming relaxed to a point somewhere between dozy and horny by episode two. But just as he was considering jerking off, his chat app on the tablet chimed with a familiar ringtone that instantly had him more alert. Ian's chats with Tris often ran for hours, but it was nearly eleven and Tris had never called him this late.

Scrubbing a hand through his hair, Ian quickly sat up, concern prickling through him as an exhausted-looking Tris came on screen, still in his work clothes and standing at the counter in his kitchen. "Hey, Chi-Town."

"Did I wake you?"

"Nah, I was chilling with some TV. You good?"

"Yup. Just wanted to talk. Although now that I'm looking at you all cozy and rumpled, I wouldn't mind just watching you."

"That's because you're creepy." Ian pushed his glasses up his nose and smiled, but he thought something was off. For the first time ever, Tris's flirting sounded forced, as if he was doing it out of reflex as opposed to any real desire to flatter. "You just getting in from dinner?"

"Sorta." Reaching off camera, Tris brought a bottle of beer back into frame, its dark glass glinting in the overhead light. "Did you know there are over two thousand restaurants in the D.C. area? Thousands of eateries in a city of over half a million people and yet somehow, I managed to run into Hannah in a random sushi joint on Pennsylvania Avenue." He dropped his gaze to the bottle in his hand.

"We've been hanging out a bit since she made the move down here—you know that. She got a job at a news outlet and the office in D.C. isn't far from Off-World's, so we meet up for drinks or dinner sometimes. We talk about stuff and it's easy."

'Talk about stuff' sounded like code for 'talk about Hannah' but Ian didn't bother asking for clarification. "Could be that not living in the same house makes it easier to be friends," he suggested, but stopped talking when Tris's expression darkened.

"I don't think Hannah *is* my friend. She's just someone I know and used to fuck. Shit, I'm sorry." He ran a hand over his head, face scrunched up in a grimace. "I don't want to be that guy."

"You're not," Ian soothed. "I'm not going to judge you for talking."

Tris exhaled noisily. "I know. Hannah was at the bar with some colleagues. After dinner and the subcontractors had left, I went over to say hello, just like I would any friend. She treated me like I was a stranger. Like we hadn't shared space in the same fucking house for almost a year and screwed around for months."

He frowned at Ian through the screen. "She did the thing

when she made the introductions, talking about how I play with toys for a living and ... I don't know." He shook his head, cheeks flushing red. "The whole thing hit different. She went out of her way to make me look bad in front of people I didn't know."

Outrage for Tris's obvious hurt flared in Ian's chest. He'd dealt with his fair share of ignorant assholes, including his bigoted parents, and tried never to carry his anger for more than a few steps. He didn't like wasting energy holding grudges. But if he ever crossed paths with Hannah What's-Her-Last-Name again, they were going to have words and exactly none of them were going to be friendly.

He caught himself reaching for the screen, the desire to touch and comfort near overwhelming. "I'm sorry. You don't deserve to be treated that way."

"You tried to tell me weeks ago." Tris's sigh sounded oh, so weary. "Said I don't seem happy after I spend time with her and I see it now, too. Hannah talks shit about my job and me being queer, but instead of calling her out, I blow it off and end up in a crap mood. But I'm not like that with other people, so what does that say about me?"

Shit. Ian hated the doubt he heard in his friend's voice more than he knew how to articulate.

"You look for the best in people," he said. "I know you wanted to see it in her. I think we're all like that to a degree, even assholes like me."

"You're not an asshole, Ian. But you think I'm naïve, don't you?"

This time, Ian didn't stop himself from reaching out to stroke Tris's cheek through the screen, prompting soft laughter from each of them.

"Not at all," Ian said. "I think you take time to know people instead of making snap judgments and that is a rare thing in this world. I mean, we're only friends because of you. You sat beside me on the train and saw through the grouchy—"

"—to the soft and gooey GB core. Yeah, I did." The stress on Tris's face lessened. "That was a good day."

"It was. I'm sorry about Hannah. Do you know what you're going to do?"

"Not really." Tris shrugged. "Not putting up with her shit anymore, so we'll see what that gets me." He drained the last of his beer and set the bottle down off camera. "I'm done thinking about her tonight. I'd rather think about you."

Ian rolled his eyes. "Sweet talker."

"You love it."

"Yeah, I do."

Smiling, Tris picked up his tablet, holding it out in front of him as he walked out of the kitchen. "Think you can stay awake with me a while longer? Just to chat or watch TV," he added when Ian didn't immediately answer. "I know I talk about cyber a lot, but I don't expect—"

"We can talk about cyber."

Tris halted mid-step. "We can?"

"Yes." Cheeks flushing, Ian looked at Tris's wide eyes and wondered what the fuck he'd just done. "I've, uh, never done it myself, but I'm not averse to the concept. I'd … do it with you if you really wanted."

"Uh, fuck yeah I'd really want." Tris barked out a laugh. He was on the move again, eyes going crinkly at the corners with his grin. "I miss your body very much, and if you don't know that already, I owe you an apology."

Now Ian felt like his whole body was blushing and God, he was a sucker for this guy. "I'm the one who should be apologizing. You've got to be kicking yourself for hanging out with my grumpy ass when you've got a whole city of people who'd be more fun."

"You're the only ass I want right now, Ian, grumpy or otherwise." Setting the tablet on the nightstand next to his bed, Tris walked off camera. "How have you never had cyber?"

Ian scooted back down into the bed so he could lay down.

"Never had to. Gus and I were together a long time, and after we split it took a while for me to be in a place where I wanted to date. The guys I met were local and we didn't need to use screens."

"You're making me feel special, GB. I like knowing you don't do watch parties with just anyone."

"You're the only person I have watch parties with, you boob. Or cook with on screen. Or eat with, for Christ's sake." Laughing softly, Ian rolled onto his side, then set the tablet on the pillow. "I thought it'd suck doing all that on camera, but it doesn't bother me. Does that make me weird?"

"Totally. But I like doing all that with you on camera too, so we can be weird together."

"M'kay, good."

A beat passed and then several more, and Ian had started drifting when a soft noise caught his ear. Tris was on screen again when Ian opened his eyes, lying on his side in the bed in a pose mimicking Ian's. He'd changed into a t-shirt and shorts and his light hair was mussed, and he looked so relaxed and beautiful Ian's breath caught.

"Hey, sleepy man," Tris murmured. "You want to call it a night?"

"Not yet." Ian's nerves kicked back up. "Do you ... Um. Have you done this a lot?"

"I have with people I met online but no, not a lot. No one since I moved here."

Since I met you.

The unspoken words made Ian's heart thump. "Been too busy, huh?"

"No." Tris smiled. "Like I said, the only ass I want right now is yours."

Ian licked his lips. "And this is safe? Like I'm not going to end up on PornHub, right?" That got him a laugh.

"This app is encrypted end-to-end, and I promise I'm not recording or catching screengrabs. You're safe with me."

"I know," Ian said, because he did. "I trust you, Tris."

"Good." Tris moved a hand against his chest, palm dragging slowly over the t-shirt. "Touch yourself if you want," he said softly, "or watch me if that'd be easier."

Boom. Heat blossomed deep in Ian's groin.

"Want that," he whispered. "Thought about it. What it'd be like watching you take yourself apart."

Tris's eyebrows rose. "You thought about me? Doing this?"

"Mmm-hmm. Earlier tonight, when we were talking."

"Oh, shit."

Tris sat up, pulling his shirt over his head, and the muscles in his torso flexed when he lay back again. He reached down and palmed his groin through his shorts, pressing the thin fabric around his erection so Ian could trace the shape with his gaze.

Holy hell, that was hot.

"Does that feel good?" Ian bit his lip. He hadn't meant to speak but God, he was losing his mind and the soft, sexy sound that came out of Tris went straight to his balls.

"Yeah." Tris's voice was throaty. "I'm hard. Started getting there as soon as you said you'd be up for this. *Fuck*, Ian, I ache." Drawing his hand up, he took hold of the waistband on his shorts and pushed them down enough to expose the rosy head of his cock and the precum shining over its tip. "See what you do to me?"

"Fuck."

Ian did see. His guy was a feast on the screen. Tris brought his hand to his mouth and licked it, swiping his tongue slowly over his palm. Ian followed that hand, goosebumps rising on his skin as Tris wrapped himself up in his fist, every motion graceful and easy. Before he could even think about what he was doing, Ian had a hand against his own groin, fingers resting on his shaft through his boxers.

"Mmm. Had a feeling you'd be a natural at this," Tris said, eyes shining when Ian met them with his.

The last remnants of Ian's nervousness faded under the

laughter buzzing through him. Because he trusted this man and the connection between them hummed strong and whole in spite of the distance. The urge to lose himself in sensation hit Ian in a mighty wave and he had to fight the urge to close his eyes, too riveted by the scene unfolding before him to look away.

Tris pushed his shorts down farther, getting them past his balls. But he didn't take them off, instead leaving them clinging at mid-thigh, where the elastic in the waistband bit softly into his skin. Something about that transformed the fire burning in Ian's belly into a blaze, every cell in his body so hot he was near panting. Seeing Tris bound, however gently, face going slack as he pumped himself, was almost too much, and Ian hadn't even done anything. Hadn't even removed a single stitch of clothing.

Fuck, that just wouldn't do.

Shifting up on one elbow, he grabbed hold of the neck on his t-shirt with his free hand, then dragged the whole thing up and over his head in a single swift move. He relished Tris's quiet groan, and went back to rubbing himself through his underwear, which was already damp with pre-cum in several spots. Ian wasn't ready to go full frontal—wasn't sure he'd ever feel *that* free while he was on camera—but he knew from Tris's appreciative hum he couldn't have cared less Ian was still in his underwear.

"You look amazing, GB. Want to touch you so bad."

"Same." Ian bit back a whine, too turned on to give Tris shit for using the nickname. "I'd take you deep if you were here, suck you hard."

Tris's eyes went wide before he quickly screwed them shut. "Holy shit." His voice sounded hoarse. "You talking dirty is my new favorite thing."

Ian didn't bother hiding his grin. He'd missed this. Sharing laughs while they got each other off and basking in the big, swoony feelings that came with such intimacy. He wished he'd agreed to this sooner. That he could be with Tris now, tangled around each other instead of alone in their respective beds. A sound like a growl came out of him.

"Want you here, Tris."

Tris blew out a shuddery breath. Lifting his free hand to his chest, he fingered his nipples, eyes slitting open again as he moved his fist faster over his dick. "Want that too. Want you to feel good."

Ian could only nod in response. Bringing his hand to his mouth, he wet his fingers and palm, then quickly slid them inside his waistband, hissing as skin finally met skin. "*Oh*."

"That's it, baby," Tris urged. "Wanna watch you."

An endless time unfurled around them, filled with ragged breaths and filthy-sweet endearments that made Ian burn. He trembled at the precipice, desperate both to come and for the moment to stretch on forever. Tris moaned steadily, fist a blur of movement now, but it was the look he shot Ian that made Ian's chest clench.

This is more than sex.
I want forever.

Ian closed his eyes. It was. And he did. With this man he craved more than he'd ever imagined possible.

Pleasure crashed through him like a wrecking ball.

"Tris," he croaked out, voice almost gone, body jolting hard as he shot over his hand, cum pulsing warm and sticky in his boxers. He floated up and up and up, borne on waves of sensation that wracked his body, made it impossible to keep his eyes from sliding closed. The next time he surfaced, Tris was watching him, awe written all over his face.

God, if only I could touch him.

Ian curled up close to the screen, his body still vibrating. "You gonna come for me?"

"Yes, yes," Tris chanted, movements losing rhythm now. "Mmm, fuck. Want you so much."

"I know, darlin'," Ian crooned. "I want you, too."

He held his breath at Tris's choked cry, desire stirring again in his belly when Tris arched into his fist and lost it. Rolling onto his back, Tris moaned softly as cum striped his torso, his hand moving slower now and his taut muscles gradually relaxing.

"What are you doing to me, Ian?" he mumbled, voice soft and so wondering Ian's throat ached.

He had no fucking clue. Was too raw from his own bombshell thoughts to even attempt a reply. But with the magical timing possessed by all goofy pets, the Wonder Dog chose that moment to leap on to the bed with enough force to bounce the tablet right off the pillow and over the edge of the mattress.

"Ho, shit!"

With the spell broken, lunacy ensued. Ian's yelp set off a play vibe in Elliott's doggy brain, and he practically launched himself at Ian, who was just trying to scramble after the tablet. There was yelping and wrestling while Tris laughed uproariously at them both, and by the time Ian finally freed himself, he and Tris were red-faced from laughing and Elliott had shifted to sulky. He stared down his snout at Ian, brown eyes filled with disdain, before stalking to the foot of the bed and plopping himself down.

"I think we've offended him," Ian said through his chuckling. "Probably scared him too with all your hollering."

Tris dashed tears from his eyes with his fingers. "Aw. Now I feel bad."

"He'll be okay." Ian rubbed Elliott's haunch with his foot and got a grumbly groan in return. "How about you, Chi-Town?" he asked softly. "How're you doin'?"

"So much better," Tris replied, and yeah, he looked far more relaxed. He'd cleaned himself up in the midst of the melee and was smiling fondly at Ian. "Needed this."

"I needed it, too," Ian whispered.

Fuck, he really had. Did. Needed Tris with an intensity that made him ache for more than a screen that was going to go dark when one of them gave in to the need for sleep.

The question was, what was Ian going to do about it?

16

April, 2022

Elliott was taking forever and a day to decide if he wanted to poop.

"I'm hungry, you know," Ian told him idly, eyes on the evening commuters streaming past in either direction. "Pretty sure we could both use some water too, so how about you get this show on the road?"

Predictably, the dog ignored him. Elliott didn't give a hoot that his human had worked an endless shift. Didn't care that they were standing by a walkway beside the Charles River and the weather was freaking hot for late April. Or that spending the last hour pulling Ian and his skateboard over miles of bike paths had left them both thirsty. Okay, maybe Elliott cared about being thirsty. He was oblivious to Ian's desire to get home though, so he could get through his list of to-dos. Which included sharing some unexpected good news with his guy. And setting up some semi-naked screen time, which Ian preferred his dog stay adorably clueless about anyway.

Who are you right now?

Ian smiled to himself. He wasn't sure he knew anymore. A

year ago, he'd have questioned the sanity of anyone even thinking he could be a guy who not only engaged in cyber but liked it. A *lot*. Then again, Ian of last year would never have imagined carrying on with a guy he hadn't been physically close to in almost two months. Or that he'd be back in Boston with a hairy beast of a dog, rediscovering the city and his friends. Feeling stronger—steadier—than he had in quite a long time and doing more than simply managing his depression.

Turning, Ian glanced out over the river. He had good days and better days, as well as not-so-great days and the occasional bad. There was no pattern. No way to be certain he wouldn't someday spiral back down again. He thought he had the tools he needed to get through if the bad days turned into something darker. But Ian hadn't had a truly *down* day in close to a year, and he was going to hang on to that tooth and nail.

Ready to steer Elliott and himself toward home, Ian bought bottled waters from a snack cart, then paused when his phone buzzed in his pocket. Maybe he wasn't going to have to wait to set up screen time after all. Ian set the board and bottles down on the grass and pulled his phone out while Elliott lay down on his belly, tongue hanging out the side of his mouth.

"Hey, you're outside!" Tris said through the screen, face scrunching up as he stared out at Ian. "And wearing a helmet? Did you buy a motorcycle and forget to tell me about it?"

Ian laughed. "Nah. This is a skate helmet. The sidewalks are finally mostly clear, so I got my boards out."

"Boards? As in ...?"

"Skateboards I ride at my leisure and sometimes to work."

"You," Tris pointed at Ian, "own skateboards."

"Two, actually. A longboard for cruising and a shorter one for when I just feel like fooling around. I prefer the longboard because it gives me room to move."

Tris gave his head a single hard shake, then blinked as if trying to clear it. He was seated in what looked like a conference room, light streaming in through a set of windows on his left, and there were three different mugs in frame, one of them visibly steaming.

"Ian? How the fuck have your skateboards not come up before?"

"I wasn't riding at all when we met because of the snow, so maybe that's why I didn't mention them."

"Makes sense. And the helmet is unexpectedly sexy." Tris's leer made Ian laugh. "How long have you been riding?"

"Since I was a kid. Now there's actually space on the sidewalks, I figured it was time to get out here. Along with every other human in the city who rides a bike, board, skates, or scooter."

"You missed it, huh?"

"Yup. More than I realized." Hunkering down beside Elliott, Ian set his phone on the grass. "Hang on a sec while I get the Wonder Dog a drink."

"Ah, I should have known you were out with the beast dog. Hi, El!"

Groaning happily, the dog snuffled at the phone's screen while Tris made silly noises back and Ian unclipped a collapsible dog bowl from Elliott's leash.

"How do you manage the board and the dog at the same time?" Tris asked.

"It's really El who does the managing." Ian poured water out for the dog who fell on it eagerly. "He towed me out to Harvard Bridge before we turned back but I know he wanted to keep going."

"Oh my God, I need to see this."

Chuckling, Ian unscrewed the second bottle for himself and drank, then picked the phone back up from the ground. "I'll see what I can do. But what's up with you, Chi-Town? It's early in the day to get a call so you're either bored or you need to talk through a thing."

Tris grimaced. "Am I that predictable?"

"No. I was going to message you anyway and see if you had

time to talk tonight. Sometime after ten?" Ian added in a slightly lower voice, then watched heat flare in Tris's gaze.

Ian didn't know how *sometime after ten* had become code for *someone's going to get naked* but it absolutely made talking about fooling around onscreen a hell of a lot easier if other people happened to be within earshot.

"I'd like that very much," Tris said with a grin. "I want to get out of here before eight tonight anyway, and I can work remotely if I have to."

Ian pulled off his helmet and ran one hand through his sweaty hair with a frown. "You need a break, kid. Like a bag of cheeseburgers followed up with a nap."

"I would be very down for either or both," Tris admitted. "But I didn't call to bitch about my workload. I called because I wanted to let you know my project is in its final stages and we should be finished by early May. On time for the most part and definitely on budget," he added with a grin. "And all signs point to a bunch of exo-suits making it into the program at Walter Reed, too."

Ian let out a whoop that drew stares from passersby and an answering woo from Elliott. "Yea-a-a-h, look at you, Tristan Santos," he said, grin so big his cheeks ached. "I'm so fucking proud, I could bust."

A flush spread over Tris's cheeks and he looked incredibly satisfied. "I'm stoked, I can't lie. And what comes after that is another thing I want to talk to you about."

Ian's enjoyment wavered. "Okay. What does that mean?"

Tris licked his lips, his expression becoming more unsettled. "You know I've been looking at graduate programs. I figure there's never going to be a better time to at least explore my options than now, even if I end up having to put it off again because of my job."

"Makes sense." Ian ran his knuckles against his beard. "So, you're not taking the offer from Off-World where you'd travel around for projects?"

"No, Off-World is still on the table. It'd take some juggling, but I might be able to work on projects *and* school because most of the programs have some virtual options. I'd still need to be on a campus at least part of the time to work on building my bots, so I just need to figure out which fucking program fits me best." He heaved a deep breath.

"I reached out to some of the schools for more info and heard back from all of them. They're *asking* me to apply because they want me in their programs."

A tender feeling rose in Ian's chest. Tris looked shellshocked. Like he couldn't believe the super nerds who ran graduate recruitment programs had immediately made him out to be the fucking star that he was. "Amazing. Your folks must be losing their minds."

"Well, Mom screeched when I told her and Rick dropped the phone, so I'd say they're excited."

Ian laughed. "Probably hoping you'll choose a school out by them, huh? Which ones are you looking at?"

Tris wrinkled his nose. "I've got it down to five. Three on the east coast, one on the west, and one back in Chicago."

Fuck. Unless one of the east coast programs happened to be in Massachusetts, Tris really was going to be gone by the end of the summer, virtual learning options or not. Goddamnit, Ian had known this was coming but he still fucking hated it.

He hauled in a breath. Tris was always supportive of anything Ian set his mind to, big ideas and small. Ian owed him the same support, even if it meant Tris not coming back after all.

Ian made a rolling 'come-on' motion with one hand. "Run them through for me."

"You sure? We can do it later if this isn't a good time."

"It's fine. I'm doing pizza and baseball with Gary tonight, but I don't need to meet him until half-past six." Ian smiled. "Plenty of time for you tell me about the programs you like before the d-o-g wakes up from his nap all ready to poop."

A COUPLE OF HOURS LATER, IAN AND GARY WERE SEATED ON Ian's sofa watching the Red Sox pound the Toronto Blue Jays while Elliott snoozed between them. They'd feasted on excellent brick oven pizza and talked a lot, all in all having a really nice evening. Yet Ian had felt Tris's absence keenly, and the list of cities he'd gone over that afternoon kept going around in Ian's head.

Seattle, Washington.
Evanston, Illinois.
Baltimore, Maryland.
Worcester, Massachusetts.
Boston.

All of the programs sounded excellent. Each of the cities had their charms. But while the programs in Worcester and Boston were clearly competitive, Seattle and Baltimore were mild climate-wise, and Evanston was just outside Chicago, a city Tris had called home in the past.

You could always ask him to stay, said a sly voice in Ian's head. *Tell him you want to have more than chatting through screens. That you dream every night about kissing him.*

Ian's gut clenched. Asking Tris to stay simply because Ian wanted him close was selfish. He wouldn't do that. Couldn't.

Could he?

Oh, man. Maybe he could. And maybe it would be wrong not to let Tris know how Ian felt so Tris could decide for himself where the hell he wanted to be.

Thankfully, a loud buzz broke through the haze in his brain, and his phone skittered a few inches over the low table in front of him. With a muttered apology to Gary, Ian plucked it up, cocking his head slightly at the message he found on the screen.

You're rubbing off on me.

I could take that a couple of ways, Ian replied, then smiled at the eye-rolly emoji that followed.

6 months ago, I'd have picked a school inside of 2 minutes, Tris wrote. *Probably the one with the largest number of hot humans and beaches.*

And now?

Questioning the wisdom of making decisions based on hot humans and beaches. That's new. And I kinda hate it.

Ian sighed. *I don't believe it. You're more mature than you pretend to be.*

Plot twist: I agree. And kinda hate that too.

Ian's heart ached a little for his friend. Tris had seemed so uncertain earlier. Like he thought it was his job to be serious about getting into a program, despite still being torn about whether it was truly what he wanted.

It's okay not to know, Ian reminded him now. *Questioning isn't a weakness—it's part of learning.*

Ian frowned down at his phone. He was doing it again, serving up fortune cookie wisdom. To a science guy who built robots! Still, he felt he was right. Believed in Tris's instincts. And felt certain that once he made up his mind, Tris would go full bore into his next new adventure with real gusto.

A string of bear emoji mixed with smiley faces popped onto the phone's screen.

Need to chat? Ian asked.

Maybe. Tris replied. *What's down in Ian Town? You still with Gary?*

Ian glanced to his left to where Gary was slouched low in his seat, Elliott's head in his lap and his attention on the game. Quietly, he snapped a quick photo and sent it off to Tris and wasn't at all surprised when his phone lit up seconds later at the same time the tablet chimed from somewhere upstairs.

Turning his head, Gary raised an eyebrow at Ian. "Is that our boy?"

"Yup," Ian replied with a laugh. "He needs a distraction. You mind if we do a watch party?"

"Nah." Gary's smile was knowing. "You haven't been

watching for the last ten minutes anyway, so I guess you need a distraction, too."

Busted.

Snorting, Ian handed his phone over. "You two talk and I'll grab the tablet," he said as he got to his feet.

But he somehow forgot Tris's voice could rouse sleepy dogs as well as humans and all it would take was a "Gary! You met the Wonder Dog!" to have Elliott scrambling up and *onto* Gary, who flailed helplessly, completely unprepared to fend off a yodeling beast who weighed over eighty pounds yet still thought he was a lap dog.

It took a while for the chaos to settle. For Gary to appear slightly less traumatized and for Elliott to chill, all while Ian tried to quell his own laughter and Tris didn't bother at all. And though they did eventually get around to watching the game, Gary said goodnight just seconds after the Sox closed it out, and the way he sort of tiptoed to the door—like he was afraid Elliott would follow—made Ian feel bad.

"I think my dog broke your friend," Ian said as he climbed the stairs to the loft. "He seemed kind of in a hurry to get out of here."

"Mmm, that was probably because of me."

Onscreen, Tris flapped a hand at himself. He'd stripped down while Ian had been locking up, and lay shirtless in his bed, clad only in dark boxer briefs. And damn, Ian liked what he saw. Wasn't quite sure what to make of what Tris had said, however, and frowned as he settled against the headboard with the tablet in his lap.

"Please tell me Gary doesn't know we ..."

"Fuck around when we chat?" Tris grinned. "I've never said anything, but the guy has an imagination, Ian, and knows I have one, too. Besides, I'm reasonably sure all our friends assume we do more than just stream media and make food together."

Ian rubbed a hand over his face. He hadn't talked in detail to anyone about the LDR thing he and Tris were trying. Still, their friends knew they talked daily now, so yep, they'd probably assumed lots of things.

"Thanks for letting me crash your date," Tris teased, his expression a mix of sleepy and affectionate.

Ian rolled his eyes. "It's not crashing if I invite you. And you know you made El's night. You're still one of his favorites among all my friends."

"I'd hope so," Tris gloated. "Funny considering he's only met me the one time."

"Speaking of which, I had an idea."

"A sexy one?"

"Yeah, no." Laughing, Ian set the tablet on the pillow beside his, and stretched out on his side. "I want to buy a PetBuddy. One of those cams that lets you feed treats and check on your pets through an app? I thought I'd set up an account for you, so you can say hi to El anytime you feel like it. If you want."

A smile broke over Tris's face. "I want. Nice that you can add virtual dog sitters alongside to the real ones, too."

"That's the idea. I might need the help for a while."

"What does that mean?" Tris snuggled closer. "Are you switching to nights?"

"No, but my hours may change, and I don't want El feeling lonely." Ian licked his lips. "I got a job offer, Tris, and it'll let me work full time at Mass General instead of splitting time between the two jobs."

"Dude." Tris's whole face lit up and he ran a finger over the screen like he was stroking Ian's cheek. "That is amazing. When did you even apply?"

"I didn't apply—I wasn't even looking. A recruiter from the hospital called me last week, totally out of the blue. That's never happened to me before, so I figured I'd take the meeting and hear what they had to say. I got an offer the next day."

"Look at *you*, Ian Byrne. Why didn't you tell me about this before tonight?"

"You're the first person I've told at all."

The first person Ian had even *thought* about telling, and man, he'd been excited. But now, knowing Tris might be even farther away before long, Ian's earlier excitement felt slightly hollow. He stifled a sigh.

"I'll tell the guys this week," he said. "But I needed to think it through, you know? Make sure that if I switched jobs it would be for the right reasons. I get that the way I approach decision-making runs counter to yours," he added, keeping his voice light so it was clear he was teasing.

But Tris shook his head, expression more serious than Ian had expected. "I get it. You were smart to think it through and make sure it felt right. And I love that you told me first. Fuck, I wish I was there to congratulate you in person."

Ian's whole body warmed for a different reason. "Yeah?"

"Yup. I've been thinking about kissing you all fucking day. Seeing you like this." Tris petted the screen again. "Relaxed and all mine for a while."

I'm yours for as long as you want me.

"Mmm." Ian closed his eyes. "Tell me more."

Tris obliged, of course. Talked sweet and dirty to Ian and got him so hot, Ian lost his head and romantical words started hovering at the tip of his tongue. Ian knew he couldn't give voice to any of them. Tell Tris he wanted this. Him. Tonight and tomorrow, and into as many tomorrows ahead as they could have.

Tris didn't want to be the right guy for Ian. Even though Ian was already pretty sure he'd never find anyone he'd want more.

17

The soles of Ian's running shoes squeaked as he hustled through Mass General's vast Emergency Department and headed for the Clinical Decision Unit, where patients underwent treatment and evaluation before being admitted or released. The place was humming, treatment bays occupied by the sick and injured and hospital staff, and—as it was also Monday evening, always a high-volume night at Mass General—the CDU seemed extra busy.

Ian scanned faces as he moved, his stomach flipping when he spied Mark step past a curtain, one hand up to get Ian's attention.

"His ribs aren't broken," he said when Ian got close. "Bruised all to hell thanks to a couple of kicks to the chest, but there were cops on the scene to subdue the guy before it all got out of hand."

Yikes. Ian winced. "How are kicks to the chest not out of hand?"

"Well, those are Gus's words, not mine."

"Sounds on brand. Can't believe he agreed to let you call me instead of the fuckface."

Mark set his hands on Ian's shoulders, squeezing lightly. "Gus didn't exactly agree. But he got cagey about who he did want to call so I made the decision, then told him what I'd done." Mark wrinkled his nose. "Guy needs an escort and, outside of the fuck-face, I don't know who Gus hangs out with these days, so you were my first choice. I'm sorry, GB."

Ridiculously, Ian had to bite back a smile. There it was again. The dumbest nickname in the world, motherfucking *Grumble Bear* and how in God's name was it his? He reached up and patted Mark's hand where it lay on his shoulder.

"You did the right thing. He'll need help, at least for tonight, and we both know it'd be a miracle if he admitted it."

Chuckling, Mark let go of Ian. "He's in a spectacularly shitty mood. Not that I'd expect otherwise given what happened but this level of surly seems extra, even from him. Also, he apparently hates the guy he's partnered with, who hates Gus right back, and they're waging some kind of war to see who can be the biggest asshat to ride an ambulance through our fair city."

Now, Ian did laugh. "Your eavesdropping skills amaze me."

"Ah, but I didn't have to eavesdrop at all. They've been snarling and spitting like angry cats since Gus walked himself in here." Mark tossed a glance over his shoulder, then met Ian's eyes. "If I was stuck in the back of a rig with those clowns, I'd probably want to do some kicking myself."

Fuck's sake. Ian wasn't in the mood for clown wrangling. Not when he had a dinner and streaming date with Tris that he'd been looking forward to just as much as the part where their clothes started coming off. But he steeled himself anyway so he could get back to his night.

Walking beside Mark into the treatment bay, he swore the air around him crackled. Gus was sitting up in the narrow bed which had been partially reclined, brown hair a mess and skin pale against the patient gown. He had it on backwards, Ian noted, wearing it the way one might a jacket so it hung open over his chest. It was an odd combination with his uniform pants and boots, but outside of an abrasion on his right cheek and the cold pack he had pressed over his sternum, Gus appeared composed. Overly so, in fact, expression flat as he stared up at a dark-haired man in Boston EMS browns that had to be the partner.

Oh, boy.

Ian knew that look. Had seen it a great deal during their last year together. The big freeze had been Gus's go-to defense when he'd felt vulnerable or out of control, and he'd become expert at throwing up walls. The harder Ian had tried to reach past them, the deeper Gus had dug in his heels to keep him the fuck out, and he'd gotten downright ruthless when Ian didn't immediately back down. Ian guessed Gus had been using some of those ruthless words on his partner tonight, because the guy's beefy frame radiated an aggrieved brand of tension Ian recognized.

"You should have said something," the partner was saying. "You had eyes on the patient, Dawson, and if you had even a second's thought he was going to be a problem, you should have told me. We should have restrained him!"

Gus gave the tiniest of eye rolls. "You saw the guy too, in case you forgot. Unresponsive to stimuli after the first dose of Narcan, which is why I went in with a second. I'm not psychic, Walt. I can't predict when a patient is going to come at us swinging."

"They're almost always confused and agitated after Narcan—"

"That's not the same thing as flipping from blue-lipped and barely breathing to Street Fighter mode in the span of three seconds." Gus scoffed. "Jesus, kid. Every patient is different, and you should *know* that."

The partner, Walt, exhaled, his cheeks mottled with color as the arguing went on, but Ian barely heard them. He was fixated on the way Gus had dismissed Walt instead, as if the conversation wasn't worth his breath. He'd called the guy 'kid,' a thing Ian had done with Tris probably a hundred times by now, but hopefully never sounding like *that*. Like Walt was a child caught out acting foolish and not Gus's peer who'd busted his ass earning the EMT patches attached to his jacket.

"All *right*," Gus snapped out, voice sharp enough that it silenced his partner mid-stream. "I don't want to do this now."

"I have to file a report," Walt said, making a frustrated noise when Gus waved him off. "You don't want to press charges against the patient, fine. But the captain's still going to want to know what happened."

"So, tell her. You were there and clearly have an opinion on how things went down. Put that in your fucking report." Gus sat up straighter in the bed, but the movement must have hurt because he winced, fingers tightening around the cold pack he had pressed to his ribs.

Wordlessly, Mark moved to the bed, rearranging the pillows and elevating it farther with quick, efficient movements. Gus looked past him to Ian, eyes meeting his gaze for the first time. The tips of Gus's ears were red, and he appeared genuinely miserable, signs he'd been caught off guard by his own pain. And just like that the walls he'd put up were gone, and Gus was simply a man Ian had known almost half his life, hurting and a little freaked out, and definitely in need of a friend.

Walt's eyes went wide when Ian stepped forward, as if he'd only just remembered he was standing in a hospital teeming with people.

"Uh." He licked his lips, genuine surprise on his handsome face. "You're not the sister."

"True, but you shouldn't assume." Ian positioned himself next to the bed. "I'm Ian, the ex."

Impossibly, Walt's eyes went rounder and the rapid blinking that followed turned Ian's stomach in a slow-motion churn. Shit. Had the guy not known Gus was gay? But that couldn't be. Gus had always been out at work and Ian didn't imagine that would ever change.

Gus leveled a cool stare on Walt, the walls back in place. "Ian is a nurse so, between him and Mark, I'm in good hands. Head back to the station, Walt." He tipped his head toward the door. "Get busy telling everyone how I fucked up."

Face going slack, Walt stared at Gus a second before he shook his head. "Goddamnit, Gus," he said, voice low. Ian braced himself for more arguing, but the guy surprised him by shifting his focus to Mark. "Are there any forms I need to sign or whatever?"

"No," Mark replied. "But if you'd like to speak about what to expect when he goes back on duty, I'm happy to do that."

Gus scoffed. "Dude's an EMT, Mark. If he doesn't already know what to expect, he's got bigger problems than a partner with a couple of janky ribs."

Mark didn't answer as he led Walt from the room, but Ian could tell he was fighting a smile. Walt, on the other hand, appeared resigned, shoulders slumped like he'd had a hell of a day. And like he was in *way* over his head dealing with Gus, who was a hardass perfectionist on his sunniest days. On the job, Gus demanded excellence of himself and his colleagues and when he didn't get it, he was not happy.

When they were alone, Ian shifted his gaze to his ex. "Always the charmer," he said quietly, then watched the corners of Gus's lips twitch.

He dropped his head back on the pillow. "At least the guy missed my face this time."

"Yay for your teeth," Ian agreed. Gus had been roughed up on the job before. The fucked-up truth about working in health care was that huge numbers of workers experienced verbal or physical abuse every day, and that was especially true for the EMTs and paramedics who staffed ambulance crews. Ian and Gus choosing to joke about it was equally fucked up. But twisted humor was how they and lots of people in their professions sometimes coped and Ian had stopped feeling guilty about it years ago.

"Are you mad?" Gus asked, frowning when Ian stared at him in silence for several seconds.

"Why would I be mad?"

"Because you have better things to do with your night than come back to the hospital to deal with me? I told Mark he shouldn't have called you."

"It's fine that he did." Ian said. "And I know you didn't get injured on purpose. Is there a reason you didn't call Ben?"

"I'm not living with him right now. Moved out a couple of weeks ago to get some fucking space," Gus said, face so even it was like he was talking about a grocery list. "Been staying at Donna's while I look for a new place."

Well, that complicated everything. Gus's sister lived out in Hyde Park, a neighborhood at the southernmost tip of the city and at least twelve miles from the hospital. Donna also worked as a training consultant and traveled most weeks of the year; if Ian had to guess, she was out of town.

He stifled a sigh. He wouldn't be eating dinner with Tris tonight. Maybe not watching a movie either. And shit, he needed to call the concierge and get someone to feed and walk the dog.

"I can give you a ride to Donna's," he said. "Give me a minute to make a few calls and—"

"You don't have to do that. Just stick around until I can get signed out and I'll order a ride. I don't want to put you out, E."

"You're not," Ian replied without hesitating, surprised to find he meant it. "You need help and I'm happy to give it to you."

Funny how Tris had said such similar words to Ian just a few months ago on a night that had changed the direction of Ian's life.

The curtain at the foot of the bed twitched aside as Mark stepped back in, this time accompanied by Dr. Walsh, one of the ED's attending physicians, and a woman wearing a Boston EMS uniform. Her shirt under the brown windbreaker was white and Ian knew from her gold badge and the bars at her shoulders that she was an officer and mostly likely Gus's shift commander.

Ducking out of the treatment bay so Gus could talk with the small crowd that had gathered, Ian headed for the waiting room to start making calls. He'd gotten as far as arranging for Elliott's care when he noticed a message from Tris that made him want to laugh and bang his head on the wall, all at the same time.

Are we still on for Manwhore Monday?

Rather than write back, he hit the Call button and got sent right to voicemail. He walked to the window and stared out at the darkening sky as he waited to speak, figuring Tris had to be on another call or possibly mid-commute.

"Hey," he said after the tone. "I can't make it tonight. I had a ... thing come up with Gus that's kind of work-related but also not and I have no idea how long it'll be before I can get online." Ian sighed, fully aware he was rambling. "If I get home before it's too late, I'll see if you're up for a call. Talk to you soon."

There was an optimism in his words he didn't truly feel. Ian knew how emergency medicine worked. Between paperwork and treatment, it'd be at least an hour before he'd even leave the hospital. And as he walked back into the treatment bay, he knew he'd also vastly underestimated how sore Gus would be because even shifting around on the bed was making him groan.

"Mother*fuck*," he bit out. "I feel like I got kicked by an elephant instead of some punk wearing a size thirteen shoe."

Ian exchanged glances with Mark. "What do you need?" he asked Gus. "I can put together another cold pack before we go."

"Let me do that," Mark said. "I'll grab his script from the pharmacy while I'm at it if you help him get dressed."

"Quit talking about me like I'm not even here," Gus grumbled. "I don't need help, for Christ's sake. I'm just stiff after all this sitting around."

Silence fell over the space after Mark walked off chuckling and Ian tried not to feel awkward. But he was standing in front of his bare-chested ex handing the guy his shirt so yep, pretty fucking awkward.

"I figure you should skip the undershirt," he said. "You'll have to raise your arms to get into it and that won't feel good." Stepping forward, he held out a hand. "Let's get you up. Make it easier to take the gown off."

"Okay," Gus replied with a sigh. "But I've been sitting for way too fucking long and this is gonna suck."

Taking Ian's hand, he eased himself off the bed until his feet met the floor then stood with a groan, swearing under his breath. Ian waited as he found his bearings, aware Gus was probably hurting all over.

"I was right," Gus ground out as he let go of Ian's hand. "That sucked all the ass."

"Good thing you're too sore to punch me because I'm sure you'll want to before we're done," Ian said cheerily. "I'll walk back to my place for the Jeep once you're dressed."

"I'd rather go with you. I can't sit anymore, and I need a distraction." Gus pulled the patient gown open, face screwed up in a scowl. "Mother *pus buckets*."

Though he was clearly exhausted by the time Mark made it back, he refused to use the wheelchair Mark had brought with him. "I'm not going to want to get out of it once I sit down," Gus admitted, and Mark quickly nodded.

"Okay." He handed a white paper bag to Ian, then looked back to Gus. "There's three days' worth of Tylenol-3 in there and you can switch to the OTC stuff for pain relief after that if you still need it. Keep icing the area for the next forty-eight hours and then alternate with heat. Don't —"

"Drive or operate heavy machinery," Gus said over him, "and call if I feel extra weird. Got it. Codeine makes me hella tired but that's usually it."

Ian frowned at him. "They fuck with your balance and sometimes your stomach aches."

"Oh." Gus furrowed his brow. "Shit, you're right."

"Are you giving him a ride?" Mark asked Ian. "He took a dose while you were on the phone and he's going to be stoned off his nut."

Gus gave him a half-hearted glare. "I always forget what a pain in the ass you are. Can I go?"

"Yes," Mark and Ian said together, the two exchanging grins before Ian led the way out.

He and Gus made the quick journey to Ian's place in near silence and with each step Ian became more unsettled. Gus was already feeling the meds. His steps were slow and almost careful, and Ian knew he'd need help balancing before long.

"Is Donna at home?" he asked as they approached his building, "or is she on the road?"

"She's in Syracuse," Gus replied. "Supposed to be back tomorrow. Or Wednesday. I think."

Shit. Gus's mom was still recovering from a nasty bout of bronchitis, but she and Gus's dad might still be up for giving him a hand.

"You remember I have a dog, right?" Ian held the entry door to his building open for Gus, then led him to the elevator. "He loves meeting new people, so he'll be, ah, hyper. Just hang by the door and you should be good. Elliott's big," he added. "I don't want him bumping into you and hurting you more."

Eyes red and heavy-lidded, Gus simply nodded. Once they were inside the apartment, however, his eyebrows started climbing because the Wonder Dog did his tail wagging, growly woo-woo thing, body practically vibrating with excitement.

"Yes, hello to you too," Ian said over the racket. He made a grab for Elliott's collar but missed and Elliott quickly zipped over to investigate the strange human by the door. "El—"

"He's fine." A small smile on his face, Gus stood quietly, hands loose at his sides while Elliott sniffed them, tail wags becoming less frantic. "Hi, dog. You are really fucking huge."

Ian chuckled. "He's a marshmallow." Pulling his backpack from his shoulder, he unzipped it and knelt. "Wouldn't hurt anything purposely, aside from his pig. He's gone through three of these already," he said, holding up a stuffed dog toy he'd bought on his lunch break. "El."

Spying the pig, Elliott yodeled joyfully. He dashed back to Ian, stopping short in front of him and bowing, the front half of his hulking frame huddled close to the floor while his butt stayed in the air, tail swaying furiously in time with his woos.

"Yeah, you want it," Ian teased, waving the pig slowly back and forth a few times before he launched it toward the other end of the apartment to be hunted down and maimed. "That'll keep him happy a few minutes while I grab my keys."

Gus waved a hand at him. "Chill. Donna's house isn't going anywhere."

"Okay, good. Because honestly, I gotta take a leak. Are you cool? Want a glass of water or anything?"

Gus shook his head. "Nah, thanks. You mind if I sit down for a sec?"

Ian should have said no. Reminded Gus that sitting down might feel good but getting back up would hurt like a bastard. Not that Gus was paying any attention to getting up at the moment because while Ian had only been gone a few minutes, that'd been plenty of time for Gus to pull up a seat, lean his head back, and fall fast asleep.

Ian bit his lip. The idea of waking the guy just seemed mean when it was so obvious he just needed to crash for a bit. But Ian couldn't leave him to sleep sitting up like that, not with injured ribs and a prosthetic that needed to come off. Gus didn't sleep with it on. And Ian's home was small and not modified to meet an amputee's needs, and he didn't own any mobility aids to make Gus's life easier when he wasn't wearing the leg. Then there was Elliott who, while very much a gentle giant, was exceptionally talented at getting underfoot when the mood struck him. Hell, Ian didn't even have a proper bed to offer Gus unless he gave up his own.

Nothing wrong with the sofa bed, Ian chided himself. *Gus just needs a safe place to crash until he's not stoned off his ass.*

Ian ran a hand over his head. He knew Gus wouldn't have hesitated to help him out had their situations been reversed.

And he really didn't like the idea of Gus medicated and alone at his sister's house without any help.

Naturally, Ian's phone buzzed with an incoming message, and he fought off a frustrated groan. He knew without looking it'd be Tris, wanting to talk about this totally screwball night. But with Gus asleep in the middle of the studio, it was going to be hard *to* talk when Tris could get Elliott from zero to zooming just with his voice.

Fuckity fuck, fuck.

Quietly, Ian made his way to the kitchen, then slid his phone from his pocket.

You wanna talk, GB? What's going on?

Minutes spun out as Ian stared at the screen and Elliott finally ambled in, nails clicking over the floor. He settled down on his haunches beside Ian, still holding the pig in his mouth, and looked up with knowing brown eyes, like he'd already guessed what Ian was thinking.

I have no fucking clue.

18

Two hours later, Ian still didn't have much of a clue nor had he responded to Tris. But he did have a plan of sorts. He'd gotten hold of Mark, and asked for oh, so many favors, which was how he'd come to possess crutches—hands-free and the regular type—and a steerable knee scooter, as well as a bench for the shower and the socks and liners Gus would need while wearing the prosthetic but also while he was not. Ian eyed the scooter askance now, hoping Elliott wouldn't regard the thing as a glorified skateboard and try to haul it, a prospect he found equal parts hilarious and terrifying.

"You want me to stay? Here?" Gus asked when Ian had presented his plan. He'd napped a solid ninety minutes, only stirring when Mark let himself in, and while his eyes had been open during Mark and Ian's conversation, it was clear now his brain hadn't been entirely online. "Why?"

"Because I don't feel like driving out to Hyde Park at this hour and you're already entrenched." Ian handed him an ice pack, and Gus took it with a frown.

"Entrenched? I'm not a tree, Ian. I can order a Lyft if you don't want to drive."

"I know. But you're going to need help." Ian watched him

press the icepack to his chest. "Your balance gets fucked when you're medicated and the idea of you being alone while Donna's out of town ..." He shook his head. "Even if your parents are feeling up to a houseguest, I think you're better off here with me and the nursing crew for backup."

Dropping his head back against the couch, Gus closed his eyes. "Yeah, okay."

Ian watched him a moment. He'd been gearing up for a Battle Royale, not quiet acquiescence, and as the need to make his case disappeared, so did some of his nervous energy. "I borrowed this stuff from the hospital," he said, "so you can get around when you're not wearing your leg. And when Donna gets back from her trip, I will run you out to her place no problem."

Gus didn't open his eyes. "Fuck. I drove in today. I need to give my captain a heads-up so she doesn't have my car towed."

"Was that her in the ED earlier?"

"Uh-huh. But I forgot to tell her about my car, and I doubt *Walt* will fucking think of it." Gus placed curious emphasis on his partner's name. "The guy kinda lost his shit today. Wanted to hit the mayday button even though there were already cops on the scene."

Ian winced. The radios carried by EMS responders like Gus were equipped with an emergency or 'mayday' button that, when pressed, alerted the entire system of a distress call so a response could be mobilized. Ian knew from Gus's stories that *lots* of cops responded to mayday calls in the city of Boston and summoning more resources today with police already present would have been a serious waste of time and money.

Still, Ian felt a twinge of sympathy for Walt. He and Gus didn't appear friendly—at *all*—but it had to be unsettling seeing your partner injured and knowing it could just as easily have been you on that bed.

"Maybe cut him some slack," he said, only for Gus to frown.

"He's been on the job at least as long as I have and rode with crews in Seattle. The guy has experience but today it was like ...

I don't know. Like he'd never seen a patient bug out before and I *know* he has. Ugh," Gus added idly, and Ian wasn't sure if the grunt was from pain or part of complaining about his partner.

"Is his name really Walt?" he asked.

"No. His last name is Walters but I call him Walt." Gus cracked an eye open. "Why?"

"Never met a guy named Walt before. It's sort of old-fashioned."

"Dude, my folks named me after a month on the freaking calendar and now I go by *Gus*."

"You could change to Auggie. Or Uhggie, since that fits you better right now."

"You make me laugh and I'll kick your ass. In four to six weeks when I'm healed." Gus's other eye flew open as a disembodied voice rang through the air.

"Gus? What happened to you?"

"Um." Gus stared at Ian. "What is that?"

"The PetBuddy," Ian said over the racket of a large dog scrambling over a wood floor. "There's a camera in it and Marco can see us."

"The fuck is a PetBuddy?" Gus mused, watching Elliott approach the foot of the stairs and sit, attention riveted to a chrome box affixed to the wall. Marco's voice floated out of it, complimenting Elliott on his doggy awesomeness before a treat shot out of a small opening, arcing through space at just the right angle for Elliott to catch it mid-flight in his mouth.

Gus turned a wondering gaze on Ian. "Did Mark spike my meds? Because I am tripping *balls* right now."

Marco rang Ian's phone while he was still laughing, and the three talked for a bit, catching Marco up on why Gus looked like he'd been hit by a truck. Ian and Gus worked together to adjust the hands-free crutch to the appropriate height for Gus to be able to use it and eventually, Gus picked it up and asked Ian to help him maneuver to the bathroom so he could piss and take a shower.

"Do you want me to come over?" Marco asked when Ian reentered the kitchen. "I know your place isn't set up for someone like Gus and I can help if you need it."

Gratitude thrummed through Ian. He got what Marco was really asking. Meeting your ex for a meal was one thing but putting the guy up overnight totally another. Especially when the history Ian and Gus shared still felt unfinished, like Ian was waiting for another shoe somewhere out there to be dropped.

Except Ian didn't feel that way anymore. And hadn't for a while.

He pulled a box of rice from one of the cabinets. Six months ago, he might have balked at having Gus in his home like this, still too raw to feel comfortable with having Gus close. But he didn't feel raw tonight. He just wanted to help. And while there'd been a time Gus had reacted badly to needing Ian's assistance, he was being unusually genial about those offers this evening. Maybe that was down to the meds. But, then again, Gus might not be the same person he'd been six months ago, either.

"Thanks, man, but I'm good." Ian ran his knuckles over his beard a couple of times before dropping his hand and meeting Marco's eye. "I'll get some food in Gus and make up the bed on the couch, and I'm sure he'll be out like a light again. Today took a lot out of him."

Marco nodded. "And you?"

"It was weird." Ian frowned. "I never expected to get a call like that about him again and I'm not going to say it wasn't unsettling. So now I'm tired and trying not to be," he said with a sigh. "Had plans with Tris tonight that I really want to salvage if I can."

"He'll understand. He's a good guy like that."

"I know. But this is a lot to explain." He cast a quick glance at the door when he heard the shower start up. "I'm gonna go so I can finish the food. Are you working tomorrow?"

"No, I'm off. You want me to hang out there when you go on shift?"

"If you could, I'll owe you forever. On top of everything I already owe you." He smiled at Marco's laughter. "I'm not on till eleven so come on over before and I'll feed you breakfast."

After ending the call, Ian mixed the rice with sweetened water in his rice cooker, then set it to boil. He went to the closet for sheets and a blanket, grabbed a pillow from the bed upstairs, and had just carried it back to the ground floor when Gus called his name.

"I'm here," he called through the door. "What do you need?"

"Your arm again," Gus replied. "My balance is totally borked."

He was standing at the sink when Ian pushed the door open, braced up against the basin, the hands-free crutch back on his leg and his prosthetic resting on the counter. Gus had dressed in the ancient Patriots sweatpants and flannel shirt Ian had set out, and the livid bruising on his chest was clearly visible through the unbuttoned shirt. He looked very tired, but his face was calm and he no longer seemed as bleary.

"You got the spins?" Ian asked.

"Nah. But everything seems kinda floaty, you know?"

"Uh-huh." Ian had heard that before. Noting Gus's hair was still rather damp, he snagged a hand towel from the rack while Gus gathered up his leg and its silicone liner. Ian offered him an arm. "Are you up to eating?"

Gus wrinkled his nose, leaning into Ian a bit as they walked out of the bathroom. "Food," he said quietly, as if considering the concept itself. "I dunno. You were right about the achy stomach. Can't believe you remembered that."

"I can't believe you didn't."

"Or that you put out these sweatpants since I know you stole them from me."

"I did not. Your mom gave me those sweatpants for Christmas like, five years ago, and *you* stole them from *me*."

They found Elliott at the foot of the stairs in the main space, tail wagging as another treat sailed out of the PetBuddy and into his jaws.

"That thing's fucking weird," Gus murmured, sounding amused. "But cool I guess, in a robot invasion sort of way."

Ian had to smile, imagining the glee with which Tris would have greeted such words, and how he'd want to talk about the scores of respected scientists who predicted it was merely a matter of time before a machine with true human-like intelligence would be a reality. But Gus wasn't up for science or robot talk, instead smiling fondly at Elliott's antics after Ian got him settled on the couch.

"You watch him through that thing when you're at work?" Gus asked as he unstrapped the crutch from his leg.

"Sometimes." Ian draped the hand towel over Gus's head. "My friends watch him more, though, whether I'm here or not. I could walk around the place naked and on fire and no one would notice."

Gus let out a groan. "Don't make me laugh."

Ian fetched him another ice pack, then grabbed the TV remote and flicked the screen on as Elliott trotted back over and hopped up onto the couch.

Gus grunted as the motion jostled him slightly, still rubbing his hair with the towel. "Good boy. Who's Tris?" he asked Ian.

Thrown slightly, Ian blinked at him a couple of times. "Huh?"

"I heard you talking earlier." Gus frowned thoughtfully. "Not on purpose. You and Marco are just loud."

"Oh. Tristan and I have kind of been seeing each other a while."

"Kind of? What does that mean?"

"He's in D.C. for work right now so it's all a bit up in the air." Ian offered Gus the remote in exchange for the towel, but the furrow in Gus's brow deepened.

"Are you moving?"

"No." Ian frowned back at him. "I'm staying here." Again, he offered Gus the TV remote. "Find something to watch while I finish the food."

"M'kay." Gus took the controller this time, but his expression remained thoughtful as Ian made his way back to the kitchen.

He was half-asleep when Ian set the tray carrying their dinner onto the coffee table in front of him but perked up after spotting the bowl of creamy rice topped with sprinkles of cinnamon. He quirked a half-smile at Ian.

"You made rice pudding?"

"Uh-huh." Ian handed him the bowl and a spoon. "I remembered you being able to eat it even when you were on the heavy meds and figured it might be okay for you again. I used plant milk and a sugar substitute, but I'm telling you right now it tastes fucking good."

Gus huffed a laugh, then winced. "Ow. Bless you for not adding raisins." He'd just stuck the spoon into the pudding when Elliott loped back in and immediately headed for Gus, sniffing the air suggestively. "Um."

"Do not," Ian warned the dog, keeping his tone easy. "You've had plenty of snacks already and you're not getting anything else."

Elliott ignored him of course, but instead of going off to sulk, he waited until Ian was seated, then pushed into the narrow space between the couch and the coffee table. He flopped down in a heap, covering the three human feet before him with his bulky body.

Gus smiled down at his dinner. "There is no more perfect animal for you than this one."

※

Okay to talk?

Ian's heart jumped in his chest. Yeah, it was okay. But when he checked the time, he saw it was past midnight and when the fuck had that happened?

Ian had messaged Tris over dinner, sharing some of the evening's gory details along with more apologies, but the chat had stayed quiet all evening. The longer the silence had dragged on, the more unsettled he'd felt, brain nagging at him like he'd forgotten to do something important and couldn't be fucked to recall exactly what.

He figured it was mostly to do with having Gus in the apartment. The space was too small not to notice an extra person in it, particularly one whose brain was mushy on painkillers. Add in a giant canine who had zero respect for personal space and the studio felt a bit full, even with Ian the only creature currently awake within its walls.

He'd sequestered himself and Elliott in the loft for the night and the place was quiet now, save for the faint echoes of traffic from the streets below. Ian had been too keyed up to sleep though and spent the last couple of hours watching baking shows on his tablet as a distraction.

Call in a sec, he wrote back, then carefully climbed out of bed.

Grabbing his earbuds from the nightstand, he checked the door, then moved around the bed, heat creeping up the back of his neck as he settled himself on the floor between it and the wall. He knew he was going overboard. But better that than have a suddenly awake and energized beast dog all up in his grill.

Tris picked up on the first ring, clearly ready for sleep himself as he sat propped up with pillows against his bed's headboard. Sure enough, his brow creased as he got a look at Ian, gaze moving over him like he was trying to make sense of what he was seeing but coming up short.

"Are you under your bed?" he asked at last, eyes twinkling despite his grave tone.

"Not quite." Ian laughed quietly. "Though if I had a closet up here, I'd be in it. I'm trying to be quiet because we both know how the animal will be if he even senses it's you."

A grin teased the corners of Tris's lips. "I guess we do. Not that I blame you either, given the time. Took a chance you'd still be up."

"I'm glad you did," Ian replied. "I should be sleeping but it's like my brain won't unplug. I've already gone through four episodes of cupcake baking and I'm starting to get hungry."

Despite his soft laugh, Tris's eyes as he looked Ian over were serious. "Tough night, huh?"

"Just chaotic. Sorry I had to cancel."

"Don't worry about it, I understand. Is Gus ...?"

"He's okay. He was assaulted in the field and got a little banged up—bruised ribs and some scrapes. He's still here." Ian drew a deep breath in through his nose and exhaled. "As in asleep on my couch right now. He's normally excellent with assistive tech but the meds he's on make him dopey and I'm legitimately concerned he might fall."

The crease had appeared on Tris's forehead. "But what about the fuckface?"

Ian snorted. "I don't even know. Gus hasn't called him. I guess Gus has been staying with his sister, but she's out of town on business and ... It's been such a weird night, Tris, I can't even explain." Ian closed his eyes, and it was as if his body suddenly remembered all at once he was tired.

"I'm remembering stuff I haven't had to think about for such a long time." Slowly, he peeled open his eyes. "Like how codeine hurts Gus's stomach and makes his thinking scattered. I made rice pudding basically on automatic pilot because I knew he'd be able to eat it and even remembered to leave out the raisins because he says they ruin everything."

Tris made a sound like a gameshow buzzer. "Well, that's just wrong. What about wine? Or chocolate-covered raisins, for fuck's sake, which clearly come from God."

A laugh came out of Ian, sudden and slightly wild, and from the way Tris's eyes lit up, Ian knew he'd surprised him. It felt *good* talking like this, finally hearing Tris's voice after the long, strange evening, and Ian felt lighter than he had in hours. And man, so fucking beat his bones felt like they were filled with lead.

Shit.

Tris's face abruptly sobered and Ian knew then he'd said some of that aloud, which made his whole face flame as he climbed back up on to the bed.

"Sorry," he murmured. "Like I said, this night has been stranger than average."

Tris waited until Ian was stretched out on his side, the tablet on the pillow beside him before asking in the gentlest voice, "Are you okay?"

"Tired. Nice hearing your voice." Ian smiled. "Needed that, you know?"

"Uh-huh." Tris scooted down on his own bed so he could lie on his side, too. "Does it bother you seeing him hurt?"

Funny Marco had asked the same question earlier; clearly, he wasn't the only one who knew Ian well.

"I don't like it, but considering what could have happened, he's not so bad off." Ian yawned, almost smiling as he recalled Gus's muttering about having janky ribs. "And this is nothing after what Gus when through with his leg. They're old friends, him and pain, and he knows how to deal. I guess I do, too.

"My training kicks in, and I want to take care of my patient, help them get through pain. It's like that with anyone. But I guess Gus *isn't* just anyone, and that's had my brain cranking harder than it usually might. Until now."

Until you.

Ian might have said that out loud if the bed hadn't dipped behind him and a warm, solid weight thumped against his back, actually shoving Ian forward a bit.

"Jesus," he muttered, aware his eyebrows were climbing as Elliott dropped his head onto the pillow just above Ian's, chin coming to rest along the crown of Ian's head. "I can't believe this is my life."

A slow smile had bloomed on Tris's face. "I can't believe I get to see it."

"Me neither." Ian heaved a big breath. "So, *anyway*, how was your day with the robots?"

"Tell you in two seconds." Tris tapped the screen with his finger. "I need a screencap to share with our friends so they can witness this moment of Wonder Dog greatness."

Ian sighed, knowing all his protests would be ignored. "If you must," he said, then laughed along with Tris as the dog shifted behind him and nudged Ian's body forward yet again.

19

"Tell me about this guy, Tristan."

Ian looked askance at his ex, unsure what to make of the question. Or the day actually, which had started just before dawn when he'd woken with Elliott half on top of him and the lights in the loft still burning, knowing right away that he'd fallen asleep while talking with Tris. He felt like an absolute shit.

The fun had continued from there, his apology message to Tris going unread while Elliott tripped him not once but twice before they'd even exited the loft. The goofy creature had zoomed around the ground floor, running literal circles around Gus who'd lain very still on the couch, expression a mix of amusement and wariness. Ian had hustled the dog out before he pounced and hurt Gus but man, he really needed to get a few minutes to himself so he could meditate and find some fucking stillness.

"Not sure what you want to know," Ian replied, voice coming out gruff. He and Gus didn't talk about their relationships, whether the topic involved that fuckface weasel Ben or not. "Told you he's in D.C. for his job, but he might be back in a couple of weeks."

"How does that work?" Gus cocked his head. "Like, you talk on the phone? Or travel back and forth?"

"Travel hasn't really been possible with our schedules."

And because I'm me.

Damn, it was hard not to feel like an asshole. But Ian had talked himself out of every invitation to visit. Told himself that sticking with the LDR plan might make it less painful when Tris eventually got bored and hooked up with someone local. Ian knew he'd eventually fade into the background because Tris had already been halfway out the door from the moment they'd met, and Ian wasn't going anywhere.

Except ... the guy Ian had gotten to know over the last couple of months hadn't gotten bored or been diverted by someone local. If anything, he and Tris had gotten closer despite the distance between them.

"We do chats," Ian said to Gus. "Have dinner together, watch movies and TV, sometimes walk the dog."

"Like with a webcam?" Gus cocked his head like he was thinking hard. "How old is this guy?"

"Younger than us," Ian replied, then left it at that because Gus was going to have to put the pieces together on his own.

"What, like thirty?"

"Nope."

"Younger? Damn." Gus whistled. "So, he's a kid."

"No, he's not." Never had Ian known it with certainty than right now. "Tris is young but he's a man, not a boy."

"A man you're dating online. *Ah.*" The tips of Gus's ears colored. "Oh-h-h-kay. I think I get what you're, thankfully, not going to come out and say. And now this is awkward."

Ian bit back a smirk. "Only for you. Do you want coffee?"

"Yup." Gus cast a glance about the place. "Have you seen my leg?"

"It's in the closet with your boots. I was afraid Elliott would get hold of it and try to kill it the way he does his pig."

One of Gus's cheeks hollowed in a way that suggested he was

biting it from the inside to keep himself from laughing. "I really hate you."

"I know." Going to the closet, Ian pulled the leg out, along with a bag holding the extra prosthetic socks and sleeves. He brought it all to the couch and set everything down beside Gus. "Elliott will be all over those socks, so watch yourself when you're handling them."

"Okay." Gus picked up the bag. "Thank you, Ian. I really appreciate you guys looking out for me. For real. I'm sorry I fucked up your night with your guy. I know you had plans."

"It's cool. We talked a while last night and he knows what happened."

"You told him about me?"

"Some," Ian hedged. He'd told Tris a lot more than 'some' of his and Gus's story of course, but that wasn't anyone's business. Still, the fib must have shown on Ian's face because Gus pursed his lips.

"Enough for him to hate me, huh?"

Ian couldn't help rolling his eyes. "Not everything is about you, August."

He made to turn for the kitchen, but stopped when Gus grabbed hold of his arm, struck as much by his serious expression as he was by the hand holding him still.

"Why won't you talk to me?"

"Um, I am talking to you?"

"Just not about your guy."

"I guess not." Ian frowned at him. "You don't see me asking about why you're living with Donna and not Ben, do you?"

"I'll tell you whatever you want to know."

"Because you haven't considered that I don't want to know anything. Look, we don't talk about guys—"

"No, *you* don't." Gus shot back, voice firm. "You don't talk about Ben or the guys you date, or how the fuck you're doing, or any of that stuff. You never want to talk about anything serious."

"Gus." Rather than peel Gus's hand away, Ian set his own

over it and squatted down with the couch's arm between them. Neither paid attention to Elliott, who made a beeline for the PetBuddy corner. "We talk about serious stuff all the time. I tell you more about some of the shit I go through than most of the people I see every day. That doesn't mean I'm going to tell you everything."

Gus made a frustrated noise. "I don't need to know everything. I just need to know ... You seem different, E. Happy, I think, the way you used to be." He waved a hand in a vague circle that made Ian smile. "It looks good on you. And I like knowing you're doing okay and not—"

Struggling just to get through the next twenty-four hours.

"I know." Ian squeezed Gus's hand where it lay on his arm. "I'm good, I promise."

Better than simply okay. And some of that conviction must have gotten through to Gus, because the tension in his face relaxed.

"Okay," he said over the PetBuddy's chime, ignoring the echo of a treat being launched into space. "That's what I want to hear."

Giving Gus's hand a final pat, Ian straightened up, grunting as his joints creaked and popped. Gus, the dick, laughed.

"You're old."

"And you need to put your leg on and get the hell off my couch, Dawson." Smiling, Ian headed for the kitchen. "Let's do coffee out on the balcony and get some fresh air. I'll make a pot so there's enough for Marco."

"Marco's coming? Ian, c'mon. I don't need a babysitter. I can call my friend, Connor, if you're really worried about me being alone."

"I'm not *really* worried," Ian called back, "but don't flatter yourself about Marco. He just wants to spend time with the beast dog."

And so it went for the rest of that day and the next. Ian helping Gus with his meds and his pain. The two of them talking about stuff both stupid and serious, including Tris and Ben. Who, it turned out, was an even bigger weasel than Ian had imagined.

What else could he call the man who'd taken the money Gus had saved toward adopting a child and blown it on a cryptocurrency scheme that had lost them every penny? Who hadn't shown any remorse over draining their savings, and instead told Gus that he needed to get over himself and start saving again if that was what he really wanted.

Gus had tried to be stoic when he'd shared that little gem, but his face had betrayed him, the raw pain in his eyes enough to make Ian's heart hurt. Ian had been gladder than ever about insisting Gus stay with him until his balance was steady again, and that the nurses kept showing up in force. They brought food and their company, plying Gus with magazines and TV shows and games. While Gus was often too fuzzy to truly enjoy himself, he accepted it all with good humor, and Elliott loved the extra company and lived his best doggy life.

The one person Ian didn't connect with very much during that forty-eight-hour stretch was Tris because no matter how hard Ian tried to sync up time for more than messaging, Tris's crazy schedule kept getting in the way. And while Ian really missed talking with his guy, he couldn't help feeling proud of Tris, too.

"I want to build stuff that'll change people's lives."

A smile tugged at Ian's lips as he looked over a half-finished chart. He'd taken Gus back to his sister's that morning and been waiting on tenterhooks since to hear back if Tris had time for dinner. He wanted to tell Tris *everything*.

How proud Ian was of him. How deeply he'd missed Tris for months, not only the last couple of days. That the connection between them was real and one of the most important Ian had ever had in his life. Because while he'd never expected to fall head over heels in love with a person he saw only through screens, Ian absolutely had.

Holy, motherfucking balls.

Slowly, Ian blew out a breath. That couldn't be right. Ian liked Tris a lot, sure. But they'd only known each other a few months and spent almost all of it separated by hundreds of miles. Feeling more than like for Tristan Santos had to be out of the question.

Except maybe it wasn't.

They spoke every day, often for hours, and by now Ian knew more about the guy on the other side of the screen than he did about many people he saw in person daily.

He knew Tris had seen his first big rock show at thirteen and remained a loyal fan of U2 to this day. That his bio dad had emigrated to the U.S. from Portugal as a teen and his mom hailed from Minnesota. That Tris had become attached to Air Station Sigonella in Eastern Sicily while his mother had been stationed there and been genuinely saddened to leave. Ian knew Tris adored Thai iced coffee and spicy cheese curls—thankfully, not together—and wore a size twelve and a half shoe. And that while he loved his stepdad dearly, he also missed his bio dad every day, even though the man had been gone for more than half of Tris's life.

Tris was the first person Ian thought of when he had good news to share or needed to talk a thing through, and he was the only person Ian had been interested in sexually for months. Once upon a time, he might've thought that weird and perhaps even sad, but fuck, cyber with Tris was so much hotter and more personal than any sex Ian'd had after Gus, he wasn't sure how he'd survive it once they could actually stand in the same room again. They just *fit*, the connection between them lighting up every time with an intensity that left Ian breathless in ways that went beyond simple orgasm and were no less devastating.

So, yeah. There *was* more going on than Ian simply liking the guy. Which would go a long way toward explaining why, after just two days of *not* talking, Ian missed Tris with a ferocity that made his chest ache.

An ache that hadn't lessened by the time he clocked out that evening, still without word about dinner. But Elliott was there at the door to distract Ian with his silly, whiny-grumble noises and kept the finally empty apartment from seeming too quiet.

Without hesitation, Ian got down on the floor with his dog. There were things he needed to do. Get Elliott walked and both of them fed, then vacuum up a metric ton of dog hair since Elliott was shedding his winter coat and there was fuzz fucking everywhere. But his body was tired and his heart heavy, and it felt nice to take a few minutes and chat with one creature who was always happy to see him. And who, for the first time in days, had been left to hang out on his own.

"Hi, guy." Ian waited until the dog plopped his butt down beside him before lightly slinging an arm round his back. "Did you have a good day?"

Eventually, they made it outside. Took a long route through the Beacon Hill streets before looping back in the direction toward home. They were nearing the MGH campus when Ian's phone finally chimed and the relief thrilling through him made his cheeks burn.

Big, sticky feelings—uncertainty, yearning, doubt—rose in his chest as Tris came into focus, dressed in a dark suit jacket, crisp shirt, and tie, looking way more put together and handsome than anyone had a right to. Tris was clearly headed out, which meant he wouldn't have much time to talk to the guy who still hadn't changed out of his hospital scrubs because he'd spent a half-hour sitting on the floor talking out loud to a dog.

God, he was so, *so* twisted up over this guy. But Ian made himself smile. "Hey, you. Feels like forever since we did this."

"Yeah, it does." Tris's voice sounded tired, but the look he sent through the screen to Ian was warm. "You walking The Wonder Dog?"

Ian nodded. "Got started late but we're headed back." He licked his lips. No sense playing dumb when it was obvious Tris wouldn't be joining him for dinner. "Where are you off to? You look incredible, by the way."

Tris smoothed his tie with his fingers, his smile bashful. "Thanks. I'm meeting up with the partners from Off-World. They're happy with the way the project turned out."

"Shit, I'd hope so. And that they're doing more than buying you dinner."

"We'll see what happens when I get my performance review, I guess." Tris waved off the praise, but Ian saw how his eyes shone. "I got here early to grab a drink and chill while I still had a chance." He lifted a glass of beer to his lips, sipping and swallowing before he spoke again. "Sorry I didn't message before now. The day got away from me."

"I understand." Ian worked to keep his tone light. "I know how busy you've been."

Tris's grin faded. "You've had a lot going on, too. How's Gus? Ribs better and all that?"

"He's healing. It'll be a few weeks before he can resume all of his normal routines, but he wants to go back on modified duty at the station next week." Ian shrugged. "He'd rather be busy than sit around his sister's place. That's where I dropped him off this morning," he added at Tris's questioning look.

"So, he and Ben are …?"

"Not together right now. Hardly talking, actually." Ian ran his lower lip between his teeth. "Some stuff went down between them over money and the question of kids and it's fucking messy. I think—no, I *know* Gus is better off staying with his sister, at least for the time being. But I'll bet Ben's still going to be pissed if he finds out what happened."

"*If* he finds out?" Tris wrinkled his nose. "You're not going to tell him?"

"I can't." Spying an unoccupied bench, Ian led Elliott over to it and sat. "I'm trying to stay out of it."

"You had your ex in your apartment for three days, Ian. That's, like, the opposite of staying out of it."

Oh-kay?

Ian wasn't quite sure how to respond. Or what to make of the sudden challenge he read in Tris's eyes. He looked angry. And like he was waiting for Ian to ... what? Apologize for loaning his couch to a friend?

Ian's bafflement must have shown because the hardness in Tris's face changed, quickly falling away. "Sorry. That was out of line."

"Maybe." Ian wet his lips with his tongue. "I let Gus stay with me because he needed help. You get that, right?"

"I do." Tris stared down at his glass. "You were trying to be a good friend."

"I was," Ian agreed, but Tris's tone sounded off. Like he hadn't truly bought what Ian was selling, even as he said the right things. "I owe him that much."

Tris eyes snapped up to meet his. "Owe him? How?"

"It's complicated." Ian stared out at the traffic moving over Blossom Street, trying to gather his thoughts. "Gus and I went through a lot together. He was there for me while I put myself through school and after my parents disowned me. And I did everything I could to support him while he did a dirty, dangerous job he loved, and I thought he was nuts for wanting.

"We never got married, obviously. Didn't care about what the law had to say about who we were as a couple. But we made promises to always be there for each other, no matter what. Gus kept me grounded when I needed it and I think I did the same for him. After his injury—after Gus almost died—it was like we forgot how to be there for each other at all."

Ian sighed. "I know the breakup wasn't all on me. Gus had a hand in it, too. But I feel like I let him down when I walked away, and I don't want to do that again."

To anyone he almost added before the thundercloud passing over Tris's face stopped him.

"Meaning you'd do it all differently if you could?" Tris asked, eyes glittering strangely.

"I guess? I'd like to think I'd do better if I got the chance."

"I don't know why you'd chance it at all. Christ, help me understand." Tris made a scornful noise and yeah, he *was* angry. "You were a wreck after Gus. Why put yourself on the line again for *anyone* knowing how it could turn out?"

Because maybe some people are worth the risk. I think you are.

Ian swallowed hard. He had to shut down that line of thinking before his ridiculous heart started spilling words Tris wasn't ready to hear.

"I know you think I'm foolish for wanting the things that I do." He nodded at Tris's barely concealed wince. "Honestly, there are days I might agree with you. But you were right when you called me a romantic, Tris. I just prefer to think of myself as hopeful and not hopeless."

"Uh-huh. Because arguing over who stole your Patriots sweatpants is relationship goals, right?"

The words landed with a thud right in Ian's gut. He and Gus had bantered about that very thing, hadn't they? But there was no way Tris could have known because he hadn't been ...

Ah.

Ian furrowed his brow. "Have you been listening to my conversations through the PetBuddy?"

"No!" Tris's eyes went wide and oh, he looked mortified. "I just ... Shit. I logged on Monday night because you said you'd be late, and I wanted to check on El. But you were there and so was Gus and yes, I heard you talking." He ran his lower lip between his teeth. "I didn't mean to do it and logged off the second I knew what I was looking at."

"You weren't looking at anything." Ian frowned deeper. "Gus was high as a kite on Tylenol 3 and needed help walking a straight line."

He knew the hurt swirling in his belly showed on his face. But Tris just shrugged like it was no big thing, voice flat when he spoke.

"Whatever. I don't care if you've got more going on with your ex than just nursing, Ian, because it's got nothing to do with me."

That ... sucked. Not that Ian had any right to be hurt. Tris had said from day one he didn't believe in the mate-for-life plan. And if Ian had thought Tris might change his mind just for him, he really was hopeless.

He turned his attention to stroking Elliott's scruff. "I know. I still hope you believe me when I say Gus is just a friend."

"I do." Tris was rubbing a hand over his face when Ian glanced up and shit, he looked exhausted. "I know you wouldn't lie. You're a good guy."

Ian ground his teeth. He *hated* this. Hated this strange, stilted conversation and how lost he felt having it. The unhappy energy pouring off Tris, right through the screen. And knowing something bad was happening and that he had no idea what.

"Tris, what's going on? I know it's been hard to connect these last couple of days but I'm here now if you want to talk."

"I can't." Tris stood straight, the fatigue in his face fading as he visibly reined himself in. When he met Ian's gaze through the screen again, it was cool like a stranger's and made Ian's heart clench. "My boss and the rest of the partners from Off-World are here."

Shit, shit, shit.

"Can we talk tonight?" Ian rushed out. "After your dinner, I mean. I think we both need that, and I just want..."

To make you feel good. Make you feel loved, if you'll let me.

For a second, Tris's expression lost its chilly edge. But then a laughing voice from off-camera called his name and he blinked, smile even and bland and just wrong on his face.

"Sorry. This is going to go on for hours. But I'll call you soon, Ian, and we can talk then."

Ian blinked as the image on his phone screen cut off and the app slowly dimmed.

What the hell had happened in the last two days to get them here?

20

The question was still dogging Ian several days later and he had no idea when he'd get an answer. Tris had stopped responding to messages, leaving Ian in the dark about too many things. Like why he'd implied Ian wanted to screw around with his ex. And why this felt like a breakup to Ian, though they hadn't really put a label on their LDR thing.

Ian stared at his chart, not really seeing it. The few messages he'd posted in their chat hadn't even been read, and when Ian wasn't busy being increasingly pissed off, he worried. What if Tris wasn't okay?

He's fine. You just need to get a clue, man. Face up to the fact the guy probably found someone new to hang out with.

Ian shoved thoughts like that away each time they surfaced, but he still seethed through his hurt. It pained him to think he'd been replaced. But so did knowing Tris had taken the easy way out by ghosting instead of just talking to Ian like a goddamned adult. If he was honest, Ian was almost more disappointed in the way his friend had handled this mess than he was over losing him.

A familiar voice cut through his funk, calling out a nickname Ian hadn't heard in far too long.

"Hey, Bones!"

Setting the chart aside, Ian smiled for what felt like the first time in days because Jenna Orloff was headed his way, grin incandescent.

"Jenna! This is a happy surprise. What brings you over here?"

"I had an appointment with my oncologist, so I was in the area." Jenna looked a bit pale, but her hug was tight, and the way she beamed at Ian when they parted was like stepping into a patch of sunlight after a storm. "The last time I was up at Post Office Square, a little birdie told me you were over here full-time, so I hoped I might run into you."

Damnit, Ian's throat was getting tight all over again. He hadn't really expected to see Jenna again after leaving the clinic. Had no idea if she'd stick around Boston for treatment or head back to Detroit to be with her family. Patients moved in and out of Ian's life all the time and that was a natural part of the job. But he loved that she was here now and looking really strong.

"I'm glad you did," he murmured, just as a tall man with salt and pepper hair stepped up beside them.

"And *I'm* glad you're here." The man glanced from Jenna to Ian and back. "I was not looking forward to hearing complaints if the great Nurse Byrne had happened to have the day off." He stuck a hand out to Ian, face wreathed in a grin that mirrored Jenna's. "Robert Orloff," he said, "Jenna's dad and the guy who pays for the Lyfts, the Starbucks, and every streaming platform known to man. Why are there so many?"

"Clearly, to make you insane." Jenna's dry tone held all the exasperation of a child long accustomed to dorky Dad jokes, but she leaned into her father as he and Ian shook hands.

"Ian Byrne, sir. It's a pleasure to meet you."

"Trust me, the pleasure's all mine." Orloff released Ian's hand, smile still wide. But his dark eyes held a *thank you* that belied his playful tone and sparked new warmth in Ian's chest. "Jenna told me how you were there for her during her diagnosis and before, and it meant a lot to me knowing she had friends to help get her through that. To support her until I could get out here myself."

He slipped an arm around Jenna's shoulders. "Took a while to convince my company to move me from Michigan to Massachusetts, but they knew I was coming anyway soon as I sold the house, job or no job." Orloff shrugged. "Guess they figured they'd keep me."

"Dad's been commuting back and forth for weeks," Jenna put in, "and I'm pretty sure he's watched *all* of the streaming platforms he likes to complain about while racking up the frequent flyer miles."

"Hush you," Orloff said over Ian's chuckling. "See how she treats me?"

"I do," Ian replied. "I'm glad you were able to keep your job and make the move. That's one less thing to grab your attention—"

"So it can be where it belongs," Orloff finished in a knowing tone. "I agree. Not having to worry about a paycheck is a tremendous relief. But, like I told my boss and my boss's boss, if I have to make a choice between working with them and being there for my kid, Jenna's going to win."

"It sucked knowing my mom had to choose between us and her job."

A lonely pang echoed through Ian as he recalled Tris's words. Tris's mother had been in the service and the choices available to Robert Orloff simply hadn't existed for her. But why was Ian thinking about Mr. Ghosty McGhostface anyway, when all that did was make him want to kick his own ass?

"Where are you all headed right now?" he asked Jenna and her dad. "I'm off duty and I'd love to catch up. Maybe grab a smoothie or something light in the cafe downstairs if you have time and your stomach's not too jumpy?" He looked askance at Jenna. "I happen to know they make a killer lemon jello."

Jenna tipped back her head and laughed. "I'm up for that if my dad is. He needs ideas about where to look for an apartment too, so maybe you could hook him up?"

"Man, that'd be great," Orloff said. "I've been staying in this corporate hotel on the company's dime and the place has about as much charm as a storage unit."

Ian rubbed his hands together and smiled. "You tell me what you're looking for and we'll see what some friends of mine can find."

"Bro. Got time for a question?"

"Sure." Ian glanced up from the platter of fruit and mochi he'd been arranging and met Gary's gaze. "What's going on?"

"I was hoping you could tell me. Because Tris has got his boxers in a big fucking twist and I'm guessing you might know why."

Ian tried not to scowl. Somehow, shitty movie night had been moved to his place, and the studio was bursting with happy people and dogs. Plus Ian who was working hard to be civil. Which, he suspected, was why his friends had taken over his home yet again. The nurses had noticed he'd had more than a few bad days in a row and banded together to keep him from stewing alone.

Most of the crew was crammed into the kitchen where Emmett and Jae were making a Korean barbecue feast, while the dogs romped around the rest of the space. Ian figured Gary had considered all that before seeking him out, waiting until Ian had gone out to the balcony so it would be easier to talk.

"I don't know, actually," Ian finally said. "Not sure I want to know why you're asking, either."

"Well," Gary murmured quietly, face set like a man ready for battle. "Tris's mood has been garbage the last few times we talked. As in he grunts and doesn't answer my questions other than to deny he's in a bad mood which is stupid because he very obviously is. Now I see you and *you're* oddly quiet, and I gotta say, that has me wondering."

Ian shrugged. "Like I said, I don't know. But I'm glad to hear he's okay."

"Uh." Gary grimaced like a man who'd stepped in something nasty. "You haven't heard from him?"

"No. Nothing since Thursday."

"Oh, man. The fuck is that?"

"No idea. Tris hasn't read the messages I've sent, and I know he'd duck a call if I made one."

"If?"

"I'm not calling a guy who blows me off, Gary. I do have some pride."

Neither spoke for a while. Ian finished the platter, laying diced mango, dragon fruit, and peaches among the soft spheres of mochi, followed by handfuls of raspberries wherever they seemed like a good idea, his brain spinning all the while. The most obvious conclusion really was that Tris had gotten bored and moved on, but Ian didn't know what to think. Tris hadn't been himself during their last conversation, emotions flitting over his features too quickly for Ian to get an accurate read. And, according to Gary, he was still out of sorts.

Looking up, Ian noticed Gary's frown, and turned a more critical eye on the dessert.

"Does it look really bad? I thought these mochi were purple but maybe I'm wrong?"

Gary's face brightened. "Nah, dude, they're purple and the plate looks amazing. I was still thinking about Tris. You said you talked last Thursday?"

"Uh-huh. It wasn't great," Ian admitted. "It turned into an argument out of nowhere, and I don't know if upset is the word but he definitely seemed bothered or angry about ... something." He shook his head, knowing he sounded confused because damnit, he *was*.

"Tris picked a fight but then backed off fast, and when I asked him what was wrong, he just shut down on me completely and ended the call."

"I knew something was up," Gary said. "Do you think this is about the ex?"

Ian picked up his glass. "Whose ex?"

"Um, yours?" Gary scoffed. "Whatever Tris is stewing about, it started last week around the time you and that Gus guy started shacking up."

Ian inhaled a mouthful of wine, and it was a moment before he could stop hacking enough to draw breath. Gary patted his shoulder in sympathy and, before long, Elliott trotted out to investigate why his human sounded like he was dying.

"I'm okay," Ian said to the dog when he could, then turned a glare onto Gary. "Gus and I were not shacking up. He was in my apartment for like, two and a half days and he slept on the couch."

"While wearing your sweatpants," Haru said, coming out to stand with them. He had a bowl of almonds in one hand and Owen at his side, and Ian rolled his eyes so hard he nearly saw stars.

Had he broken some unwritten rule about loaning people clothes?

"Tris logged on to the PetBuddy and accidentally spied on them," Gary said to Owen who, unsurprisingly, grimaced at Ian.

"Cringe."

"Nothing was happening," Ian protested. "I was helping Gus walk back to the couch while we debated who had or hadn't stolen a pair of fucking sweatpants, and suddenly it's like that was somehow a crime."

"To be fair, I saw your ex when I logged on to the PetBuddy and he's hot as hell." Haru set the bowl of nuts on the table, shooting a playful grin at Gary who looked like he didn't know whether to agree with his boyfriend or be irritated.

Ian just groaned. "God, not you, too."

"It's not like he's wrong." Gary shrugged. "You do understand we see you on camera, right? Like, we log on to shoot treats to your dog, but you make for nice eye candy in the background."

As if in agreement, Elliott yawned, then flopped onto the deck by Ian's feet.

"There's a pool," Owen said, smile wry as his own dog trotted out and started sniffing at Elliott. "We bet on when you'll walk around in your underwear, eat spaghetti naked, watch TV with a turkey on your head. The list is both extensive and detailed."

As if eating spaghetti while naked would indicate otherwise.

Ian counted backward from ten. Objectively, he'd known he could be seen through the PetBuddy. He'd just never really thought about what that would mean from a practical standpoint. A massive miscalculation given he'd passed a virtual key to his home to a bunch of crazypants people and left them to their own devices.

"You're all disturbed," he said, which just made his friends laugh.

"For what it's worth, Tris doesn't bet in the pool," Haru said. "Which is funny when you think about it, since he sees you in your apartment way more than anyone and could probably win the whole pot." He glanced around their small circle. "Anyone need a refill on drinks?"

Ian shook his head, busy mulling over the details he'd just learned. Obviously, Tris had misinterpreted the glimpse or glimpses he'd gotten of Ian and Gus. But to assume there was something going on there—that they were together in any way other than platonically—seemed a bridge too far.

Didn't it?

"Balls," he murmured quietly as Haru headed back to the kitchen. "He really thinks Gus and I are—?"

"I don't know," Gary replied. "He hasn't come out and said anything specific, but think about it, Ian. Gus isn't just any friend to you. You'd still be partners if things had worked out."

"But they didn't." Ian ran his knuckles over his cheek. "Gus and I broke up. I don't want a future with him anymore and Tris knows that."

Trouble filtered over Owen's handsome face. "Does he? Did

he ask why Gus stayed at your place instead of going home to that fuckface Ben?"

Now Gary was frowning too. "Who?"

"Gus has a boyfriend," Owen replied. "Ian and Mark and the guys call him the fuckface."

Ian snorted. "Gus and Ben aren't together right now, and Gus has been living with his sister. Wait." He looked between Owen and Gary. "Are you saying Tris thinks Gus wants me back?"

"He might." Gary's face grew thoughtful. "Tris doesn't have a ton of experience dealing with exes of any kind—boyfriend, girlfriend, hookup buddies gone bad. A lot of that is down to him moving often enough he doesn't have to navigate the friend zone with someone he used to get with. Look at what happened with Hannah. They were basically frenemies after the hooking up stopped, but then she followed him to D.C." He grimaced slightly at Ian. "She wasn't excited when Tris told her he still just wanted to be friends because he was in an LDR with you. And I think it threw him, having her around when he hadn't expected to see her again."

Well, that explained why Tris's friendship with Hannah had faltered again. But Tris clearly didn't have problems dealing with *every* ex-partner, either.

"What about you?" Ian asked. "You and Tris seem to get along great."

"We do, but that wasn't always the case. We stopped seeing each other over my decision to move to Boston." Gary looked down at his glass. "Tris was against it—he was already hooked on doing the short-term thing in different cities chasing after work that he wanted and thought I should keep moving with him. When I went for something more settled in my career, he took it as me selling out. Which is insane given I'm me and not some famous gamer schmuck." He smiled wryly. "Anyway, things were awkward for a while. And after I met Haru, it was awkward times a hundred."

Ian frowned. "Really? Tris told me you and Haru are two of his best friends."

"We are. Just took a while for Tris to stop squawking about me putting my personal life over my career. The only reason I didn't haul off and smack the guy was because I could tell he felt rejected and didn't know how to deal with it." Gary shook his head. "Tris and I didn't have anything like a grand romance, but I don't think he expected Haru and me to get serious. We had plenty of time to work on getting back to being friends before he moved out to Boston, so there weren't any gray areas to navigate by the time he showed up."

"Unlike Ian and Gus where there's a whole lot of gray," Owen put in. "Plus, Tris doesn't even know Gus."

"There is no gray," Ian insisted. "Gus and I know where the lines lie."

"But I doubt Tris does." Owen's firm, gentle tone halted Ian's bluster in its tracks. "For all he knows, Gus is still the love of your life. Maybe that makes it easy to imagine all sort of shit, especially when Tris is four hundred miles away and Gus is right there in your apartment."

"I'd like to think I could do better if I got the chance."

Well, fuck. A chill slid down Ian's spine. He'd said those words. Had meant them rhetorically about relationships as a whole but it wasn't hard to imagine how they might sound like he harbored regret over how things had ended with Gus. That he might want a second chance. And now everything Ian's friends had been saying fell into place.

"I don't know what to say." He shook his head slowly. "But if Tris thought Gus and I were screwing around, he could have talked to me instead of icing me out. That seems—"

"Childish," Owen finished quietly. "I know it does. I did it to Mark once. Backed off, stopped taking his calls and messages. I knew it was stupid, but I got scared and it felt easier to cut him off than face it."

Ian glanced from Owen through the windows to where Mark

was chatting with some of the others by the couch and appeared, as usual, like he had few cares in the world.

When Ian looked back to Owen, he found him watching Mark with an expression so tender, it was like witnessing an intimate act. "What were you scared of?" he asked.

"Loving him." Owen met Ian's eyes again. "Knowing he didn't feel the same way. Mark told me all the time he didn't believe in love and, for a while, I was okay with that. Until I wasn't." He smiled down at his beer. "I thought that if I didn't walk away, he would break me to pieces."

Pain shot across Ian's chest. "That's not what's happening here. It's Tris who doesn't want more. He's said it all along."

"I'm sure he has," Gary replied. "But I don't think he means it. He *likes* you a lot, Ian. And I'm not sure I've ever seen him this dopey over anyone, even me."

Ian wanted to chuckle along with the joke but found that he couldn't. He was still coming to terms with his own feelings for Tris. And if Tris was cutting Ian out because he didn't believe Ian wanted him ... well. Nothing about this conversation struck him as funny at all.

His hurt must have been painfully obvious because Gary's whole face softened. "You like him too, don't you?"

"It's more than like," Ian admitted, warmth splashing over his cheeks and neck. He hadn't planned on outing his hopeful romantic self to Tris's BFF. But Owen's fond smile helped Ian go on.

"I care about Tris more than I should. I'm still getting used to the idea. But even if I'd figured it out ages ago, I wouldn't have told him. Wouldn't have thought I could. I have no idea what it would mean if I did now." Ian wet his lips with his tongue. "What if you're wrong and Tris doesn't want more?"

Or want me at all?

"For the record, I don't think I'm wrong." Gary's expression was kind. "But it's your decision to fess up about loving him, Ian, and I'll respect whatever you decide." He squeezed Ian's shoulder. "Just don't write him off yet, okay? Tris acts like he can't wait to move on, but he misses us and Boston. You in particular. And I honestly think he's trying to figure out what to do about that."

Ian felt Tris's absence deeply as the evening wore on. He sat with his friends, sharing good food and cheer, and missed Tris's light and laughter so much he wanted to facepalm himself. He was still pissed and hurt at being ghosted. But Owen's words about being afraid of loving without being loved in return had rung true. Falling for someone might be as easy as drawing a breath, but it was fucking terrifying if you weren't ready to put your heart on the line.

Ian had been there. Told himself a hundred times not to get attached to Tris and taken none of his own advice. But he couldn't bring himself to regret it. Not when Tris had somehow gotten Ian to look at the world in ways he'd almost forgotten he could.

Tris carried a lightness with him that he shared without expecting anything in return. He made Ian laugh every time they spoke. Never judged him for being different or needing to prioritize his own mental health. And not only did Tris truly listen to Ian when he spoke, he trusted Ian to do the same. Hear and know him in ways others might not.

Ian didn't want to lose that trust. Didn't want to lose Tris. Which meant he was going to have to put his heart on the line and try like hell to do better.

21

"Release any unnecessary tension. Gently bring your awareness to your breath."

Eyes closed, Ian did as he was instructed.

"You need only observe the movement of air in and out of your body, not to change anything."

He acknowledged the steady, low roar of engines still audible beneath the meditation track and vibrations rumbling through the cabin floor beneath his feet, then let them go.

"Allow your attention to travel with the air passing through your nose and throat to your lungs, feeling the expansion of the chest and belly."

And inhaled the arid, musky scent of pressurized air being breathed in and out by dozens of other people.

Okay, that was gross.

Ian stuck with his practice anyway, allowing the errant notion and those that followed to drift away. Yes, he hated flying. And yes, breathing recirculated air was disgusting. But he didn't need those thoughts right now. He listened to the coaching words and mellow chiming of bells on his audio track instead. And when he surfaced at the end of the fifteen-minute practice, his head felt a bit more settled.

His stomach, not so much.

Ian glanced out the porthole to his right, watching the clouds as they streamed by. He set his fingertips atop a small tin of mints on the tray table before him, the gesture more out of reflex than discomfort. His queasiness wasn't strictly motion related. He'd pulled on a pair of sea-bands during the ride to the airport and had a full arsenal of anti-nausea tricks in his bag. Ian's wobbly insides were all about nerves and knowing he had a shit ton to do *after* his roughly ninety-minute flight concluded.

A ding rolled through the cabin, followed by the melodious voice of the pilot.

"Passengers, we've begun our initial descent into Washington, D.C. and the flight crew has turned on the fasten seatbelt sign."

Ian opened the tin and fished out a mint as the rest of the pilot's announcement washed over him. He didn't know what he was about to walk into down here. Whether Tris would want to talk or if the ghosting he'd done so well over the past week and a half would carry over into real life. But Ian had slightly over twenty-four hours to figure things out, so he popped the mint in his mouth and folded the tray table away.

He wanted to know why Tris had cut him off cold. To tell Tris how much he'd hurt Ian and why. Which would mean fessing up to his big, sticky feelings.

You flew four hundred miles on a random Saturday morning to talk to a guy who's been ignoring you, buddy. Pretty sure your hand's been tipped.

Okay, that might be true. But Ian wasn't taking anything for granted, given assumptions—his and Tris's—had gotten him into this mess. He'd own that. He'd been so sure in the beginning that he'd simply been infatuated with a charming young man who'd eventually grow bored with him. That he and Tris were too dissimilar to build a lasting connection beyond screwing around. He'd doubled down on his assumptions after Tris left Boston, certain neither of them was capable of forming an attachment to someone they saw only through screens. Ian had expected the LDR to flame out as the weeks turned into months, particularly since Tris hadn't wanted anything beyond laughs and great sex.

Except ... Maybe Tris did want more. Something lasting in addition to the laughs and sex. Which could mean Ian's assumptions had been fundamentally flawed from the beginning.

He wouldn't know unless he and Tris actually talked, of course. And Ian was going to make damned sure that happened before he had to leave.

⁂

THE FUNNY THING ABOUT CONFIDENCE IS ITS unpredictability. Ian never knew when he'd feel it, like an energy boost that lifted him high. Or, as was the case right now, when it would desert him and leave him hanging out on a figurative ledge. That's about where Ian was emotionally as he stood outside Tris's apartment building, trying to figure out what to do next and terrified of choosing wrong.

He'd gotten through deplaning and riding out to Bethesda, then made a quick stop at the hotel where he'd reserved a room. At just past eight in the morning, it'd been too early to check in, but a cheerful young woman at the desk had given him a map of the D.C. area and a list of nearby cafés in case he'd wanted breakfast.

Too wound up for coffee, Ian had settled for walking the three blocks to Tris's building and promptly gotten stuck in his head, leaving him staring up at the gleaming glass facade while his knees went all kinds of wobbly.

He wasn't even sure Tris was home. He'd almost certainly be working this weekend, and could already be out at Walter Reed or the Off-World offices. He might not have more than a few minutes to deal with Ian. Might be pissed with him for showing up unannounced. Or worse, not care at all.

And here Ian had thought he'd been done with making assumptions.

Sighing, Ian pulled his phone from his pocket and did what any sane person on the verge of freaking out would do; he called his dog. Which actually meant logging on to the PetBuddy in Mark and Owen's apartment since that was where Elliott would be until Ian got back, enjoying an extended playdate with Popcorn and no doubt mauling another stuffed pig.

The lights were on in the wide space that held Mark and Owen's living and kitchen areas, which made it easy to see the dogs curled up together on a sectional couch in the foreground while the humans puttered around farther back, clearly making breakfast and exchanging the occasional kiss.

Ian kept the app's volume muted, but the image was peaceful and sweet and so homey that longing thrummed through his chest. He wanted that in his life. To share coffee and kisses with someone while their beast dog snored on the couch. To make decisions about decor and dinners together and gorge on the occasional tub of ice cream and give each other shit about the cheesy TV shows they loved.

Ian might not get any of it, even if he managed to get this thing with Tris back on track. They were still very different people. Still had wildly contrasting ideas about what they wanted from their careers and in their lives. Tris wanted to get out into the world while Ian felt content hanging back.

None of that had changed. Ian had, though. And he was ready to stop assuming his and Tris's differences would doom them to failure and embrace them for what they were. Whatever that meant, since Ian was pretty sure they'd still be making it up as they went along. Oddly enough, not knowing how that was going to work didn't bother him much at all.

Quickly, he caught a screencap of the dogs with his phone and logged out of the app. He didn't expect much as he flipped over to chat, intent only on sharing the photo with Tris. Who hadn't sent any new messages. But who'd read the ones Ian had sent. Read them early that morning if the time stamp on the screen was correct, while Ian had been mid-flight. And as Ian watched, the tiny dots that indicated Tris was replying started to bounce, up and down and up and down, before they fell still once again.

Holy balls.

The energy firing through Ian made his hands shake.

I'm in town till tomorrow PM, he quickly tapped out. *Would really like to talk if you can.*

For long seconds, the chat stayed quiet, and Ian swore he could actually feel Tris's shock. Moving with purpose now, he went round to the building's front door, pulling it open just as his phone buzzed in his hand.

In town ... like Bethesda?

Yes, Ian replied. *Downstairs in your building now but can meet wherever.*

No answer came and, after counting backward from ten, Ian looked up from the screen, heart slowly sinking again. Tris might not be alone up there. They'd never spoken about being exclusive and just because Ian hadn't wanted to see anyone else, didn't mean he should expect Tris to feel the same way. Besides, even if he was wrong about Tris having company, he didn't think he could just hang out in the lobby indefinitely. Exchanging messages was a good start but waiting around for Tris to turn up felt too much like stalking and that had Ian crossing the wide lobby to the concierge.

"Hello." Nodding at the uniformed man standing behind the counter, he tried not to look or sound like a guy bugging out, which he one hundred percent was. "Would it be all right if I left a message for one of the residents? I'm in town overnight and not sure if my friend is at home, but I thought I'd leave him my contact info anyway."

The concierge smiled, not perturbed in the least by Ian's request. "Of course." He set a pad of stationery and pen in front of Ian, then placed an envelope beside them. "If you'd write the resident's name on the envelope, I'll make sure it's delivered to their door."

"Thank you." Ian dropped his backpack between his feet and picked up the pen, ignoring the way his face flamed. He knew he could simply send the info to Tris's phone. He was just stalling by writing it down on paper in hopes that if he gave Tris enough time, he'd come downstairs and they could talk face to—

"You don't have to do that, Ian. I'm here."

—face.

Joy squeezed Ian's chest as he turned and simply drank Tris in. The pretty eyes, wide with uncertainty. The platinum hair flopping onto his forehead. Mouth relaxed in an almost smile. For a second, everything was perfect. Until Tris blinked and his gaze turned shuttered and cool.

Unease slid down Ian's spine. He watched the little line form between Tris's eyebrows, whole body practically telegraphing his wariness. Like he was trying to figure out why a cyber-fuckbuddy Tris hadn't seen in person for months was standing in the lobby of his building.

Oh, boy.

Turning back to the pad of paper, Ian tore off the sheet he'd written on, folding the page before pocketing it. He slid everything else back over the counter to the concierge with his thanks, then stooped to pick up his backpack, not really focused on what Tris and the man were saying to each other than to note the exchange sounded friendly.

Shouldering his bag, Ian met Tris's eyes once again. "Can we talk for a minute?"

To his credit, Tris didn't miss a beat. "Sure." He inclined his head toward an entryway that sat beyond the counter and to the left. "We can head out back."

As Ian had expected, Tris was dressed for work, casual but still polished in a black jersey and jeans. He appeared entirely confident as he led Ian into what turned out to be a common area for the building's residents to gather, plush couches and chairs dotting the space, while flatscreens on the walls broadcast a stream of home and garden improvement shows. Herbaceous aromas perfumed the air, undercut by sweeter notes, and Ian caught sight of a juice bar set in the back corner servicing a small line of people.

"Nice," he murmured without thinking. He'd heard plenty about the building from Tris, but it felt strange and not entirely comfortable to be standing there now.

Or perhaps that was more the vibe pouring off Tris, who was watching Ian so closely.

"Yeah." Tris clasped his hands in front of him. "I don't spend a ton of time down here other than to grab a smoothie or bowl but it's not a bad place to hang out." He glanced toward the bar then, eyebrows coming together. "Do you want something to drink? They make a great watermelon cooler with mint and there's also decent, basic coffee if you don't want anything sweet."

His careful courtesy made Ian ache. God, he was so far out of his depth he was practically drowning, and he had no idea where to start. Not with Tris so obviously ill at ease. It was obvious he didn't want Ian here; he was just too polite to come out and say so. Which meant Ian really needed to say his piece and leave.

"I'm okay, thanks." He rubbed his knuckles over his beard, unsurprised when Tris's eyes narrowed.

"What are you doing here, Ian?"

"That's a great question." Ian's laugh was creaky. "I came to see you. I know I should have given you a heads-up before walking in here, but I didn't know whether you'd pick up if I called or listen to voicemail if I left one."

Immediately, Tris's cheeks flushed a dark red. "I'll own that," he muttered before dropping his eyes to his feet. "I shouldn't have—"

"It's fine," Ian cut in, quickly shaking his head when Tris looked at him askance. "Well, no, it's not *fine*. Like, at all. But I don't want to talk about that right now. I want to apologize."

Tris's head snapped up so quickly Ian wanted to wince. "Apologize for what?"

"For not being better at this."

A long pause followed as Tris ran his bottom lip between his teeth, clearly taken off guard. "I don't know what you mean," he said, voice surprisingly gentle. "What do you need to be better at?"

"Making you understand I liked being with you. Because I'm pretty sure you have no idea just how much I did and that's my fault. I should have done more to get that through your head. Came down here to see you before now." Sighing, Ian forced himself not to look away. "I wanted to, every time you asked me. But I didn't because I thought it was better to keep some distance."

A frown settled on Tris's brow. "I think I got that."

"But you don't know *why* I thought it and I think you should. I owe you that much."

"You don't owe me anything."

"I disagree," Ian pressed. "I told myself a million times it was just a fling. Friends who have sex, right?" he added with a weak smile. "And I was so sure you'd lose interest in the long-distance thing. Especially when you started talking about applying for graduate programs again. We got lucky finding time to hang out, but with the extra burden of classes on top of your work, I couldn't see how we'd do it. Plus, you in another new city with like-minded people, stuffing your brain with information, me back in Boston being me ..." He shook his head.

"Our worlds are so different. *We* are so different. I didn't want to get attached because I knew it'd come back to bite me. But I fucked up. Got attached before you ever left Boston," Ian murmured. "And fell for you a little more every day."

Tris's eyes went comically wide. "Ian."

"I know it sounds ridiculous, but I still thought you should know." Ian stuck his hands in his pockets. "Even if you think I'm fucked up for feeling the way that I did. For thinking you were worth the risk."

Goddamn, he was an idiot. Whose motto for the day was *go*

big or go home, the second of which Ian would be doing in just a few minutes even if it meant paying extra to change his flight. And provided Tris didn't fall over in shock, which was a real possibility given how pale he'd suddenly gotten. Ian had to fist his hands in his pockets to keep from reaching out.

"I wanted to say that to you the last time we talked—that you were worth risking it all. I didn't because I knew you wouldn't want to hear it. But when you went dark, it occurred to me I might never get a chance to tell you anything ever again. Like how I'm teaching myself to make mochi. And that I bought a new longboard. About the girlfriend Elliott made at the dog park." He watched Tris's face light up with his first real smile and almost smiled himself.

"I wanted you to know I missed our talks. And that you changed my life. You do that for people every day with your work, but you also do it just by being you. You made my life better, Tris, and I don't think I'll ever be able to adequately thank you for that."

"Jesus." Tris sounded almost dazed. He made a helpless little hand motion that cracked Ian's heart, like he wanted to reach out but had stopped himself. "You don't have to thank me for anything. All I ever did—"

"—was be my friend," Ian finished. "I know. I should have been a better one to you. Because if I had, you'd know I'd have chosen you." He watched Tris's mouth fall slightly open. "Even knowing you think this is all incredible bullshit." Ian's voice wobbled dangerously on that last word, and he swallowed hard before going on.

"We talked once about how I was looking for the right guy. Well, I think you could have been him, Tris Santos, even though you didn't want the job."

Blindly, he pulled the folded-up sheet of paper from his pants pocket, desperate to get out of there before he lost his shit. "I'm sorry about showing up like this, but once I'd figured myself out, I didn't want to waste any more time telling you. I've got a room in town till tomorrow if you want to talk more. I wrote the details down here and—"

"Are you out of your mind?" Tris was regarding Ian with wide eyes. "You can't just show up, be all hopeful romantic but use the past tense, then walk away. That's not how this works, Ian."

"Yeah, well." Ian's eyes stung. "Not sure I know how anything works anymore. As for using the past tense, I don't know. I have no idea where we stand. You went dark on me after you told me you wouldn't and I'm ... *really* fucking pissed at you for doing that."

Tris took a step closer, expression shifting into regret. "I know."

"Good." Exhaling hard, Ian scrubbed a hand over his face. Truthfully, he felt drained now that the nervous energy that'd carried him through the last several hours was starting to ebb. He was still mad though, and seemingly incapable of hiding it. "What you did sucked."

"I know it did. And I'm sorry. I just—" A loud chime came from Tris's pocket, and he screwed up his face. "*Crap.* That's my boss. Can you hang on a minute while I check in?"

"Of course." Ian glanced down at the note in his hand. "Do you want to meet up later? Meet at my hotel after you finish work?"

"Uh-uh. Not letting you out of my sight." Grasping Ian's arm gently, Tris started leading him back in the direction of the lobby. "Come up to my place and we'll figure out how this is going to go."

A half-hearted protest bubbled up in Ian's brain. He and Tris needed to *talk*. Get on the same page and hash out the weird vibe that'd hobbled their last conversations and, he assumed, made Tris turn cold. If they could do that, maybe they really would be able figure out how this was going to go, not just today but tomorrow as well.

Ian wanted that desperately. To know he and Tris had tomorrows together even if the shape the future might take wasn't yet clear.

He just wasn't sure he'd *want* to talk if he got Tris alone. Ian might be smarting over the way Tris had treated him, but it'd been so long since they'd inhabited the same space. Just walking next to the guy was enough to make Ian feel almost dizzy, senses heightened to everything Tris. He breathed in the light spice of Tris's cologne, very aware of the hand on his elbow pressing warmth through his shirt and into his skin. Of Tris's attention on him as he spoke into his phone.

Ian's skin prickled with the need to touch and connect. And it wasn't about sex, though that'd be very welcome at some point. Right now, he just wanted to hold the guy so tight it'd be impossible to tell where one of them ended and the other began. Stroke Tris's arms and shoulders and back, smoothing the flat planes of muscle with his hands. Stir that soft hair with his fingertips. Be held. Kissed until his bones turned to jelly. Stretch out together somewhere and just be.

Ian let himself be herded onto an elevator, then watched Tris pocket his phone.

"Sorry." Tris's mouth quirked into a half-smile. "It's been nonstop for the last couple of days."

Ian nodded, forcing himself to take a mental step back. He wanted time with Tris, but not if it meant getting in his way. "We don't need to do this now if you can't. Go in, and we can talk later."

"I don't want to put it off." Leaning forward, Tris hit the button for the twelfth floor. "I've been thinking too, Ian. And with you here, I'm done waiting to do anything with you."

22

Silence unfurled between them as the elevator ascended, broken only by the chimes marking the floors that they passed. Ian tried to find his chill. Not read too much into Tris's serious expression and the crease in his brow. Or kick his own ass since it was entirely possible Ian had already screwed up again and just didn't know it yet.

They exited onto the twelfth floor and Tris fished his keys from his pocket. But once they were inside his apartment, he spun to face Ian and the look on his face stopped Ian in his tracks.

"Tris?" He'd never seen Tris look so unnerved, like the ground had dropped out from right under his feet. "What is it?"

Tris licked his lips. "Downstairs, when I asked what you were doing in Bethesda, you said you were here to see me. But you're here for a conference or work or whatever, right?"

Slowly, Ian shook his head. "I'm here to see you. Which," he said carefully, "is either totally romantic or just plain bananas, depending on how you look at it. But I came to you so you'd know I was serious. About choosing you, over anyone. Except the dog, because I couldn't live with myself if I didn't put Elliott first," he added, smiling at Tris's strained laugh.

"I'm not saying I have anything figured out," Ian went on. "Like how we'd get your work and life to mesh with mine and still make sure we're each getting what we need. That'd mean not always living in the same city and relying on screens, but we've been doing that for a while now and I thought it worked out okay."

"I did, too." The hope in Tris's eyes sent a wave of tenderness washing through Ian. "You didn't seem so sure about it in the beginning."

Ian shrugged. "My brain still stutters over the idea sometimes. But I could be down for whatever came next using screens or whatever."

"You're down for anything," Tris teased. "I like that you're not using the past tense anymore. But seriously, you got on a plane? You *hate* flying. And after the way I treated you ..."

"Like I said, I might be bananas." Ian frowned. "Or stupid. You hurt me, Tris."

Tris's face fell. "I know I did. I'm so sorry, Ian. I wish I could make you understand how much."

Ian stared down at his shoes. His anger at Ghosty McGhostface was still there, simmering under the surface. It might be a while before it faded completely. But then Tris stepped close and pulled Ian into his arms and it was like every cell in Ian's body sighed with relief.

Damn it, he was a sap.

Ian buried his face against Tris's shoulder. Breathed him in, grateful for the strong arms around him. And Tris wrapped him up tighter, his hand coming to rest on the back of Ian's neck as he repeated the apology, voice hushed.

"I've been trying to get up the nerve to call you for days." He said at last. "But the longer I waited, the harder it got to figure out how the fuck I was going to explain myself. Gary reamed me out for being a phenomenal asshole."

"Shit. I didn't know he did that." Ian pulled back enough to peer into his friend's red-rimmed eyes.

"He was ripshit. Told me I'd hurt you. That I was being fucked up and shitting all over a good thing. That you seemed sad." Tris winced. "I'm guessing everyone knows what happened, huh?"

"More or less. It all came out during the last shitty movie night."

"Oh, good. That explains why the group chats have gotten so quiet." Tris blew a breath out through his nose, expression resigned like he was waiting for Ian to lay into him. "I'm not going to make excuses for being a shit. I made a crap decision and didn't do anything to make it better. But how do I fix this? Because I want to, so much."

Hearing Tris own his bad behavior helped loosen Ian's hold on his hurt. And now that they were talking, he wanted to focus less on the blame game and more on understanding why Tris had shut him out in the first place.

"What happened?" he asked. "It might help if I knew. Might help us both to talk about it."

"We can talk about it. And get the hell out of this hallway while we're at it." Tris gave him a weary smile. "Emotions are exhausting and I want to sit down."

He led Ian down the short hallway past a galley kitchen that opened into a furnished living space with floor-to-ceiling windows looking out onto some fabulous views. It was all familiar to Ian from his and Tris's chats, and yet oddly sterile, one step up from a hotel room vibe. Tris's belongings stood out vividly against the chic decor, his laptop on the coffee table, black silhouette of Godzilla adorning its lid. A pair of red canvas high-tops standing sentry outside a door on the opposite side of the room. A gaming headset on the coffee table parked alongside a stack of technical manuals, each one thicker than the last.

"Want that coffee now?" Tris asked. "Or I could brew up some herbal tea." Smiling, he shrugged at Ian's soft huff of laughter, the tips of his ears flushing pink. "You and that thermos of yours really did get me hooked."

"Tea would be great, thanks."

Ian parked himself at the island in the kitchen while his friend got busy heating up water, and a hollow feeling came over him as another silence stretched over the room. This wasn't like them at all; he and Tris didn't do stiff and awkward, yet here they were acting like strangers, grasping for words but failing. Then Ian caught sight of several boxes of tea by the stove and started to see flashes of himself in the apartment, too.

A cookbook he'd recommended for eating well on the cheap, tucked in beside the tea. The coffee mug he'd sent as a housewarming gift, knowing the dancing robots on its sides would make Tris laugh. Printed photos of the Wonder Dog stuck to the refrigerator door, most captured through the PetBuddy app.

"I'm not looking to get back with Gus," Ian said, without preamble or forethought. "I don't know what you saw through the PetBuddy, but—"

"You don't have to explain." Tris made a face. "I swear I never used that thing to spy on you. Elliott yes, but that's sort of the point of having it. I just took it as a bonus if you were there when I logged in, too." His lips stretched like he wanted to smile, but it faded before really taking hold.

"Lately, logging in has been like watching home movies. The ones families make just for the hell of it, you know? Except I wasn't a part of the movies because I was here, and the rest of the family was somewhere else. Including Gus."

Ian could tell where this was headed. "It bothered you that he was around. Which means you lied when you said you didn't care if I had more going on with my ex than just nursing." He wasn't surprised at Tris's cringe.

"Yeah, I lied. And that was a shitty thing to say to you. But it was weird seeing Gus with your friends. With your dog. Shit, napping with El on your couch, curled up all snug." Tris dropped tea bags into the mugs of hot water. "I always hopped off the PetBuddy real quick. Chucked a treat at El and made sure he was happy. But I saw Gus with you. Eating dinner or watching TV, giving each other crap. That's stuff you and I do all the time. And I don't know, Ian. Gus fits with your crew. I guess I started wondering where that left me."

Guilt prickled along the back of Ian's neck. He'd known Tris had been feeling disconnected. That for all his ambition and excitement about where the work he liked so much might take him next, Tris missed his friends. Missed Ian too.

Ian had seen longing in the looks Tris had given him. Heard it on the edges of the late-night murmurs they'd exchanged. Recognized it in the silly messages he'd sent that weren't about anything but keeping the connection between them alive. But Ian had never suspected Tris might feel insecure about where he fit in. And he should have.

Ian knew this guy. Recognized the sweet soul that lay beneath Tris's confident exterior. The military brat who'd watched his mom literally sail away over and over again and lost his dad before really having a chance to know him. He knew Tris was used to not calling anyplace home for very long and that saying goodbye to friends he made in each city had become a part of his life.

Ian suspected Tris had also picked up a habit of walking away to keep from being hurt and *that* was what had spurred him to cut Ian off.

Ian waited until a mug of tea was in front of him before he spoke again. "Gus asked me about you."

"Uh." Tris's whole body seemed to shift into slow motion as he settled onto the stool beside Ian. "He did? What did you tell him?"

"Not much at first. I'm not really a big sharer," Ian added quickly, hating the way Tris's mouth tightened. "Been like that my whole life. I'll talk about personal stuff, but there are things I like to keep just for me."

Some of the tension left Tris's face. "I get it. You like your privacy."

"Around most people, yeah. But it's different with someone I trust. And especially you. I told you more about myself during those weeks we rode the train together than I have some people I've known for years." He smiled past his tight throat.

"I had no idea why I kept talking and talking to a guy I barely knew. Maybe it was the way you trusted me with the mints and acupressure on that first ride. I was pretty grouchy if memory serves. But you took it in stride, that morning and then again at the pub."

Tris looked almost sad. "I just wanted to talk to you."

"And you made me want to open up." The gratitude that rose in Ian made his ribs ache. "Let you get to know me and the parts of my life that I don't always share because they can be a mess. Somehow, I knew you wouldn't hold them against me. And that you'd trust me to do the same. Listen. Hear you. Be the friend you needed or try to be."

"You are that friend, Ian." As if unable to stand the distance between them anymore, Tris reached over and grabbed Ian's hand. "I know people all over the world who I might call friends but there's only one person like you. It could be that's what you meant by keeping some things just to yourself. Honestly, I think I do it sometimes without realizing." His grin was sheepish. "Like when I crashed your Sox night with Gary because I didn't like that he could have time with you when I couldn't."

"Idiot. You can always have time with me." Smiling, Ian linked their fingers together. "And it's not crashing if you're invited.

"Anyway, Gus," he said. "He asked who you were. Then asked me again the next day. I was pretty floored because we don't talk about guys, his or mine. But I guess I shouldn't have been surprised at all because Gus has known me a long time. He probably sees a lot without me having to say anything. And he noticed I'd changed just by knowing you. Said I seemed happy and that he thought it looked good on me."

"Shit. Shit, shit, shit." Eyes squished shut, Tris drew the words out, the 't' sounds sharp as slaps. "I heard some of that through the goddamned PetBuddy. Gus saying you seemed different and how he was glad you were okay. But I thought it was because of *him*. Because Gus was there with you and that's what you wanted." He appeared a little green around the gills when he re-opened his eyes and Ian didn't feel much better. "I'm so sorry. I fucked up so much."

"That makes two of us. I need to do something about that stupid, dog-sitting robot."

"Don't hate the bot."

"I do what I want, Santos." Grunting, Ian gave Tris's fingers a squeeze. "Listen, I'm sorry, too. I've been so focused on not scaring you off with my romantical stuff that I didn't say things you needed to hear. Like that you matter to me. And I choose you, whether we're just friends who have sex or more. That there's a space for you that no one else can fill wherever I am."

"I thought you knew all that." He sighed. "Figured if Gus could see it after just a few hours, you *had* to know. But something must have got lost from one end of the chat to the other because you didn't."

Tris jerked the stool he'd been sitting on closer to Ian with enough force to knock it into the island, sending some of the tea in Tris's cup sloshing onto the counter.

"I don't need apologies." Leaning in, he cupped Ian's face with his palms. "I just want to make this better. I hated not talking to you or seeing you. I went to delete our chat and the app and couldn't. And I know I hurt you." He bit his lip. "When I read your messages today, I was so ashamed. Probably drafted fifty apologies before you messaged to ask if I'd come downstairs and I swear, I almost shit my pants."

"Yay, me." Ian glanced down with a laugh, unable to bear the fire in those pale eyes a second longer. "I saw you writing a reply. Didn't know what else to do except take a chance."

"I'm glad you did. So glad. You're one of the bravest people I've ever met."

"Mmm, no. I stood outside of your building and freaked out for longer than I want to admit."

Chuckling, Tris got to his feet and gathered Ian up in a hug. "After flying down here like a total badass, the guy who doesn't like planes. Not sure I'd have had the balls to do it. Fuck, I was terrified to even go down and face you."

"Terrified of me?"

"No, not really of you. But of fucking things up even further? Yes," Tris said against Ian's hair. "I don't want to do that anymore."

"I second that." Ian smiled in spite of himself, then sat back so he could ask a question that had been stuck in his brain since their strange almost-argument had sent Tris running. "What *do* you want, Tris?"

"You," Tris said simply. "In my bed, in my life, in my chats—fuck, wherever you want to be." He smiled, but his eyes were serious. "You matter to me too Ian, and I care about you so much. I hate that it took thinking I could lose you for me to comprehend all of that. To see what I'd be missing out on if you weren't around."

Ian bit his lip. "I like what you're saying. But you have to know there's more going on here for me than just sex and good feelings. I meant it when I said I fell for you, and I'm done pretending otherwise. If you really want me, I need to know you can handle the epic romance stuff that comes out of my mouth. Because if you can't and decide to cut me off again, I won't want to forgive you."

"I can handle the romantical stuff now. I ... *like* that you say those things. That you feel them about me." Tris's Adam's apple bobbed. "But I still have no idea what I'm doing. I don't know how to be somebody's right guy, Ian. The closest I ever got was with Gary and I'll bet you already know how that turned out. I don't want to be the guy who hurts people he cares about because I get scared."

"So don't."

The room lit up with Tris's laugh. "Man, I missed you." Carefully, he traced a finger along Ian's forehead. "These too. The Grumble Bear eyebrows give me life."

Emotion swamped Ian, so intense it made his eyes burn. He bowed his head, his heart almost choking him when Tris set a hand on his back. Neither spoke for a minute, Tris's hand rubbing warm circles into the space between Ian's shoulders while he pulled himself together.

"What's wrong?" Tris asked, voice hollowed out and oh, so careful. "I feel like I said the wrong thing."

"Just the opposite," Ian murmured. "You called me Grumble Bear. Wasn't sure I'd get to hear that again and fuck me if I didn't miss it." He glanced up. "Don't tell Dennis I said that."

Tris's smile was a bit broken. "I won't. Your secret's safe with me. And so are you." He leaned in and nuzzled Ian's temple tenderly. "I'll do whatever it takes to make you believe it."

"I know you will," Ian replied. "I'm going to work just as hard to make sure you trust me back."

They stayed like that a while longer, Ian perched on the stool by the island while Tris held him together. He'd started to really feel the long morning, body drained by the early wake up and flight, not to mention the high emotions that'd come from the reunion and intense talk. The untouched tea mugs were no longer steaming when Tris stepped back at last and his expression as he looked Ian over was adorably shy.

"Can I kiss you?" Tris asked, a sweet echo of their evening back in the Weymouth house when they'd stood in a different kitchen with truckloads of snow falling from the sky outside.

Ian smiled back, pulse quickening as he got to his feet. He meant to say 'Yes.' But the word got lost somewhere between his brain and his mouth as he stepped in and slotted his mouth against Tris's. Because then it was like Ian could really breathe for the first time in days, and the kiss was each 'hello' and 'missed you' and 'sorry' he'd wanted to say or hear.

A soft sound rose in Tris's chest, and he kissed Ian deeper, hands tightening on Ian's shoulders, his fingers digging in. Electricity bolted through Ian as Tris opened his mouth, and Ian slid his tongue over Tris's, already lost and buzzing with an overflow of good feelings.

Every trace of fatigue in his body transformed into a buoying lightness that made him crave ... more. More kisses and touches. More conversations about work and life and nothing at all. More walks with Elliott and dinners with friends. More nights spent twined around each other and mornings sharing coffee and low-sugar biscuits.

More Tris, in every moment that filled Ian's life.

23

Tris was the one who seemed shaky when they finally came up for air, voice quietly awed as he spoke. "Damn, Ian. Really glad you're here." He glanced down, running his hands up and down Ian's arms and seeming to draw as much comfort from the gesture as he gave. "Can we move this to the couch? I know we're not done talking but I want to be more comfortable."

Ian smiled and nodded. He walked on ahead to the living room while Tris washed their cups, then went to the window to look out at the park below them. Catching sight of a young man with a dog, he remembered the screencap he'd caught of Elliott and Popcorn cuddling and drew his phone from his pocket. He'd just gotten the photo app open when Tris appeared at his side.

"When is this from?" Tris ran a fingertip over the screen, hovering for an extra second over Elliott's sleeping mug.

"Today," Ian replied. "Sounds silly, but I miss the doofus. Not going to see him in person again until I can pick him up Monday morning."

"Monday? I thought you were flying back tomorrow."

"I am. And going straight to the hospital from the airport

because *this* guy—" he mimed to himself "—is working graveyard this week."

Tris's face fell. "You traded with someone so you could come here. Fuck. You're going to be wrecked. You should nap while I'm at the office. Stockpile sleep while you can." He slid a hand around Ian's. "In the meantime, bring your pretty ass over here and we'll work on relaxing you."

Ian tucked his phone away again. "Okay. But don't you need to go in? I can go back to my hotel and crash, then catch up with you tonight if you have free time."

"I don't need to be anywhere until noon, and I will have all the free time tonight. I have a metric ton of laundry to fold." Tris drew him to the couch. "Trying to get my stuff squared away this weekend so it's ready to pack up. I should be back in Boston next weekend."

"No shit?"

"None at all."

He collapsed backward onto the couch, pulling Ian with him, and Ian's squawk echoed loudly over Tris's laughter. But then Tris's lips met his, and Ian forgot about everything else.

Deep and drugging, the kisses cycled between hungry and tender as Ian and Tris stretched out on the cushions. Ian savored the feel of the lean body against his and loved Tris's eager sounds. His dick plumped in his jeans, straining at the zipper, and he hummed when Tris slid a knee between Ian's, shifting so his hard length was pressed against Ian's hip. Ian followed suit so they could grind into each other slowly, stoking the blaze between them.

Head spinning, Ian buried his face in Tris's neck, dropping a soft kiss against the tender skin there. His body burned, balls throbbing and dick so stiff he ached, and he felt amazing. Content, really, because he didn't need anything more than to simply luxuriate in being close to someone he wanted so badly and make him feel wanted, too.

They needed this. Needed time to reconnect and smooth

over the cracks that had formed between them. They weren't done talking by a long shot, but this was important too, touches and kisses like affirmations they were in this together. Ian and Tris.

Ian could tell Tris needed those assurances, feel it in the way he gripped Ian tightly, eyes intent when he pulled back enough to look into Ian's face. Ian slid a hand into Tris's hair, leaning in to murmur soft words against his lips between kisses.

"I'm glad I'm here, too."

Tris grabbed Ian's hand with his own. "Ian." His voice was tight, and the remorse in his eyes pierced Ian's heart. "I wish I'd ..."

Ian gave Tris's fingers a quick squeeze. He got it. They'd both made mistakes, some bigger than others. But they had to get past feeling guilty if they were going to move forward. "No more apologies, remember? We're going to figure this out."

They made out a long time, kissing until Ian's lips were sore, sometimes breaking off to laze like a pair of big cats in the sunlight pouring through the windows. Neither made a move to go further than the delicious, sensual grinding, and Ian was so drunk with it his limbs turned to mush. Tris was right there with him, drowsy and intoxicatingly warm, stroking Ian's back and shushing him when he startled awake, abruptly aware he'd started to doze.

"Shit. M'sorry."

"Don't be." Tris brushed the tip of his nose over Ian's. "I'd be so down to nap with you if I didn't have to go into the office." With a sigh, he checked his watch. "Shouldn't take long. I'm just stopping in at Off-World to tie up a few loose ends."

"Okay. I'll walk out with you." Ian stretched, ready to rouse himself, but froze when Tris shifted his weight and pinned Ian down. "Um."

"You're not going anywhere." His grin was impish, and his mouth and chin were reddened from brushing against Ian's

235

beard. "Seems silly for you not to stay when you're already half asleep."

"You sure you don't mind?"

"I'm sure. I like knowing you'll be here."

"As opposed to having to look at me through a screen?" Ian meant the words as a tease, but Tris's face grew thoughtful.

"I never minded the screens. I mean, they made me feel closer to you." A blush crept over his cheeks. "Made it easy to see how much you liked being in your new place and having friends just around the corner, and that taking care of Elliott *totally* makes your day even when you're grouching about it."

Ian wasn't sure how to respond. Knowing Tris had seen so much through a screen blew him away at the same time it sobered him. Perhaps Gary had been on to something when he'd insisted Ian not write Tris off as already gone on to the next best thing.

"He misses us. You, in particular. And I think he's trying to figure out what to do about that."

After Tris had headed out, Ian drifted a while but couldn't let go of his meandering thoughts long enough to surrender to sleep. He got up and made a quick meal of eggs and coffee, wondering if a movie would settle his brain. He'd wandered back into the living room when a flash of red caught his eye and the sight of Tris's sneakers on the floor reminded him there was laundry to deal with, a chore he seized with true enthusiasm.

It took three trips to haul everything from the laundry room back out to the couch, and soon Ian was surrounded by what he assumed was every garment, towel, sheet, and sock Tris owned, save what he'd worn out the door. Ian turned on the TV, then spent a long while folding and organizing while a bunch of beautiful people in Regency costume onscreen did their best to pretend they weren't totally into each other.

The light in the room had faded when a gentle touch on his cheek roused him, but Tris's grin more than made up for it.

"Hey, sleepy guy."

"'Sup, Chi-Town," Ian murmured, eyelids still at half-mast. "You watchin' me sleep again?"

"Possibly."

"That's still kinda creepy."

"And you're still kinda cute."

Ian would have retorted that forty-year-old men were not cute had Tris not leaned in and kissed him, lips sweet and wonderfully soft, lingering several beats too long to be truly chaste.

He felt far more awake when Tris sat back and he ran his knuckles against the side of Tris's leg, rubbing a line of warmth through his jeans. "Can I buy you dinner?" Ian asked. "We've never really done that—like, sat down for a meal in a restaurant with menus and waitstaff and such. Snacks at the pub in South Station don't count when we both know I was barely civilized."

Tris chuckled. "You were, too. Are you up for Indian? I found a place in Penn Quarter that does keema with chicken. Not as tasty as the curry you made but it'll do."

Ian smiled up at him. "Sounds nice. I've got a change of clothes in my bag that'll help me look more human. Speaking of which, I folded your stuff."

"I saw." Tris bit his lip, expression an adorable mix of pleased and bashful as he glanced over the piles that filled both the laundry basket and the cushions at the far end of the couch. "Can't believe you did that."

"I can't believe you own more socks than God. And don't thank me yet." Smirking, Ian straightened up in his seat, pointing at a mass of dark shapes he'd draped over the top of the basket. "Not sure how well I did matching up colors, so I'd do a sanity check if I were you."

༺❀༻

THEY ATE AN EXCELLENT MEAL AT THE CAFE IN PENN Quarter, sharing portions of food from each other's plates while

Tris brought Ian up to speed on the upcoming apartment shift back to Boston.

"Your stuff's still in storage with Zac and Aiden, but have you settled on where you want to stay?" Ian tried to sound casual as they strolled toward the Washington Monument, the city's lights shining softly all around them. With everyone having moved on from the house in Weymouth, Tris was a bit at loose ends, though several friends had already offered to put him up. Ian himself wanted to strike a balance between *'you do you'* and *'my house and everything in it is yours,'* but he'd never been very good with subtleties.

Tris, thankfully, didn't appear in the mood for subtleties either. "Ela and Sully said I could crash in their spare room for as long as I need," he said, "which means I'll only be a few blocks from your place until I can find one for myself."

Wait, what now?

"You want an apartment in Boston?"

Tris cocked a brow at him. "Well, I can't stay with Ela and Sully forever. Don't want to if I'm honest."

Ian smiled. "That's not what I meant. Unless I heard wrong, it sounded like you were planning to set up base in Boston."

"You heard right. I do want that. Haven't decided on a neighborhood yet, but definitely near the Orange Line and maybe close enough to walk. Yo, you could teach me to ride a board."

Ian grinned now. He loved the idea of a skateboarding Tris. In Boston, no less, where it sounded like he planned to be on a somewhat regular basis. Ian still tried to temper his excitement and shove his assumptions aside.

"So, you're staying with Off-World for now?"

"Yup. There's a ton of interest in getting the exo-suit into more rehab programs." Tris gave his head a slow shake. "Like projects to keep multiple teams busy for the next two years and beyond."

Ian sighed happily. "Look at you, Tris."

"Yeah, look at me." But Tris looked like he was stuck

between preening and cringing. "I'm still trying to wrap my head around it. There's talk of forming a division at Off-World specifically for this type of work. Possibly going international. And *I'm* part of it, the guy who plays with toys for a living."

More like the guy who needs to get Hannah's crap out of his head.

Out of reflex, Ian glanced around them. He'd learned to be careful about being an out gay man in places he wasn't familiar with, but he didn't hold back now, reaching over and taking Tris's hand in his own.

"You're still not seeing yourself clearly," he said. "This opportunity didn't happen out of thin air. You and your team kicked ass getting the exo-suit into the program at Walter Reed, and the people you work with know it. I'll bet they're already lined up to talk to you about new projects." He smiled at Tris's unguarded laughter. "Am I wrong?"

"No. I have a meeting with a team in a couple of weeks about a feeding device for people with spinal cord injuries or neurodegenerative diseases like ALS. I'm stoked to see what they've built."

"I can't wait to hear about it. But what does this mean for the travel you thought you'd be doing?"

"Still happening. But I want to think out the details before I agree to anything. This is uncharted territory at Off-World, and nobody's got a blueprint for someone like me."

"Shocking."

"I know, right?" Tris grinned. "But they want to help me figure it out and I told them I want to make Boston my base." He paused then, considering Ian for a beat. "I'd still do on-site work like I've been doing here, but I'd be back home between those assignments, just like we talked about."

With you.

Ian bit his lip. Tris hadn't said the words out loud, but the hopeful glint in his eyes said he was thinking them. Even so, Ian held himself back. Something was different in Tris, that much was clear, but whether it'd come about during the days they'd spent not talking or developed over time, Ian didn't know. He did recognize that it was important.

He brushed his thumb over Tris's knuckles. "What changed? You haven't mentioned making Boston your base since you came down here. You talked about graduate programs instead, and the majority of the schools weren't in Massachusetts. Last week it started to feel a little like you were already gone, but now that we're talking again, you make it sound like you always planned to go back."

"I did." Tris turned earnest eyes on Ian. "I don't have the capacity for a graduate program right now, not with all the work in my pipeline. And I refuse to feel bad about that."

"You shouldn't feel bad. But you see where I'm coming from, right?"

"I do. I was—*am*—going back to Boston after this project. Not sure when it happened but the place started to feel like home, and I want to hang on to that."

A breath caught in Ian's chest. Twice Tris had used the word 'home' to describe Boston and Ian knew he hadn't done so carelessly.

"I love working for Off-World and the people I've met through the Mass office," Tris said. "But my best friends live up there too. Gary and Haru and Ela and Sully ... I miss them. Thanks to you, I have new friends too, and while we've met only once in real life, we talk all the time, and I can't wait to know them better." His expression grew infinitely more caring.

"I don't want to give that up. My friends, my work, my life in Mass. You. You're there, Ian, with my favorite dog ever. And I want to keep you. The talking and the laughs and the way we just click. God, the sex." He chuckled at Ian's small, strangled noise. "Maybe it's weird I've never wanted to be with someone like this before, but I don't care. I just want you."

Ian shook his head. "And you say *I'm* the romantical one," he muttered, heart thrumming when Tris leaned into his side.

They held hands during the journey back to Bethesda, not

parting unless forced to, fingers linked as they passed through the lobby of Tris's building and into the elevator, up the twelve floors and through his front door. And then Tris was on Ian, the corners of his mouth quirked up in a small smile. Still, the look in his eyes was raw, and his voice when he spoke was soft and plaintive.

"I missed this."

The words pricked Ian's heart. Stepping closer, he slid his arms around Tris's waist, smiling back at him. "I missed it, too."

Leaning up, he kissed Tris, holding him close while Tris held him right back. Awareness washed through him, and Ian let himself fall into it, savoring the pleasure. It was a while before they came up for air, and by then he felt dazed, Tris's shirt fisted in his hands. Tris grinned at him, big and dopey, but it wavered abruptly as he seemed to come back to himself.

"How the hell are we in this hallway again?"

"Not sure." Ian smirked. "Thought you'd picked up a kink and wanted to wait for the right time to tell me."

Tris tipped his head back and laughed. Arm in arm, they walked through the apartment, stopping every few feet or so to exchange more kisses. Once in the bedroom, they stripped down to t-shirts and boxers, then curled up on Tris's bed, petting and making out, driving the heat between them higher.

Shifting his weight, Tris grabbed hold of the neck of his t-shirt with one hand and jerked the garment up over his head in a rush. Ian eyed the miles of skin and muscle as Tris tossed the shirt aside, stroking Tris's ribs with one hand, his own body thrumming. Tris settled back and kissed him again, teasing with his tongue and small nips of teeth now before he went deep with his tongue, kisses slow and so feverish Ian couldn't contain his groans.

He caressed Tris's bare shoulders and back, pulse jumping when Tris palmed him through his boxers, smiling against Ian's lips when Ian swore softly.

"Like that?"

"Yes." Ian cupped Tris's cheek with his hand. "Love it," he said between kisses. "Love being with you."

Tris wrapped his fingers around Ian through the boxers, just barely stroking, his touch everything Ian wanted and absolutely maddening. "You feel so good," he whispered before taking Ian's mouth again.

Grunting, Ian brought a knee up, curling it around Tris's hip, and Tris responded eagerly, rolling more fully on top of Ian. He let go of Ian's cock so he could reach back and loop the arm around Ian's knee, and he pulled the leg tight against his side, pressing his fingers into the meat of Ian's thigh. Ian's eyes rolled in his head at the change in heat and pressure against his dick.

"Fuck," he murmured, skin pebbling at Tris's answering hum.

Fire lit Tris's eyes when Ian opened his own, his lips swollen and wet from kissing. He leaned over Ian, reaching toward the nightstand, and Ian didn't hesitate to take advantage of the beautiful torso before him.

Propping himself up slightly, he closed his lips around Tris's right nipple, sucking at the already rigid nub. Tris's body jolted, his gasp slicing through the quiet room, and Ian's balls throbbed. He looped his arms around Tris's waist, drawing Tris closer as he gave himself over to the pleasure of making his partner feel good.

"God, Ian." Tris's voice sounded wrecked.

Ian rolled them onto their sides and tongued Tris's left nipple, desire coiling deep in his groin. He sucked, long and slow, until Tris's whole body trembled, his breaths coming in fast little puffs. When Ian pulled back at last, Tris's eyes were wild, and a possessive urge unfurled in Ian as he looked his man over.

He'd done that. Made Tris groan and sigh, his dick so hard inside his shorts and leaking precum onto the cotton.

Tris's mouth tilted in a wry smile. "Smug looks good on you, GB."

"Thanks." Ian huffed out a laugh. "Never been with someone

whose nipples are hardwired to their dick. Think you could come like this?"

"That's never happened before but yeah, I think I could with you." Tris's laugh was a bit shaky. "Try not to let it go to your head."

"Too late!"

Growling playfully, Tris pushed Ian onto his back and their laughter dissolved under more kissing. Ian found the tables turned against him as Tris mounted a full-on assault, frotting against Ian slowly, the friction against his cock so fucking good without being enough to get him off.

He could feel himself glaring when Tris broke away again, but Tris shot him a look of his own before retrieving a small bottle of lube from the nightstand.

"Tried to grab this a minute ago," he chided. "Wanted to make you feel good. But then you and that devil mouth of yours took most of my brain offline and oh, now look who's sorry."

"Not sorry," Ian murmured. "Can't be when I'm with you like this."

Tris grinned. "Sweet talker."

"You love it."

"I really do."

Ian pulled his own t-shirt up and over his head, then lifted his hips so Tris could slide the boxers down over Ian's thighs, calves, and feet. He waited until Tris had stripped off too before reaching for him again, splaying a hand on Tris's thigh.

"Come here, darlin'."

He watched in silence as Tris wet his fingers, then spread his knees wide, hands coming up to catch Tris's waist as Tris lined up their bodies again. Tris took hold of their cocks in one hand, then braced himself up with the other, and the combined pressure of his touch and the hard, silky length against Ian's was sublime.

Ian groaned, sparks shooting through him when Tris rolled his hips, the motion slowly sliding his cock against Ian's. His scent and needy sounds swamped Ian, and he brought a hand up to the nape of Tris's neck, hanging on to him tight with his fingers. A familiar ache pooled in Ian's balls, pulsing outward in waves each time Tris moved against him.

"Love this," he said, only just managing to not add *'and you,'* even though everything in him wanted to. It was true. Ian loved this brilliant, funny, beautiful man and the time they shared, whether together in person or over long distance. They fit, messy, mismatched lives and all.

Ian didn't dare say those words out loud. They were too big and too soon and he and Tris still had work to do to get back on the same page. But Tris was right there with Ian, holding him with an adoring expression. Gaze open and unwavering. Hopeful. Loving.

Orgasm rolled through Ian in a blast that leveled him. He moaned, cock pulsing over Tris's hand and their shafts, the hot slick of cum heightening the exquisite sensation of each movement. Tris followed moments later, neck and chest flushing red, thrusts becoming slow and languid as he rode his pleasure out until he finally lowered himself onto Ian's body with a heartfelt groan.

Ian held him, wrung out enough that he started to doze. He peeled his eyes open when Tris stirred at last and watched him roll himself up to sit. Tris grabbed his t-shirt from the foot of the bed and cleaned them both off, and when Ian caught his eye, gave him a smile that hit Ian square in the chest.

I love you.

"I can come to you sometimes," Ian said. "When you're living in another city for project work, I'll use the days off I earn to come see you, so we're not always looking through screens."

Lying back down, Tris pillowed his head on one arm, setting his other hand over Ian's sternum. "I'd love that. *If* and when trips worked for you. And for El. But you know you don't have to, right? I'll understand if you can't take those trips."

"I know. But I want to take them. Meet you halfway when I

can. Being together shouldn't mean you're the one making all the changes Tris, not when I can make some, too."

"Okay." Tris smiled. "Just know I'll still want to come back to you, too."

"Yeah?"

"Mmm-hmm." Tris caught his bottom lip between his teeth. "It's been a long time since I've been homesick for a person, but I've felt it for you."

Ian couldn't speak. Not long ago, he couldn't have imagined it possible to feel homesick for people. He knew better now. Had learned that 'home' wasn't always a place where you laid your hat, but sometimes a person you trusted to hold on to your heart and keep it safe.

24

November, six months later

"*Amtrak Acela Express train number 172 with a 3:20 PM time of arrival is now on track 8, arriving from 30th Street Station, Philadelphia.*"

Ian eyed the doors that led to the platforms. "This is ridiculous," he muttered. When he looked down and met Elliott's brown eyes, he got the distinct feeling the dog might agree.

It was almost old hat now, staying in Boston while Tris worked out of state for weeks at a time. But every time Ian did this—welcomed Tris home from Chicago, Austin, Philadelphia—his eager, joyful rush mixed with a healthy dose of nerves.

"Okay, so *I'm* ridiculous. And I get that," Ian added, tone conversational as Elliott whapped the marble floor with his tail. "I'm a man in his forties who talks out loud to his dog, and I took a half day of vacation so I could meet up with a guy who willingly boarded a train over flying because he was feeling nostalgic." Ian frowned to himself. "Maybe that makes Tris the ridiculous one."

Hearing a favorite name, Elliott let out a rolling woo-woo

that echoed through the terminal, but Ian just laughed and reached down to pat him.

"I know you missed your buddy, big dog. And you can love all over him in just a few minutes, I promise."

"He can love on me right now," said a familiar smiling voice, and there was Tris with a megawatt grin for them both. "You two are the best thing I've seen all day."

Pleasure swooped through Ian, lighting him up head to toe. He had a moment to just take Tris in, bright eyes and floppy hair —a darker ash blond now that he'd stopped stripping it platinum —jeans and thick sweater somehow pristine despite the hours of travel. But then Elliott yelped and surged forward, and his leash pulled a dumbstruck Ian along for the ride.

They made quite a scene as they collided, Elliott crashing into Tris's legs and yanking Ian bodily against Tris in the process. Tris clutched at Ian for balance, the duffel bags he'd been carrying already tumbled onto the floor, but then Elliott reared up on his hind legs to rest his paws on Tris's chest, his noises loud and joyful. Passersby stopped and stared, smiling as Ian did his best to keep all of them from toppling over while he and Tris cackled uproariously.

With effort, he finally got Elliott back down to all fours, but he kept an arm around Tris anyway as the beast dog whined and wriggled against their legs. "Sorry 'bout that," he managed. "I probably should have left him at home."

"No way. This is great!" Squatting down, Tris opened his arms to the dog, scrubbing at Elliott's coat with his fingers and spluttering when he got his face licked in thanks. "Best welcome back ever with my favorite people."

"I hope you're ready to see the rest of your faves." Ian smiled when Tris looked up in question. "There's a whole party of folks at Ela and Sully's waiting on us for an early Friendsgiving Dinner."

Tris straightened back up, the confusion on his face

morphing into pleasure. "Seriously? How come no one said anything?"

"The plan only materialized over the last couple of days. Ela mentioned getting together before folks go out of town for the actual holiday and we thought tonight with you getting back would be perfect."

Tris slipped his arms back around Ian. "Love it. And being back, too." He sighed. "Feels nice to be home."

Closing his eyes, Ian leaned into his touch, breathing in the scents of coffee and light spices on clean skin, along with a sweet edge of peppermint. "You still poppin' those mints?"

"Of course," Tris replied. "They remind me of you."

"You always assign smells to people you like?"

"Nope. Only to you, Grumble Bear."

Ian didn't bother trying to hold back his laugh. "Sweet talker."

He kissed Tris, warmth flooding his person as the world around them slipped out of focus, station, passengers, and even the dog at their feet fading. A soft hum rose in his chest when Tris brought a hand to Ian's cheek, and his goddamned toes literally curled in his sneakers.

"Jeez, get a room!" someone hollered, and while there was laughter in that stranger's voice, the words were enough to bring Ian back down to earth.

Tris didn't come as easily, however. "Oh, come on!" he called back, which naturally set Elliott off. "It's not like there was tongue!"

Choking on laughter, Ian scrambled to gather up Tris's things. "C'mon," he urged. "Let's get out of here before you two get me banned from the T."

Back among the crowd at Ela and Sully's, Tris practically shone, eating and talking with gusto and seeming hungry not only for food but for contact. He hugged and squeezed shoulders and ruffled Haru's glossy black hair, then scooped Ginger the cat up from the floor so he could cradle her close as he chatted.

But he had Ian in his sights too, and the promise in his grin as he crossed the room made Ian blush.

"This is really nice," Tris said. "You can stop pretending it wasn't your idea, by the way. Ela already told me you did most of the planning."

"I helped," Ian allowed. "Are you having fun?"

"I am." Smiling, Tris found Ian's hand with his. "This is just what I needed."

He stayed close after that, and Ian was surprised to hear Tris beg off when plans were made to move the festivities to a nearby tavern.

"You sure you don't want to come?" Gary asked. They were working together to clear the long table that had boasted most of the food, Ian holding a tray for the plates Tris and Gary were gathering. "The bar's on the way back to your place if that's what you're worried about."

Tris gave him a grin. "I'm not worried. But we've got El and it's bedtime for good little poochies."

"And for good little robot nerds, too?" Gary's expression turned sly. "I see how it is. We'll leave you to it, then. Game night at our place tomorrow if y'all are free and somewhat recovered from screwing each other's brains out."

"Shut it, you," Tris shot back, shooing Gary with both hands while Ian snorted on laughter.

"No, I will not." Clearly pleased with himself, Gary leaned over and pressed a kiss against Tris's cheek, then took the tray of dishes from Ian. "Glad you're back, doll. Things aren't the same without you around."

"You sure you don't want to join them for a drink?" Ian asked after Gary had moved off. "I can get El back to my place and we can meet up afterward."

"I know." Tris's gaze was intent. "But I don't know why I'd go to a bar when I could hang out with you instead."

Ian smiled. "I'll make our goodbyes."

After exchanging promises with the others to meet up for

games, he got them out of there, holding on to Tris's hand as they strolled the chilly streets, taking it slow to give Elliott time to do his business.

"I had lunch with Hannah earlier in the week," Tris said. They were waiting at an intersection to cross Cambridge Street, and something in his voice caught Ian's attention.

"What did you do?"

"Nothing! You know how she is."

"Consistently disappointed in you." Ian shook his head. "What was she doing in Philly?"

"Working, I think, and visiting friends. I didn't have time to get the whole story before she started in with the same old bullshit."

"Damn."

"Meh." Tris shrugged. "I told her you and I were still all romantical and she lost her shit."

"But she knew we were together!"

"Yup. Guess she assumed it was a phase." Mischief made Tris's eyes gleam. "She actually said the words 'I can't believe you picked the gay over me.'" He smiled at Ian's barking laugh. "So, I told her if she couldn't be supportive, she could get the fuck out and she did, stuck me with the bill and everything. Which was totally fine since I was starting to legit fear for my balls."

Ian pulled Tris in for a kiss. "I'm sorry she was a douche again," he said. "You deserve better."

"Fuck yeah, I do," Tris kissed him back. "I told her that too."

Heading onto Staniford Street, they traversed the gentle slope leading downward toward North Station, and Tris smiled big when he caught sight of Ian's building.

"Is it weird that I miss your place more than I do mine?"

"No. But you just feel that way because the dog is in mine," Ian joked. Tris lived a mere four blocks east and they tried to split time evenly between the two apartments when he was in town. And Ian didn't really care where they ended up so long as he had time with his guy.

Once upstairs, Tris went immediately to the huge windows that made up the apartment's west wall. "You feel like stepping outside for a bit? I know it's kind of cold, but I've gone from one tiny box to the next all day and more air would be nice."

"Of course." Ian smiled. "Go on out and I'll grab some drinks."

In the kitchen, he checked the dog's water bowl and left out a few treats, then pulled two bottles of a low sugar soda he liked from the fridge. He popped the caps before heading back out, tiptoeing his way to the balcony door past Elliott, who'd sprawled out on the couch for a nap.

Tris glanced back as Ian joined him, though he didn't straighten up from where he'd been leaning his elbows on the balcony railing. "Love this," he said with a nod to the nightscape before them and moonless sky above. Light pollution made it hard to see many stars, but they were up there if he looked closely enough. "I'm glad we get to share it."

"Me, too." Ian handed Tris a bottle of soda and watched him a moment. Something was up with his guy. Tris seemed unsettled now, like a million thoughts were keeping that big brain of his busy. Despite the unease curling in his gut, Ian forced a smile.

"Everything okay? You're the one with the grumpy eyebrows and I'm not sure if that's a good omen or bad."

Tris bumped Ian's hip with his own. "Not bad. But I feel like I should be the one asking you if you're okay. You said you'd be good with the travel I've got going with Off-World, but I can't help wondering if you feel differently now that we've been doing it awhile."

Ah.

Ian's instincts had been right on about Tris and his big brain. And while answering Tris's question would take more than a simple yes or no, he appreciated being asked.

"I'm not unhappy with your travel," Ian replied. That wasn't a lie. He'd come in to being more than just friends who had sex knowing he'd have to say goodbye to Tris every few weeks. But they made it work. Used tech to keep the lines of communication open and traveled to each other on weekends or days off when time and money permitted. If the distance wasn't too great —like during Tris's recent stay in Philly—Ian brought Elliott along too, just to make Tris and their silly pooch happy. "I don't *love* it when you're not here," he added, "but I'm really okay with it because I know you'll come back."

"Okay." Tris tilted his face up to search out the stars. "I had lunch with my brother this week, too. Not at the same time Hannah was bitching me out, thankfully." He looked back to Ian. "Jim asked how you were doing. Wanted to know how you felt about me only being around part time, that kind of thing. And I started thinking about how much it bothered me watching Mom leave on her deployments. About how I'm doing it to you."

"Oh, darlin'." Stepping closer, Ian let go of Tris's hand and curled the arm around Tris's waist. "They're not the same thing at all. You know that, right?"

"One part of me agrees but another not so much." Tris sighed. "You've been working the graveyard shift way more than usual, and I know that's so you can get time off to come see me. I worry about that. Like what if all those late hours mess with your biorhythm circadian thing and your brain starts thinking its Daylight Saving Time all year round?"

"Shit, that sounds like a plot from a horror movie." Ian chuckled, but it sounded weak to his ears. Not because he didn't find Tris's meandering thoughts amusing, but because they made his heart squeeze. Tris was so loving. So genuinely caring about Ian's mental health over his own that Ian felt humbled to his core every time he thought about it.

"My cycle is fine," he said. "I'm being careful about not screwing up my body clock too much and doing the right things with nutrition and self-care. I'd tell you if I started to feel like it was catching up with me."

"Okay." Tris rested his temple against Ian's. "You mean so

much to me, Ian. I hate the idea of making you unhappy or hurting you."

"I know. But I wouldn't have agreed to the part-time LDR if I wasn't sure I wanted it. Not when the hopeful romantic in me is all fired up to try."

His breath caught as Tris leaned down and fit their mouths together. His beard stubble lent a welcome edge to the lush softness of his lips, and Ian slipped his arms around Tris as they kissed, tasting the vanilla soda Tris had been drinking.

They stood beneath the night sky, clinging to each other like they had all the time in the world. Which, for the moment, they did. When their groins met through their jeans, the movement over Ian's hardening cock made his knees wobble, and he let out a tremulous laugh.

"Damn," Tris muttered against Ian's cheek. "I know we saw each other in Philly only a couple of weekends ago but I fucking missed you."

Ian understood perfectly. He loved the time they spent in their chats and knew Tris did too. But they'd learned from mistakes they'd made early on during Tris's stay in Bethesda. Nothing compared to being in the same space. And coming together physically—the way they always were emotionally—was a critical part of making them work.

They crept inside finally, mindful not to disturb Elliott, Tris stealthily climbing the stairs to the loft while Ian latched the dog gate behind them. Following Tris, Ian slid the door to the bedroom closed too, and they shared a smile, Tris reaching for the hem of Ian's shirt. The lust in his eyes seared Ian, and Ian was aware of his heart pounding like it would beat its way out of his chest.

They undressed and Ian went to the bed and lay down, pillowing his head in his hands, unable to keep from showing off a little when Tris looked at him with such hunger. He held his breath for a beat as Tris sat beside him, his hand scorching against Ian's belly. Then Tris bent and kissed Ian deep, swallowing Ian's moan, his dick already rigid against Ian's thigh as they stretched out together.

"Want you," Tris murmured against Ian's mouth.

He teased the sensitive skin of Ian's pelvis with his fingers before wrapping them around Ian's cock and the lust that flooded through Ian made his head spin.

"Want you, too."

He linked his arms around Tris's neck and turned his attention there, licking and sucking, thrilling in Tris's small gasps and grunts. He worked his way lower, grumbling when Tris let go of his cock and rolled onto his back, but then he ran his teeth gently against Tris's ribs and smiled at his soft laughter. Tris brought a hand up to rest on Ian's head, slipping his fingers into Ian's hair. But before Ian could continue his way south, Tris gave a gentle tug and guided him back up his body.

"Need to see you," he whispered before taking Ian's mouth in a blistering kiss that nearly stole Ian's breath.

Jesus.

Rolling Ian onto his back, Tris reached between Ian's legs and tugged at his balls, the sting scorching him. Ian broke the kiss with a gasp, arching his body up into Tris's, need crawling all through him.

"*Tris.*"

"I know, baby," Tris whispered. "I've got you."

He kissed Ian again, gentler now, and it was a long time before he pulled away. Ian kept a hand on Tris's thigh as he got the lube from the nightstand, and his cock throbbed at the telltale *snick* of the cap. Tris spread Ian's thighs, eyes dancing, and the fucker took his time wetting his fingers, making enough of a show of it that Ian fixed him with a mock glare. But his playful ire faltered the second Tris slid a finger inside him, and all Ian could do was gasp.

Tris bent down and pressed a kiss to his chest, voice almost reverent. "Love you like this."

Ian loved it too. Sweat broke out over his skin as another

finger slid inside him and he groaned, unable to keep quiet. His nerve endings sparked as Tris stretched him, and the bliss razored through him with a sting that he loved. Suddenly, it got hard to breathe.

"Oh." He bit his lip, overwhelmed by the sheer volume of feeling. Sensation, yes. But emotion even more, his love for this man so intense it almost hurt. "Need. I—"

"Okay," Tris murmured.

Slipping his fingers away, he lowered his torso over Ian's, shushing him with kisses when Ian whined. Tris lined their bodies up and Ian pulled his knees to his chest, hanging on to his knees with his hands. He groaned softly when Tris bumped Ian's hole with the head of his cock, and then Tris was pressing forward into Ian so slowly, eyes fixed on Ian's as he panted through the stretch of being split in half. They groaned as one when Tris bottomed out, and Ian closed his eyes, reveling in the weight of the body on his and of being so fucking full.

Tris rocked into him, dropping murmured words of praise along with kisses over Ian's cheeks and forehead and closed eyes. Letting go of his knees, Ian grabbed on to Tris, holding on tight and meeting his thrusts. The burn in his ass deepened, become an ache he craved, and he hooked his heels around the backs of Tris's thighs. The change in angle pressed Tris's hard belly against Ian's dick at the same time it sent his cockhead scraping across Ian's gland, and Ian dropped his head back onto the pillow with a gasp. Lightning flashed through him, crackling down every nerve.

"*Fuck!*"

His cry pulled a rumbling growl out of Tris. Setting his forehead against Ian's, Tris drove into him faster and harder, finding his rhythm as he nailed Ian's prostate with each thrust. Ian urged him on, babbling now as his body barreled toward the edge, the sensations near overwhelming. Then Tris hauled him closer, and the pressure against Ian's dick broke him wide open.

His body jerked hard and he moaned, cum smearing over

their bellies as Tris's bodyweight milked him, and all Ian could do was hang on through the waves of bliss smacking into him.

"So fucking hot," Tris whispered, his own body trembling as he neared his peak. "Can't ... oh, God."

He fucked into Ian harder, thrusts losing rhythm, while Ian hung on, clumsily trying to return Tris's kisses, soothing Tris when he came apart and lay wrecked in Ian's arms.

They stayed like that awhile, exchanging touches and kisses until their breaths had quieted and the sweat on their bodies cooled. Ian coasted near dozing until Tris eased off him, settling onto the mattress beside Ian and snuggling up close.

"You want your boxers?" Tris asked. He sounded sleepy, and Ian ran a hand over Tris's thigh.

"Nah. Too comfortable to move." He smothered a yawn against Tris's shoulder. "But just so you know, El's got a new trick where he wakes up at dawn and does the yodeling thing until I get up."

Tris huffed a laugh. "That'll be fun." He sighed, but it sounded content and Ian smiled to himself. "Hey, what do you do at Thanksgiving?"

"I'm usually working." Opening his eyes, Ian watched Tris's brow furrow. "It's a given I'll work some holidays with this job and I usually pick Thanksgiving. Hospitals always put on a huge spread for the patients, and I like being there for them. Making sure they know someone cares about them when they can't be at home or with their loved ones."

"Ian ..." Tris's eyes were soft and fond. "You're something else. You know that, right?"

"I'm just doing my job. Don't make me out to be a hero." Ian smiled. "Besides, the holiday pay is *great* and the nurses and docs at MGH put together a potluck just for staff that is now legendary."

Tris laughed. "I like how you make it sound fun."

"It's *not* terrible. I already know I'm working days that week, so I may be home and in my jammies by six." He brushed the hair back from Tris's forehead with his fingers. "What about you? Do you head to Hawaii to see your folks?"

"Usually yeah, but not this year." Tris leaned into Ian's touch. "Including Boston, I've lived in five different cities this year and I don't want to get on a plane or a train for a while." He smiled at Ian. "So, I made a deal. Told the fam I'd fly out and see them for New Year's if they'd come to Boston next week and help me put on a Thanksgiving spread in my dinky little apartment. Would you be up for meeting them?"

It took a second for Ian to put the words together in his head. "Meet your folks?" He blinked. "For Thanksgiving?"

"They want to meet El too, of course," Tris said quickly. "I told them you two are a package deal. Jim's actually flying into town a couple of days early and asked if we'd wanna hang." His cheeks turned a dusky shade. "Said he can't wait to meet the guy who told Hannah to go fuck herself."

Ian's mouth fell open. "I never said that!"

"Not out loud, no," Tris agreed, "but you've gotta admit that you said them in your head, GB."

Eyes narrowed, Ian poked Tris in the ribs, then tickled him without mercy until Tris's laughter echoed loudly around the room. That turned into wrestling, Ian emerging as victor by sitting astride Tris's chest, pinning his shoulders to the mattress with his hands.

"Oh my God, get *off*," Tris groaned. "You weigh a ton, you fucking beast. You have got to stop working out."

"And you need to get outside more." Relenting, Ian let go of Tris's shoulders, then helped him lever himself up into a sitting position. "Touch grass, breathe smog, ride the fucking board I bought you."

Tris wrapped him up in a hug. "I like it when you're bossy," he joked, though his smile had turned shy. "Do you want to think about meeting Jim and my folks? Because you don't have to if—"

"I'd love to meet them. Thank you for asking me." Ian hauled in a deep breath. "Really I'm glad you're telling me now, so I have time to freak out before they fly into town."

"Come on." Tris kissed Ian's shoulder. "You're, like, the perfect person I could introduce them to. A nurse who adopted an abandoned dog, for Christ's sake." He paused as a high-pitched whine made it past the loft door, then frowned at Ian. "Is that—?"

"A four-legged bag of bones who wants to come up here and can't because the dog gate is locked? Yup. And I can tell he's winding up for a howl." Ian sighed and heaved himself out of Tris's lap. "I'll go get him or we'll never have peace."

There was hardly peace once the dog gate was open, however. Because the beast dog flew past Ian up the stairs, then launched himself at Tris who fell backward under the dog's ecstatic attentions. Ian laughed so hard he almost fell over, and it took a minute to calm everyone down.

"I can make him get down if you don't want to share," Ian offered as he got back under the covers. "He knows he has a bed of his own."

They eyed the furry lump taking up space at the foot of the bed, then laughed together as Elliott whooshed a huge sigh through his nose.

"Not sure I could live with myself if I did." Tris set a hand over the center of Ian's chest. "Besides, it feels right having him here. Feels like home."

Throat aching, Ian covered Tris's hand with his own. "Yeah, it does," he agreed, closing his eyes as Tris snuggled closer and they welcomed each other home without needing to say a word.

-Fin-

BONUS SCENE
SO THIS IS LOVE

April, 2023

Tris Santos got to his feet as the Amtrak Acela Express coasted to a stop inside Back Bay Station, and once the doors were open, he headed for his subway connection. He'd been in Manhattan all week and couldn't wait to get home.

Well, that wasn't entirely true. Tris didn't plan to stay long at *his* place. He'd empty his bags and stow them in his closet, but he planned to be out the door and headed for his boyfriend's immediately afterward. Never mind the mountain of laundry he had to do.

He smiled to himself as he boarded an Orange Line train, duffel slung over one shoulder and messenger bag over the other. He'd used public transportation all over the world, but there was something special about the trains that moved in and out of this city. Maybe because he'd boarded the commuter rail one wintery day while the city had been half buried in snow and sat down beside someone who'd changed his whole life.

Several stops later, he exited Haymarket Station into a cool spring afternoon and made his way onto Canal Street and toward the building that held his studio.

"Hello, Computer," he called as he closed his door behind him, not bothering to watch the smart speaker on his kitchen counter pulse blue and green as it woke up.

"Hello, Tris," it replied in a friendly, measured tone.

"Play Driving at Night," he said, toeing off his shoes as the playlist started up and downtempo house music filtered through the air.

When Tris was in town, he typically stayed overnight in the studio once or twice a week. Otherwise, he stopped in for changes of clothes or to pick up the odd technical manual for work, fully aware he treated the apartment like a glorified storage unit. It was a nice little place, with sleek lines that pleased his aesthetic sensibilities and a great kitchen. The building boasted a shared roof deck and Tris's neighbors were both friendly and quiet when they needed to be, the kind of folks who arranged regular potlucks and bakeoffs, just for fun. Tris like the place well enough, but it didn't feel like home.

Home was four blocks to the west in Ian's apartment, one of the places Tris liked best in the world.

Enough to share it with Ian?

Tris furrowed his brow. That voice in his head was a pain. Partly because it sounded too much like his ex-friend, Hannah, who'd never, ever cut Tris any slack. But more so because the voice tended to pester Tris about thoughts he tried to ignore. Like why he was still renting this apartment when he should probably move in with Ian since by Ian's side was where Tris wanted to be.

He carried his duffel to the laundry closet and set it on the floor. They'd been together a year now and Tris couldn't imagine anyone more perfect for him. The guy put up with the highly ridiculous nickname Tris had given him, blithely accepting of both *Grumble Bear* and *GB*, even in public. Tris's friends loved Ian and his folks and brother adored him, just as Tris had known they would. Because Ian was perfect in all the ways Tris needed him to be, and when he looked down the road to the future, Ian was there, too.

"Computer, call GB at home," he called, squatting down to unpack his bag. He lifted out small stacks of clothes as the music cut off and the speaker dialed an identical device—nicknamed Evil Bot 2—that sat in Ian's apartment. The call went unanswered though, then flipped to voicemail, and Tris ended it without leaving a message.

Odd. Ian had offered to cook dinner. It was possible he'd gotten distracted by a task or gone out to buy beer or the low-sugar soda he liked. A task Tris had meant to offer to do himself and then promptly forgotten.

I suck.

"Computer, call GB at mobile." He set the bundle of clothes in the laundry basket, then headed for the bedroom end of the space, smiling when the call connected and a familiar harried voice answered.

"Hey, Tris. You back?"

"Yup. How you doing, Grumble Bear?" Tris opened his closet. "Wanted to see if you need me pick anything up on my way over."

Ian sighed. "Damn. I should have called earlier."

Eyes on the clothes in front of him, Tris frowned. "That doesn't sound good. You're not stuck at work, are you?" Ian's job as an orthopedic nurse at Mass General Hospital kept him so busy, there were times Tris wondered how the guy functioned.

"No, not at work. Just dealing with ... something right now."

"You need any help?" Tris pulled a gray, long-sleeved t-shirt from the closet. He'd heard Ian hesitate over the word 'something.' And Tris paused when the line stayed quiet, turning to look at the speaker when Ian stayed silent for what felt like way too long. "Ian? Are you okay?"

"It's Elliott," Ian said then, and now Tris heard concern in his voice. "He came out of the dog park with a wound on his paw and I didn't wanna leave it until tomorrow."

Tris put the t-shirt back in the closet. Elliott the Wonder Dog was a Malamute-Husky mix and one of Ian's favorite life forms on the planet. One of Tris's too, and his stomach went tight at the idea of Ian hauling the beast dog around on his own.

"Where are you guys?" he asked.

"The vet's office on Charles Street."

"I know the one you mean."

"But you don't need to come down here—"

"I'll be there in fifteen minutes," Tris said over him. "Can I bring you anything?"

"Nah, I'm okay. Well … Could I borrow a hoodie? Mine's a mess. Something dark you're not fond of?"

Tris went back to pulling clothes out of the closet. "Got it. Be there as soon as I can."

Ian sighed again. "Thanks, Tris. I owe you one."

Tris's frown deepened as he swiftly changed into a pair of older jeans and a weathered sweatshirt from the University of Chicago. The idea Ian would feel beholden to Tris for *anything* didn't sit right at all. Friends might owe each other favors, but he and Ian were much more than friends. Then again, a real gentleman lurked inside Ian, and he could be charmingly old-fashioned when he felt in the mood. Like being on the lookout to do a chivalrous deed for Tris in return because that was just how he was.

He loves you, the voice in Tris's head said, more gently this time.

Tris's insides quivered a bit as he pulled on a pair of old Converse, but he knew it was true. Ian did love him. Had told Tris so a month ago, right in the middle of the organic foods aisle of the freaking grocery store of all places. He'd chuckled when Tris's eyes went wide, then kissed him softly and told him not to panic. Said Tris didn't need to say it back and put a bag of chia seed in the cart, so they could go about the rest of their day like nothing had happened. Ian hadn't said the words out loud again. But Tris sometimes thought he heard Ian whisper them under his breath when they were twined around each other in bed, making each other gasp and moan. And Tris felt crushed flat every time.

He hadn't said the words back, of course. Tris had never been in love. In deep like, sure. He'd felt that way for his ex, Gary, a mix of fondness and lust and generally heightened enjoyment anytime they were together. Tris and Gary had been the best of friends the whole time they'd screwed around and, with the exception of a small window of time, stayed tight after Gary had moved to Boston and started a new relationship. Hell, Tris was better friends with Gary now than he'd been when they'd been fucking.

The idea of not being with Ian, though ... Tris's stomach dropped at the thought.

Tris had known Ian was special to him for a long time. But something had changed in him after Ian had said that 'I love you.' Like his heart had gone soft and open in the best possible way. He felt it now as he bundled a t-shirt and dark blue hoodie for Ian into his bag and headed for the door. It was there when he met Ian's smile. When they cooked or gamed online together, and when Ian asked Tris to check out his clothes because Ian couldn't always discern shades of blue and yellow and green. When he came home from a long shift at the hospital and kept Tris company in front of the TV despite being tired, his body a snug, welcome weight at Tris's side. When Tris slid inside Ian and made him come so hard he couldn't speak.

Is this love? Tris wondered.

Was that the thing turning him inside out as he jogged out the door toward the vet's office? Knowing a man like Ian loved him still stunned Tris. Because Ian was extraordinary. One of the smartest, kindest, most real people Tris had ever met, and so fucking strong it humbled him just thinking about it. God knew what he saw in Tris. Yeah, Tris had a great job and was smart as hell, and his ass was spectacular, if he said so himself. Still, he had a way to go before he'd be a real adult. Before he'd be as together as Ian.

But maybe ... maybe that wasn't entirely true. Tris licked his lips. Ian said often enough Tris was more grown up and capable than he gave himself credit for. That he didn't see himself clearly. And perhaps Tris's doubts about himself were just that—doubts and not reality.

His inner musings ground to a halt the moment he stepped into the vet's office where Ian sat on a bench in the otherwise empty waiting room. He glanced up, looking tired and worried, his dark hair messy like he'd been running his hands through it. He was still stupidly gorgeous. And when he spotted Tris, he smiled, and everything in his face said Ian was very glad to see him.

Ian stood and Tris crossed the space in five steps, quickly wrapping him up in a hug. He closed his eyes when Ian squeezed him back hard.

Fuck, Tris had only been gone five days, but he'd missed this so much.

"Hey," Ian murmured as Tris pressed a quick kiss to his cheek.

"Hey. How's the Wonder Dog?" Tris pulled back enough to meet Ian's eyes. Only then did he notice blood smears and dirt mixed in with the dog hair that was all over Ian's army green hoodie, as well as an abrasion on his chin. "The heck happened to you?"

Ian glanced down at himself. "The blood's not mine."

"And the chin?"

"Oh." Ian's expression grew sheepish. "Took a spill off my board a couple of days ago. Nothing some Tylenol and antiseptic couldn't fix."

Tris raised a brow. "I leave you guys alone for less than a week and everything goes to hell."

Ian snorted.

The man loved his skateboards and he was good on them—like, really good. Ian always wore pads, guards, and a helmet, but even they weren't enough to keep him one-hundred percent unscathed when he took the rare fall. And while Tris didn't like that, he knew better than to complain right now.

"What's going on with Elliott?" he asked Ian again.

"Dr. Ling said he should be okay with a couple of staples and a bandage." Ian stepped back, then tugged Tris down onto the bench beside him. "The wound is deep, but the edges are clean, so we think he stepped on some glass or a piece of sharp metal. I don't know."

He frowned and ran a hand over his hair, mussing it further. "We were at the dog park on Myrtle Street. I didn't see anything happen or hear him make a noise that would have tipped me off. Which is weird given he's so fucking loud all the time." His lips quirked at the corner when Tris laughed, but it wasn't quite a smile. "Everything seemed fine until he walked over and I noticed him limping. I had some water with me, so I cleaned the paw and knew I had to bring him here when I saw how deep the wound went."

"There's nothing you could have done." Tris rubbed Ian's back. "We should post a note at the dog park to give other people a heads-up."

"Cora was there with Shay—she said she'd do it," Ian replied. He and Elliott had met Cora and her German Shorthaired Pointer shortly after moving to the West End, and they met regularly for doggy play dates. Ian thought Elliott was a little in love with Shay, and his glee when he'd delivered that declaration still made Tris grin.

Ian's hazel eyes held only regret right now, however. "I'm sorry I didn't call about dinner," he said. "But I got everything ready before I took the beast dog out for a walk, and it won't take long to get it going once we're back at my place."

"God, GB. Don't worry about dinner."

"You were on a train all afternoon."

"I was on a train for three-and-half hours." Tris shrugged. "I ate some snacks on the ride, so it's not like I'm about to fade away to nothing."

Ian scowled gently. "You might."

The muttering made Tris grin. Ian was always after him for not eating enough and clearly today would be no exception. He pitched his voice to soothe.

"Go wash up and change." He undid the flap on his bag and pulled out the t-shirt and hoodie he'd packed. "We can talk about the logistics of dinner *after* we get the beast dog back home."

"All right." The corners of Ian's lips twitched up in a real smile this time. "Thanks for this. And for coming to meet me, too. Missed you, Chi-Town," he said, then leaned in to press a kiss against Tris's mouth.

※

WHILE IAN INSISTED HE COULD CARRY ELLIOTT TO KEEP THE stress off his stapled and bandaged paw, Tris ordered a car back to Ian's apartment, very aware Ian might actually herniate himself toting eighty-plus pounds of canine for a second time that day. Tris held on to the bag of antibiotics and changes of bandage while Ian focused on keeping the dog calm in the back of the car, but the sweet, easygoing side of Elliott's nature shone through any discomfort he might have been feeling and made the trip less burdensome. Ian was clearly spent by the time they made it up to his apartment though, practically panting as they walked down the hall to his apartment door.

"Guess I can skip going to the gym tomorrow," he said, then chuckled when the dog licked his face. "Gah, no."

Tris ushered them in and closed the door behind them. "You're going to need a hot shower and a massage, and possibly a chiropractor." Smiling, he watched Ian squat and set the dog down, then straighten back up with a groan. "What do we tell his legion of fans?"

"Fucking hell, I don't know. I'll shut the PetBuddy off for the night and think about the rest of it tomorrow." Ian arched his back and sighed. "You are heavy, big dog." He scritched behind Elliott's ears and the dog made a rumbling noise of contentment.

Tris joined in with the petting. "How about you wash up while I order some food?"

"This is the second time you've asked me to get clean tonight, you know." Ian sniffed. "You're gonna give me a fucking complex."

"Please," Tris said. "You stink like dog park and you're bruised and covered in fur that's not yours, but you're still the best thing I've seen all week."

Ian raised a brow to retort, but Tris pulled him into a kiss before he could speak. Ian stilled and drew in a sharp breath, but then brought his hands up to grasp Tristan's waist and opened his mouth to Tris, hot and wet and so goddamned good. Fire flashed under Tris's skin, and he had to force himself to break the kiss and press his forehead to Ian's.

"Missed you, GB," he murmured.

Elliott uttered a couple of low woo-woos, and they both glanced down and laughed.

"We missed you, too," Ian said, and dropped a hand to Elliott's cheek, stroking lightly with his knuckles while the dog thumped the floor with his long tail. "You can love all over Tris while I get your food ready," Ian told him, "and then I am gonna shower because Tris's got a point—I smell worse than you and that's just not right."

Once Elliott was fed and medicated, Ian headed off to the shower while Tris placed an order at a nearby sushi place, dashing out to grab the food and returning just in time for Ian to emerge clean and newly energized.

They sat at the tiny bar in Ian's kitchen, catching up over nigiri and tempura while Elliott snoozed in a corner of the couch with his favorite stuffed pig, his injured paw swathed in a bright pink bandage and tucked up close to his nose. Pleasure thrummed through Tris as he simply listened to Ian speak his mind, the sensation of being near him again both thrilling and familiar. Tris always felt like this around Ian—content and alive and filled with more desire than he knew what do with. He blinked when Ian stopped talking, realizing he'd long ago lost the thread of their conversation.

Tris gave him a grin. "Sorry, what was that again?"

Ian cocked an eyebrow at him. "You haven't heard a word I've said, have you?"

"Not for a couple of minutes, no," Tris replied, feeling not one shred of guilt as he grinned. "Your fault for being so stupid handsome."

A slow, knowing smile spread over Ian's face. He set down his chopsticks and laid a hand on Tris's thigh, the simple, wordless gesture sending a bolt of lust straight to Tris's balls. He pushed his plate away and his chair back, stepping up between Ian's legs so he could cradle Ian's face in his palms.

Heat flooded Tris as he kissed Ian, and while he'd only had a single glass of wine with dinner, his head spun as if he were tipsy. His cock hardened at Ian's rumbling hum, and when Ian slipped a hand up under the hem of Tris's sweatshirt, touch wonderfully rough over Tris's skin, Tris had to bite back a groan.

They left their plates behind and climbed the stairs to the loft where they quickly undressed, Ian chuckling as Tris pulled him in for another scorching kiss. He clung tightly to Tris, like he couldn't get close enough, and his voice as he murmured was urgent.

"Want you so much."

Tris's chest ached. Walking Ian backward until his calves hit the bed, he tumbled them both down onto the mattress. Their laughter faded into sighs and groans as Tris reached down and settled a hand over Ian's cock.

Ian shuddered. Shifting, he rolled them onto their sides, then hooked a knee up around Tris's hip. Their kisses were slower now but no less intense, each burning Tris from the inside out. He met Ian's stare when they finally broke apart, and the world came to a standstill around them.

"Fuck, you're gorgeous," Tris whispered, biting his lip at the passion he saw in Ian's face.

Letting go of Ian's dick, Tris shifted, quickly pushing up onto his knees. He grabbed the lube Ian kept in the nightstand, but kept his eyes trained on Ian when he could, gaze lingering on hard planes of muscle and golden skin gone pale after another long winter.

He wet his fingers with lube before tossing it down, then lay beside Ian once more. Ian moaned when Tris took him in hand again, and the sound made goosebumps rise along Tris's skin.

"Missed this," Ian told him. He slipped his arms around Tris's neck, dipping his head to suck at Tris's collarbone, and Tris closed his eyes, pumping Ian lazily as the soft mutters continued. "Missed touching you. Hearing you when we're like this."

"Missed you too, baby."

Ian kissed him, sweet and deep, and the longing in those kisses tugged at Tris's heart. He nearly gasped when Ian broke away, and when he opened his eyes, Ian's were burning. He set his hands on Tris's shoulders and pushed, urging him onto his back.

"Need you in my mouth."

Desire pooled in Tris's gut, his balls throbbing at that very welcome suggestion. Letting go of Ian, he closed his eyes, aware of Ian reaching for the bottle of lube. His skin tingled when slick fingers wrapped around his shaft and Tris moaned without shame.

"God," he got out, shivering as Ian ran his thumb over the head of Tris's cock. "Feels so good."

Ian chuckled and shifted his weight, and Tris peeled open his eyes again, smoothing his hands over Ian's body as he got himself turned around, so he was facing Tris's feet. He settled over Tris and took hold of Tris's hips, his cock standing red and rigid against his abdomen, only inches from Tris's face. The need rising in Tris's chest nearly crushed him.

Together, they rolled onto their sides, and Tris pressed his face into the juncture between Ian's hip and groin, breathing in a heady mix of soap and sweat and something uniquely Ian. He licked Ian's skin, tasting salt, and nuzzled the dark curls at the base of Ian's dick, his own cock twitching. He cursed low when Ian licked his cockhead, the teasing touches like the best kind of torture. But then Tris opened his mouth and swallowed Ian down, loving the weight on his tongue and bitter tang of pre-cum, and Ian inhaled sharply.

Tris's bones turned liquid, his heart thundering in his ears as Ian took him deep. He slid slick fingers along the cleft of Ian's ass to his hole, teasing his rim, aware of Ian's now steady moans. Ian hauled Tris closer, driving himself down Tris's throat, and Tris wrapped his arms and legs tight around Ian, greed buzzing through him.

Breaching Ian, Tris sank two fingers deep, groaning at the way Ian jolted, his near shout muffled by Tris's cock in his mouth. Ian bucked his hips, thrusting hard, and Tris's eyes rolled behind his lids, the world beyond melting under the feedback loop that spun out between them.

God, he loved this. Ian's wanton groans, like he couldn't get enough. The way he grabbed Tris's ass and thrashed in Tris's hold, his solid body trembling as he chased his pleasure.

Tris curled his fingers inside Ian, tapping his gland again and again. His chest squeezed at Ian's broken sounds, and Tris fucked and sucked until Ian went rigid, back arching and his dick pulsing over Tris's tongue.

Moaning desperately, Tris rolled his hips, heart lurching when Ian's arms tightened around Tris's waist. Ian took Tris impossibly deep, and the pleasure coiled deep in Tris's belly snapped without warning, rolling through him in huge waves. Gasping, Tris pulled off, cheek coming to rest against Ian's thigh as Ian swallowed his cum. Ian's groans were soft and pleased, and Tris smiled as he floated, only rousing after Ian had pulled off and buried his face against Tris's belly.

Carefully, Tris got himself turned around on the mattress so he could gather Ian up. He held him close, sharing kisses with him until their breathing evened out. Eventually, they'd need to get up. Clean themselves and clear away what remained of their dinner, and determine if the Wonder Dog would need to be hauled bodily into the loft. But Tris chose to linger beside Ian a bit longer, and he liked that Ian made no move to pull away either, instead tracing shapes over Tris's torso with his fingers.

"You ever think about living together?" Tris asked him.

Ian's touch stuttered to a near stop before resuming. "Sometimes," he said, voice rather quiet. "But I also think about not pushing my luck."

Tris frowned. "What does that mean?"

Stopping his tracing, Ian rolled back enough that he could meet Tris's gaze, his face suddenly somber. "I've got a good thing going with you. Really good. But I don't know how I got so lucky. I still struggle sometimes understanding why you want to be with me."

"I have thoughts like that about you," Tris said. "Had them tonight before I called."

"Idiot." Ian's smile was loving. "You could have anyone."

"So could you. But I don't want anyone who *isn't* you."

"Yeah, well." Ian's lips twisted slightly, the grin becoming rueful. "There are still days my brain doesn't want to believe that. But, more importantly, I don't want you to feel pressured to make our relationship something it's not."

This is why he doesn't say 'I love you' out loud.

The uncertainty in Ian's face hurt Tris's heart. Knowing Ian felt a need to hold himself back—that he doubted his own worth—hurt. But Tris already knew there were times Ian didn't see himself clearly and Tris wanted to fix that.

"I'm where I want to be, Ian. With you." He leaned in for a

kiss. "I want more of that. I want to travel a little less and do more project work remotely."

Ian brought his eyebrows together. "Really? But I thought ... You like working in new cities and being around new people."

"I do. But I miss being here even more," Tris said. "Miss seeing those clowns at Off-World. My friends and El. You." He rubbed Ian's hip through the sheet with his palm.

"There are days I can't wrap my head around my life either. Like how I ended up on a commuter train, seated next to the hottest grouchy guy ever. Who talked to me, even though I could tell he didn't really want to talk to anyone. Nursed me with peppermints when I said I felt gross and was nice about my snoring." Tris grinned as the tips of Ian's ears flushed red.

"You sure know how to find the silver lining in a cloud," Ian said, his voice low and pleased.

"Or maybe the clouds are silver to begin with and you didn't notice because you thought they were pink," Tris laughed at Ian's eyeroll. "You gave me a second chance after I got scared and ghosted, and we both know you didn't need to do that. So, it could be that *I* should shut up and be happy with my fucking awesome life."

He laid one hand over Ian's where it rested on the bed. "I still want more with you. I love you, Ian. And I don't want to miss out on making you believe it."

Emotion streaked over Ian's face, lighting his eyes with stars. Affection. Desire. Love. "I do believe you. I love you so much," he said at last, rough voice tender. Turning his hand up so his palm met Tristan's, he wound their fingers together. Then he kissed Tris, sweet and slow, and the press of his lips made Tris's heart feel too big for his chest.

Yeah, Tris was in love all right. And it made him feel more alive than he'd ever known he could.

AUTHOR'S NOTE

I hope you enjoyed Ian and Tris's story! I would be honored if you would consider leaving a short review and let me know what you think.

Like many people, Ian suffers from depression, a treatable medical condition. Different people experience different symptoms of depression, but help is out there. Call, text, or chat 988 to be connected to trained counselors at the 988 Suicide & Crisis Lifeline or call 1-800-273-TALK (8255).

https://988lifeline.org
https://findahelpline.com/i/iasp

ACKNOWLEDGMENTS

"The opposite of depression is not happiness. It is vitality." — Andrew Solomon from his TED talk on depression.

TRADEMARK ACKNOWLEDGMENTS

Grumble Bear and Jimmy and the Pulsating Mass - Housekeeping Games

Mad Max - George Miller, Byron Kennedy

Halo - Microsoft Corporation

ReWalk - ReWalk Robotics

Ritz Crackers - Mondelez International

Jeep - Fiat Chrysler Automobiles

Blue Moon - MillerCoors

Law & Order: Special Victims Unit - Dick Wolf

Inferno (part 1 of *Divine Comedy*) - Dante Alighieri

Mountain Dew - PepsiCo

Big Gulp - 7-Eleven

SpongeBob SquarePants - Stephen Hillenburg

LinkedIn Corporation - Microsoft Corporation

PornHub – MindGeek

Street Fighter - Capcom

Godzilla - Tomoyuki Tanaka, Ishirō Honda, Eiji Tsuburaya

So This Is Love - Mack David, Jerry Livingston, Al Hoffman

Gus Dawson uses an expression from *Ghostbusters*.

Tris Santos makes several comments inspired by the movie *Mean Girls*.

Ian Byrne makes at least one comment inspired by the movie *Die Hard*.

HOOKED ON YOU

If you enjoyed this book, check out *Hooked On You*, available in paperback and ebook on Amazon and Kindle Unlimited.

Hooked On You

*What's a straight guy to do
when he falls for his new friend?*

Paramedic Connor Devlin is a stressed-out tower of a man. Hoping knitting will help him unwind, he visits a local craft shop, where he's overwhelmed by the yarn selection but more so by his feelings for shop owner Judah.

Judah Bissel is tired of falling for unavailable men. He can't help his crush on Connor, though, or wanting to get closer to the big, gentle bear. And that just might spell trouble because pining for straight guys is not Judah's style.

As a blizzard pummels the city, the men hunker down together to wait out the storm. When the spark between them ignites, will the revelation that Connor feels more than friendship for Judah bring them together or tear them apart?

Hooked On You is a 72.8K friends-to-lovers MM novel. It features a stressed-out paramedic who's figuring out he's not quite straight, a yarn shop owner with a bad habit of falling for unavailable guys, lots of knitting and snowdrifts, and a sweet, happy-sigh HEA.

CHAPTER 1

Thursday, January 3

You are in way over your head, buddy.

Connor Devlin had never seen so much yarn. Literal boxes of it, cubbies stacked floor to near ceiling on the walls of Hook Me, a knitting supply shop in Boston's North End and only a few blocks from Connor's apartment. He'd walked by the shop dozens of times on his way to work but had never been inside it until tonight. And he had very little idea of what he was looking at other than so. Much. Yarn.

Eyebrows drawn together, Connor peered into the cubby nearest him and its neat stacks of wooly bundles, vibrant hues ranging from deep rose to shocking pink. Movements tentative, he fingered one of the bundles, his frown growing deeper as he considered the colorful, organized chaos. Where the hell did he start?

"Do you have a particular pattern in mind?"

Connor almost jumped out of his skin. For a guy who stood six-foot-four, he'd always been easy to startle, a personality flaw many of his co-workers exploited with great glee. Forcing himself to take a breath and peel his shoulders down from

CHAPTER 1

around his ears, Connor turned to the guy who had appeared at his side. Still, his surprise must have shown because the guy's face immediately scrunched up in a wince.

"I'm *so* sorry," he said to Connor. "I didn't mean to sneak up on you."

"You're fine," Connor murmured, blinking rapidly as the guy's lips quirked into a smile.

Oh, crap. Fine was an understatement.

This guy was nothing at all like the caftan-wearing ladies Connor had imagined working in this store. Mr. Hook Me was maybe five years younger than Connor's thirty-two, with striking gray-green eyes and a Pride pin attached to the collar of his black shirt. He'd been behind the counter when Connor had walked in and Connor's attention had been on the yarn. No chance of ignoring the guy now that they stood only a foot or two apart, however, especially with Mr. Hook Me smiling at him. Connor was abruptly glad he'd exchanged his Boston EMS uniform shirt and jacket for street clothes before leaving the station.

Wait, what? What difference did it make what Connor wore?

"I noticed you'd been standing here for a while," the guy said, then gestured toward the wall of cubbies. "I thought I'd check in, make sure you were finding everything you need."

"Thanks." Connor pushed his hair back over his shoulder, his cheeks on fire as he caught himself staring. He hoped his beard hid at least some of his blush. This guy looked like a film actor for crying out loud, all slim and sleek, his form graceful compared to Connor's meaty body. Not that Connor should be thinking about Mr. Hook Me's body. Or any man's. Except he was. And why?

Ugh.

Shifting his focus back to the wall of cubbies, Connor cleared his throat. "I'm, um, honestly not sure what I need."

"Is that why you were talking to yourself?"

"Say what now?"

Mr. Hook Me's smile grew a little wider when Connor

CHAPTER 1

glanced back, and his eyes crinkled at the corners. "You said 'Where the hell do I start?' A question I hear often, by the way. People talk to themselves all the time in this store. I suspect it's a knitter thing."

"Oh, I'm not a knitter," Connor said. He looked away again, his face blazing hotter. He was making himself sound awfully stupid. Not to mention talking out loud to no one in a public place. "Or at least not yet. I wasn't kidding when I said I have no idea what I need, though. I've never even held a pair of knitting hooks."

"They're called needles," Mr. Hook Me replied, his tone easy. "A hook is what you'd use for crochet, which is different from knitting entirely." An encouraging expression crossed his face when Connor met his gaze. "Or maybe that's what you want to do instead?"

"I'm ... not sure."

With a shake of his head, Connor glanced at the door. He could leave. Call this outing what it was—a mess—and go home and fix himself a sandwich for dinner. He'd only come in here because his coworker Olivia was convinced that a hobby would help wrangle some of Connor's anxiety. He could find a different yarn shop. Maybe do some googling before he ventured in, and hope it was staffed with safe, caftan-wearing ladies who didn't make Connor's insides go both tight and melty when they smiled.

"Don't worry about it," Mr. Hook Me said, his voice soothing. He cocked his head at Connor. "Can I ask what brought you in here tonight? That might help me understand what you're looking to do."

Connor gave a terse nod. "Right. Well, like I said, I've never knit or done crochet before, so I guess I'm more looking to get started than anything else."

"That makes sense." The guy's forehead puckered, and a thoughtful air came over him. "Is there a project you're looking

CHAPTER 1

to work toward once you understand stitches and the mechanics of needlework?"

"Yeah, actually. How did you know?"

"Lucky guess. A lot of people have an idea in mind when they decide they want to learn to knit, be it a scarf or socks, or even a winter hat."

"I want to knit a baby blanket," Connor blurted. He drew a rectangle in the air with his index fingers, then almost rolled his eyes at himself—what the hell was wrong with him tonight? "I'm not really sure what size would be best, though."

"No problem. We've got books of patterns that could be of help if you'd like to look through them." Mr. Hook Me tipped his head in the direction of the counter.

"That'd be great, thanks."

"Of course. Knowing what you'll need to create your final project may help me too, so I can direct you to the right yarn or recommend specific stitches. I also have plenty of suggestions about how to get started with the learning part. Oh, man." Bowing his head slightly, Mr. Hook Me set a hand over his heart. "I'm being super rude. I'm Judah and this is my place."

"Nice to meet you, Judah." Connor shook the hand Judah extended. This guy was something. Confident but genuine, too, and so good at not making Connor feel like a big oaf. "My name's Connor. I'll take any advice you can give me on the learning and the blanket and whatever else I might need to know about knitting. Or crochet. Hah." He huffed out a breath. "I'm sure I sound like a complete dope wandering in with zero idea of what I'm doing."

Judah gave a soft chuckle. "Not at all. People walk in here all the time with an idea of what they'd like to make and no concrete knowledge of what it will take to get there. It was a daily occurrence in the run up to Hanukkah and Christmas! That's where I come in." He gestured Connor toward the counter. "How about we get started with the patterns and go from there?"

CHAPTER 1

Thirty minutes later, they'd come to the agreement that Connor wanted to learn to knit and not crochet, at least for the time being. Judah had settled Connor in a big, overstuffed chair near the counter at the back of the store and Connor was paging through a book of patterns. Glancing up, Connor caught sight of Judah talking quietly with a customer, his expression bright and interested.

It's nice in here.

Connor blinked, aware then of how heavy his eyelids had become. What the heck? Clearly, he was overtired, but he was in a yarn store, for crying out loud. While it might be cozy, what with the comfy chair and the chill house music, it was no place for a nap.

Sitting up straighter, Connor flipped the page of the pattern book and stopped, sure he'd found exactly what he wanted. He got to his feet and walked to the register, intent on showing Judah the pattern once the man was free to talk, when an abrupt increase in noise drew his attention to the door. Several women of varying ages trooped in, chatting among themselves. They waved cheerily at Judah, calling out greetings as they approached him and his customer, but the conversations stuttered when they spotted Connor. The women's eyes went wide then, and sudden smiles crossed their faces, two or three giving him a none-too-subtle once over. Connor quickly glued his gaze back on the book of patterns, heat licking along his cheeks again.

"Please go on in and make yourselves comfortable, everyone," Judah called out, much closer to Connor than he had been only moments before. "There is plenty of coffee and tea as well as some very nice cookies from our favorite bakery, and I'll be down in a few minutes. How are you doing over here, Connor?" he asked in a quieter tone as he walked behind the counter.

"Doing okay," Connor said over the chatter rising from the women once more. Glancing up, he watched them head through a door to the right of the register and disappear from sight. A quick look around told him the rest of the shop was now empty

285

CHAPTER 1

and Connor checked his watch. Quarter to six? He'd been in Hook Me for nearly an hour. "What time do you close?"

"Officially, we close at five-thirty," Judah said. "We host classes and social circles in the basement most evenings, however, including tonight from six to eight. That's what everyone who's come in for the last five minutes is here for—socializing while they knit or crochet." He raised his hand in greeting as another trio of women entered with a man just behind. The women did the same deer in the headlights upon noticing Connor, who turned his attention right back to the knitting pattern. "I'll be right with you," Judah said to the new arrivals.

"Damn, I didn't mean to stay so late." Connor could almost hear Judah's shrug as he replied.

"No worries. You couldn't have known and, obviously, other customers have been in. Besides, you were busy with your pattern hunting. Did you find one you like?"

"I think so, yeah. What do you think?" Spinning the book around, Connor nudged it closer to Judah and watched him eye the pages with a smile.

"This is an excellent choice. The garter stitch is not difficult to master at all—it's the first stitch you'd learn as a knitter and once you've got it down, this pattern will go quickly. That said, you'll be using two strands of yarn, so the blanket will be soft and squishy and super warm when it's finished. Perfect for a baby."

"Great. I really like all the colors." Connor ran his fingertip over the photo in the book, then pursed his lips. How the heck did you get purple, lilac, and pretty, soft green into one blanket? Before he could ask, the young man who'd just entered peeled off from the group and joined them, his eyes very like Judah's though more brown.

"Hey, bro," he said to Judah. "Just wanted to say hi. Who's your Viking friend here?"

The tips of Judah's ears turned pink. "This is Connor," he

said in a tone that held a lightly chiding note. "He came in tonight to shop for knitting supplies." Judah looked almost abashed as he glanced back to Connor. "Connor, this is my brother Levi."

"Hello." Connor nodded but Levi surprised him by quickly pulling off his gloves and thrusting out a hand.

"Hiya." Levi gave Connor a firm shake before letting him go. He tipped his head toward the nearby door as the women he'd walked in with disappeared through it. "You going down to hang with the knitting nerds, Connor? I keep telling Judah it'd be nice to have some dudes around on these nights to break up the estrogen-fest."

Connor made himself return Levi's smile. "Uh, no. I don't actually know how to knit yet."

"Meh, that's okay. You could just join in for coffee, cookies, and gossip because, seriously, that is what the stitch-and-bitch is all about. You should sign up for the Knitting 101 class." Levi gave Connor a knowing look. "People come in here all the time who can't knit for crap, but once Judah and Molly get a hold of them, they find their inner skills."

Judah sighed. "I'm not sure you're doing a good job of selling it, bro."

"Says you." Levi made his eyebrows go up and down in an exaggerated manner that made Connor chuckle. "Anyway, I have homework and *you* should get down there before the circle goes all *Lord of the Flies*, Jude. You know what they can be like when you're not around to make sure everyone plays nice with the cookie platter."

Judah let out a laugh. "I do. I'll see you for dinner, okay?"

"You bet." Levi turned for the exit again but called back to Connor as he headed out. "Good meeting you, Connor—I'll see you around!"

"See ya, Levi." Connor watched him go, then set his hands on his hips with a small frown. "Judah? How many classes does a person have to take if they want to master Knitting 101?"

"There are four classes in the course, and each is two hours," Judah replied. "Most people can knit a garter stitch proficiently by the end of their first class, though, and I know plenty who've taught themselves to knit by watching YouTube."

Connor bit back a groan as the door opened once more, admitting a twosome of teenaged girls, one of whom let out a noisy "*damn*" as she ogled Connor.

"Jeez." Judah looked as though he was trying not to lose it laughing and waved them on. "I'm sorry about that," he said to Connor. "As Levi said, we don't get a lot of men in the circle, particularly not guys like you."

Connor pursed his lips, his stomach going tight. "Guys like me?"

Judah's expression softened. "You know you look a little like a real-life Thor, right? And the fact you might be even remotely interested in needlework ... well, you must see how that might make an impression on a group of crafting nerds." His small smile cut right through the awkwardness that threatened to overwhelm Connor.

"Fair." Connor said. "It's not the first time someone's ..."

"Admired you?" Now Judah smirked. "Yeah, that tracks."

Way to make yourself sound like a conceited ass.

Connor chewed the inside of his cheek. He knew he wasn't a bad-looking guy. He'd never understood why any woman would want to ogle him, though, and every time it happened, he just felt mystified and vaguely uncomfortable. Luckily, Judah seemed completely unfazed by the whole thing.

"Back to your question about knitting class," he said now to Connor. "New sessions start this week if you're really interested in attending."

"I'm interested. I think it'd be good for me. I want to finish the blanket *before* my partner's baby is born and I'm not sure I'll be able to do that by watching videos." Granted, Olivia wasn't due for another five months, but Connor had no idea how long it'd take him to knit a potholder, never mind an entire blanket.

"Got it," Judah said. "Not everyone likes to learn from a screen, and I respect that."

Heading past Connor, he rounded the counter so he could flip through a set of hanging folders. Plucking a sheet of blue paper from one, he turned back and laid it on the counter in front of Connor.

"Here we go." Judah tapped a calendar on the sheet with one finger. "Knitting 101 happens on Tuesday evening from six to eight, Saturday morning from ten to twelve, and Sunday afternoon from four to six. Most people sign up to come once a week, but if your schedule allows, you're welcome to attend multiple classes. They're held in the basement about ninety percent of the time, but now and then we'll have one up here in the store, just for a change of scene."

Connor nodded but couldn't help feeling something was off. Judah's demeanor had changed somehow, grown more closed off in just the few seconds it had taken him to find the class schedule, and damn if Connor knew why. What the heck had just happened?

"Okay," he said, rubbing his hands against his dark brown cargo pants. "And are you the teacher? Or would it be the person your brother mentioned?"

"Molly?" Judah's face relaxed a bit. "Most of the time I'm the instructor, yes, but Molly and I sometimes switch off when she's in town. Molly is my mom."

"Really?" Connor looked around the store again. "So, you run this place together?"

"Yep. We have a shop up in Stowe, too, and my mom and stepdad live there. My stepdad's an accountant, by the way, and he still can't tell the difference between a knitting needle and crochet hook, but my mom has never held it against him." He smiled. "They come down on Sundays for dinner with my brother and me, and Mom likes to teach class when she has time." Judah paused as a burst of loud laughter echoed through

CHAPTER 1

the door leading to the basement. "Um. I should make sure they're not doing anything too off the wall down there."

"The more I hear about this circle the more interested I get," Connor said. He picked up the class flyer. "Okay if I take this?"

"Absolutely." Judah walked back around the counter. "The class signup is online at hook me dot-com. Oh! I almost forgot." He doubled back and grabbed a small, brown paper shopping bag from beside the cash register and handed it to Connor.

"This is a beginners' knitting kit. Needles, a small ball of soft yarn, and a sheet with lots of links for tutorials."

Connor peered down into the little bag, a warm buzz filtering through him. "Whoa, thanks. How much do I—?"

"Not a thing." Judah shook his head. "You can practice on your own and, if you do end up coming to class, just bring it along and I'll upgrade everything."

"Oh, I'll be back," Connor promised. "I still need the pattern for the baby blanket."

The corners of Judah's eyes crinkled as he laughed. "True! I'll make a copy for you and keep it here at the counter. Guess I'll see you around, Connor."

Connor sketched a wave as he headed for the door, but he carried the sparkle in Judah's eyes out of the shop right along with him.

ABOUT K. EVAN COLES

K. Evan Coles is a mother and tech pirate by day and a writer by night. She is a dreamer who, with a little hard work and a lot of good coffee, coaxes words out of her head and onto paper.

K. lives in the northeast United States, where she complains bitterly about the winters, but truly loves the region and its diverse, tenacious and deceptively compassionate people. You'll usually find K. nerding out over books, movies and television with friends and family. She's especially proud to be raising her son as part of a new generation of unabashed geeks.

K.'s books explore LGBTQ+ romance in contemporary settings.

For more books and updates: https://kevancoles.com

- amazon.com/K-Evan-Coles/e/B072L7L8BZ
- bookbub.com/profile/k-evan-coles
- instagram.com/k.evan.coles
- twitter.com/K_Evan_Coles
- facebook.com/kevancolesauthor
- pinterest.com/kevancoles

ALSO BY K. EVAN COLES

Wicked Fingers Press (Self-Published)

Stealing Hearts
Thief of Hearts (Novella)
Healing Hearts (Novella)
Open Hearts (Novel)
Hopeful Hearts (Novel)

Hooked On You (Novel)

Overexposed (Novel)

A Hometown Holiday (Novella)

Moonlight (Short Story)

Pride Publishing (Totally Entwined Group)

Boston Seasons (Novels)
Third Time's the Charm
Easy For You To Say (TBD)

Tidal Duology w/ Brigham Vaughn (Novels)
Wake
Calm

The Speakeasy w/ Brigham Vaughn (Novels)

With a Twist

Extra Dirty

Behind the Stick

Straight Up

※

Off Topic Press (Self-Published)

Inked in Blood w/ Brigham Vaughn (Short Story)

https://kevancoles.com

Made in the USA
Columbia, SC
06 February 2025